"WHAT!" My voice surprises even me. I clear my throat. "I'm sorry, but did you just say that Callie Reyes would be working at the gym?"

Mom and Inga shake their heads. I do, too.

Positive thoughts. Think positive thoughts.

But this is going to be—

Positive thoughts, I remind myself. *Positive thoughts.*

Nope. Hard as I try, I just can't imagine a world where the next few months working with Callie aren't miserable. Maybe Callie isn't the biggest bully in school, but she's not what I would call nice either.

It will only be as bad as you allow it to be, a small voice inside me says.

But the voice is too small to affect my growing sense of doom.

PUDDIN'

JULIE MURPHY

Balzer + Bray
An Imprint of HarperCollins*Publishers*

Balzer + Bray is an imprint of HarperCollins Publishers.

Puddin'
Copyright © 2018 by Julie Murphy
Emoji icons provided by EmojiOne
All rights reserved. Printed in the United States of America.
No part of this book may be used or reproduced in any manner
whatsoever without written permission except in the case of
brief quotations embodied in critical articles and reviews. For
information address HarperCollins Children's Books, a division of
HarperCollins Publishers, 195 Broadway, New York, NY 10007.
www.epicreads.com

Library of Congress Control Number: 2017954051
ISBN 978-0-06-241839-5

Typography by Aurora Parlagreco
19 20 21 22 23   PC/LSCH   10 9 8 7 6 5 4 3 2
❖
First paperback edition, 2019

For Ashley. Our friendship is my favorite rom-com.

If you don't like the road you're walking, start paving another one. —Dolly Parton

"She's my friend because we both know what it's like to have people be jealous of us." —Cher Horowitz, *Clueless*

PUDDIN'

MILLIE

One

I'm a list maker. Write it down. (Using my gel pens and a predetermined color scheme, of course.) Make it happen. Scratch it off. There is no greater satisfaction than a notebook full of beautifully executed lists.

A long time ago, I decided to make a list of all the things I could control, and what it came down to was this: my attitude. Which is probably why I've been able to psych myself into thinking that a 4:45 a.m. wakeup call is humane. Listen, I'm a morning person, but 4:45 doesn't even count as morning if you ask me, and I'm an optimist.

After swiping away the last alarm on my phone, I roll out of bed and pull on my fuzzy baby-pink robe with a scrolled *M* embroidered onto the collar. For a moment, I stretch my whole body and yawn one last time before sitting down at my desk and pulling out my floral notebook. Across the hardcover front in gold letters, it reads MAKE PLANS, and below that, in cursive, *MILLIE MICHAL-CHUK*.

I smack my lips together to rid myself of the taste of sleep. Normally, I'm militant about brushing my teeth, but the other day Amanda said she read online that if you're experiencing writer's block, you should try writing first thing, before your brain even has a moment to turn on. I figure it can't hurt to try. With my mint-green GIRL BOSS pencil poised in hand, I examine all the false starts I've scratched through this week.

I believe in the power of positive thinking.
Most people don't know what they want, and that's the real reason they're stuck. Me? I know exactly what I want.
Webster's Dictionary defines journalism as the activity or job of collecting, writing, and editing news stories for newspapers, magazines, television, or radio. I define journalism as

I turn to a fresh page and I sit and I wait. I stare down the blank page, hoping for the lines to morph into words, but instead they stay perfectly static.

I'm a good student. Not as great as Malik or Leslie Fischer, who was destined to be our class's valedictorian the moment she won the third-grade spelling bee when she was only in first grade, but I'm in all AP classes and I'm doing better than most of my peers. I rarely feel daunted by an exam of essay questions or even a timed trigonometry test. But this personal statement is turning out to be an entirely new kind of beast. In fact, it's got me feeling more like a girl failure than a girl boss.

After ten minutes and nothing to show for my time except a few crossed-out words and a doodle of two stick figures who I imagine are out on a date and who might even be me and a particular someone . . . I shove my note-book back in the drawer of my desk.

Tomorrow. Tomorrow will be the day when the right words come to me. I open my laptop and scroll through my video library until I settle on *When Harry Met Sally.* This is one of me and my mom's favorites—the kind of rom-com we can quote in our sleep—even if my mom does fast-forward through the orgasm scene and we still watch the VHS copy she recorded years ago. (My mother has yet to discover that I can just watch the full-length version online.)

Above my computer hangs a cross-stitch I copied from Pinterest. An intricate floral vine weaves around the quote YOU HAVE AS MANY HOURS IN A DAY AS BEYONCÉ. (I made one for Willowdean that replaced Beyoncé's name with Dolly Parton, both of whom are goddesses in my humble opinion.)

Beside that is a piece of découpaged wood that reads WHEN I LOOK INTO THE FUTURE, IT'S SO BRIGHT IT BURNS MY EYES. —OPRAH WINFREY. Above that is another cross-stitch that reads LIFE IS TOO COMPLICATED NOT TO BE ORDERLY. —MARTHA STEWART. And those are just a few of my masterpieces.

I got my love for inspirational quotes, cross-stitch, and crafts from my mom. Our whole house is lined with hand-made embroidered pillows emblazoned with encouraging quotes and watercolor prints of Bible verses that are darn near good enough quality to be sold at The Good Book, our local Christian bookstore.

It's like me and my mom are a pair of birds, always adding to our nest, and the project is never quite done, but with each addition we feel a little more at home. At least that's how it's been until now. But in the last few months, my hopes and dreams are growing in the opposite direction of what my mom wants for me. Slowly, I've been redecorating my nest.

The cross-stitches and découpages hanging on my wall today are a departure from the inspirational diet quotes I surrounded myself with last summer and the eight summers prior to that at Daisy Ranch Weight-Loss Camp. YOU HAVE NOTHING TO LOSE EXCEPT THE WEIGHT was always a personal favorite.

Fat camp. Yes, I went to fat camp. But that's all history, because for the first time in nine years, I'm not going back to see my friends or Ms. Georgia, my counselor, at Daisy Ranch. Entering and winning runner-up at the Miss Teen Blue Bonnet Pageant changed the game for me. I did things I never believed possible. I played my ukulele for a crowded theater and walked the stage in a beautiful gown—not to mention the swimsuit portion of the competition! I even went to a dance with a boy. I did all that in this body. Which is why I can't afford to waste another summer weighing in every morning and eating rabbit food in the hopes that someone will notice that I've dropped six pounds on the first day of school.

Now if I could only just figure out a way to explain that to my mom. And then, watch out, world! Millicent

Michalchuk, trusted news anchor, is coming to a television screen near you.

But first I've gotta finish this dang personal statement for the Broadcast Journalism Boot Camp at the University of Texas in Austin.

I know it's going to take more than summer camp or even a degree. We're talking internships and years of grunt work. But I'm willing to do all that, because I want to be the face people come home to every night—a voice they can trust. A voice that will inspire. And maybe even change the world. I guess that's a silly thing to expect from a news anchor, but my grandparents are as religious about the local news as they are about, well, religion!

I hear them talking about things people have said on the news channels they watch, and there are times that I don't even think we're living in the same world. It's got me thinking that sometimes it's about more than the facts. Sometimes it's about how and which facts are presented. Like, when same-sex marriage was legalized, all the news outlets I pay attention to online treated it like a celebration, because it was! I went over to my grandparents' house, and by the sound of their television, you would have thought we'd been invaded by a hostile enemy.

Maybe it's different for everybody, but people like my grandparents? Their opinion of the world is shaped by the person who delivers their news. That's real responsibility, and I don't take that lightly.

I know. They don't put fat girls on the news. Well, they

didn't let fat girls win runner-up in the Miss Teen Blue Bonnet Pageant either. But everything happens for the first time at some point, so why can't that first time be me?

After I've removed all my curlers, I reach for the black leggings and mint sweatshirt I laid out for myself last night. The sweatshirt is the result of a Mother-Daughter Craftur-day Saturday—a fading monthly tradition, now that I'm working for Uncle Vernon—and has a fabric-paint-lined iron-on transfer of a puppy with a butterfly on its nose. (It's as adorable as it sounds.)

I add a touch of light pink lip gloss and close my laptop, leaving Harry and Sally behind. Lastly, I get the coffeepot started for my parents before driving to work.

At 5:45 in the morning, Clover City is just barely buzz-ing awake. The only evidence of life is the flickering light that spills into the street from Daybreak Donuts and Coffee and the handful of runners I see before pulling into the parking lot of Down for the Count, my uncle Vernon and aunt Inga's boxing gym.

Dad tried telling them that the name of the gym felt a little defeatist, but they weren't hearing it. Uncle Vernon and Aunt Inga connected on a Rocky fan-club message board. Inga was a recent transplant from Russia living in Philadelphia, and they met for the first time at the top of the infamous Rocky steps at the Philadelphia Museum of Art. (Against my entire family's protest, because no one in my family except me can really wrap their head around falling in love on the internet.)

I've never been to Philly, but Inga has promised me that

we'll go after graduation—a true girls' trip. I just hope it won't take climbing all seventy-two Rocky steps for me to get the happy ending to my own love story.

I park in the spot right in front of the gym. Inga always nags Vernon and I for us both parking in the front spaces, but I like to think of it as my employee-of-the-month parking. Even if I am their only employee. Hey, the pay is crummy. I've got to take my perks where I can find them.

Stretching above the windows in our corner of the shopping center is our light-up sign. It reads DOWN FOR THE COUNT with a set of boxing gloves hanging next to it. Below that I can still see the shadow of letters where it once read LIFE CLUB FITNESS.

Bells jingle above my head as I open the front door and run behind the counter to turn off the alarm.

I go through my opening duties: counting out the register, sharpening pencils, printing off new member applications, checking the locker rooms for towels and toilet paper, and doing a quick walk-through and equipment check. I make a game of weaving in and out of the punching bags and tugging on each of them to make sure they're just as sturdy as they were yesterday morning. Bouncing on my toes, I give the last bag a quick one-two punch.

The bell above the door rings, letting me know someone's come in.

"Looking good, Millie!"

Sheepishly, I glance over my shoulder. "Morning, Vernon." My uncle was once the kind of guy parents begged their daughters to stay away from. Thick muscles

7

and sandy-colored curls. But these days he's more sleep-deprived dad than small-town bad boy. He's got a few clusters of white in his reddish-blond beard, and his smile lines are more deep set now, but he's just as sturdy as I always remember him being.

"Your stance is getting pretty solid," he says. "I don't think I'd want to mess with you in a dark alleyway."

I shake out my hands. "I'm just messing around," I tell him as I head over to the counter and grab my car keys. Learning how to box for real is on my long-term to-do list, after getting into broadcast camp and making out with a boy. (Hey, Oprah says to name your goals, and she's never led me astray.)

He shrugs. The circles under his eyes and his day-old T-shirt tell me he was up all night with the twins. Not only that, but the gym is really up against the ropes at the moment. (Pun totally intended.) Up until last month, this place was part of the Life Club Fitness franchise, which has specialty gyms (tennis clubs, CrossFit, indoor soccer) all over the country. This meant we had additional resources for marketing and equipment and even doing things like sponsoring local sports teams.

But LCF filed for bankruptcy without any warning, so now Uncle Vernon and Aunt Inga are on their own with this place, and without a safety net. Between all the investments they've already made here and newborn twins, the success of this gym has turned out to be more important than ever. Last time I was at their house, I saw a stack of late notices from the water and electric companies, and I just can't shake the image. This place is their last hope, and I'm not about to let it fail.

I point to a puke stain on Vernon's shoulder. "You've got some clean shirts in the office."

He glances at the stain. "I don't, actually. This was the last one." He plops his head down on the counter. "Nothing will ever be clean. Luka and Nikolai had the toxic shits last night. We might just have to condemn the whole house. All is lost, Millie. Poopocalypse has claimed every last soul."

I try not to laugh, but I can't help smiling. Vernon is the only person in my family who cusses, and something about him doing it in front of me makes me feel somehow older and cooler than I actually am. "I washed the shirts in your office with the towels last night." He picks up his head, and I get a good whiff of him. Toxic is about right. "Maybe hop in the showers, too? We normally don't see anyone for another twenty minutes anyway."

Vernon lifts his arm up and sniffs. "Well, guess I don't wanna scare off any potential new members."

I muster my most encouraging smile. "Right! Now, you know where the new membership packets are, and we're starting that promo with Green's Vitamins, remember? Those flyers are on your desk. And just . . ."

"Don't take no for an answer," he says, finishing Inga's business mantra. (Well, really, just her mantra in general.)

"Yes. Exactly."

"Inga's been slashing our budgets like crazy lately. She could star in her own horror movie. Or maybe she could be a wrestler. Invincible Inga the Budget Assassin." He turns and shuffles toward the showers, his shoulders sloped. I decide not to tell him about the brown mystery stain on his back.

"Just throw that shirt in the dirty towel hamper," I call as I let myself out the front door.

I slide into the minivan and glance up to the *Down for the Count* sign flickering above, with the *W* in "Down" completely out—something I take a mental note of for our long list of needed repairs.

As I pull out into the street, I hit the call button on the steering wheel. "Call Amanda!" I shout.

"Calling Panda," the robot car voice responds.

"No. End call. Do not call Panda. Call Amanda."

"Searching for Panda Express."

"No!" I moan and turn the whole radio off and on before trying again. "Call Amanda!"

There's a long pause before the robot voice answers me. "Calling Amanda."

"Finally," I mumble.

The line rings for a moment before Amanda groans into my speakers.

"Good morning, beautiful!" I say. "You are smart. You are talented. You are kind."

"There is nothing good about mornings," she says, her voice muffled by what sounds like a pillow. "But at least you got the beautiful thing right. Smart? Talented? Kind? I'll work on those."

"All mornings are good," I tell her. "It's those afternoons

that ruin everything." I chuckle at myself, but Amanda's silence is evidence that she doesn't find my humor cute. "Daily affirmations. I read about it last week. You speak the things you want to be. I figured it'd be easier if we affirmed each other. Spice things up!"

"I can play this game," she says. "I just say good things for you to be."

"Pretty much."

"You are a plate of hash brown. You are a waffle. You are a cinnamon roll."

"Amanda!" I roll my eyes. "Take this seriously."

"What? I'm hungry and no one is taking that seriously." She huffs into her receiver. "Are you on your way?" she asks. "Get out of my room, Tommy!" she growls. "Sorry. My brother."

"Be waiting for me outside. I've got morning announcements." I grin. "Be there in ten. And maybe we can stop for breakfast."

"I'm awake, Mom!" she shouts again. "Please hurry," she whispers into the phone.

"You owe me three affirmations!" I remind her as I press down harder on the gas. A friend in need is a friend indeed.

CALLIE

Two

Melissa and I sit on the floor of the gym, facing each other with our legs spread and our feet touching. Our hands clasp together as we stretch, pulling each other back and forth. She sits up, and her dark burgundy ponytail on the very top of her head swings forward as she pulls me toward her. I'm trying really hard not to breathe in, though, since the gymnasium floor seriously smells like balls.

"Our after-school practices next week were bumped to the band room," I tell Melissa.

She looks up from her stretch. "Are you shitting me?"

"Nope. Coach Spencer is scrambling because the football team's indoor facility isn't done yet, so they're moving everyone's practices around so the team can have the gym and the weightlifting equipment."

"But the band room has no space! What have they even done to deserve an indoor training facility? And it's not even football season."

I shrug. "In Clover City, every season is football season."

She blows her bangs out of her face. "Man, screw the athletics department."

"Finally, something we can agree on."

Melissa tugs me so far toward her that my whole upper body is lying flat on the ground. My inner thigh muscles sting, but I make no move to let her know that she's over-stretching me, because Melissa knows exactly what she's doing. She's testing me, and I'm not about to show any signs of weakness.

It's not that I don't like Melissa. I've known the girl half my life, and while neither of us has ever excelled at friendship—especially me—we've always done a good job of playing the part for each other. But what Melissa doesn't get is that in order for me to succeed, she must fail. At least in regard to our school's dance team, the Clover City High School Shamrocks. We're textbook frenemies, and I don't even mean that in a bad way. But next year, only one of us can be captain.

I rotate my neck, my cheek hovering over the floor. *Yep, still smells like balls down here.* Hanging just above us are various athletic banners, boasting of district championships and even a couple of state wins, too.

The biggest banner watching over us, though, is practically a family heirloom. The title of 1992 National Dance Team Champions belongs to none other than the CCHS Shamrocks. Not only was it the only time we won Nationals in any sport, it was the only time CCHS made it to a nationwide competition at all. And the most extraordinary part? The team was led by my mother. It also happened to be the year a huge judging scandal was uncovered in the dance world, on all levels from district to Nationals. Lots of teams were temporarily banned, but I've seen the tapes. The 1992 Shamrocks were on fire.

The Rams, our football team, has one of the worst records in Texas, and still they get a brand-new state-of-the-art indoor training facility, while the Shamrocks, the most winning team on campus, are relegated to practicing in the band room. Like my mama says, if it smells like bullshit, it probably is.

"Sam is late again," Melissa tells me over the cacophony of female voices echoing through the gymnasium.

"You wanna be the one to call her out?" I ask.

Melissa rolls her eyes and shakes her head. Sam is a senior and our team captain. What Melissa doesn't get is that Sam is late on purpose. She's testing us. Melissa and I are both second in command to Sam, as co–assistant captains, which means we are next in line to the throne, but only one will ascend. And I never lose.

Until then the two of us have to do a pretty decent job of working as a team, at least until Sam is ready to name her replacement.

But it's not all competition. Pieces of what Melissa and I have are the real deal. Like when her parents got divorced in ninth grade and she spent three weeks at my house, because things at home were way too lethal. Or the time Mrs. Gutierrez, Melissa's mom, began speaking to me in Spanish when she found out I was half Mexican. I was a little embarrassed because I can only pick up on a few words here and there and I'm definitely not confident enough to have a conversation. Melissa, on the other hand, comes from a large, traditional Mexican family. In fact, they lived here before Clover City could even be considered Texas. I swear, she could speak Spanish and read English while doing a Shamrock routine at the same time. But when Melissa saw my cheeks flush, she cut in, casually translating what her mom had just said. She never even brought it up after. Just pretended like nothing had happened.

Melissa pulls me even deeper into the stretch. "We're supposed to meet with Mrs. Driskil after practice." I twist my hands free and pop up on my feet.

"Whatever," she says. "That woman's just phoning it in. She doesn't care about being our faculty sponsor. All she cares about is the stipend from the district."

"It'd be so much worse if she actually gave a shit, though," I remind her. "Remember when she suddenly decided our bikini car wash was inappropriate and she made us do the whole thing in rain ponchos?"

Melissa laughs. "Okay, that was totally tragic. But it was hilarious when you just cut circle holes around your boobs and ass. She had no idea what to say." She laughs again, pointing a finger at me as she imitates Mrs. Driskil. "Young lady, your goodies are hanging out."

I bump hips with her. "At least my goods are worth seeing," I say. "Voted Best Ass three years running and Hottest of Them All this year. Don't you forget it."

She rolls her eyes. "Yes, we know. You would never let any of us forget. All hail Callie Reyes's ass."

I grin devilishly and clap my hands together once, silencing the rest of the team's chitchat. "Y'all! Let's get this going. Sam's running a little behind, so we're gonna start. Melissa," I call, "cue the music."

I begin rotating my hips a little to loosen up. "Okay, ladies, State is in three weeks, and we've got some serious ground to cover. We slayed at Regionals, but let's be real: our competition wasn't stacked the way we know it will be at State. So let's run through the routine two or three times, and then I'm going to step out and diagnose the problem areas."

The music starts. It's the perfect mash-up of pop songs everyone knows by heart and EDM that no one has ever heard of. Sam's got good taste. The opening verse of "Bad Girls" by M.I.A. kicks us off.

I close my eyes for the first few counts. I can practically feel the San Francisco breeze. I've never actually been to San Francisco. In fact the only person in my family who's been farther west than New Mexico is my older sister, Claudia, who went to San Diego for an opera singing competition when she was still in high school. But since Nationals are in San Francisco this year, that won't be the case for long. Last year we came in a heartbreaking second place at State, but Copper Hill, the team that took first place, is in total shambles after half their team was caught hazing their incoming freshmen.

My plan is to at least make it to Nationals, so we can build early momentum for next year. Maybe we'll even place. And then next year, we'll be in Miami for my senior year, and I'll lead the team to first place. I'll be accepted at the college of my choice, and I'll get the hell out of Clover

City before the ink on my diploma even has a chance to dry. That's the plan.

I enter the stage—well, actually the gymnasium floor—in the second wave of dancers. Our first run-through is a little clunky, but it's only our first go, and yesterday was a conditioning day. Already I can feel Melissa's frustration mounting. If she had it her way, she'd have torn into these girls already. But that's also why she'd be a shitty captain.

"Okay!" I shout the moment the music stops. "That was a decent warm-up, but we gotta pick up the pace. I think some of you are still having trouble with that triple pirouette. Jess, can you get out here and show us how it's done?"

Jess, a tall black sophomore and my pick for captain when I'm out of this hell hole, steps forward. She spins and spots effortlessly, which is most likely because she moved here from Dallas, where she went to some fancy-ass ballet school. The rest of us grew up at good old Dance Locomotive, which isn't really known for putting out quality dancers.

Jess slows it down and answers a few questions about momentum, hand placement, and spotting before we do our routine a couple more times. After that, Melissa and I sit out and watch, taking notes.

"I'm still not sure about that jeté combo," Melissa says. "I just don't think we can get even height on the jump. I mean, Jess's jump is way too high. She has to scale that back for the rest of us."

This choreography is my baby, and Melissa knows it.

"Maybe it's not about changing the choreography," I say. "Maybe we just all need to be better. Like Jess." I turn to her. "And do you wanna be the one to challenge Sam?"

Melissa shakes her head. "You're right."

After we give our notes, the whole team stands in a huddle before we break for the lockers.

"Look at all those tight asses!" Sam shouts as she jogs in to meet us. Sam is the kind of girl who, unlike me, actually looks like she could be related to my blond mom and even blonder little sister, and a small part of me hates her for that. Tall, white, strawberry-blond hair, and a straight frame built for ballet and the type of dresses that just graze your skin.

Sam squeezes into the circle. "Sorry I'm late, ladies. Had a few captain admin things to attend to."

I step aside to give her the floor. The key to a successful transition of power? Always know your place.

She smiles at me. "Wrap it up, Cal. You got this."

Melissa bristles beside me, but I don't flinch.

I close the team huddle and say, "Don't forget. Next week, we're performing at city hall for the mayor's American Heroes ceremony. Remember grades, y'all. I don't want to hear that any of you bitches are on academic probation just before we're going to State. I don't care if you have to cheat. Shit. Last week, Jill wrote her vocab words on her thigh."

All the girls laugh, but Jill, a short white sophomore with light brown ringlets, just shrugs. "It smudged a little, but I still passed. Apparently *fiduciary* means relating to or of the legal nature of *trust*. Not rust."

"That's the spirit!" I say. "Okay, hands in, y'all. On three. One, two, three!"

"SAN FRAN OR BUST!" we scream in unison.

I glance up to the bright red banner casting a shadow over us. *Watch out, '92. We're coming for you.*

As the team heads for the lockers, me, Melissa, and Sam sit on the bleachers.

"Thanks for taking the lead today, y'all," says Sam.

Melissa and I both nod.

"Hey," I say, "we might want to look at the jeté. Jess gets such crazy good height. It makes the rest of us look like total newbies, ya know?"

Melissa turns to me with a bitter smile. "I agree," she says dryly.

Sam squints, like she's running through the combo in her head. She nods. "You're so right, Callie. We'll look at it tomorrow."

What can I say? Some people are just born to be leaders.

Sam continues, "So listen, Driskil is about to come in here, and I already know why she wants to talk."

"What's up?" asks Melissa.

Sam rolls her eyes. "You know that dinky-ass gym that sponsored us this year?"

We both nod.

"They pulled their funding."

"Oh my God," I say, "what does this mean?"

Sam's normally sunny expression is grim. "Well, Driskil's gonna try to paint a pretty picture."

The door to the gym opens, and Mrs. Driskil shuffles inside.

"But basically we're fucked," whispers Sam before Mrs. Driskil is in earshot.

"Good morning, ladies," says Mrs. Driskil. "This will take just a moment."

Mrs. Driskil is a mousy woman who wears long skirts that collect dust along the hem and bulky cat-hair-coated grandpa cardigans with seasonal brooches. With the whiskery wrinkles around her mouth, not only is she a cat lady, she looks like one, too. She's nice enough, but she keeps her distance, which is exactly what we need in a faculty adviser. Her name might be on all the paperwork, but we're the ones running this show.

"Hey, Mrs. D," I say. "Nice sweater."

"Oh," she says in a sugary voice. "This was my aunt Dolores's. We almost buried her in it, but I was able to find her favorite just in time for the viewing."

Melissa clears her throat. "What a . . . memorable story."

"So what brings you all the way to the gymnasium?" I ask.

Mrs. Driskil coughs into her fist. "Well. It's, um, one of your sponsors. They had to back out, and it appears they were your primary sponsor. That sweet little boxing gym. Down for the Count?"

"Wait," I gasp, feigning surprise. "What did you say?"

"Well, I guess the owner is just having a rough go of it, and he's cutting costs." She speaks slowly and loudly, as if I was being literal about not hearing her.

"Okay," I say. "But can't we just, like, get another sponsor? My boyfriend's dad owns a couple car dealerships. I'm sure he could help us out."

Sam shakes her head.

Driskil rings her hands together. "Well, it's not that easy. The district bylaws say that a sponsor must be approved before the school year, and that the student is responsible for any additional funding needs. And so I'm afraid that means the cost of travel and accommodations for State and Nationals would fall to you ladies."

Panic swells in my chest, but I refuse to appear anything less than calm. "Who can even afford that?" I ask.

"Definitely not me," says Melissa.

Mrs. Driskil continues, "It looks like we have almost half of what we need for State, but if we make it any further than that, we're going to have to raise funds."

I sputter for a moment. "But . . . but how much does it even cost to go to Nationals?" The expense of a big trip like that is almost as unfathomable to me as the cost of college.

"Well, it isn't cheap. At all," says Sam. "I mean, a single car wash barely paid for just one of our uniforms. Airfare to California is astronomical. We could maybe charter a bus, but the district would have to give us tons of extra time off."

Silence settles as I let this news sink in.

Mrs. D clears her throat. "I don't think you should be too worried, girls. You ladies are all so talented, but . . . but Texas is a big state."

I'm almost impressed. I didn't think Mrs. D had it in her to make a dig like that. But I'm mostly pissed, to be honest.

"We've made it before," says Melissa. "And we came really close last year. We shouldn't have to limit ourselves just because some stupid gym flaked on us."

I nod. "This is our year. I can feel it. And it's Sam's last year." I shake my head. "Hell no. Not on my watch. Ya know, no one talks about the budget when the football team has an away game. If those boys ever made it to post-season again, the whole town would be throwing money and panties at them."

We wait for Mrs. Driskil to say something, but all she gives us is a look of pity. I'm so angry my fingers are trembling. Maybe if Mrs. Driskil wasn't so used to people treating her like crap, she wouldn't let the dance team get treated the same way.

Sam stands up and starts walking to the locker room without waiting to be dismissed, and Melissa and I follow her.

"Girls," calls Mrs. Driskil. "Girls! I think it's best we not tell the team for the time being. It might not even be an issue! And I just think it would cause unneeded distress. We ought to discuss next steps."

The three of us just keep walking.

★ ★ ★

I spend second period as an office aide. Not because I requested the job, but because my mama did. Actually, she's more of a smother than a mother, but she's *my* smother.

As I try to sneak past her into the copying room, the sound of a thick southern twang stops me. "There's my Callie Honey. Baby, come here. Give your mama some love."

I double back and stash my backpack under her desk before plopping down onto the little stool she keeps behind her desk for filing. She pulls my face close to her with both hands and gives me a kiss on the cheek, leaving her mark: Revlon Certainly Red 740, the color my mama has worn every day since her mama took her to the drugstore on her thirteenth birthday to buy her first real adult makeup.

"Has your sister emailed you?" she asks. "I tried to get her on the FaceTime chat, but I can't make sense of the time zones in Germany."

"Mama, it's just FaceTime. Not the FaceTime chat. And no, Claudia hasn't emailed me." I don't tell her that I haven't emailed her either. It's not that I don't love my sister, but we're busy, and if Claudia's not answering Mom's phone calls, I'm sure more than time zones are to blame. Claudia is a student at USC but is spending the semester at the opera house in Dresden. I'm happy for her, but I miss having someone in our house who looks like me. When she left for college, I didn't anticipate what it might feel like to be the only brown person in our otherwise white household.

Mama sighs. "How were the girls looking this morning?" she asks.

I nod. "It wasn't bad. We're going to start meeting after school next week to gear up for State."

She taps a pen to her lips. "Is that going to interfere with your work schedule?"

I prop up my elbows on her desk and rest my chin in my hands. "It'll be tight, but it's just for two weeks. And everyone at work is cool about dance stuff."

She licks the pad of her pointer finger before flipping through attendance sheets. "And what about homework? You won't be leaving much time for Bryce either."

"I'll make it work with homework, and Bryce will see me when he sees me. It's not like he stresses out about fitting me into his schedule during football season."

"That's my girl." She hands me a stack of late slips to stamp. "I'm gonna get with some of the parents and Principal Armstrong about arranging a fan bus down to State. We got to be sure to decorate y'all's bus, too, with shoe polish and whatnot."

My smother would be the ideal candidate for faculty adviser, but seeing as she's the school secretary and not an actual teacher, her level of involvement is limited to enthused parent. Which is for the best, I guess. Between my stepdad, my sister Kyla, trying to keep tabs on Claudia from halfway across the world, and her job, the woman barely has a moment to shower. I can see her age showing, too, but maybe that's just 'cause I remember what she looked like when it was just me, my dad, Claudia, and her.

When I think of her then, I remember her black high-waisted jeans and her thick black belt with its shiny silver buckle and her tight, lacy tank tops. She was like the West Texas version of Olivia Newton-John's Bad Sandy from *Grease*. She'd swivel her hips across the kitchen—which always smelled more like her DIY perm than any food we ate—to old Selena songs while my dad made horrible bachelor-type food for us, like hot dogs wrapped in tortillas.

Now the only self-imposed requirements of my mama's wardrobe is that it "drapes nicely" and covers up any lumps or rolls she's found herself with over the last few years. The lipstick, though, still remains.

She presses her fingers to my forehead, massaging my furrowed brow away. "You're gonna need to start using my antiaging cream if you keep wrinkling up your forehead like that. Now tell me what's got you so worried."

I look over my shoulder and beyond her where students wait to be seen by the principal, vice principal, or guidance counselor. "Well," I say quietly, "shit's sorta hitting the fan. It looks like the dance team lost one of our major sponsors, and now we're pretty much screwed. We're gonna have to do a few emergency fund-raisers before State, but there's definitely not any money for Nationals."

She tucks a loose strand of hair behind my ear. "Oh, goodness. Well, that just won't do. What'd Mrs. Driskil say?"

I roll my eyes.

She shakes her head firmly. "That woman's more useless than fuzz on a peach," she whispers, tapping her red-painted pointer fingernail against her chin. "Mama's gonna get you in to see Vice Principal Benavidez. Y'all girls have worked too hard for some silly little money to stand in your way. And Lord knows most of us can't just spring for a trip to San Francisco."

I bite down on my lower lip to stop myself from smiling. I can see her going into full-on Mama Bear mode, referring to herself in the third person. I know there's not much she can actually do other than make the vice principal have a sit-down with me, but there's something about seeing an adult actually *try* that makes me feel better. Even if it's only momentarily. And if I can solve this problem on my own, Sam will have no choice but to name me captain.

"Thanks, Mama." Before I get to work on picking up attendance sheets, I dig through her desk drawer for a makeup wipe to scrub away the lip print on my cheek. She may have her nose in every corner of my life, but sometimes having a smother isn't all that bad.

MILLIE

Three

At lunch, Amanda and I sit in the courtyard at our usual table while she devours the Amy Poehler autobiography I lent her—or I guess I should more accurately say I rehomed it, since my mother was not too pleased when she cracked it open and got an eyeful of some of Ms. Poehler's language. Amanda chuckles to herself every few minutes, and it takes everything in me not to ask what part she's reading.

As my eyes roam the courtyard, I spy Willowdean peeking her head out the door and waving frantically. Following her gaze, I find Bo, her boyfriend. Her very cute boyfriend with—as Amanda puts it—a peach butt. Just the thought of a boy's behind has me blushing.

Will's eyes sweep the rest of the courtyard, and she waves at Amanda and me before ducking back into the building. I wave back and make a note to myself to talk to Willowdean about my current . . . situation. I'm hungry for any type of advice that will move me from Crush Corner to Boyfriend Boardwalk. (Surely I'm not the only person who imagines life in terms of board games like Monopoly or Candy Land.)

See? This is why I need to talk to Willowdean. I'm going bananas here.

But our opportunities to chat are sadly limited. I wish Willowdean, Ellen, and Hannah at least shared a lunch period with me and Amanda. That'd be a good excuse to see them.

I don't know what I expected after the pageant. Actually, that's a lie. I know exactly what I expected. I thought that we'd all be friends. Me, Amanda, Willowdean, Ellen, and Hannah. We'd be this renegade group of mismatched friends that didn't always make sense, but somehow works. Our shared experience would have bonded us like in *The Breakfast Club* or some other great ensemble cast. Except that's not quite what happened. And, to be honest, I've spent a lot of time wondering if the Breakfast Club even hung out again after those credits rolled.

I open my thermos and pour the chicken soup into the lid, resigning myself to lunch with a distracted Amanda. "I miss the pageant."

I'm answered with silence except for the sound of the table rocking back and forth as she bounces her feet.

"Did you see that the school newspaper did a big exposé about how the cafeteria meat loaf doesn't actually contain any meat?"

Nope. Nothing.

"I was thinking we could sign up for a belly-dancing class together?"

Silence.

I reach across the table and slowly pull the book away.

"But—but I was reading that."

"Well, I was also trying to engage in conversation with you. And you've been headfirst in this book since I picked you up this morning. And!" I add. "This is my book!"

She sighs and dog-ears her place in the book. "You're the one who made me read this thing in the first place."

I try not to cringe. Dog-earing a book feels like a violation of some sacred unspoken rule. "What I was saying is I sort of miss the pageant, don't you?"

She laughs. "Not even a little bit. Those people never appreciated my skills and charm anyway."

I try not to smile. Amanda's soccer display for the talent segment of the pageant was inspiring, but the judges didn't really know what to make of it. I think the comment section of one of her scorecards said something along the lines of "Didn't quite fit the tone of the pageant. Maybe try juggling next time? Or try going out for the soccer team?"

The soccer team. A sore subject with Amanda. She, her parents, and the administration at school have gone back and forth with the soccer-team coach, Ms. Shelby, who can't seem to look past Amanda's physical differences to see the talent she possesses.

Amanda's been ridiculed for years about her LLD (leg length discrepancy) and about the heel lift she has to wear. But if Amanda can hear or see people making fun of her, you would never know. Her theory is that she sets the tone for how the world treats her. And in her own words: if she wants to be treated like a bada**, then she should act like a bada**. But I know it must get to her sometimes.

"You're totally right," I finally say. "But I don't even mean the pageant. I'm talking about all of us just hanging out, ya know?"

She shrugs, her whole body flopping. "Yeah, I guess. But I kind of like it when it's just us."

For a moment her words make my heart burst. Amanda and I haven't been friends forever like Will and Ellen, but being the butt of everyone's jokes for much of middle school and high school has bonded us together in a way that is stronger than time. "Me too. You know that. But I just wish we all had a reason to get together every once in a while."

She squints a little, looking past me at some memory of the last few months. "Yeah, we were like our own kind of club, I guess. Like, a badass lady gang that totally upped the cool factor of that pageant."

I smile at the thought, but then it hits me. "A club! Oh my God! Amanda, you're a genius!"

"Well, that's news to exactly no one, but explain yourself," she demands in a British accent as she holds her pencil up like a sword.

"Hang on." I pull my cell phone out of my backpack, which has been emblazoned with all kinds of stitchwork, including flowers, clouds, stars, a few emojis I tried my hand at, and even a little fat mini me on the very bottom of the front pocket. I fire off a quick text to Amanda, El, Will, and Hannah.

Amanda's phone immediately dings. "You didn't have

to text me, too. I'm sitting right here." She rolls her eyes before reading the message out loud. "MAYDAY! MAYDAY! MAYDAY! MEET ME IN THE COURTYARD AFTER SCHOOL AT 3:15!"

The first bell for next period rings. My phone dings in rapid succession as I get two responses.

ELLEN: I'll be there.

WILLOWDEAN: DITTO! Plus El and Tim are my ride home.

HANNAH: I'll be there but only because I don't have anything else to do. 💩

I drop my phone into my bag and pour my leftover soup back into my thermos.

"Are you even going to tell me what your idea is?" asks Amanda.

"You'll see at three fifteen." The second bell rings. "Oh, darn. I gotta go."

Amanda waves me off, and I dash over to my next class. Anyone with short legs knows the value of speed walking, and with my AP Psychology class clear on the other side of the school in the temporary buildings, I barely make it before Mr. Prater locks the door.

Mr. Prater doesn't mess around with his attendance policy, and tardiness is not tolerated. He's a very serious guy who is also guilty of making seriously bad jokes.

"Okay, last one," Mr. Prater says as he shuts the door behind me. "Why was Pavlov's hair so soft?"

The only response he gets as I walk to my desk is a few groans.

"Come on, y'all!" he says. "Classical conditioning!"

I chuckle as I sit down at the back of the class next to Malik at the fat-kid table. (Well, it's not just for fat kids. A few kids in wheelchairs use them too, but I lovingly think of it as the fat-kid table. Amanda prefers cool-kid table. She's not wrong.) Everyone else has those little desks you slide into, but I don't quite fit—at least not comfortably. I guess it used to bother me to be singled out, but one size doesn't actually fit all. (Oh my gosh. That is totally my next cross-stitch.)

Malik isn't fat, but I am, and he's my go-to partner on group projects. He is also my crush. In fact, I think he might be THE CRUSH TO END ALL CRUSHES. So, yeah, I like him. But the better news is he might like me. I think. Amanda says yes, definitely. He went with me to Sadie Hawkins last fall. We even held hands. But no kiss. To say he's sending mixed signals would be the understatement of the year.

My hopes were all but deflated until he volunteered to be my escort for the pageant. I thought maybe then, after seeing me win runner-up, that it just might be the night our lips locked. But instead I got a hug, a pat on the back, and a yellow rose. Nothing says "just friends" like a yellow rose. (And nothing's wrong with being friends, but what I feel for him is different than friendship.) Not only that, but we have these wonderful hours-long conversations every night via chat or sometimes text. And then I show up to school and I'm lucky if he says more than fifteen words to me.

"Hey," I say, catching my breath for a moment before adding, "Almost didn't make it."

Malik shakes his head. "Explain to me how Clover City can afford to build an indoor training facility for their mediocre football team, but the AP Psych class has to meet in a temporary building that can barely withstand a windstorm, let alone a tornado, and has no windows."

My cheeks warm. My stomach tingles. That was a lot of words. From his mouth. Using his talky lips that also double as kissy lips. "I swear you should run for city council."

Malik turns to me, his face a little flushed, like he's just realized that whole rant was said out loud and not in his head. Or online.

I feel like my insides are glowing, and if I'm not careful, they'll glow so bright everyone will be able to see.

There may or may not be a small notebook in my room with a furry seafoam cover that is dedicated to all the reasons I find Malik crush-worthy. (I like organizing things, okay? Including my feelings.) There are lots of things I might put on those pages in list form.

1. His thick, commanding eyebrows that perfectly match his shiny black Fonzie-like hair.
2. His square tortoiseshell glasses that perfectly complement his deep brown skin and the fact that he keeps a dustcloth folded in his wallet to clean them off a couple times a day.
3. The way he wears penny loafers and puts real,

shiny pennies inside them.

4. How he rolls his jeans at the bottom and always wears subtle but seasonally appropriate socks.

5. The way he irons his T-shirts and always wears them tucked in with a cardigan in the fall and a leather bomber jacket in the winter, like a hot South Asian greaser with a little bit of dad sensibility mixed in.

But perhaps the thing that really makes my knees melt is Malik's drive. I'd be lying if I said I hadn't spent a fair share of our AP Psych classes daydreaming about how we'd make the perfect power couple. Me on the six o'clock news and him running for local office. Or maybe even Congress or working as some kind of documentarian/philanthropist.

His leg brushes against mine as he reaches behind his chair to grab his textbook. "I think we're doing that open-book quiz today."

"Shoot," I whisper before I can even dig through my bag. "I knew I was supposed to stop at my locker. You even mentioned it last night."

He slides his book toward me. "We can share."

I smile. There goes the fluttering again. "Okay. Thanks."

I tear out a piece of notebook paper as Mr. Prater turns on his projector and lowers the lights. He plugs in the twinkly lights strung overhead. He hung them himself due to the lack of windows out here in the temporaries, which means no natural light for note-taking while the projector is on.

I realize this wasn't Mr. Prater's intention, but it's all sort of romantic. Sharing a book with Malik underneath the low lights as our thighs touch so frequently it's more than an accident . . .

I have to force myself to concentrate on the quiz questions displayed on the slides, but it's hard not to let this breathless feeling overtake me completely.

Is this what liking someone is supposed to feel like? Because if this is a crush, I don't know if I can handle the intensity of actually *loving* someone. Or maybe this *is* love. I don't know. What I do know is that whatever I feel for Malik goes way beyond just friends.

That afternoon, Will and El are waiting in the courtyard with Tim and Bo. Amanda's close on my heels as we make our way to their table.

"I don't want to step on any toes," I call out to them. "But this meeting is girls only."

Tim shrugs, and Ellen gives him a quick kiss on the cheek with his face glued to his phone before he walks off toward the parking lot. "I'll be at the car."

"His latest obsession is that geocaching app with those little trolls and gnomes," Ellen explains.

Bo gives me a quick nod. "Hey, Millie." He turns to Willowdean. "I'll pick you up for work if you want?"

"I think El and Tim are gonna drop me off actually, but

I'll take a ride home tonight," she says, her golden curls tangling in the wind.

He nods before giving her a kiss on the lips and then jogs to catch up with Tim.

"Not a bad view," says Amanda, watching him go.

El sputters with laughter, and Willowdean's whole face looks like it's about ready to catch fire. "Can't say I disagree," she finally says.

I smile. "Anyone seen Hannah?" I ask.

"I'm here," someone groans.

I turn to find Hannah wearing a front baby sling with an anatomically correct baby in it. Her once-overgrown bangs have become swoopier than they were, so you can actually see her face. Her charcoal eyeliner is jagged and a little smudged, but the look works for her. Based on her medium brown skin, most people at school just call Hannah black or African American, but she actually prefers Afro-Latina. One of the ladies running the pageant told Hannah that was a mouthful when she included it in her pageant intro, but Hannah told her she should try harder. I tend to agree.

Of everyone from the pageant, I see Hannah the least. Not because I don't want to, but because she goes out of her way to be unseen. Plus she has lots of slightly older friends who don't even live in Clover City. Her elusiveness makes me want to try even harder to be friends with her.

"What the hell?" asks Will.

Hannah rolls her head back, stomping to the table where the rest of us sit. "I signed up for that life-skills class thinking it would be dumb stuff like online banking and applying for jobs, but no. It's basically a home ec class." She sits down and slams the doll on the table, triggering sobs from the speaker on the back of its head. "Our final," she says, like we're gathered around a campfire telling horror stories, "is a casserole."

Ellen, Amanda, and Will nearly fall out of their seats in hysterics, and I bite my lip, trying not to laugh along with them.

Hannah gives them all a half-baked dirty look, but it's the best she can do not to smile herself.

"I'll dig through my mom's recipe book if it'll help," I offer.

She turns to me. "If you really want to help, you'll make the damn thing for me."

Willowdean nudges me with her elbow. "So what's all this about? Did you gather us all here to corrupt another time-honored Clover City tradition?"

They go quickly silent with all eyes on me. Suddenly I feel very, very dumb. Self-doubt washes over me, and I am immediately positive that I like all of them much more than any of them like me. That's just the worst feeling. It's like showing up to a costume party where you're the only one who dressed up.

But then I look at Amanda, and she nods, and I know that at the very least, I can always count on her.

"I miss y'all," I finally say. "A lot. And that's what this emergency meeting is about. I know that we're all busy with different things and the pageant is long gone."

"Thank God," says Hannah, stuffing her baby and sling into her messenger bag.

"But I sort of hate that, ya know? Because I just never see y'all anymore, and, well, a lot of good things came out of the pageant. But the best part was all of us becoming friends."

Willowdean smiles. "Well, not to be self-centered, but I sort of feel like the best part was when I wore a cardboard Cadillac on stage."

"Okay," I say. "Yes, that was pretty great. But back then we saw each other all the time," I say. "Because we had a reason to, so if we need a reason to get together, I'm creating one."

Ellen squints at me suspiciously.

"I'm not a big organized-activities person, in case you hadn't already discerned that about me," says Hannah.

"What's your idea?" asks Amanda.

I inhale deeply. "Slumber parties. Every Saturday until the end of the school year. We'll all take turns hosting."

It's so quiet I can hear the cheerleaders practicing in the gym.

Ellen speaks first. "Every. Single. Saturday. Night?"

"Well, sure," I say, my answer coming out more like a question. "But with slumber parties. We can do face masks. And crafts. And play games. And exchange ideas."

"Exchange ideas?" asks Hannah. "What? Like the Slumber Party United Nations?"

"It has to be every Saturday night?" asks Willowdean.

"That's prime date-night real estate."

Amanda shrugs. "The only date I've got is with my TV and my cat. I'm in."

A small bit of relief sparks in my chest, but no one is quick to follow her lead. I nod. "Okay. What about every other Saturday?"

Hannah works diligently at peeling off her dark purple nail polish. "We all have to take turns hosting?"

Ellen turns to Will, and in a quieter voice says, "This is like what we were talking about the other night. More time for us. Without the guys, ya know?"

I can see Will turning this over in her head. She's the kind of person who is economical with her time and her love, and I can appreciate that. Sharing Ellen is hard for her.

She looks to me. "Let's try it for a few weeks. But no hard feelings if it gets to be too much, okay? Just with work and school and . . ." Will sighs. "Bo, and trying to be a good friend and not go crazy. It's a lot."

"I get it," I say.

Ellen grins. "You know the deal. We're a buy-one-get-two kind of thing. I'm in."

And as a surprise to absolutely no one, Hannah is in no hurry to respond. She picks the polish off her entire thumbnail before speaking. "We're not, like, having pillow fights or anything, okay? And if anyone tries to give me a makeover, I'll cut off their hair in the middle of the night."

I swallow. "Understood." I force out a laugh to lighten

the mood a bit. Laughing on command is something that happens to be my number-one talent, and one of the things that will make me a great news anchor one day.

I volunteer to host first and promise to text everyone more details before the weekend. A part of me is nervous, like somehow they'll all decide they don't like me anymore or that this will all turn out to be one big embarrassing disaster. But we only have one year left of high school, and the anxiety inside me tells me that if I don't solidify our friendship now, the five of us will just drift away from one another eventually.

But mostly I'm just bubbling with excitement.

CALLIE

Four

After school, I hang back for a little while to try to talk to Vice Principal Benavidez about the dance team's sponsorship dilemma, but he's no help. I guess he *pretended* to be helpful. He promised me stuff I know he won't deliver on, like that he'd check with the superintendent or ask Principal Armstrong if there's any room in the budget. When I asked to speak to the principal myself, he fed me some crap about Principal Armstrong being a very busy woman, like she's the freaking president or something.

My back pocket vibrates, and when I check my phone, I find a text from Bryce.

BRYCE: babe im outside where u at?

Just as I'm about to type a response, I collide with a pastel ball of dough. My whole body bounces back as my phone slips out of my hands and slides across the floor.

"Oh my goodness!" squeaks a voice.

I glance up to see Millie Michalchuk, someone I am very much aware of. To be honest, you can't miss the girl. Freshman year she was crowned the Nottest of Them All according to the Hottest and Nottest List. Luckily for Millie, her name only popped up on the list one year. I believe this year the honor went to Hannah Perez.

I groan. "That phone better not be broken."

"Oh gosh, I hope not," she says as she retrieves the phone from the floor. "Shipshape!"

I hold out my hand. "Lucky you."

She grins. "You're right about that!" The phone vibrates in her hand as she gives it back to me. "Sorry," she says. "I was just in here to give your mom the morning announcements to proofread for tomorrow, but I guess I missed her, huh?"

I shrug. "Yeah, I don't really keep up with her schedule." Lie. She's gone to pick up Kyla and take her to dance class. I glance down at my phone to see another message from Bryce. "Right, well, I gotta go."

Millie steps forward, blocking my path as if she didn't even hear me. "What a beautiful necklace," she says, lightly touching my thirteenth-birthday gift from my dad.

The gold circle pendant with an engraved *C* hangs from a thin gold chain. It's something I only take off for dance competitions. Besides the tiny diamond studs Bryce gave me for Christmas, it's the only piece of real jewelry I own. I clear my throat. "Uh, thanks."

"Tell your mom I stopped by?"

I squeeze past her. "I'll try to remember."

Millie just makes me uncomfortable. It hasn't always been that way. Before the pageant last fall, she was just some random fat girl who always kept to herself and who . . . okay, yes, me and my friends sometimes made fun of. At least not to her face. At the pageant, especially during the swimwear component . . . I don't know. It was just, like, hard to look at her. It wasn't like when I'd made dumb jokes about her in the past. This time I just wanted to cover her up and save her the embarrassment. Except Millie didn't seem embarrassed. Anyway, I guess the judges pitied her, too, because in the end, she got runner-up.

I shoot off a reply to let Bryce know I'm on my way. I sigh with momentary relief.

I love Bryce. Between my mom, my stepdad, my little sister, and sometimes Claudia, my house is constantly in motion. And there's my dad, too, and all my worries about him ever finding someone and my abuela getting older. Then the never-ending Shamrock drama.

But Bryce. I never have to worry about Bryce. We've been together since freshman year. Bryce is The One. We've had our hiccups, but what long-term couple hasn't?

As I push through the doors leading into the parking lot, I find Bryce leaning against his sparkling cobalt-blue Dodge Charger with shiny new dealer plates. Despite what everyone might think, I'm not a materialistic person, but I've got to admit: there's something hot about having a boyfriend with a flashy car. And Bryce has a new car every few months—a perk of his dad being none other than Clay Dooley, owner of not one but four local dealerships. Clover

City doesn't even have a damn Target, but we have almost as many car dealerships as we do gas stations. Anyway, with the last name Dooley, he's Clover City royalty. If he's a prince, I'm his princess.

He greets me with a kiss—an open-mouth kiss for everyone to see. His hands grip either side of my waist, and he literally sweeps me off my feet.

We can't keep our hands off each other. I know it can be obnoxious and over the top. But I spend my entire day 100 percent in control of my life. When I'm with Bryce, the buzzing in my brain eases and I can operate on autopilot.

He twists his hand into my ponytail and tugs playfully. "I missed you today."

"Well," I tell him, "you've got me for two whole hours before my family gets home."

"Say no more," he says, and smacks my ass.

I yelp, trying to force a giggle. I might be down for public displays of affection, but that's not exactly my flavor. Whatever. It's not a big enough deal for me to make a thing of it. And I'll totally get him back tomorrow and embarrass him in front of his friends with some sappy-ass baby talk or something.

"Hey," he says as we're getting into the car. "There's Ellen."

My gaze scans the parking lot, and there she is. For a brief moment, regret pokes at the pit of my stomach. "Gimme a sec," I tell him.

Ellen was my sad attempt at branching out for more female friends while Bryce was busy with football season.

She was in the pageant and we worked together at Sweet 16. She's the kind of girl everyone wants to be friends with. I am so not that girl. But I am the girl who gets what she wants, and I wanted El to be my friend.

But the pageant ended. I didn't win—even though Bryce's dad, who served as a judge, swore I had his vote. I thought for sure I'd at least get runner-up like Claudia had a few years ago. And then a couple weeks later, Ellen left Sweet 16 for a higher-paying job at Cinful Rolls, the cinnamon-bun stand in the food court. So I decided that I don't need friends. I don't even have time for them, honestly. But something about Ellen still makes me feel like a failure, and that really pisses me off.

"El-bell!" I call, but she doesn't flinch. She probably can't hear me over the engine. "El! Ellen!"

She doesn't turn around as she walks arm in arm with her friend Willowdean—who, by the way, hates me for no reason other than that I was a good friend to Ellen when she wasn't—to the other side of the parking lot, where Tim's Jeep is parked.

"Ellen!" I yell a little louder but immediately regret the decision. It feels desperate, and on the list of things I hate, that is nearly number one.

She freezes, but Willowdean doesn't hear me and instead trips on a chunk of gravel as Ellen inadvertently yanks her back. Ellen laughs, and so does Willowdean, their heads knocking together.

For a brief moment something that feels like jealousy crawls up my spine.

Finally Ellen turns around and searches the empty parking lot for a second before she sees me. I offer a short wave, and from all the way on the other side of the lot I can see that she's surprised it's me, and not necessarily in a good way.

"Hey!" she shouts back. "How's Sweet 16?"

"Good," I say. "Same as it's always been. I haven't been working as much since it's dance-competition season."

"Cool!"

If it's even possible to share an awkward silence from across a parking lot, we do. I immediately feel foolish for thinking that she and I could be friends. Or that I need friends to begin with.

"Babe!" says Bryce from inside the car as he gently revs the engine.

Willowdean tugs at Ellen's hand and whispers something in her ear. A feeling that is only faintly familiar creeps up my neck. It's the kind of feeling I get when people assume I'm dumb because I'm on the dance team or because I'm pretty. Or when Bryce took me home for the first time, and his dad called me a pretty little señorita. (I've spent many sleepless nights fantasizing about the perfect comeback to that, by the way.) It's that feeling like you're the butt of the joke.

I don't say good-bye or wave. I just turn around and slide into the passenger seat, slamming the door behind me.

"Whoa," says Bryce. "Careful." He pats the dashboard, soothing the car.

I close my eyes and shake my head. "Sorry. Let's hurry

up before my family gets home."

The tires squeal as we take off out of the parking lot and blow straight through a stop sign. Bryce rests one hand on my thigh, and we break so many speed limits that this dumb town becomes a blur.

Bryce lies sprawled out on my floor while I sit cross-legged on my bed with my laptop balancing on my knees. He's spent the last thirty minutes nuzzling and kissing me, trying to distract me from my task: figuring out how the hell to fund the rest of the dance team's season. Bryce, tall, white, with broad shoulders, and bright green eyes, makes for a very tempting distraction, but my focus is unwavering.

He groans, rolling back and forth on my mauve-colored shag carpet. "Are you almost done?"

"I don't know." I bite back a grin.

He's being annoying, but there's something I love about seeing him in my room, in my old house with its fading carpet and popcorn glitter ceilings. You would think he would care about how outdated this place is or that he'd rather be at his fancy new house that looks more like the Parthenon than anything that belongs in Clover City. But he's here. With me.

He sits up, trying to get a glimpse at my computer screen. "What are you even doing?"

I open my mouth to speak, but I get lost in a blog post about a high school band that sent themselves to Nationals by having a twenty-four-hour marathon drum circle. No, thank you.

"Babe," says Bryce. "Babe, your phone is ringing."

"Oh." I blink quickly.

He tosses me my phone from where it sits on the floor, and I catch it like a hot potato.

"Hello?" Why do I always say it like a question?

"What's a dad got to do to get his girl to answer her phone? I already pay the damn bill."

I laugh, but my shoulders slump. I have a great dad; however, I'm not always the best daughter. "Sorry, Dad. I've been crazy busy with practice and—"

"I know, I know. You've got a life. I get it. But maybe you could make it over here for a weekend visit soon, yeah? Your abuela has been nagging the hell out of me about you coming down for your birthday."

I can't even think that far beyond my immediate problems right now, but instead I just say, "Tell her I miss her."

"You can call her and let her know yourself. I think I hear from Claudia more than I hear from you."

I sigh into the receiver. "You're really piling it all on, aren't you?"

He yawns and groans, like he's stretching after a long day at work. "Watching your kid's life unfold on Facebook doesn't really cut it, if you know what I mean. So how's Bryan or Reese or whatever his name is?"

I giggle, and Bryce looks up from his phone as if he can sense my dad talking about him. Dad isn't one of those fathers who thinks his daughter isn't dating until she's forty-three or that I'm completely void of hormones. But Bryce, with his flashy cars and show-stealing (and casually racist) dad, isn't really someone my dad, who values things like a smartly organized toolbox and almost any Nicolas Cage film, especially *National Treasure*, has patience for.

"Bryce," I say, overenunciating his name, "is actually right here."

"So you guys are at the library or something, right? Because I know your mom and Keith aren't even home from work yet."

"Actually, we're in my room doing homework."

"With the door open, I hope."

"Dad, no one's home. If I want to have sex with my boyfriend, do you think it matters if the door is open or closed?"

Bryce's face turns ghostly white.

Dad huffs. "Why do you have to go and point out logic like that?"

"Love you, Dad."

"Just . . ." He clears his throat. "Make sure you're careful and all that."

"I've been on the pill since I was—"

"Yup. Okay. I hear ya. Loud and clear. Message received. Good job."

"The dance team lost funding," I blurt out before realizing I hadn't even told Bryce yet.

"You didn't tell me that," says Bryce.

I glance at him apologetically before continuing to fill him and my dad in simultaneously. "We've got State in two weeks, which we can barely cover, and Nationals after that, which isn't even an option at the moment. And we actually have a shot at going all the way this year."

"Oh, baby," he says. "Maybe I could talk to my boss and see if they could throw some sponsorship dollars your way, or maybe I could even cut a check to make a tiny dent."

I smile. "Thanks, Dad. I'm going to brainstorm some options and see what we can do."

"What happened for you to lose a sponsor? You girls getting into trouble?" he jokes.

"This dumb, dinky little gym offered to sponsor us for the first time this year, and they just bailed on us right in the middle of the competitive season."

"Can they even do that?" he asks.

"What are we gonna do? Bully them into giving us the money?"

He grunts. "That's pretty much what you and your sisters do to me and your mother."

"Not funny," I tell him.

"A little funny."

"Maybe a smidge funny."

"Well, you let me know if I can help, okay?" he says. "And your birthday, too. I need ideas. Unless you want another transistor radio with a wind-up flashlight on the end."

"I think I'm good."

"That was a great gift," he says, defending himself. "A good thing to keep in your trunk for emergencies."

My dad has a love for all things simple and utilitarian. In fact, I think I've gotten him the same mustache comb for three Christmases in a row, but he doesn't mind since it's one less thing he needs to replace. "Dad, I don't have a car."

He chuckles. "Prepare for the life you want, mija, not the one you have, right?"

I roll my eyes even though he can't see. "I'll send a list," I tell him. "And I'll call Abuela. Love you."

"To the moon," he says before hanging up.

Bryce clears his throat. "What was your dad saying about me? I think that guy hates me." It's a fleeting moment of weakness from Bryce, who is very used to receiving male approval.

"He doesn't *hate* you," I say. "He just doesn't know you."

"You're right. Everybody loves The Bryce." He laughs to himself. "By the way, did you say the dance team is broke?"

"Well, yeah. We're kind of screwed." I crawl onto the floor next to him, and he practically pulls me into his lap. I tell him all about my shitty day and how unhelpful Vice Principal Benavidez was and how Down for the Count just pulled the rug right out from underneath us. I find myself tearing up a little, which only makes me angrier. "I really hate to ask this, but do you think your dad's dealership would think about sponsoring us?"

Bryce's brow furrows. "My dad's old-school, ya know? He still thinks cheerleaders and dance teams only exist for the sake of halftime shows. He doesn't really get the purpose of a competition that doesn't involve one team scoring points against the other. He's pretty set on his football sponsorship."

My shoulders slump as I nod. I hate being compared to the cheerleading team. Our cheerleading team is noncompetitive, which means they live for football and basketball games. I don't mind doing halftime shows, but when it comes down to it, those things are just extended practice times for us. While some cheerleading teams kick serious ass, ours seems to exist for the sole sake of giggling and chanting for boys fumbling around with balls. The Shamrocks exist to win.

"But I guess I could ask if he wants to sponsor another team," says Bryce. He doesn't sound confident, but I appreciate the effort.

"Really?" I ask. "You would do that?" If anyone can afford it, it's Mr. Dooley. Despite the handful of cars in his garage, he has a chauffeur drive him around from morning until night. When we were in elementary school, before his driver upgraded to a huge luxury SUV, Bryce's dad would come through the pick-up/drop-off line in a limo.

He shrugs. "I'll just have to catch him at the right time. He's been weird lately. Wants me to start spending more time at the dealerships, figuring out how things work. Hey," says Bryce, cradling my chin in his hand. "I know what'll make you feel better. Or at least distract you for a little while."

"Yeah?" The pit of my stomach hiccups as he spreads kisses along my jaw, both of us leaning back onto the floor. Instead of returning to my research, Bryce and I take advantage of my seldom-quiet house.

After Bryce leaves, I fall asleep on the end of my bed with my American Lit reading assignment clutched to my chest.

When I finally wake, I feel groggy and heavy. The sound of my sister shouting at Shipley, our pit mix, and the smell of my mother cooking dinner flood my senses.

"Callie!" calls Kyla from the other side of the door. "Mama said you would help me with my reading homework!"

"After dinner!" My door begins to inch open, and I throw a pillow at it. "After dinner!" I shout again.

Kyla pushes the door open anyway and sticks her head in. Her long blond hair is split into two French braids. Over Christmas, she had a growth spurt, and even though she's only eleven, she's nearly taller than me. "Is that a hickey on your neck?"

I throw my second and last pillow, but this time I hit her right in the face. "I'm telling Mama!" she growls before slamming my door shut.

I groan and plop back down on my bed, letting my brain slowly come back to life as the sleepy fog evaporates. I reach for my phone and find an alert telling me I have eighty-seven missed text messages.

HO-LY SHIT.

I open my messages and find one long thread with at least half the dance team on it. As I skim through, I find that news of the sponsorship fiasco has spread to the rest of the team. *Melissa.* She probably spilled the beans.

HAYLEY: We worked so hard for this. I haven't eaten bread in three months.

ADDISON: Why should we even bother practicing anymore?

JILL: And what's the point of even trying to compete at State if we can't go to Nationals? GREG BROKE UP WITH ME BECAUSE HE FELT LIKE I WAS TOO BUSY WITH THE SHAMROCKS.

GRETCHEN: Greg was a punk anyway, BUT THIS IS STILL BULLSHIT.

WHITNEY: I missed my grammy's funeral for Regionals!

BETHANY: The football team gets a new training facility and we can't even afford to compete?! 🔥

ZARA: Does this mean I can eat carbs again? 🌙

SAM: Zara, no one said you couldn't eat carbs.

Reading these messages is like watching the five stages of grief play out, and by the time I get to the end it's obvious that the team has hit the anger stage and they're out for blood.

Sorry, I type, **just got caught up on all these messages. Maybe we should all take a breather and reconvene in the morning.**

JILL: We don't need a breather. We need revenge.

My phone buzzes over and over again as my text is lost in a sea of new messages.

ADDISON: We can't let that trashy gym do this to us!

BETHANY: We've worked our asses off. This is bullshit.

LARA: I say we let them know exactly how we feel.

MELISSA: Y'all, we gotta be strategic right now. Revenge isn't getting us anywhere.

I almost jump in to try to defuse the situation with her, but to be honest: I'm pissed as hell, too. And I can't believe this grody-ass gym is the thing standing in the way between us and a shot at Nationals.

I click the cursor in the message box.

Y'all are right. This is bullshit.

SAM: We're trying to work on solutions. But this might be the end of the road this season, y'all.

JILL: Tonight. Midnight. Wear all black. Meet in the alleyway behind the gym. Bring toilet paper and eggs. They don't even have to be fresh.

I start a new thread, and this one is just me, Sam, and Melissa.

ME: Did y'all see Jill's plan?

MELISSA: This could end badly.

SAM: Everyone's pissed. I think a harmless prank will get it out of their system.

ME: Should we go? Like, is it better or worse for the team leadership to be there?

MELISSA: I think we should let them act on their own.

ME: I don't know. Will they feel like we're abandoning them?

SAM: Listen, y'all, it's my senior year and this season is already going down in flames. I feel like we might as well make it memorable. But either all three of us go or none of us go. Y'all know where I stand.

ME: I'm in.

MELISSA: Guess I am, too. I don't like this.

MILLIE

Five

After I get home from closing up the gym, I hang my keys on the hook by the front door. My house smells like someone passed gas and low-fat cheese, which means my mom is probably cooking one of those dishes that she likes to call a sweet little compromise. This usually means zucchini alfredo or mashed potatoes made of cauliflower.

"I'm home!" I call as I brush past the dining room, where Dad is setting the table.

"What's for dinner?" I whisper.

Dad's expression is full of dread as he shakes his head. "You don't want to know."

"Eggplant parmesan with this dairy-free cheese I found in the refrigerated section of the vitamin store," answers my mom over the sounds of the kitchen and the television.

I swear that woman hears everything. It's her superpower.

Despite Dad's disdain for Mom's cooking, I'm lucky as all heck. My parents love each other.

They met when my mom came back from Daisy Ranch the summer after her senior year. She only went for one year, but it was enough for her to drop forty-four pounds and shrink to a size ten—sometimes even an eight, depending on the cut and fabric. She wasn't that fat to begin with, but the way she tells it, she was a whale. Literally hours after she returned home from camp, she met my dad in the parking lot of Harpy's Burgers and Dogs on a Friday night. He was a few years older and had just graduated from the University of Texas at El Paso. He told her she was the most beautiful girl he'd ever seen. Not only was my mother suddenly beautiful, but she was seen. Daisy Ranch, she swears, changed her life.

The big deception between them is that my dad secretly hates my mom's cooking. It's pretty bad. Her cooking is a mash-up of all the casseroles and Americana dishes she grew up on as a kid, with all the good stuff substituted for things like zucchini or cauliflower. Some of it isn't bad, but much of it is an abomination.

I know a lot of people look at fat people like we're gross slobs who are just constantly shoveling fatty foods in our mouths, but I could probably pass any written test for a dietitian or personal trainer. For so long I obsessively consumed any information I could get my hands on in the hopes that maybe one new little piece of knowledge would be the magical truth that changed everything.

But that never happened, and I don't think it ever will. My magic truth—the thing that has changed everything for me—is this: the body I have shouldn't change how deserving I am of my dreams. I stopped obsessing over my body being too round or too wide or too lumpy. Because

I'm not too much of anything. I'm just enough. Even when I don't feel like I am.

After dropping my backpack in my room, I head back to the kitchen to help my mom set up dinner. It still smells less than great, but I can appreciate how much effort she puts into every meal, even if my taste buds cannot.

Maybe it's corny that we have family dinners like this every night. Amanda says that her house is a fend-for-yourself situation. I felt bad when I heard that and invited her over one night, but all it took was my mom's zucchini-and-quinoa lasagna to show her that the grass isn't always greener on the other side.

We all hold hands for a quick prayer. Tonight's my dad's turn, and he always makes a joke of it.

"Rub-a-dub-dub, thanks for the grub. Yay, God!" he prays.

My mom tsks in his general direction.

He smiles. "The Lord has a sense of humor, Kathy."

"Is that what the doctor told your mother when you were born?" she asks.

I laugh. "Nice one, Mom."

She winks at me.

"How was your day, sweets?" Dad asks me as Mom serves each of us a piece of eggplant parmesan. "Working on any neat projects at school?"

"It was good." I clear my throat. Every time we sit down for dinner, I tell myself that this will be the night I tell my parents I'm not going back to Daisy Ranch and instead hope to go to journalism camp at UT.

Mom won't take it well. That I know for sure. Some mothers and daughters communicate via makeup and pedicures or shared hobbies like tennis or even horseback riding. My mother and I have crafting, romantic comedies, and above all else, diets. Diets are our love language. And it's not been such a simple thing to shake. The truth is I've spent most of my life thinking of food in terms of point systems and calorie charts, and, for me, exercising only existed for the sake of becoming someone I'm not instead of taking care of who I am.

I know I'm not changing my mind, but I still don't know how to break the news. Instead, I go for a smaller request. "I was wondering if I could have friends over this Saturday? For like a sleepover?"

"Of course!" my dad says prematurely.

"Well," my mom says, "who'd you have in mind? I think my brother and Inga were going to come over on Sunday afternoon with the babies. And Gran and Pop-Pop, too, probably."

"Oh, everyone would clear out before then. And we wouldn't make a mess, I swear." I take a bite of my dinner and swallow it down with a gulp of tea. "Well, Amanda, obviously. And that tall blond girl I met doing the pageant, Ellen. Also Hannah and Willowdean."

My mom twists her lips to the side. "You know Amanda is always welcome here. And that Ellen seems like a very sweet girl. Such a pretty thing. But I just wonder if Hannah and Willowdean aren't the best influences?" She pauses for a minute. My mom does this thing where she tries to plant an idea in your head and make you think it's your idea, except that the only person it works on is my dad. "Especially that Hannah. So much dark makeup. It's not flattering. You know, a good friend would tell her so."

I put my fork down and count to ten. Lots of people would never guess this about me. But I have a temper. Well, I have a temper when dealing with my mom. "They're my friends, Mom. And Hannah is awesome. No matter how she wears her makeup."

"I just want to see you surround yourself with positive people, baby."

My mom put the weight back on and then some after she had me, which was only a year and a half after she and my dad met. These days she's closer to my size than her post–Daisy Ranch size ten. Ever since then, though, she's been trying to become that girl again—"the most beautiful girl he's ever seen."

The irony is that she has always been that girl to my dad.

Dad clears his throat and touches my knee under the table. "We trust your judgment, Millie," he says, his eyes steady on my mom. "And we would be glad to host your friends."

My mom sighs into her dish. "I'll pick up some extra snacks at the store on Friday."

I almost just nod and say thank you. I don't want to push my luck. But I do anyway. "Maybe they could be like regular snacks and not just rice cakes and stuff."

Dad chuckles. "I think we can make that happen."

"Finish your dinner," my mom tells me. "You probably have a lot of homework piled up." After a moment, she adds, "I've got *Runaway Bride* on the DVR."

Later, in my room, while I'm putting the finishing touches on my trig homework, a chat message from Malik pops up in the bottom corner of my computer screen.

Malik.P99: Have you looked at the psych essay questions yet? That last one feels like a trick question.

aMillienBucks: Not yet! I'm saving that for the weekend. :D :D

Maybe the second smiley face is overkill. *Chill, Millie.*

Malik.P99: Speaking of this weekend . . .

Malik.P99: Well, not this weekend. A weekend.

Malik.P99: My birthday is coming up.

aMillienBucks: Oh yeah! That's right!

Malik.P99: My mom is having this big birthday party and now she's got a bunch of family coming into town and she wants me to invite friends.

Malik.P99: She knows I don't really have a lot of friends.

aMillienBucks: I'm your friend! Amanda, too.

Malik.P99: It's not going to be fun. Not even a little bit.

aMillienBucks: Not to brag or anything, but I'm sort of known for my morale-boosting skills.

Malik.P99: Mils, really. It's not going to be fun. There will be aunties everywhere all up in my business, so if you're not up for an in-depth interview and a lie detector test, I get it.

Mils. He only calls me Mils online when we're chatting like this at night without anyone around. It feels so . . . familiar.

aMillienBucks: Okay, well if this is you inviting me, then I would love to go to your birthday party and have no fun at all and meet all your aunties. I'll even bring Amanda if you want.

Malik.P99: Thank you so much. At least we can suffer together.

A burst of fireworks go off in my chest. We chat like this almost every night, leaving our chat windows up from after dinner until one of us falls asleep. It's almost like being in one of those relationships that's all lived-in, where silence isn't uncomfortable.

But then the next day at school, reality always sinks in. I'm constantly left to wonder if the people we are online will ever materialize in real life.

I'm extra rushed in the morning, trying to pull together some semblance of a breakfast while still remembering to turn on the coffeepot for my parents. I overslept and didn't even have time to work on my personal statement for journalism camp.

After I pull out of the driveway, I have to double back down the street because I forgot to close the garage door. It's just one of those mornings. My hair is frizzier than normal. I feel ridiculous in my clothes—black leggings with white polka dots and an oversized red sweatshirt, like I'm channeling my homemade Minnie Mouse Halloween costume from fourth grade. Even though I wore this outfit three weeks ago and loved it! It's like some days you just wake up and your body doesn't seem to look right in any of your clothes.

By the time I get to the gym, I'm on autopilot. I unlock the door and race over to the security keypad to shut off the alarm, not noticing the glass crunching beneath my feet or the fact that the alarm was never even beeping. Did I turn it on last night? Suddenly I have no memory of the little buttons lighting up for the last week—maybe even two!

I turn around and look up. Oh my gosh. If I were a cussing person, now would be a good time for a whole slew of dirty words.

The whole front of the gym is normally a tinted glass storefront, but this morning the entire panel of glass is missing.

Well, it's not missing. It's all over the floor in pieces. Someone broke in, and as my eyes begin to wander, I see that not only did they break into the gym, they vandalized the equipment, mirrors, and walls. Spray paint, eggs, toilet paper, and shaving cream. Everywhere. And those eggs smell way worse than anything my mom's ever cooked up.

My heart is pounding. A cold sweat forms on my neck. I'm frozen. It's one of those moments that begs for action, but I feel like everything is a nightmare and my limbs are suddenly weighed down with lead.

I think so many things at once. What if the intruder is still here? Why would someone do this? How are we going to clean all this up?

The police. I need to call the police. I reach for my phone, and out of pure habit, I dial the numbers for my parents, Amanda, and Malik before forcing myself to concentrate.

"Nine one one," I say out loud to no one except myself—at least I hope so.

After two rings, the operator answers. "Nine one one. What's your emergency?"

"My job—it was broken into."

"Ma'am, are you safe? Is the intruder still on the property?"

"No. I don't think so," I sputter. "I mean, I don't think they're still here, but yes, I'm safe. I work at a gym. Down for the Count."

"Stay on the line. I'll have a squad car there in less than ten minutes."

While I'm on the line with her, I send out texts to my parents, asking them to call Uncle Vernon and Aunt Inga. This will gut them.

My dad beats the cops there, which means he must have sped, and if there's anything my dad has respect for it's *Star Trek* and speed limits. My dad doesn't take the time to tiptoe around the glass. He comes straight toward me and squeezes me tight.

"Are you okay?" he asks.

I nod, unable to come up with words.

"Have you checked the office or the lockers?"

But before I can answer, Officer Barnes, my elementary school's former D.A.R.E. officer, walks through the gaping hole in the storefront. "Millie?"

"Yes, sir. And this is my dad."

I confirm with the operator that the police have arrived and hang up.

"You two stay here," Officer Barnes says as he heads into the locker room with his gun in hand.

Soon after he checks the whole building, there are a handful of police officers, including Sheriff Bell, but my family quickly outnumbers them. My mom's in the janitorial closet, gathering cleanup supplies, while Pop-Pop and Gran follow Officer Barnes, double-checking all of his work. And poor Vernon is on the phone with the insurance company, with baby Nikolai strapped to his chest, while Inga circles around him with baby Luka on her hip as she shouts Russian cuss words directed at the adjuster on the phone.

A younger officer approaches my dad and me while the two of us sit helpless behind the counter. "Uh, ma'am? You're the one who found the place this morning."

I nod. "Yes, sir. I am."

"I see there are cameras set up out here. Those the real deal or just for show?"

A frown settles on my lips. "A little bit of both. They only keep footage for twenty-four hours."

"Would you mind walking back there with me so we can take a look?"

I nod, and while the officer gets a head start, I turn to my dad. "I feel so bad for Vernon and Inga."

My dad grips my knee. "You didn't do anything wrong."

I walk back to the office with Dad as he gently guides me with his hand on my back.

"Looks like Pop-Pop is on the case," I say as he questions Officer Barnes about why they aren't dusting for fingerprints.

Dad lets out a half grunt, half laugh. "At least he's got a new distraction. This might be the most excitement the old guy has seen since we let him help us pick out new grass for the yard."

The office is small and can barely fit two people when it's cleaned out, which is not its current state. I take a seat at the desk, and Sheriff Bell and Dad hover behind me.

I search through the system and save the footage starting with me locking the door last night up until now. As we fast-forward through the evening, I stop just after midnight as I spot some shapes blocking out light from the parking lot. It's only a few minutes before the first window cracks. And then the next. And the next. Soon a handful of people spill in over the broken glass. All of their faces are covered with scarves, hunting masks, and a few Halloween masks, too.

Sheriff Bell leans down over my shoulder. "Those . . . those look like a bunch of teenage girls. You don't recognize any of them, do you?" he asks me.

"It's hard to say." There are only a few of them on the actual footage, but you can tell they're talking to a bunch of girls outside. And then something shiny catches the light from the parking lot. I hit pause and zoom in on a shorter girl in black shorts and black T-shirt. Her face is covered with a hunting mask, but beneath the mask a small necklace hangs down.

I gasp.

"What is it, Millie?" my dad asks.

I look up at him. Dread swells in my chest. "I know that necklace. I know who that is."

Sheriff Bell coughs into his fist. "Let's get you on the record."

My mouth feels like a desert. I don't want to get anyone into trouble. But someone—a lot of someones—really wrecked this place. And this isn't just some gym. It's Vernon and Inga's dream and livelihood all wrapped up into one.

Over the next hour or two, I answer endless questions. It's dizzying. I listen as officers go back and forth with Vernon and Inga about pressing charges and how it would be best to go after the one person that they can identify instead of the whole group.

"Well, if Millie is correct," says Sheriff Bell, "I'd say the girls in the video are all on the school dance team." He clears his throat. "Especially after the, uh, financial difficulties you detailed, Vernon."

It appears that not only did Inga and Vernon skimp on their security system fees this month, but they also had to drop their sponsorship of the Shamrocks, making for a convincing motive.

When the police finally leave, I sit down behind the counter to make sure that nothing was taken from the front desk. I feel like I've been awake for days. All the adrenaline that's kept me going for the past few hours is starting to dwindle.

My phone buzzes from inside my backpack, and I find eighteen missed calls and forty-two text messages from Amanda. I can see she's allowed her imagination to escalate quickly as the texts move from calm to panic within thirty minutes' time.

AMANDA: Did you oversleep?

AMANDA: Am I getting ditched right now? 😠

AMANDA: Should I get my mom to take me to school?

AMANDA: OMG ARE YOU DEAD YOU NEVER MISS SCHOOL WHERE ARE YOU 🚨 💀

"Darn! I totally forgot it was a school day. I was supposed to pick up Amanda. And there goes my perfect attendance record! Great. Just great." I groan. "And I missed getting to school in time to do morning announcements. Mrs. Bradley probably thinks I'm a total flake."

Unfortunately, my flakiness probably won't be the worst news Mrs. Bradley gets today.

CALLIE

Six

I woke up today with what can only be described as a hangover. I was late to practice—as was most of the team. So that was a wash.

My stomach is all knots and my heart stammers against my chest. I'm good at doing bad things. I've gotten away with my share of unspeakable acts. But that's because I'm careful. I'm a planner. Last night? Last night did not go as planned, and this town is way too small for what happened to stay secret for long.

Honestly, I feel like my life is a Lifetime movie and I just got away with murder, but justice is lurking at every corner. (Okay, I might have a thing for Lifetime movies. Thanks to my mama.) But seriously. Nothing turned out the way it was supposed to last night. It was only going to be some toilet paper on the gym sign out front and maybe a few eggs on the windows. Until Jill threw a freaking rock through the window. Jill's that person who takes every joke too far, so I would like to say I'm surprised, but I'm not.

I'd also like to say that when I saw those windows

shatter, my first instinct was to put a stop to everything or, at the very least, to run like Melissa, but adrenaline masked as rage took over. Call it mob mentality or whatever you want, but we trashed the place. I even took the rock used by Jill and went to town on the mirror stretching across one of the walls. It was sort of pretty the way it shattered slowly at first, like a crack in an icy lake, and then came crashing down all at once. We destroyed the equipment, the bathrooms, and even the boxing ring. I think the only thing left untouched was the cash register.

So, yeah, last night got way out of hand. No one wants to get in trouble, obviously, but some of those bitches would gladly rat out the rest of us if it meant saving their own asses. I trust Sam, but seeing as Melissa was nowhere to be found last night after shit got real, I'm just waiting for her to rat me out. If she really wants to secure her title as captain next year, this is probably her best shot of getting me out of the way.

I spend my office-aide hour staring into the bottomless abyss that is the attendance filing cabinet as I think through several different scenarios and how they might play out.

The phone shrieks, sending me nearly two feet in the air.

"Sweetie, can you get that?" my mom calls from the other side of the office.

I nod and pick up the phone. "Clover City High front office."

"Uh, yes, this is Todd Michalchuk. I need to speak with someone about my daughter, Millie, being out sick today."

"One moment please." I press the hold button. "Mom, it's a parent with an excused absence."

"Oh, I better take that," she says, pushing her red-glitter reading glasses, which perfectly match her nails and lips, into her curls.

I hand off the phone and find something to alphabetize.

"Oh, I knew something must have been really wrong when she didn't show up for announcements this morning," says Mama. "Well, I'm so sorry to hear that, but I hope they find whoever did it so they can pay the consequences."

Oh God. That doesn't sound good. Sweat gathers at the nape of my neck. But there's no way Millie has anything to do with that gym. I doubt that girl's ever even seen workout equipment outside of a late-night infomercial.

Slowly, I reexamine every detail from last night. We wore all black and a mix of ski masks and molded Halloween masks. I twisted my hair into a sloppy bun and donned a Richard Nixon mask Jill had in her truck, among the piles of masks she'd stolen from her brothers. None of us were even slightly recognizable.

I've gutted my phone for any text messages that might incriminate me, and I should tell everyone else to do the same. But isn't covering up evidence somehow even worse? And don't they have technology to recover deleted stuff from phones?

I shake my head. It doesn't matter. A chilling sense of resignation settles down my spine. What happened last night is done. I can't change that. I can only protect my team and whatever shot we have left at State and Nationals.

"Well, that's just awful," says my mom as she hangs up the phone. "You know that little gym, Down for the Count? The new one behind the Chili Bowl?"

I nod but keep my eyes focused on my work. If anyone will notice something's up with me, it's my mom. "I think so." The words feel like nails on a chalkboard.

"Well, that was Todd Michalchuk, and he says his brother-in-law owns the place and his daughter, Millie . . . you know Millie. That . . . bigger girl who was in the pageant last year with you. She's such a gem. Does the announcements for me every morning. I was worried about her this morning."

"Mmhmm."

"Well, she was opening the gym up for her uncle and found the whole place ransacked. They're not sure if people were looking for money or what, but the place is trashed." She sighs. "Things like that just don't happen here."

I'd hoped that somehow this whole thing would exist in a bubble and never work its way back to me, but suddenly it's here. It's simply a matter of time before this is the only thing the entire town is talking about.

Because Mama is right. Our local police department keeps busy with things like drunk drivers and domestic disputes. As trite as it sounds, this is the type of place where you can leave your doors unlocked. In Clover City, an incident like this is front-page news.

I am front-page news.

She sits down at her computer and opens up her attendance

software to mark Millie as having an excused absence. "I tell you," she says, "little places like this can only hide from big-city crime for so long. It's like watching a way of life become extinct like the damn dinosaurs." After a moment, she adds, "I hope they find whoever is responsible and lock 'em up for a good long while."

Later that day, I excuse myself from US History to take the attendance slip to the office, mainly as an excuse to eavesdrop on any possible gossip related to the incident at the gym. I can barely sit still or even process my surroundings. Words melt together until all I hear is a low, dull buzz. Mouths open, and all I hear is static.

On my way back to class, I stop in the bathroom, and as I'm walking out of the stall, the door swings open, and there's Melissa, still in the same black clothes she wore last night. Her eyes are wide and crazed, like she's just been roaming aimlessly for the last twelve hours.

"We need to talk," she says, still framed by the doorway of the stall. She yanks me by the elbow and pulls me into the narrow space, locking the door. I wedge myself into one of the corners.

"You disappeared last night," I say, my voice low.

She squats down to check for feet in the other stalls before whispering, "Well, when it went from a silly prank to an actual break-in, I figured the dance team wasn't really worth having a criminal record."

The minute that window broke, Melissa was gone. All anyone saw were her taillights leaving the parking lot. I notice the dark circles beneath her eyes. But I can't find it in me to feel even a little bit sorry for her. "So what's there to talk about then?" I ask. "Besides you totally ditching us. Sam had to squeeze Natalie and Gretchen into her backseat with three other girls, by the way, because you weren't around to give them rides after driving them there in the first place."

"So there weren't enough seat belts!" she says. "What's another broken law after breaking and entering?"

I roll my eyes, trying to maintain the cool and collected exterior I'm known for. "No one's gonna find out it was us." Though saying it out loud makes me realize how unsure of that I actually am. "That place didn't even have a working camera."

"You know I can't get in trouble again," she says through gritted teeth.

Ah, yes. In eighth grade, before Melissa had transformed into a pretty little rule follower with dance-team ambitions, she was caught shoplifting thousands of dollars' worth of designer cosmetics, sunglasses, and clothing from Levine's department store. She had to do endless hours of community service and even had a parole officer.

"How do you know for sure the camera wasn't working?" she asks.

"There wasn't a little blinky light," I say. The moment the words are out of my mouth I feel silly.

She throws her hands up. "That means literally nothing."

"You're overreacting," I tell her. But all I want to do is flail right back at her, because I smell a rat. "And you smell guilty . . . and like BO."

"I saw the sheriff in the front office during my lunch period."

My heart stops. I swallow and take a deep breath. "He could be at school for any reason."

She looks at me pointedly. "You should've stopped them."

"I'm not anyone's mother. And I didn't see you trying to be the voice of reason."

"They listen to you," she tells me.

"We're both co–assistant captains," I remind her. "They listen to both of us."

"Cut the crap," she says. "You know they don't listen to me the way they do with you."

My little world is on the verge of being hit by an asteroid, and still some part of me feels satisfied to hear her admit this. I hate myself for it.

I shrug, feigning nonchalance. "Our faces were covered. There's no proof. As long as everyone can keep a secret, we're all in the clear. And you can keep a secret, can't you, Mel?"

Later that afternoon, we have an emergency practice to make up for poor attendance this morning. Not all of them were there last night—it was mostly juniors and seniors— but word spreads fast enough that everyone might as well have been there.

We all meet on the bleachers outside the track. With so many voices talking at once, it's nearly impossible to get anyone's attention.

"Hey!" I shout. No one even blinks.

"Y'all!" Sam barks.

And they all freeze, turning to her. It's a reminder, even for me, that she is still very much the team captain.

Sam motions for everyone to move it in.

All our bodies press together to create a tight, sweaty circle.

"You wanna know what makes us great?"

"Jess's pirouettes?" says someone.

Sam smiles, and just that small act of normalcy sends a wave of ease through our huddle—myself included. "Well, that, and the fact that before we're a team, we're a sister-hood. And sisters have each other's backs. No matter what."

And that's all she needs to say. Mentally, I file this moment away. This is how a captain does her job.

After a grueling practice, including a three-mile run, we all collapse on the grass at the center of the track ring.

"Okay, ladies," says Sam. "I've lined up a car wash at one of the Clay Dooley service-repair departments for next Saturday."

"Oh," I blurt.

Sam and Melissa both eye me.

"Sorry," I say. "News to me."

Sam smiles. "Callie's boyfriend, Bryce, was sweet enough to set that up with his dad." She glances to me. "He told me just before lunch. I'm sure he meant to tell you first."

I nod, feeling unease about the whole team witnessing this interaction. The admiration I'd just felt for Sam melts into suspicion. "Totally," I say, trying to shake it off.

It's weird that Bryce forgot to tell me, but it probably slipped his mind. I guess he just wanted to help out after seeing how stressed I was last night, so I can't fault him.

Sam clasps her hands together. "And not to be too mushy or anything, but the end of the year is almost here, and it's my last year as a Shamrock. I'm going to miss y'all so much. Once a Shamrock, always a Shamrock, right?"

The whole team whoops and cheers.

I lean over to Melissa. "And Shamrocks don't snitch."

After practice, Bryce drives me home. I haven't told him about last night. It's not that I don't trust him, but I'm playing it safe for right now.

He takes the long way home through downtown Clover City. A few of the shops are boarded up, and while much of downtown maintains its mom-and-pop charm, a few places have been replaced with chain stores and restaurants.

I hold my hand out the window, letting my fingers drag through the warm breeze, and this is the first moment of real calm I have all day. But it's gone faster than I can count. "Hey," I say, "so you set up a car wash for the dance team and forgot to tell me?"

He grins. "Just trying to do my part to get my girl to Nationals."

"Well, you couldn't tell your girl about it instead of letting her find out in front of the whole team?"

He shakes his head. "You're making this into a thing. I just texted Sam because I knew she would be the one you'd have to run everything by anyway."

I start to argue, but instead I take a deep breath. I'm on edge today. That's all.

In the alley behind my house where he always drops me off, we share a long kiss that is quickly turning into more when my stepdad knocks on the passenger window.

The two of us knock heads as we disentangle.

Keith opens the door, ducking down to speak to Bryce as I gather my backpack and purse.

"I'd invite you in," says Keith, "but tonight is family dinner."

Bryce nods. "Understood, sir."

I squint my eyes at Bryce for a minute, and I find myself almost making a comment about how he never makes any effort to call my real dad sir. Both Keith and my dad work blue-collar jobs—the kind of things Bryce will never find himself doing. The only difference between them is that one of them is white and the other isn't. But I shake it off and decide it's just more paranoia. Bryce isn't racist.

Keith shuts the door behind me, and I follow him in through the back gate.

"Maybe cool it with the protective-dad act," I tell him.

"Aww, come on," he says as he locks up his work truck. "You can't expect me to catch some guy getting handsy on my stepdaughter and not to step in."

I laugh. Keith and I used to butt heads quite a bit, but we've come to an understanding in the last few years. At first, though, he was just some tall blond dude who married my tall blond mom and the two of them made a cute little blond baby named Kyla. Claudia and I were the odd ones out—short with curves that announced themselves the moment we hit middle school and deep brown hair with a slightly darker complexion that stood out against the rest of the family's freckled skin.

For the longest time, I looked at family portraits and didn't see a family. All I saw was two half-brown girls intruding on a perfect little white family of three. It never bothered Claudia as much. Maybe because she was older and can remember how viciously Mama and Dad fought. I guess I'm mostly over it now. But sometimes I still look at the portraits lining our walls, and I wonder what it might be like to see one of me, my mom, Claudia, and our dad framed like it was something worth remembering.

I follow Keith onto the porch and into the kitchen. He stops abruptly, and I practically walk right into his back. "Sheriff," says Keith.

My heart rattles, nearly pounding out of my chest. *Shit. Shit. Shit. Shit. Shit.*

I peer around Keith's arm to find my mother serving Sheriff Bell a glass of sweet tea.

"Baby," Mama says to Kyla, "take your homework upstairs." Her tone is soft, but her lips are pursed into a thin line, and everything about the way she stands, from her squared shoulders to her arms crossed over her chest, her red nails drumming along her forearm, tells me that I'm fucked.

"Is Callie in trouble?" my little sister asks.

Of course I'm in trouble, you turd.

"Upstairs," Mama says, her voice firm this time.

Okay, save the panic for later. Now is the time for logic. What are my options? I can just rat on the whole team. I can deny, deny, deny. I can take the blame. Or I can pin it on someone else entirely. It all depends on what Sheriff Bell knows.

The four of us watch as Kyla takes her time gathering her papers and pencils, walking toe-heel, toe-heel like she's been taught in dance class, before stalking upstairs in a huff for being dismissed. If Mama and Keith think they have their hands full with me, just wait until that one hits puberty.

Not until my mother hears Kyla's bedroom door shut does she say, "Callie, sit down." She turns to Keith, her expression softening slightly. "You too."

I think that if my life were some kind of courtroom drama, this would be the part when we call a lawyer. But my mom and Keith went to high school with Sheriff Bell. The guy was my mom's homecoming date once, so yeah, no one's calling a lawyer for my defense anytime soon.

"Callie," says Sheriff Bell.

My mom dabs her eyes. She hasn't cried yet, but she's going to. My mom cries a lot. I hate crying. I hate when I do it, and I hate when other people do it. It makes me uncomfortable. Some primal thing in me labels it as weakness. Maybe that sounds cruel, but to me it just feels like a private thing. Even when my mom's tears are genuine, they feel like manipulation. We can go toe to toe, but as soon as she sheds a tear, I bend to her will, because who wants to be the asshole who makes their mom cry?

"Is there anything you'd like to share with me?" asks Sheriff Bell. "Anything about where you were last night?"

I look to my mom. Still with the dabbing. *Seriously.* And then to Keith. His lips are pressed together.

"No, sir," I say. There's no way he has proof. I recite it to myself over and over again. *There's no way he has proof. There's no way he has proof. There's no way he has proof.*

"Well, your parents here—"

"My mom and my stepdad," I correct him. "Keith is just my stepdad." I don't look, but I hope that made Keith flinch. I feel like a cornered cat, and my claws are out. "My real dad isn't here right now."

"Well, you better believe I've called him," says my mom, her voice shrill and shaking. "He is very disappointed in you, as am I. We never had problems like this with Claudia."

I roll my eyes. Claudia practically came out of the womb balancing a checkbook. That's how angelically responsible she is. Mama comparing us is nothing new, but it's a game I'll never win.

Sheriff Bell folds his hands on the table. "Listen," he tells me. "That gym on Jackson Avenue was trashed last night. Broken glass everywhere. Rotten eggs. Toilet paper. Damaged equipment. I'm pretty sure I know who did this, and I'm pretty sure you do, too. And if you're thinking of playing cat and mouse here with me, I'm just gonna put it out there and tell you the whole thing is on camera."

My heart pounds, and the kitchen is so quiet that I'm scared everyone else can hear it, too. I try not to react to this news. I don't want to do anything to further incriminate myself.

"I can't make out much," he continues, "but I got a head count. And by the looks of it, the whole bunch of 'em were girls. I also happen to know that the gym was the primary sponsor for the dance team until very recently. Ya putting things together here with me, girly?"

I open my mouth to—I don't know? Deny?

He holds a hand up. "How long have you had that necklace, Callie?"

I tilt my head to the side and press my fingers to the *C* pendant. My nerves fizzle out for a moment. "Years. It was a thirteenth-birthday present from my dad."

Sheriff Bell nods. "And you've never let anyone borrow it?"

"No. Never," I say, realizing all too soon that I've given myself away.

"Jared," says Keith. "Say Callie was there and she can tell you who else was with her."

His head dips down a little as he says, "Well, here's the deal. We know you were there, Callie. But you're the only one we can identify, and you shouldn't have to pay this price alone."

My mom says, "He's right, baby." It's the first inkling of nondisappointment I've gotten from her yet.

This is a sinking ship. Hell. I *am* the sinking ship. But

I won't bring down the rest of the team. I remember Sam and what she said at practice today. I normally don't fall for all that fluffy BS, but the Shamrocks are my life. If that's not a sisterhood—a really dysfunctional sisterhood—then what is? "I was there," I say in a sweet voice. "But it was so dark, Sheriff. I wouldn't have the faintest clue who else was with me."

Sheriff Bell holds my gaze for a long moment, and I can tell this is my last chance.

The sound of my mom bursting into tears pierces the silence in the kitchen. Yup, right on cue.

I groan and cover my face with both my hands, not bothering to be careful of my makeup.

All the things I stand to lose stack up like a pile of dirty laundry. The team. State. Nationals. And then—my God—what if I'm arrested? My weekend job at Sweet 16. Time with Bryce. My standing on the social food chain. What if I have a criminal record? Can I even get into college?

"What do you need from me?" I finally ask.

Sheriff Bell clears his throat. "Well, I'll be speaking to the owner to see if they'd like to press charges. And of course we'll have to speak with the city attorney."

"Do we need a lawyer?" asks Keith.

My mama lets out another yelp.

"It's not like I killed someone," I say. "It was just a joke that got out of hand."

"A joke that's going to cost a pretty penny to repair," says Sheriff Bell sternly. "And as far as a lawyer goes . . . well, they're not my favorite sort of people, but it wouldn't hurt to have one in the wings."

Keith nods. "We, uh, appreciate you coming over and not just picking her up at school and making a scene of things."

"Oh Lord, yes," Mama chimes in.

That is possibly the only thing that could've made this worse. Me getting arrested at school, with me making a scene in the attendance office.

Sheriff Bell nods and scoots his chair back, putting his broad khaki-colored sheriff hat back on.

"I trust y'all will be keeping an eye on Callie here until I have more information."

"Of course," says Mama as Keith shakes the sheriff's hand. "The girl is so grounded, she's halfway to the center of the earth."

Keith walks the sheriff out to the front of the house, where his police truck is parked. The door shuts behind them, vacuuming out all the air in the house.

Mama turns to me.

I can feel her getting ready to unleash.

"What were you thinking?" she asks, her eyes dry now and her voice low and angry. In this moment, nothing about her red lips is sweet and familiar.

"I didn't start it," I tell her honestly. "And it really was just supposed to be TP and eggs. Just a dumb prank."

Mama shakes her head furiously. "That is the exact reason why you should not have gone! These things always get out of hand. Christ, baby. You should've told someone. Stopped it somehow. I'm raising you girls to be leaders, not followers."

"We didn't mean to do any real damage. I swear."

"Callie, it does not matter what you meant to do. Only what you did do. You've worked so hard for the dance team to make it this far, and now it's all over for you. Doesn't that mean anything to you?"

It's all over for you. Her words ring in my ears. My hands begin to tremble, and I can feel every muscle in my body tense as it tries to suppress tears.

The front door creaks as Keith lets himself back inside, pulling me back into the moment.

"Does that mean anything to me, Mama?" I'm shouting now. My eyes begin to burn as I blink away tears. I use the heels of my hands to wipe them away. "This means everything to me! And yeah, I wish it hadn't happened, but if you think I'm 'bout to cower 'round here with my tail between my legs like some kind of poorly trained puppy— well, then you don't know what the hell kind of daughter you raised."

She crosses her arms over her chest with Keith standing a few steps behind her. "No phone. No Bryce. I will take you to school, and you will leave with me when I'm done with work. I will call Sam, Melissa, and Mrs. Driskil to let them know you will not be at practice."

I knew it was coming. I knew that when the woman said I'd be grounded, she meant it. And still every word hits me like a perfectly placed punch, but one specific thing stings the most. "I can't just miss practice," I tell her.

"Oh, can't you?" She rests her fists firmly on her hips. "You did this. You had every chance of making it to

Nationals. I would have loved nothing more than to see my daughter follow in my footsteps. You could've been a legacy."

Where's my tearful mother now? Suddenly this has nothing to do with me.

"I don't know who you think you are," she continues, "but in this house we do not commit crimes and expect things to go back to normal. There will be consequences, and one of yours is that you are grounded from the dance team until further notice. I will always be a Shamrock, but above all, I am a mother." She holds a finger up to stop me from responding. "And I will arrange for you to apologize to the vice principal, the principal, and later on, the school board. We will apologize to the owner of the gym as well. That is your punishment. For now. Until we hear more from Sheriff Bell. And for the record," she adds, "I know exactly what kind of daughter I raised, and whoever you are right now is not it."

I push past the both of them to stomp up the stairs. All the tears I'd tried to hold back are falling freely now. Mascara burns my eyes and runs down my cheeks.

Mama follows me, stopping at the bottom step. "Phone," she says.

I turn on the landing and throw the dumb thing down the stairs.

MILLIE

Seven

Me, my mom, Inga, and Uncle Vernon all sit around my mother's breakfast bar on Saturday morning with the twins in their carriers on the counter. The moment one of them stops crying, the other starts, like they're tagging each other in and out of the ring.

My mother coos at a sobbing Luka. "He does that howl you would do when you were a baby, Vernon. Just crocodile tears. It's a wonder you never fried your vocal cords."

"Ah," Inga says, "so this is his fault. I was a good baby, you know. Slept and ate. Slept and ate. I was a dream. But no, they had to inherit their father's temperament."

"Okay," I say. "Y'all eat and I'll entertain the twins."

Neither Inga nor Vernon argues at that. The two of them pick sparingly at my mother's oatmeal and topping selection while I make ridiculous faces at Nikolai and Luka as I bounce their carriers back and forth.

The gym has been closed to the public since Wednesday, when I showed up to find the place a complete wreck. Since then I've felt inexplicably anxious. It's not that I feel unsafe, but I feel . . . out of sorts.

"Have they figured out what they're doing with the girl Millie caught on camera?" my mom asks.

"We have," says Vernon, using that voice he so often uses with my mother. It's that you-won't-like-this-but-you-can't-change-it voice.

"We!" exclaims Inga. "More like *he*! I had no part in this decision." Both Nikolai and Luka sob in unison. Inga circles around to them, relieving me of my brief duties. "I know, babies. Your father is a spineless do-gooder."

"Thanks," says Vernon. "I'm sure they'll respect me for life now."

"Do something respectable," she says. "Earn respect. Simple."

He sighs. "I offered to let the girl work off the damages at the gym."

"What!" My voice surprises even me. I clear my throat. "I'm sorry, but did you just say that Callie Reyes would be working at the gym?"

Mom turns away from her waffle maker. "Oh, Vernon, you don't even need help at the gym. It's not like she'll be saving you any money."

He shrugs. "The girl didn't act alone, okay? I spent a lot of years getting into trouble. Maybe if someone would've given me a shot like this, I would've gotten to the finish line a little sooner."

Mom and Inga shake their heads. I do, too.

Positive thoughts. Think positive thoughts.

But this is going to be—

Positive thoughts, I remind myself. *Positive thoughts*.

Nope. Hard as I try, I just can't imagine a world where the next few months working with Callie aren't miserable. Maybe Callie isn't the biggest bully in school, but she's not what I would call nice either.

It will only be as bad as you allow it to be, a small voice inside me says.

But the voice is too small to affect my growing sense of doom.

CALLIE

Eight

I didn't realize how chaotic my world was until this weekend. Keith locked my cell phone away in the safe where he keeps his hunting rifles. I thought that was tragic, but then my mom locked me out of all the computers in the house, changed the Wi-Fi password, and added parental controls so that all I can watch is the History Channel. Somehow that last thing was what pissed me off the most. And that was only Friday.

I spent all evening Friday pacing my room like a prison yard. I knew my necklace gave me away, but it's just a simple *C* necklace. Someone must have tipped off the sheriff. It was Melissa. That was something I had absolutely no doubt about.

By Saturday afternoon, I'm wondering what the rest of the team knows and how they've reacted. Surely more of them will come forward once they know I got caught. *I mean, if everyone just owns up, they can't disband the whole team.* Sam wouldn't let that happen. I wish I could just get a text out to her. At the very least I would tell her not to trust Melissa.

That afternoon my mother hands down my official punishment. She knocks on my door, not waiting for me to tell her to come in.

I sit on my bed with my Algebra Two homework spread out around me.

Mama only takes two steps in past the doorway.

"I've spoken with Sheriff Bell and Vice Principal Benavidez. The owner has graciously decided to hold off on pressing charges, so long as you work off the cost of the damage by helping out at the gym after school and sometimes on the weekends."

I stand up, my arms crossed. "That won't work. I can't do that. Not with Nationals coming up. I can't just continue to skip practice."

She doesn't even bother acknowledging my protest. "And Vice Principal Benavidez spoke with Principal Armstrong. They've both come to the conclusion that it would be inappropriate for you to continue on with the Shamrocks."

The floor drops out from beneath me. "What—what does that mean?" I stutter. "Like, as co–assistant captain? What about next year?"

Mama shakes her head. "No." And for the first time, I see the slightest sign of sympathy in the way her brow furrows. "Baby, you're off the team for good."

It takes a moment for that news to sink in. I feel silly for not realizing that I would get kicked off the team. I guess I just assumed I would serve my punishment and things would go back to normal.

But no. I have to lose something. It's like Melissa said. Someone would pay a price.

Mama leaves, shutting the door behind her. I plop down on my bed with my arms limp at my sides. Every day of my life since I was a little girl has been spent working toward the moment when I would finally be able to call myself a Shamrock. And now it's gone in a moment.

The whole room feels like someone sucked out all the air. I remind myself to breathe, but with everything I've worked so hard for evaporating right before me, even the simple act of pushing air in and out of my lungs feels impossible.

MILLIE

Nine

My room is way too small to hold this many people, but it feels full in a good way, like a bustling restaurant on a Friday night.

I'm sitting in my huge wicker chair, which feels more like a throne. Amanda and Hannah sit on my bed with their legs crossed, and Ellen and Will are curled up on the floor like two cats.

"Good night, girls!" calls my dad as he pads down the hallway, and the light pouring in beneath my door disappears.

We kicked off the night with pizza—courtesy of my dad—and a plethora of online quizzes. (Yes, I did google "slumber party activities." No, I did not expect to be inundated with pornography.) But for now everyone's just kind of vegged out with their phones. I guess this isn't a bad slumber party, but it's not exactly what I had in mind when I imagined us all bonding.

Hannah, in her black leggings and oversized battle of the bands T-shirt, yawns with her entire body as she flops onto her side. "I think I'm actually a forty-year-old trapped in a seventeen-year-old's body. Is it too early to go to sleep?"

I groan. "Y'all. Come on. We're all just on our phones, and Hannah, yes, it is too early, okay? It's only ten thirty."

She hisses at me but sits up.

"Maybe we should watch a movie," offers Amanda.

Ellen yawns. "I would just fall asleep."

"You say *sleep* like it's a dirty word," says Hannah.

Willowdean pops up into a seated position. Her curls sit piled on top of her head and vibrate at even the slightest movement. "Y'all wanna play a game?"

"You hate games," Ellen says.

"Okay," says Willowdean. "Well, yeah. But I was just trying to contribute or whatever." She touches the speck of toothpaste on her chin. "Are you sure this is going to work?" she asks me.

"According to Google, toothpaste is the perfect topical remedy for a pimple," I say.

Willowdean groans. "This is like one of those horrible under-the-skin ones that just throbs. Can a pimple give you a headache? Is that possible?"

"No," says Hannah, biting down on her freshly pierced lip. "But you talking about it enough will."

Amanda leans in a little closer to Hannah. "On a scale of one to OH MY GOD I FEEL THIS PAIN IN MY SOUL, how much did your lip piercing hurt?"

Hannah bites down on the ring again. "The pain wasn't half as bad as the lecture I got from my mom when she saw it. Changing the rings out is sort of uncomfortable, but Courtney got a piercing apprenticeship, and she needed to practice on something that wasn't made of silicone. She could've used a pig's ear, but she's a vegan."

Ellen shivers. "That's some serious trust."

Hannah holds back a smile, but her rosy cheeks give her away.

"Hey, how about that Two Truths and a Lie game?" asks Amanda.

"Yes!" I say a little too loudly. "Everyone, on the floor. Come on!" I tiptoe around Ellen and Will to turn off the bright overhead lights, so that the only sources of light are my two bedside lamps. The room feels instantly more intimate and somehow safer—perfect for secret keeping. I grab the sheet face masks I bought at the drugstore this morning and pass them out.

"What are these?" asks Amanda.

"Face masks," says Ellen.

Amanda and Hannah stake out their spots on the carpet and I sit leaning up against my bed. We unwrap our face masks and carefully try to place them on our faces, matching up the eye, nose, and mouth holes.

Willowdean screeches. "This thing is freezing."

Ellen reaches over and helps her smooth out her mask. "Don't be a baby."

"I probably should've washed the toothpaste off my chin," Willowdean says through gritted teeth, to stop her mask from slipping down her face.

Hannah looks around at all of us and then glances at her reflection in the reverse camera on her phone. "We look like serial killers."

Amanda leans over her shoulder so she can see herself, too. "Oh, yeah. Like we're wearing the skin of our victims or something."

"Well, I hear these things are very moisturizing," I say. "And better to look like a serial killer than actually be one, right?"

Hannah looks at me, a faint grin teasing her lips. "I think maybe there's such a thing as too optimistic."

"Okay, okay!" says Ellen. "Enough serial-killer talk. Time for Two Truths and a Lie! Who's going first?"

Hannah shrugs. "Might as well be you."

"Fine," says Ellen with a hint of defiance in her voice.

"Better make it good," says Will. "I know all your secrets."

Ellen squints, studying the ceiling for a moment, as her tongue just barely sticks out. This must be her thinking face.

"Okay! Okay! I got it. One, I have bigger feet than my boyfriend. Two, a few weeks ago . . . after we, ya know, did it and were cuddling, I farted."

We all erupt in laughter.

"Oh man," says Amanda. "That's gotta be true. Why else would you own up to that?"

El shakes her hands, trying to silence us. "Wait! I'm not done. Three, I started my period at my twelfth birthday party."

"Well, that's not very interesting," says Hannah.

Ellen shrugs. "Harder to tell if it's a truth or a lie then."

Will opens her mouth to speak, but Ellen slaps her hand over her lips before she can say a word. "And you have to sit this round out."

"Mop bare," says Will, her mouth still covered.

"What was that?" I ask.

Will pulls Ellen's hand away. "Not fair."

"I'll allow it!" I say, mimicking the courtroom dramas my dad watches every Thursday night. "Okay, so let's see." I eye Ellen's feet. "You *are* pretty tall."

"So having bigger feet than your boyfriend wouldn't be that weird," says Hannah. "But your feet don't look *that* big."

I try to hide my excitement at Hannah's slight eagerness. She's like a stray cat—only attracted by disinterest.

"They're pretty big," says Willowdean, assuring the rest of us.

"Hey!" I say. "You're not supposed to be playing this round."

She mimes zipping her lips together.

"Or maybe he just has abnormally small feet!" says Amanda as she fishes around a bag of gummy bears for her favorite flavor, pineapple.

"And like Amanda said, why would you make up that story about . . . passing gas?" I ask, preferring the more polite phrasing. "But maybe it's a red herring!"

Willowdean bounces a little, her eyebrows skipping up and down.

"Okay, okay," says Ellen. "Time's up."

Amanda licks her lips. "Uhhh . . . hmmm. Okay, the period at your twelfth birthday party is a lie!"

"I'm gonna say the gastrointestinal incident," I say after a moment of deliberation.

"I think . . . ," says Hannah. "I think . . . I agree with Millie."

"So which is it?" I ask.

"Her period is the lie!" shouts Will. And then she gasps. "Oh my God. I forgot your parents are asleep."

"It's okay," I say, knowing that really my mom is probably lying wide awake in bed, thinking of all the ways Hannah and Willowdean might be corrupting me.

Ellen swats at Willowdean's arm. "I can't believe you remembered. I got my period at my *thirteenth* birthday party. Not my twelfth!"

"Oh, come on!" says Amanda. "That's a technicality!"

Hannah holds up a finger. "So wait. This means you farted on your boyfriend after doing the nasty?"

Secondary mortification turning to molasses in my chest. "What did you say?"

"Uh, yeah," says Willowdean. "I can't believe you didn't tell me this!"

Ellen shrugs. "I pretended to be asleep. And hey, if he wants allllllll of *this*"—she motions to her body. "Then he can't pick and choose what he gets. People fart! Girls fart!"

Amanda holds out her fist for Ellen to bump. "Respect. Is it weird that I was hoping the fart was the truth?"

Ellen laughs. "Only if you're weirded out that it

happened, I guess?"

"Why are bodies so weird and gross?" asks Willowdean. "Like, just the phrase *body fluids* should be illegal. Right up there with *moist*."

Ellen leans her head on Willowdean's shoulder. "You just have a weird complex right now because . . . well, you know . . ."

"You know what?" asks Amanda.

Willowdean holds her hands over her face. "Bo and I have started talking about doing it."

"And what exactly do you mean by 'it'?" asks Amanda. "I mean, if you're gonna do it, at least be able to say it."

"Sex! Okay?" says Willowdean. "We're talking about maybe-probably-sooner-than-later having sex, but, like, there are just so many awkward things to think about. And I'm not even talking about him seeing me naked, because, well, we've nearly gotten that far." She sighs. "Isn't it someone else's turn?"

I try to pull myself together. But I know my cheeks are beet red. Sex. Wow. I just . . . the thought of being naked in front of someone else. I want to be ready for that one day, but that day is not today. "Okay," I say. "Amanda's up next."

Amanda wiggles on her rear end. "I don't know if I'm interesting enough for this game."

"Everyone's got dirt," says El.

Amanda nods into her chest, and I think it's the most serious I've ever seen her. "Okay. One, I pulled the fire alarm in middle school to sabotage a pop quiz in Earth

Science and blamed it on Patrick Thomas. And I never got caught."

"Oh my God," says Willowdean. "Please let that be true."

"For real," Hannah chimes in. "That would be straight-up shero status."

I hate the thought of someone carrying the blame for something they never did, but Patrick Thomas is an exception. He's the kind of person that probably gets on the internet just to be mean to people he's never even met. I can't walk by without him oinking like a pig. Now I just ignore it, which would be fine if I didn't have to suffer through the pity stares people give me every time it happens.

Amanda clears her throat. "And number three—"

"Oh, wait! I missed number two," I say. "Sorry. My mind wandered."

"It's okay," Amanda says as she tears open a bag of Runts and digs around for her favorite flavor, banana. "Number two was that I'm adopted."

The lie. I try not to smile. Amanda isn't adopted, but her youngest brother, Tommy, is.

"And number three!" she says with a mouth full of banana Runts. "I . . . have never really been sexually attracted to anyone."

Will sits up, her posture straight as a fence post. "What does that even mean? You talk about Bo's peach butt all the time. I mean, don't get me wrong. It's a great butt."

My brows furrow, because I know this is one of

Amanda's truths, but I've got to admit it's not something that makes much sense to me. We've talked about it before, and the two of us had just figured she hadn't met the right person. Or maybe I figured that, and Amanda just let me believe it.

"I can appreciate a good butt." Amanda shrugs. "And who knows? Maybe that's the lie."

Hannah's eyes narrow in on Amanda. "You're not adopted."

"What!" says El. "How do you know?"

Hannah tilts her head to the side, like she's seeing something completely new when she looks at Amanda. "I don't."

"I'm recusing myself," I announce.

"Okay," says Will. "I think the last one is a lie."

El's whole face twists into a knot as she studies Amanda. "I was going to say number one, but I think you're ballsy as hell, so I bet you did it. And number two . . . I feel like you wouldn't make that a secret. I mean, some people would, but you're the kind of person who treats the world like you've got nothing to hide. But number three . . . it's too specific to make up." She pauses before giving her diagnosis. "Number two is the lie!"

"You would be a great investigator," I tell Ellen.

She turns to me. "Yeah? I've been thinking about going to school for criminal justice."

Will plugs her fingers in her ears. "Lalalalalala we are not talking about college and how we're going to live a bajillion miles away from each other lalalalalala."

Ellen rolls her eyes and then looks to me. "We can talk

later," she whispers before yanking Will's hands from her ears. "Okay, Amanda. Give us the deets."

Amanda pulls in a deep breath. "Number two is the lie."

Ellen pumps her fist in the air. "Yes! I was right."

"Okay, okay. Back up," says Willowdean. "You've never had the hots for someone?"

Amanda pulls her knees in to her chest, doing her best to make herself smaller. "Oh, I've totally had crushes." She rests her chin between her two kneecaps. "I can still look at people, like Bo or even girls, too, and find them attractive. But there are lots of different kinds of attraction. And I think I want to be in a relationship one day. I just don't know what that will look like for me yet. I guess what it comes down to is I don't experience sexual attraction, and also I don't really have any interest in sex. At least not right now. I think if I knew someone really well and was attracted to them in other ways, that might change."

I can feel myself blinking too much, like I'm trying to process this information, but my body is malfunctioning. I know Amanda has never had a boyfriend. Or girlfriend. But I've never really thought anything of it. I've heard of girls not meeting anyone until college or even after. I just figured it wasn't a priority for Amanda.

I form my words carefully, like I'm tiptoeing around the edge of a cliff. "Do you—do you think you'll always feel this way?"

Amanda smiles. "Do you think you'll always have a crush on Malik?"

My cheeks spark into flames.

"Sorry," she says. "I just meant that I don't really know, but it feels pretty permanent for now."

Hannah lets out a long groan. "Y'all need to get on the damn internet or something. Amanda is asexual. Aren't you, Amanda?"

Amanda's gaze connects with Hannah's and something inside me feels hollow. Amanda is my best friend, and I want to understand her as well as Hannah does in this moment, but I feel like I'm a few steps behind.

"Well," says Amanda, "technically biromantic asexual. I think."

"Not to be a total ass," says Will, "but can someone translate, please?"

Hannah opens her mouth to speak, but Amanda says, "I got this."

Hannah smiles—a real smile!—and nods.

"So what that means," explains Amanda, "is that I can experience different kinds of attraction, but I personally don't have sexual feelings for anyone." She turns to Will. "Maybe it sounds complicated. But it feels pretty simple to me. And I guess that's all that matters."

"But you said you might want to have sex," says Will, "so how can that happen without sexual attraction?"

Hannah opens her mouth again, but looks to Amanda first, who nods an approval. "It's like not being hungry, but still being okay with eating pizza or even enjoying it. And then there are some people who just don't like pizza no matter what."

Amanda cracks a smile as she nods. "Totally."

Will nods. "Okay. Okay. I think I get it."

Hannah smirks. "Congratulations!"

Ellen shrugs. "Sounds good to me."

And then Amanda looks to me, waiting for me to say something. And the truth is Amanda could be sexually attracted only to people who have detached earlobes, and I wouldn't care. My mom and dad . . . they have a hard time understanding anything that's not boy + girl = marriage, house, and baby, but that never worked for me. So I'm not sad that Amanda is asexual. But I'm just sad she never told me. Or maybe it's that I wasn't listening closely enough when she did try to tell me.

"It's great!" I finally say, my voice too high and too loud. "Whatever makes you happy makes me happy."

Amanda smiles, but it's a little strained.

Ellen gasps. "Oh my God! I totally forgot to ask you about your uncle's gym, Millie!"

I nod, glad for the change of subject. "It's been such a mess. But the police think they caught the person who organized the whole thing." *Well, actually, they definitely have and I'm the one who cracked the case.* But I don't exactly want that going around school. I don't mind attention, but I don't need that kind.

"Are you serious?" asks Will. "Our police department can solve actual crimes?"

Hannah chuckles.

I smile and nod.

"Well, who was it?" asks Ellen eagerly.

I guess everyone will find out soon enough. "Callie Reyes," I say. "One of the dance-team assistant captains."

"That bitch!" exclaims Willowdean. She turns to Ellen. "I told you she was awful."

Ellen rolls her eyes.

"She is pretty horrible," Amanda says.

"Won't fight you on that one," says Hannah. "I heard her best friend hooked up with her boyfriend and she stayed with him and dumped her best friend."

Ellen sighs. "That's not actually true. Mainly because she doesn't really have any friends. But he is kind of a jerk. Super showy about money, and he speeds through school zones, and for some reason that just really pisses me off."

I shake my head. "No, thank you," I say.

"Well," says Ellen, "she's not exactly a basket of sunshine herself."

I shake my head. "Now she's my new coworker."

"Are you serious?" Willowdean's eyes go wide with horror.

I nod. "That's the deal. She wouldn't rat out anyone else she was with—"

"Are you serious?" asks Hannah. "I didn't peg her for the loyal type."

"Of course it was the dance team," says Amanda.

I cross my arms over my chest. "That's what makes the most sense with the gym dropping out as a sponsor, but Callie was the only one we could identify on camera, and she wouldn't give up anyone else. So Sheriff Bell, Uncle Vernon, and her parents agreed she would step down from the dance team and work off the damages at the gym. And I get to train her. When her debt is paid off, Uncle Vernon will drop all charges against her."

Willowdean shakes her head. "If there's anyone I'm sorry for here, it's you. That girl is like a ball of prickly burrs all tied up in a bow."

I smile halfheartedly. I've already promised myself to give her the benefit of the doubt, but the truth is I'm mad. I'm really, truly angry. I feel violated, like this one little space I had to call my own—this dirty, smelly gym—is no longer safe. It's no longer my own. And it's hard not to take offense to the fact that working with me is part of her punishment. I shrug, trying to get beyond the negativity. "Well, if anything, she's lucky my uncle was generous enough not to press charges."

Amanda nods. "You're not kidding."

A brief quiet settles. This slumber party needs a hit of adrenaline.

"Ice-cream sundaes!" I say, the words coming out like more like *Eureka!* "I think it's time for an ice-cream sundae break."

Hannah laughs, pushing her bangs out of her eyes. "Well, that's something I don't hate."

Willowdean nods. "A-plus slumber party, Millicent Michalchuk!"

Sprinkles make everything better, and for a whole night I even forget about Daisy Ranch and how in the world I'm ever going to get into broadcast journalism camp.

CALLIE

Ten

The wheels of my mom's Tahoe barely come to a stop outside the gym before I swing the door open and jump out. "I can't believe you agreed to this without consulting me," I tell her. This is the constant argument we've had for the last few days, which I've spent at home serving suspension. Every time it fizzles out, one of us sparks it right back up again, like two trick birthday candles.

"Well," she shouts as I slam the door. The automatic window buzzes as it rolls down, so she can be sure she's heard. "I still can't believe you *vandalized* a place of business like some damn hooligan."

"You don't think I've already been punished enough? Everything I've spent the last few years working for has basically evaporated." My voice grows louder with each word, and a few people in the shopping center, including a couple of men exiting the gym, pause to watch our interaction.

My mom, fully aware of our audience, doesn't bother to indulge me. "I'll pick you up at six," she says. "I love you, honey."

I spin on my heels and shout, "Sure you do." I go out of my way to make eye contact with absolutely every person I pass in the parking lot. It takes everything in me not to snap at each of them. *Keep staring*, I think. Watch the pretty girl's life unravel before your very eyes. And that's really one of the shittier parts of this whole thing. When you're at the top, people just love to watch you fall.

The bells above the door jingle as I walk into the gym, and Millie is the first person I see. *Perfect*, I think.

Popping down from her stool behind the counter, she waves and says, "Hiya! You're Callie."

"Thanks for reminding me," I respond dryly. "Hi, Millie."

You would think a girl like Millie would do her best to stay out of the spotlight, but I swear to God the girl does everything in her power to not be missed. Like today. In her lavender leggings and hot-pink tunic dress with sneakers that appear to be hand-painted with flowers and kittens.

She claps her hands together. "Welcome to Down for the Count! I don't know if you remember me, but I do the morning announcements for your mom at school."

"Well, we collided in the office the other week," I tell her. "You were in the pageant." Couldn't miss her, really. "And we've gone to school together since elementary school. So, yeah. I know who you are."

She smiles, but her lips are stiffer than they were a moment ago. "Well, I try my best not to make any assumptions, and I didn't want to embarrass you in case you had forgotten me."

Oh, this girl is good. Her passive-aggressive game is next level. It's so good that most people would just mistake it for manners. "Right," I say. "Well, let's get this over with."

I haven't seen this place in the light of day. The brand-new window stretching across the store front is shiny and tinted. Much of the equipment has signs on it that read TEMPORARILY OUT OF ORDER, and the women's locker room is currently under construction . . . which is probably from the damage incurred last week. I know that I should feel bad, but I'm too pissed off to care.

Millie takes me behind the counter and pulls out a label maker and a blank plastic name tag. "First things first! A name tag. C-A-L-L-I-E?" she asks.

"Yep."

"Callie and Millie," she says, testing our names out in tandem. "We sound like a crime-fighting duo."

"Except in this duo, I'm the actual criminal," I remind her.

Her cheeks turn even pinker than they already are as she repositions herself back on her stool. "There's another stool under the desk for you."

I watch as she carefully taps my name out on a label maker, and while it prints, she reaches under the counter for a backpack. Her hands emerge with sheets of stickers. "To decorate your name tag!" she says.

While she applies the label to my name tag, I finger through the pages of mini holographic stickers and settle on a smiley face, which I apply upside down to signify that

I'm in mourning for the life I once had. RIP me.

"You know what?" says Millie. "You and my friend Hannah would really get along."

"Okay?"

She smiles. "So Friday afternoons are on the slow side for us. Well, to be honest, almost every time of day is on the slow side for us at the moment. My uncle Vernon and aunt Inga own the place. Uncle Vernon is pretty chill and has been okay . . . through all of this, but Aunt Inga . . . well, you could say she holds on to things for a little longer."

"Inga?" I ask. "What kind of name is that?"

"She's Russian."

"Right," I say. "So avoid the bitter Russian lady."

"Well, I never said bitter." Millie smiles stiffly. "But yes."

"Okay, what else?"

"Well, when members come in, they give us their card and we file it in this little box while they sign in on the clipboard." Millie holds up what appears to be a small recipe box. "And when they leave, we hand them their card back." She goes on to explain the procedure for when someone forgets their card and how to sign up new members.

"So you guys are just a boxing gym?" I ask.

"Well, under the franchise we were, but we're trying to expand now and just be a regular . . . gym."

I look around. It's not like the dance team did this place any favors, but it wasn't exactly nice to begin with. We have another gym in town, Rick's Total Body Fitness, which is undoubtedly the nicer of the two. Bryce and his dad have a membership, and Bryce added me as their permanent guest.

"Maybe you guys should get some tanning beds like they have in the locker rooms at Rick's? Or what about some spin classes or Pilates?" I feel my eyes growing bigger. I could make this whole damn place over. That would be some do-gooder stuff that would make my mom happy and maybe even get me back on the dance team. Shit, I'll make over Millie while we're at it. She could be my pièce de résistance or whatever.

"We don't want to be that kind of gym," Millie says plainly. "Uncle Vernon wants this to be a no-frills kind of place, where you come in just the way you are." Her gaze travels over the unoccupied machines and the rows of punching bags behind the boxing ring. "There's nothing wrong with being tan and going to Pilates." She shrugs. "But that's not our thing." She grabs a bucket full of cleaning supplies. "Now's a good time to sanitize the weight machines."

Deflated, I yank the all-purpose cleaner from the bucket and tuck a roll of paper towels under my arm. This is what I get for trying to find the bright side. Note to self: the only bright side I've got left is Bryce.

Later that afternoon as I'm following Millie to the back room, my arms weighed down with some seriously foul sweat towels, I ask, "So do I, like, get a break at some point?"

"Oh!" squeaks Millie. "Well, it's usually just me, so I hadn't really thought about that, but yeah, I guess you should. What do you think, like fifteen minutes or—"

"I was thinking more like an hour."

She opens the lid to the washing machine, and I nearly gag as the whiff of BO hits me one more time as I release the towels from my arms.

"How about we call it a compromise and say thirty?" She glances down at her cell phone. "We close in an hour anyway, so letting you go for an hour-long break would just be flat-out silly, don't you think?"

"Yeah," I say. "That would be super . . . silly. You think I could borrow your phone?"

She doesn't even take a second to think about it before handing it over and leaving me there in the back room.

I know only two phone numbers by heart: 911 and Bryce. I punch his number in as quick as I can.

The line rings and rings and rings. "Come on," I whisper. "Pick up."

On the eighth ring he answers. "Hello?" His voice is slow and sleepy.

"Babe!" I almost scream. "Babe! It's me. I've got thirty minutes right now, but you've got to come to me."

"Hello?" he asks again.

"It's me, Callie. Were you sleeping? I'm sorry to wake you up, but I've been on lockdown for days."

He clears his throat. "Sorry. I stayed out last night and totally missed school today. Last night was wild."

"You had a wild Thursday night?" I ask. "You know

what? Never mind. Can you come get me? You gotta hurry, though. I only have a little bit of time."

"Yeah, sure thing," he says. "And whose number is this?"

"You wouldn't believe me if I told you."

"I've been trying to call you for days. I even swung by the house, and your stepdad made me leave. Did you really trash that gym? Why didn't you tell me? Patrick's telling people you must have been high as hell."

"Just get here, okay? I'll explain everything."

It never takes more than ten minutes to get anywhere in Clover City, which is why I'm all kinds of ticked off when Bryce's ten-minute drive takes twenty. By the time his tires squeal to a stop in the parking lot, I've already wasted most of my break sitting on the curb.

As I get in the car, I slam the door shut behind me.

"Hey, babe. Gentle on the door? This girl is fresh off the lot." He leans over and kisses his way up my neck. "You wanna grab some tacos or something?"

"I only have ten minutes," I snap, jerking my body away.

"What kind of break is that?"

"Well, I had thirty minutes. But you took your fucking time."

"Well, this isn't the reunion I'd imagined." He pulls around to the back of the parking lot. "But we can do a lot in ten minutes."

"Not gonna happen," I tell him. "You were out last night? Did someone have a party? Whose party?" I feel so cut off from the world without even the ability to stalk everyone on social media. "Is Patrick really telling people I was on drugs? What are people saying?"

"Yeah. Kirsten. You know, Volleyball Kirsten. Her and Sam had a thing because Kirsten's parents were out of town."

"You mean Volleyball Kirsten with her ass cheeks hanging out of her shorts? Yes, I know Volleyball Kirsten." I cross my arms over my chest.

"What's your deal?" he asks. "Are you pissed at me for going out? I've heard nothing from you for days, okay? Radio silence. All your mom would say was that you were paying your debt to society. I heard Sheriff Bell tried to get you to snitch, though, and you were a steel trap. That's my baby."

"Well, keeping my mouth shut has gotten me absolutely nowhere." I shake my head, because in this moment of weakness right now, I'm pretty sure I'd drag the whole team down with me if I could. "Bryce, I've lost everything. The team, my social life, my job. It'd be nice if I didn't have to worry about you and Volleyball Kirsten, okay?"

He drags his fingers up the length of my thigh. "Baby, you don't have to worry about me. I can fend off the ladies when you're not around to mark your territory."

Somehow that doesn't make me feel better. "What about Sam?" I ask. "Has she asked about me?"

He studies the leather of his steering wheel before shaking his head.

I glance down at the time on his dashboard. "I only have four minutes left."

"Why the hell are you working here, by the way?"

I bite down on my lip. "I could explain, or we could make out for four minutes."

He laughs. "Option two, please."

MILLIE

Eleven

Judge not, lest you be judged. Judge not, lest you be judged. Judge not, lest you be judged. I repeat Matthew 7:1 over and over again in my head. It's one of my favorite verses, and one I often find is either misused or ignored altogether.

I knew working with Callie would test my patience. She's just one of those girls. The kind of girl who I'm sure is smart, but gets by on pretty. She doesn't have to go out of her way to be polite or sweet to anyone, because she's not trying to make up for something else. I know people think I'm just a ball of cheer, and I am. Sometimes. But I don't exactly get to be moody or snappy when I don't feel like putting on a happy face, because when most people meet me, I'm already starting out with a deficit. Fat girls don't get that luxury.

I take a deep breath as the door swings open and Callie returns from her break. *Judge not, lest you be judged. Judge not, lest you be judged.*

Every muscle in my body has been spun tight since this afternoon. Even my jaw is starting to throb. Ow! I hold a hand to my cheek. "How was your break?" I ask.

Callie pulls down on her shirt around her waist and checks her makeup in the mirror behind the front desk. "It was whatever."

What does that even mean? "Was that your boyfriend?"

"Yeah, Bryce." Something about her voice feels far away, and suddenly I wonder if we don't speak such different languages after all. "We haven't spoken for days," she adds.

"Were y'all fighting?" I ask a little too quickly.

She looks up. "Nope. Just been grounded. From absolutely everything. I can't even go back to school until Monday."

"Why are you grou—"

She smirks bitterly and motions around. "Why do you think?"

"Sorry," I say automatically, even though I don't have a darn thing to apologize for.

"Not your fault." She plops down onto the stool beside me, like she's resigned herself to this.

I suck in a breath through my teeth. I wonder if she knows that I was the one who identified her.

"What about you?" she asks. "Got a boyfriend?"

The way she says it almost reminds me of that taunting singsong voice I've spent so much of my life hearing when I walk by. I watch her from the corner of my eye for a second before turning to face her. "It's complicated."

She nods. "It always is."

"So we went to the Sadie Hawkins together in the fall." I immediately feel ridiculous for spilling these details she didn't even ask for. But once I start thinking about Malik, my brain turns into a fire hydrant that I just can't manage to shut off. And with cleaning the gym and catching up on schoolwork, I've barely even been able to talk to him for the last week. "And there was a kiss. Well, a peck. But nothing since then. Nada!"

She crosses her legs, holding her chin in her hand with her elbow rested on her knee. It's like she's a doctor giving me her prognosis. "So it started with the Sadie Hawkins dance, which I'm guessing means you asked him. The ball's in his court at this point."

"Right. And we talk. But there hasn't been any kissing. And I like the talking. But I really would prefer the kissing."

She shrugs. "When it's good, it's good."

I nod longingly as I remember that moment with Malik in the parking lot of the school, the lights above us creating little glowing pools as we stood at the edge of one. "Tonight is his family birthday party, and he invited me and my friend Amanda. So maybe something will happen tonight?"

"Hmmm." She muses to herself for a moment. "Him inviting your friend tonight too is a major friend-zone sign. It's been a while now since the dance, though, and you can't just wait around for him forever."

Oh my gosh! She gets it! "Right?" Maybe she isn't as awful as Willowdean said.

"Give him one more shot," she says. "But you gotta be smooth about it. Put yourself out on a limb for him just once more, and if nothing comes of it, at least you know you did everything you could." She rolls her eyes. "It's such bullshit the way we're made to think that only boys can go after girls. What about what *we* want?"

"Yes! Why should I have to sit around and wait for him to be brave enough? Maybe I'm plenty brave for the both of us."

Callie slinks back a little, like something about what I've said or my voice or something has just reminded her who she's talking to: Millie, the fat girl. And not the cute fat girl. Not like Willowdean. I can practically hear Patrick Thomas oinking in the distance.

My jaw throbs again, and this time I wince.

"Are you okay?" asks Callie.

I hold my hand to my cheek again. "Yeah. Just a tooth-ache. You think you're okay out here for a minute?"

"What's the worst that could happen?" she asks.

I look at her for a moment, and she rolls her eyes. "I promise not to trash the place while you're gone, okay?"

I nod, secretly thankful that she put it out there before I had to. I shuffle to Uncle Vernon's office, holding my cheek. I can feel the pain all the way down to my toes. I've had a toothache before, but this is something different altogether. I sit down at the desk and just close my eyes for a few moments as the throbbing thrums through me like a tuning fork.

Finally I reach for the first-aid kit, but find the bottle of ibuprofen completely empty. I reach for the office phone and do what I've done anytime something hurts more than

I can handle. I call my mom.

She answers after only half a ring. "Millie?" she asks, recognizing the gym number on her cell. "Is everything okay, sweetie?"

I don't normally call during work, and she's been a little on edge since the place was vandalized anyway. "I'm fine," I answer automatically. "Well, no, actually I'm not. My mouth is throbbing, Mom."

"Is it a toothache?" she asks. "You didn't crack a tooth, did you? Your grandmother did that once on a piece of hard candy."

"No, it feels worse than a normal toothache. This is more at the back of my mouth. And Mom, it just hurts so bad. I can barely keep my eyes open."

"Oh dear," she says. "That would be your wisdom teeth."

I don't know exactly what this means, but it doesn't sound good.

"Let me call Dr. Shepherd." Before I was born, my mom was one of Dr. Shepherd's dental hygienists, and she's never been shy about calling in a favor.

"Mama, it's almost six o'clock on a Friday."

"Well," she huffs, "I don't expect that your wisdom teeth know or care what day or time it is."

"But I'm supposed to go to Malik's birthday party with Amanda."

"I'm sorry to break it to you, but I don't think you're going anywhere but the dentist today. Just stay put in that back office, and I'll be up there in a jiff with Vernon so he can lock the place up."

The moment we hang up, I slump forward, laying my head on the desk, and the next thing I know, my mom is guiding me to her car and I'm mumbling to Uncle Vernon to teach Callie how to close down the gym and then I'm in Dr. Shepherd's office.

The last thing I remember hearing are the words "emergency wisdom teeth removal" as I lie absolutely helpless with Dr. Shepherd's fingers in my mouth and a bib around my neck.

Everything after that is fuzzy, like how I imagine it would be to live in a place where snow falls so endlessly you can't see more than two feet in front of you. Snow in my hair. Snow melting on my cheeks. Snow in my eyelashes. Snow everywhere.

CALLIE

Twelve

If I didn't have to bear the brunt of Inga's wrath, I'd actually respect the woman. When she and Vernon showed up with their two screaming babies, she didn't even acknowledge me. Her chief concerns were helping Millie to the car and counting the register to be sure I hadn't stolen anything.

While she did that, Vernon rocked both their twins back and forth in their huge double stroller. I use the word *twins* generously. Those boys are little screaming demons. I don't know what kind of contract with the devil Vernon and Inga inked to get stuck with two beet-faced howlers.

"Callie," says Vernon, "could you double count the register while Inga prepares the deposit sheet?"

"Uh, no sir," says Inga. "This criminal is not touching our money." She elbows me out of the way.

"Whatever you say," I grumble. While I don't like being referred to as a criminal, it's kind of nice to come across someone who's finally saying exactly what she thinks.

Inga snaps her fingers, and over the continuous wailing, she says, "I see fingerprints all over this glass. What have you even been doing all day?" She licks her thumb to count the bills in the register and leans a little closer to me. Too quiet for Vernon to hear, she says, "If your fate had been up to me, I would have thrown your spoiled ass in jail."

I liberally squirt the glass cleaner all over the counter and look to her. In my most deadpan voice, I say, "You can't fire me. I work for free."

Inga snarls and closes out the register. She calls out each of the closing duties and uses the stopwatch from Vernon's office to time me. For no reason at all. Except that she can. I hate the woman, but I'm also taking notes.

After we lock up, I find my mom outside in her Tahoe waiting for me. I watch as she gets out. I drag my finger across my neck in an attempt to get her to stay in the car, but she's already bustling over to Vernon and Inga.

"I'm Callie's mama," she says, the words spilling out of her like a confession.

"Oh," says Inga.

Vernon gives her a knowing look. "Babe, you wanna get the boys settled in their car seats?"

Inga nods firmly and walks away, but not before glaring at me from over my mother's shoulder.

Mama's face falls into a deep-set frown. "I just want to let y'all know how sorry I am. And so is Callie's dad, and her stepfather, Keith. We just . . . we didn't raise this type of girl."

Vernon glances over her shoulder to where his two hellions scream as Inga buckles them into their car seats. "I'm new to the whole parent game," he says, "but something tells me that the quicker you figure out that not all your kid's mistakes are your mistakes, the better."

Mama's frown softens. "Wise words from such a new parent."

Vernon laughs. And I can see now that he might be closer to my parents' age than I thought. "Well, if my parents had taken all of my screw-ups personally, they'd be repenting for a whole slew of speeding tickets, property damage, and trips to the ER."

"I've gotta thank you, too," Mama says. "If it weren't for your mercy, there's no telling what kind of legal trouble Callie would be in right now."

"Well, I tell you one thing," he says. "The girl is passionate. I sure was sorry to drop the gym's sponsorship."

"Well, we thank you for your understanding and kindness. Don't we, Callie?"

No cell phone. No dance team. No Bryce. The only people I've gotten quality time with are Millie and Inga. Maybe I would've been better suited going to court and serving community service or something. I'm a minor. Aren't those records sealed or something? No one outside of this awful town would've ever had to know.

Mama clears her throat. "Don't we, Callie?"

"Yes, ma'am," I say, sounding more like a parrot than a human girl.

The whole ride home, Mama is mostly quiet. It's not until we pull up to the driveway that she says, "Baby, Vernon was right. You're passionate. So passionate. Like your mama. You just gotta learn how to direct that passion."

"You mean you don't want my passion in life to be smashing windows and vandalizing businesses?"

She tsks to herself as she turns off the ignition, and we head inside.

That night I lie awake in my bed for hours, hoping for sleep. I'm so used to falling asleep scrolling through my feed or watching videos that this silence is something I'm still not used to. The quiet stillness of night means being left alone with my own thoughts. It's like seeing yourself naked in a mirror with bright fluorescent lights overhead.

When all I've got left is what's in my head, my thoughts spin out. Bryce cheating on me at whatever huge party is happening this weekend. Sam confessing to Melissa that the job of captain was always going to her anyway and that she just kept me in the running to be nice. Whispers as I walk down the hallway about how I was never really that talented or that pretty.

But worst of all is the realization that I've spent so long building my life around dance. From the moment I found my mom's yearbook when me, her, and Claudia moved into that little apartment after she and Dad split up. That picture of her on the football field in her white skirted uniform and matching jacket with its blue-and-red trim and her white boots. I knew I wanted that life. I wanted to wear that uniform. I did everything I could to carry myself to that moment in ninth grade when I auditioned for the team. And so did my mom. Even as a single mother, she sacrificed to send Claudia to voice lessons and me to dance class. She'd buy me new dance shoes, which I was constantly growing out of.

And now my closet is made up of more dance-team uniforms than it is real clothes. Everything from our signature red, white, and blue cowgirl outfits to our shimmering green leotards with *Shamrocks* written in gold sequins. Because up until a few weeks ago, I defined myself in two ways: dance team and Bryce. Only one of those remains.

I sit up in bed. Maybe if I could just talk to Sam. Maybe there's some big plan I don't even know about to get me back on the team next year. It's a small, stupid hope. But sisterhood. She called us a sisterhood. I barely believed it at the time, but I don't have much else left to believe in.

I tiptoe down the stairs to the drawer in the kitchen where Keith leaves his work phone. It used to be that'd he'd get calls at all hours of the night. Finally Mama put her foot down and said their bedroom wasn't big enough for her, him, and the phone. So from the hours of eleven p.m. to seven a.m., this is where his work phone lives. I've saved the chance to sneak a call on the phone for something important, and this is important. Keith won't notice a random outgoing call.

I go into the living room and throw a blanket over my head to muffle my voice.

The line rings six or seven times before a voice answers. "Hello?"

"This isn't Sam," I say immediately.

"Callie?" asks Melissa. "Is that you?"

"What are you doing with Sam's phone? Are you, like,

stalking her now? Don't worry. You're a real shoo-in for captain now."

"We've been trying to call you. I even went by your house, but your stepdad said you were grounded. And not that it's any of your business, but I'm spending the night at Sam's. We're discussing the future of the team."

"Oh really?"

"Yeah, the administration is all over our asses," she says. "We can barely sneeze without them noticing."

Well, being nice was fun while it lasted. "All over your asses? I got kicked off the damn team."

She sighs. "That was really shitty, but, like, are you surprised?"

"I'm surprised that everyone let me take the fall on my own."

She's quiet for a long moment. "You can't be calling us, Callie," she says. "We can't have you associating with the team. We need the school board to think you were the only one from the dance team there. Especially with State in a few weeks."

I can barely process all that she just said, but State? How? "Y'all are going to State?"

Her tone changes. It's that voice she uses to trick Sam into thinking she has everything under control. "The car wash was, like, a super-big success, and Bryce's dad agreed to triple whatever we raised. He says we can do more car washes if we make it to Nationals, and he'll triple what we earn every time."

My shoulders sink. "Oh."

"I have to go," she says. "Sam's coming back."

"I need to talk to her."

"No," she says. "You don't. The dance team can't be associated with you. The sooner everyone forgets that you didn't act alone, the better."

"But . . . but I didn't act alone. You were there, too, Melissa."

"I left," she reminds me. "And no one cares who was there as long as someone pays the price."

"I know you're the one who ratted me out." It feels good to finally say it out loud.

The phone cuts out. I yank the blanket off my head and squeeze my hands into two tight fists. Oh, I'm passionate, all right. And right now my passion is making Melissa's life hell. I'm gonna burn it all down.

MILLIE

Thirteen

I sleep for days. I think. I have vague memories of my parents coming in and out of my room and cotton balls in my mouth and bloody drool. One reccurring dream haunts me: an out-of-body experience where I watch myself writing my personal statement for journalism camp. Except every time I finish, the page is blank, like I've been writing with invisible ink. And then another where I'm doing my audition tape 100 percent naked.

When I do come out of it, I wake up in a panic. My bedroom is hot with afternoon sunlight. I reach for my phone on my nightstand, but it's not in the pineapple-shaped charging cradle where I set it every night like clockwork. After taking a moment to rub my eyes and pry myself out of bed, I stumble out into the kitchen, where my mom is chopping celery and simmering chicken stock for chicken noodle soup.

I open my mouth to speak, but my jaw punishes me immediately with a shooting pain. Cradling my cheek, I groan.

My mom spins on her heels. "You're up! Oh, sweet pea,

I could've brought this to your room. Do you need something?"

I sit on the bar stool across the breakfast bar from her. "My mouth hurts." My throat nearly cracks from dryness, and my tongue feels heavy and swollen in my mouth. "What time is it?"

My mom glances at the microwave. "Three thirty in the afternoon. You've been out since we got home from Dr. Shepherd's last night."

I nod. "Did he give me anything for the pain?"

"Awww, sweetie," my mom coos. "Yes, he did. And you're due for a dose in about thirty minutes." She comes around the other side of the breakfast bar to smooth out my hair a little. "You slept good and hard."

"I didn't see my cell phone on my nightstand. Did I leave it at the gym or something? I could've sworn I brought it home."

She reaches into the pocket of her apron. "Well, it was just the weirdest thing. Amanda called the house phone last night and said I oughta take your phone away from you. Immediately. She wouldn't say why, except that your life depended on it. You know I like Amanda, but she's a touch dramatic."

"Huh." I run my fingers through my hair, trying to detangle some knots. "And you did? Take my phone away?"

"Well, I thought she was just being funny. You know I can never tell when Amanda is joking or not, but she said your social life depended on it." She chuckles to herself. "So I took it out of your room. I figured better safe than sorry." She winks as she twirls around to grab a jar of dried parsley off her spice rack.

I hit a button on the side of my phone, lighting up the screen to see that I'm almost out of battery. "I'm gonna go brush my hair and charge this thing for a bit."

"Okay, sweets, this soup will just simmer for a bit longer before it's ready. And I've got some prescription toothpaste and mouthwash for you when you're ready to brush your teeth."

I smack my lips together. If my breath smells half as gross as my mouth feels, I'm in pretty rough shape. "After the soup," I tell her.

She smiles sympathetically. "I must have dropped at least eight pounds when I had my wisdom teeth removed, so that's something to look forward to."

Somehow it always comes back to weight loss. But I'm too uncomfortable and groggy to engage with this right now. "I'll be in my room."

Back in my room, I search for a charging cord so that I can charge my phone and use it at the same time. I quickly scroll through my text messages. What could have possibly been so horrible that Amanda would call my mom and tell her to take my phone away?

The first text message exchange is between Willowdean and me.

ME: hey youuuuu

WILLOWDEAN: Millie? Hey

ME: what if there was an app that texted you every day to tell you something awesome about yourself but what if the

app was like real stuff like it knew you but not in a creepy robot way

WILLOWDEAN: That sounds awesome, but are you okay right now?

ME: I AM GRAND

ME: like if I were the app robot I would say Willowqueen, you have balls of steel and that makes you awesome have an awesome day love your awesome app robot

ME: so genius

WILLOWDEAN: Balls of steel? Am I being pranked? Did someone steal Millie's phone?

ME: boop boop beep boop

ME: that's robot for shhh good night

"Oh my God." I clap a hand over my mouth. My cheeks burn with instant embarrassment. *Balls of steel*? I don't think I've ever even said the word *balls* out loud.

I've heard of this happening. People just totally out of it on painkillers and doing or saying ridiculous things. But I was so tired. I barely even remember coming home last night.

Still, I'm scared to dive into whatever other messes I might have gotten myself into. But it's a car wreck. And I can't look away. Plus I've got to get into damage-control mode at the very least. What if I said something rude or hurtful? Or accidentally told someone's secret? Or my own secrets?

I scroll down to the next message. Amanda.

ME: my feelings ache

AMANDA: Huh?

ME: it's like a stomachache, but with my heart and not the one in my body I mean the feelings heart. the heart-shaped heart not the fist-shaped heart

AMANDA: Millie?

ME: i want you to always feel like we can talk

AMANDA: I can't believe I'm asking this, but are you drunk?

ME: I like you for always okay but I felt like a bad friend for not knowing that you're asexual

ME: I had to have my wise teeth taken out but only the very smartest ones and that's why i missed malik's party, but it's okay i told him i wouldn't be there and that we should kiss for fun

AMANDA: OMG MILLIE WHERE ARE YOU

AMANDA: Throw your phone. Do it. Right now. Throw it as far as you can. THIS IS NOT A DRILL.

I clutch my phone to my chest. Oh Lord Baby Jesus. What did I do? I need to talk to Amanda. I can't believe I told her my feelings were hurt—when I had no right to even have hurt feelings to begin with! And Malik.

I take a deep breath and hold the phone out in front of me as I click on my message thread with Malik.

ME: no party for me :(

MALIK: Oh ok. Did something just come up? You seemed excited the other night.

ME: I was excited but were you is the real question

MALIK: I don't get it. Did I do something wrong?

ME: if being cute and wearing your stupid pennies in your stupid loafers and always having a kissable face is wrong

then yes you do all the things wrong mister sir

I roll over onto my side and pull the blankets over my head. With my face pressed deep into my pillow, I scream as loud as I can. The world is a cruel, cruel place. And what's even worse is that those were only the first few in a very long series of messages. After a few more screams, I emerge from my blankets with my hair even more mussed than it was to begin with.

I inhale for two deep breaths, taking my time to exhale each time. My breath is truly unpleasant.

MALIK: Wow. Well, this party would be a whole lot better if you were here. That's for sure.

MALIK: And I think you're cute, too. And pretty and basically every synonym for pretty.

I gasp, and the rush of air actually hurts the wounds on my gums, but holy cannoli! Did Malik say that? And he wasn't even doped up on painkillers. He was just regular Malik, sitting around at his birthday party full of people, telling me I'm pretty.

ME: well if that's true you could've kissed my face after the dance and not just pretended like it never happened you weirdo

I pump my fist into the air. "You go, girl!" I say, my voice no louder than a stage whisper. It's like I'm reading a really good book—the kind that makes you feel like you've swallowed fireflies—except this time I'm the main character of the book. I'm the love interest! I'm the girl who gets the guy! And girls like me? You don't find us in fairy tales or on the covers of romance novels.

Slowly I can feel myself shaking away whatever bit of embarrassment and shame I'm still clinging to.

MALIK: Would you believe me if I said I was shy?

ME: would you believe me if I said I believe you but that it's still a dumb reason

MALIK: I better get back to this party. I wish you were here. My sisters are driving me crazy and my mom keeps asking for you.

ME: well maybe if you get better about kissing my face, we can celebrate your birthday together next year

MALIK: I like that possibility.

ME: how many cotton balls can you fit in your mouth? However many it is I can beat you.

MALIK: Challenge accepted.

I hold my phone to my chest. My lungs are swelling and I'm scared they might just burst. In a small way, I feel like a fraud. An imposter. I'm not that girl. I can't even find it in me to tell my mom about broadcast journalism camp. I'm not the kind of girl who would just message Malik and tell him to kiss me.

But I did that. I was that girl. For a short, drug-induced time, I was that brave girl I've wished to be for so long. And I'm embarrassed—a little horrified, even—but that girl knew what she wanted and she took it. I remember my talk with Callie yesterday afternoon. "Why should I have to sit around and wait for him to be brave enough?" I said that. Just yesterday.

So maybe that girl who sent all those text messages last night—good and bad—is me after all.

★ ★ ★

Without me to corral the troops on Saturday night, our slumber party at Ellen's house was postponed until next weekend. Secretly, I was pleased, because fear of missing out is a real thing and I suffer from stage four.

On Monday morning, Uncle Vernon goes in early to open up the gym, so I can sleep in a little bit before going back to school. If this is the kind of special treatment that having wisdom teeth removed affords me, I'll take it.

Even though I've already ruined my perfect attendance for the year, I pull myself out of bed. I've gone through my prescription of serious painkillers and am only on a regimen of Tylenol now, but Mom still insists on driving me to school.

When I inherited Mom's minivan, she and Dad agreed it was time for her to get her dream car: a champagne-colored Volvo. They had to drive five and a half hours for the closest Volvo dealership, but between the safety ratings and the buttery-leather interior, I think it's safe to say that my mom might leave all her worldly possessions to this car instead of me.

Mom is wearing one of her matching-set velour track-suits with a pair of her Cloudwalker Deluxe tennis shoes, because after she drops me off, she will kick off her morning routine with a trip to Cinch It!—the women's-only circuit gym located in the mall and wedged between the only two plus-size stores in Clover City. (Both of which should be called Old and So Old You Might as Well Be Dead. Thank goodness for online shopping.) And after her trip to the gym, Mom will power walk with her girlfriends to the food court, where they'll each get their own personally formulated smoothie at Juice Monster, with the perfect cocktail of vitamin boosters, fiber, and protein powder.

We approach a school zone and the Volvo slows to a crawl. "Dr. Shepherd says the puffiness in your face should go down over the next few days."

I laugh. "My face is eternally puffy."

My mom doesn't respond. "The girls at Cinch It! have been asking after you," she finally says. "I told them all about your job at Uncle Vernon's gym, and they all just think it's so great that you're taking the initiative to work at a gym."

I look to her, but she keeps her eyes trained on the school zone ahead, and I'm actually thankful she can't look at me when I say, "Mom, you know that's not why I'm working at the gym, right?"

A small boy darts out across the crosswalk, and she slams on her brakes. "I swear! That crossing guard isn't paying attention to a thing!"

"It's really just to help out. Uncle Vernon and Inga need all the help they can get since the twins were born. And I like boxing okay," I tell her. "It's fun, ya know? Uncle Vernon gives me a few pointers every now and then. But I don't do it to become some after-picture version of myself. I do it 'cause it makes me feel good. You know that, right?"

She smiles and accelerates as we leave the school zone.

And that's it. I wish I could figure out a way to just say

it in the most blatant terms: MOM, I DON'T WANT TO OBSESS ABOUT DIETING WITH YOU ANYMORE. But instead, I've just sort of slipped away from her and have begun avoiding all the things that once bonded us. Now, the void between us feels so wide that I often wonder if our bond only ran as deep as our obsession with bodies we'll likely never have.

In front of the school, we share a hug and a kiss. "Oh, I printed off the application for this summer at Daisy Ranch," she tells me. "I'll just need you to fill it out so we can send in the deposit. I'll leave it on your bed for you, okay? This is the year, baby. I can feel it."

This is the moment when I should just rip off the dang Band-Aid. "I'm not going to weight-loss camp." Seven words. That's all it would take. But instead I nod and say, "Sounds good, Mom."

A cloud of hurt and anger at no one but myself follows me through the carport and into the school. I'm so scared of bursting this unspoken bubble between my mom and me, when in reality, it would be the best thing for both of us. I've spent so much time wondering who my mom would be without all the fad diets and the calorie counting and the absurd workout plans. Honestly, I've wondered the same about myself. Some part of me is scared that she's spent so long living this life that if she stripped it all away, there'd be nothing left, and surely in some deep recess of her brain, she fears that, too.

I head straight to the front office to do morning

announcements, hoping to find that spring in my step but failing.

Between first and second periods, I find Amanda waiting at my locker, tugging the straps of her backpack and twisting her toe into the linoleum. A wave of embarrassment washes over me as I relive my wisdom-tooth text-message fiasco. I might've been drugged, but I made something that was very much about Amanda about me and my feelings. I should've reached out to her over the weekend, but I didn't know where to start. I take a deep breath and tuck all thoughts of my mom and Daisy Ranch aside. Trying to fix more than one thing at a time usually means I can only give half a mind to a whole problem. So first: Amanda.

"Hey, are you okay?" she asks immediately.

I nod and touch my cheek. "A little sore. Mom said she can't believe I had to get my wisdom teeth out. Her and Uncle Vernon never did."

She nods, but there's something about her that feels off.

"We should talk," I offer.

She waves her hand and her whole body bounces back, like she'd just as soon tiptoe around the issue. "Psh! Nothing to talk about. Well, I mean, between us." She leans down and whispers, "But oh my God! What did you send to Malik?"

I release a heavy breath, but I can't hide my smile. "Well, I've got some damage control to do, but it shouldn't be too bad." I've backed out of one tough conversation already this morning; I won't do it again. "You know those texts I sent you about my feelings?"

She nods silently.

"That was just about me wanting you to always feel like I'm here for you and not about me thinking there's anything wrong with you being . . . asexual." I test out the word, wanting to be sure I'm using it in the right way. I take a step closer and cup her arm with my hand. "You're my best friend. The only one who's ever willing to go all in on my ridiculous plans and the only one whose faith in me is unwavering. I want you to be able to tell me everything. And if it's something I don't understand, I want to learn. And I know it's not on you to teach me about it."

Her lips split into a half smile. "It's not that I didn't want to tell you. I just didn't know how. And . . ." She shakes her head. "When we were playing Two Truths and a Lie, it felt like a good time to just get it out there. Like, it wouldn't be some big deal. It's just my sexual orientation in the same way that you're straight and Hannah's a lesbian. I wanted to tell you, but I also know that you're always looking for a solution. So I was scared you'd think this was something that needed fixing."

"Oh, no. Not at all. I don't think you're broken," I say. And I mean it. "I love you because you're Amanda," I tell her. "And that means loving all the little and big things that make you—you!"

Amanda throws her arms around me and squeezes relentlessly. We've never been the type to hug much. Not like Ellen and Willowdean. But in a way, I'm okay with that. Because this hug—this suffocatingly tight hug that Amanda has perfected from years of wrestling with her brothers—means so much more.

After lunch, I rush over to AP Psych in the hopes that I'll catch Malik a little early and maybe we can talk. If I'm being honest, I have totally daydreamed about this moment. Us in Mr. Prater's dark classroom with the twinkling lights. Except in my daydream, no one else is there. We would talk and talking would turn into kissing and kissing would turn into love and love would turn into forever.

I know, I know. But aren't daydreams supposed to be embarrassing?

I settle into my seat and wait for Malik. Slowly students begin to trickle in, and my daydream begins to dissipate. The second-to-last bell rings, and Mr. Prater strolls in with a fresh mustard stain on his tie. He waits in the doorway for any stragglers, and just as the final bell rings, Malik squeezes in past him.

He plops down beside me and says, "Hey."

"Hey," I echo. Our eyes lock for one . . . two . . . three seconds before he looks away and we are right back where we started.

I turn away and reach into my bag for my textbook. I squeeze my eyes shut as hard as I can, because if I don't, I might just cry.

When Mr. Prater isn't looking, I shoot off a quick text to the one person I know has carried the weight of a truly painful crush.

ME: I'm having a CRUSH-911.

She responds almost immediately, which surprises me, even after all this time, because I've always felt like she's way too cool for me.

WILLOWDEAN: Operator. What's your emergency?

CALLIE

Fourteen

Life without a cell phone is a desert without water. It's killing me.

I literally asked Kyla to play Scrabble with me the other night. (For the record, I won. Obviously.) The only lifeline I have to Bryce is school, and my mom's been checking in on me in every single class. The woman is a hawk.

I stand behind the counter at the gym wiping down the same spot of glass over and over again to give the appearance that I am indeed very busy. Millie and her uncle are doing some routine maintenance on the weight equipment. Today, Tuesday, is her first day back since her emergency wisdom-teeth removal, and I nearly hugged the girl when I saw her.

While she was gone, I was left to finish my training with Inga. She tried to fire me four times, despite the fact that she's not paying me, and even made me go stand outside in the giant muscle suit while I waved around a big NEW MEMBERSHIP SPECIALS sign. When I asked her why, she said I was breathing too loudly.

The bell above the door chimes and, shockingly, a

customer walks in. I nearly jump off my stool and recite the greeting Inga drilled into me. "Hi, welcome to Down for the Count. Are you a member or a first-time guest?"

The guy—tall and broad and on the huskier side—clears his throat before responding. "Uh, yeah. I'm not a member."

Out of the corner of my eye, I see Millie rush over to the desk beside me.

My brow wrinkles for a moment as I try to place his face. Rosy cheeks, soft blue eyes, and a few acne scars on his chin. His blond curls have a reddish undertone, and something about his face feels boyish. "You're in my grade, aren't you?"

"Mitch, right?" Millie pipes in. "I think you know my friend Willowdean."

His already bright cheeks turn a deep shade of red. "Uh, yeah."

Mitch, Mitch, Mitch, Mitch. I squint. There it is! "You're on the football team! With my boyfriend! Bryce. I knew I recognized you."

Mitch has always been that big dopey guy who tags around with Bryce, Patrick, and all the other guys from the team. I don't really know him, but now, stuck in this gym and phoneless, I feel like freaking Ariel from *The Little Mermaid.* I nearly scream, "I want to be where the people are!" Like this big burly dude is some kind of lifeline to my previous life.

But instead I just bite my bottom lip while Millie gives him the lowdown on all of our membership packages.

I take his cash as he pays for the first three months of his membership.

He looks at the cash longingly as I deposit it into the register.

"We appreciate your business," I say, "but the way you're looking at this cash, I sort of feel like I'm forcing you to pay a parking ticket."

"A birthday gift from my dad," he explains. "So I can get in some extra training before next season when the weight room at school is closed."

"Senior year," I say. "Surely you've had some scouts interested." Unlike Bryce.

He shrugs. "Yeah. Guess so."

"Well," says Millie, "we'll laminate your card while you work out and hand it back over before you leave. Towels are in the locker room and on the wall by the punching bags. My uncle Vernon—Vernon, wave!"

Vernon offers a quick wave but doesn't look up from his duties.

Millie smiles sheepishly. "He's a certified trainer and offers one-on-one sessions as well. If you need help operating any of the machinery, just ask Vernon or me for assistance. Callie here is still a newbie."

I chuckle. "You're a pro on the workout machines?"

I expect Mitch to laugh, too, but his lips turn into a straight line.

The color drains from Millie's face, but her voice is defiant when she says, "Yes, actually. I am."

"Okay." It was a joke. The girl can barely get through a

sentence without giggling, but suddenly she's taking herself seriously?

Mitch clears his throat again. "Well, I guess I better get my dad's money's worth."

Without a word, Millie takes his card to the back office to be laminated as Mitch adjusts one of the leg machines.

I sit down on the stool, and something about my whole body feels heavy. It's guilt. It settles into my stomach and turns to concrete. What I said to Millie was dumb, I know. But it was funny! I mean, any other guy in Mitch's crowd would have totally laughed.

I watch as Millie walks back up to the front desk.

I open my mouth to speak, but I don't know what to say.

It doesn't matter, though, because before I even have a chance to form a word, she slaps the card down on the counter and says, "Don't forget to give him a welcome bag."

"I won't." My voice squeaks.

I should've said I was sorry. I know that. But something inside me rears up, and I find myself somehow annoyed instead. It was just a dumb joke. And probably way more mild than what she's used to hearing. She should just get used to it. The world is a tough place. Especially for people like her. She could at the very least get a sense of humor.

Everyone stands out in some way. It's not like I don't get upset every time some stranger thinks I'm not white enough or not Mexican enough or when someone thinks I'm Kyla's babysitter and not her sister. Millie needs to toughen up, and I say that as someone who has had to do the same.

The next day at school, while I'm walking from English to World History, Bryce rushes up behind me and kisses my neck. I shriek from the shock and because I am super ticklish.

"Bryce!" I yank his arm and pull him up beside me. "What the hell are you doing? My mom has eyes in every crevice of this place."

"I miss you." He pouts.

"I miss you," mimics his friend Patrick as he passes us in the hallway with Mitch close behind.

Bryce laughs and flips him the bird.

"Eat shit, Patrick!" I call.

Mitch offers a slight smile, and I nod my chin in his general direction. Yesterday I was thrilled to see him, but we're not the kind of people who would actually acknowledge each other in public.

"You could come visit me at work," I tell him.

"That place stinks," he says. "And where would we have any privacy?"

"Well, maybe you could just power through the smell and maybe—just maybe!—we could hang out for a little while without you stuffing your hands up my shirt?"

He grunts. "You've never complained in the past."

"Well, that was before my whole life was one giant prison sentence." I squeeze his hand. "What have you even been doing without me?"

He lets go of my hand as the hall is about to split in two different directions. He bites down on his lip, and for a moment, I see him the way I did on the first day of tenth grade. My knees feel like Jell-O and I have to stop myself from pulling him into the handicap bathroom across the hall.

"I've found ways to keep busy," he says.

A brief panic weighs on me. I trust Bryce, but I know every day I'm grounded is another day our relationship is at risk. It's time to get creative. I stand up on my tiptoes and give him a soft, closed-mouth kiss. My mama and her snooping abilities be damned!

"I'll figure something out. I promise." One more kiss. "I swear!"

MILLIE

Fifteen

I follow Willowdean up the steps leading to the second story of her house.

"Dumplin', I just brewed up some fresh sweet tea!" her mother calls from the kitchen. "Come and get it!"

Willowdean throws her head back, her eyes rolling. She sighs. "It *is* good sweet tea."

She doubles back and leads me to the kitchen.

Ms. Dickson sits at the kitchen table in black-and-white polka-dot scrubs, her legs crossed, while she clips coupons. The moment she sees me, her eyes light up. "Millicent! I didn't realize you were coming over! I thought that was Ellen sneaking upstairs."

"It's good to see you again, ma'am." From what I know about Willowdean and her mother, they've had a bumpy relationship. Ms. Dickson isn't perfect by any means, but I think that when I won runner-up at the pageant, the only people cheering louder than she was were Dale and Lee from the Hideaway. (Dale and Lee . . . well, Dale and Lee are a long story.)

"How's your mama doing?" she asks, gripping my dangling hand as Willowdean pours us each a tall glass of sweet tea.

"She's good, Ms. Dickson," I say. "A little overprotective, but good."

"Baby, call me Ms. Rosie." She looks at me with sympathetic eyes. "We just want the best for our babies."

"Except your best isn't always our best," chimes in Willowdean.

Ms. Rosie rolls her eyes. "Pains me to say it, but you're not wrong."

Willowdean doesn't bother hiding her satisfaction. "We're going upstairs," she tells her as she hands me a glass with a striped bendy straw and a slice of lemon floating on top.

"Millie, you don't be a stranger," says Ms. Rosie. "And I hope we see you in the pageant again this fall," she adds.

I grin wildly. "You just might." But first things first: journalism camp. Well, actually: Malik. Then camp.

Upstairs, as I'm following Willowdean down to her bedroom, I linger for a moment in front of a room that would best be described as crafting heaven. A beautifully refurbished sewing machine sits in one corner with a long cutting table on the other side. Clear plastic cabinets sit against the other wall. Each drawer is color coded and full of fabric, thread, and yarn. There's even a drawer labeled GLITTER, which is undoubtedly calling my name.

"Aunt Lucy's old room turned pageant-prep/sewing

room," says Willowdean, once she sees that I'm still at the other end of the hallway.

My eyes drift up, and that's when I see that every inch of spare wall space is covered with Dolly Parton paraphernalia.

Willowdean treks back down the hallway toward me. Her gaze travels the room, and her expression is a cross between longing and satisfaction. "Our Dolly Parton shrine," she says. "Well, really it was Lucy's, but it's ours now. We did all this during the Christmas break. Whatever's not hanging in here has found a home in my room."

"It's magnificent," I tell her.

In her room, Willowdean hovers above a record player as she cues up an upbeat Dolly Parton song. "It's called 'I'm Sixteen,'" she says as she turns it down just a bit. "A new favorite, but more importantly it'll stop my mom from eavesdropping so easily."

We sit on opposite ends of her bed, sipping on our sweet tea.

"Your mom is so cool," I tell her.

She sputters out a laugh. "You're kidding, right?"

"She's, like, so nice and probably doesn't even care that you date Bo."

"Honestly, I think Bo might be her new favorite thing about me."

"My parents could barely handle me entering the pageant against their wishes," I tell her. "A boyfriend? That is definitely Not Until You're Thirty-Five territory. I can't even muster up the courage to tell them I want to go to a different camp this summer."

"Hey," says Willowdean, "I imagine it's a whole lot easier to be the cool parent when the person who thinks you're cool isn't even your kid. So this boy trouble nine-one-one? What's going on?"

"Oh, right!" I'd nearly forgotten why I was here in the first place and the text I had sent. I set my tea down on her nightstand and flop backward. "It's Malik."

"Y'all are so cute. And you asked him to the Sadie Hawkins with your ukulele! What could possibly be wrong with y'all?"

"Well, that's sort of the problem," I say. "There is no 'y'all.'"

"Ohhhhhh." She lies down from the other side of the bed, so that our heads are side by side, her golden curls spilling out and tickling my shoulders. Before this year, I spent a lot of time wishing I could be Willowdean. It's like she never has to overthink or try too hard.

"Malik and I talk almost every night," I tell her. "And during the day at school it's like . . . he's nice, but it's like all those in-depth conversations we have at night never even happened." I let myself pout. "I'm just ready for something to happen already. I mentioned it to Callie, and she thinks I should just make my move, but . . . but she . . ."

"She's skinny?" Willowdean asks, attempting to fill in the blank. "Well, I have a feeling boys have never been an issue for Callie. And not to say that they have for you, but it's different."

"I get it. Boy, do I get it."

She turns her head toward me. "But Callie's awful. You know that, right? She is not to be trusted. You're too good to people, Millie. You put too much faith in people who don't deserve it."

I roll my eyes. "She's not that bad."

She huffs. "But in this one case, she might not be so off the mark. You know Malik likes you, right? All the signs are there."

I nod. Except . . . I'm scared to even think it, but what if Malik is so different in person because he doesn't want to admit he likes a fat girl? Maybe he just needs a little push."

"You know, me and Bo . . . things didn't start out so good at first. But there came a time when he put it all out there. He wasn't pushy or rude, but he knew what he wanted and he was pretty sure I wanted it, too. But if it had been up to me to make that first move . . . well, we might still be having angry make-out sessions behind the Dumpsters."

I wrinkle my nose.

"I gotta tell you," she says. "Once you're in the heat of the moment, the smell sort of goes away."

I chuckle. "So is it true what Ellen said the other night? About you and Bo?" I glance back to the door to make sure it's shut all the way and double-check that the record is still playing. "Having sex?" I whisper.

Her cheeks turn an alarming shade of pink and her hands fly up to cover her face. "No. Yes. Yes, yes, yes!"

I squeal to let her know I'm just thrilled for her, but inside I'm doing everything I can not to put myself in her shoes, because that's flat-out terrifying.

"I just . . . Millie, you can't tell anyone this—oh my God. I can't believe I'm talking about sex with Millicent Michalchuk."

My eyes widen. "Honestly, I can't believe it either."

She laughs. "The thing is . . . and I don't even know how to talk about this with Ellen. It's taken a lot for me to feel okay with Bo touching me. Especially in places that remind me that I am definitely fat. That probably sounds weird."

"No." My voice comes out like a sigh. "That's not weird at all." I roll onto my side and prop myself up on my elbow. She's got my undivided attention.

"Now that I'm sort of over that . . . honestly, though, some days I am and some days I'm not. But I guess what I'm saying is, I want him to touch me and anytime I don't it's because of me and not him. Except now I have to think about him seeing me naked and—" She covers her face again.

I think for a long time. I think about the exact thing I would want someone else to say to me in this moment. "Willowdean, I know you're fat. We all know it. Ellen does. So do Hannah and Amanda. And Bo does, too. You're the same person you are with your clothes on as you are with them off. If you want to have sex—if you're ready for that, and the only thing holding you back is the thought of yourself naked . . . well, if I had to guess, every person in the history of sex has had that same thought."

She shakes her head. "And I'm the one who invited you over to give you boy advice. You obviously don't need me."

Except I do. I need Willowdean so much. Because if I ever feel like I need permission to do something that people in my body aren't meant to do, I just look to Willowdean. She's all the reminder I need that the only person who can give you permission to live life and to live it big is yourself.

"Oh, I need you," I tell her. "I need you like Oprah needs Gayle."

CALLIE

Sixteen

Maybe there is a God. I'm not really doing a very good job of praying to Him (or Her?), because on Thursday morning during Anatomy, I experience nothing short of a miracle when Ms. Santana hands me a note from the attendance office.

I unfold the note in my lap.

Had to leave early today and take Kyla to the doctor's. Her fever is back and the school nurse won't keep her in the infirmary again. You have my permission to get a ride home from Bryce, but that is it. A single car ride! School and home! That's it! I swear, Callie, if I hear you left early or pulled some kind of hijinks, you will see my wrath. And if you think this is my wrath, this is only the warm-up, baby. Be safe. Wear your seat belt. I love you.

Mama

I fold up the paper just the way it was given to me, and I almost have to stuff the damn thing in my mouth to stop myself from screaming with joy. My arm shoots up in the air, but I don't even wait to be called on. "Miss! I need to use the restroom."

Ms. Santana motions to the hall passes hanging on the back of her door. "Make it quick."

I speed out the door, and as soon as it shuts behind me, I make a dash for Bryce's locker, where I scribble a note on his dry-erase board.

Meet me in the wrestling mat room at noon.
Come alone. —C

I rush back to class, where I completely tune out the rest of the lecture and instead make romantic plans for my romantic afternoon, right down to what snacks I'm going to get from the vending machine for our reunion feast.

I use the dance-team sweatshirt from my locker as a tablecloth to lay out our vending-machine spread of Flamin' Hot Cheetos, pork rinds, a sleeve of Oreos, Skittles, Funyuns, and two Dr Peppers. Hmmm. Maybe we should make out before partaking?

The wrestling-mat room isn't ideal, seeing as the mats are years old and carry their own specific stench, but the one thing this place guarantees is privacy. Especially since wrestling season ended early when no one qualified to move on past District.

I watch the clock above the door as the last lunch bell rings. I wish I would've worn something cuter today, like a little dress and some strappy sandals. But instead I wore the cheer shorts I slept in last night, an old homecoming T-shirt, and knee-high gym socks with a pair of hot-pink sneakers. I glance down at what I have to offer. It'll have to do.

Thirty minutes into lunch, and still no show. That's when I break into the Oreos. The polite thing to do would be to brush my teeth before any making out—Oreos have this miraculous way of working themselves into every crevice of your mouth—but Bryce is already late as hell, and I'm starting to fume. He'd be lucky to kiss my chocolate-crusted mouth at this point.

By the time the final bell for what should be my economics class rings, I contemplate going on a search for him. Maybe he never made it to his locker? Or maybe he got held up by a coach or something. But I don't have a phoooooooone. And if he shows up and I'm not here, we'll just be missing each other again.

I crumple down on a mat and spread out like a snow angel—not that I have much experience making those.

The next bell rings for last period, scaring my whole body to life. And then the door creaks open and I shoot up. Bryce stands in the doorway, with Patrick peering over his shoulder.

"You were supposed to come alone," I say through clenched teeth.

Bryce looks to my rations on the floor. He laughs at my one empty can of Dr Pepper lying on its side next to a half-empty sleeve of Oreos.

"And at lunchtime," I add.

His shoulders flop as he shrugs. "I wanted to go to Taco Bell with the guys. I figured you would wait."

I stand up, shaking the crumbs off my shorts. "And what is Patrick even doing here?"

Bryce looks over his shoulder and shrugs again.

"Hey, are y'all lovebirds gonna eat those pork rinds?" asks Patrick.

I roll my eyes and toss them in his general direction. "Get lost."

He tears the bag open and pops one in his mouth. "Good luck, dude," he says between bites.

The door closes behind him and I immediately ask, "Good luck with what?"

Bryce takes a careful step toward me. "Baby, we need to talk." He drops his partially zipped backpack on the mat and a few things spill out, including his cell phone.

"Well, yeah, that would be nice! I mean, I've barely seen you in the last two weeks."

He nods. "See. You get it. I knew you'd get it."

"Get what?" For the first time, doubt ripples in my stomach. Doubt in us. High school sweethearts for a year and a half now. When people talk about living the dream, we're the dream they're talking about!

"I just feel so disconnected from you lately."

"Well, baby," I say, trying my best to keep my voice measured and even. "I've been grounded for three weeks. The whole no-phone-and-house-arrest situation makes it hard to communicate, but that's not a forever thing." I take a step closer and drag my fingers down his elbow. "And maybe I can leave you with a few good memories to get you through until this whole ordeal is over."

He crosses his arms over his chest. "It's just like, with you not on the dance team and working at that piece-of-shit gym . . . it's like we're living in different worlds."

My stomach drops and my vision blurs. I close my eyes, blink hard, and pull back from him. "Excuse me?"

"I just, like, think we should maybe quit or take a break."

"What does that even mean?"

"It's like you're not one of us anymore."

"One of who?"

He holds his mouth in a firm line, refusing to further incriminate himself.

I dart to the ground for his cell phone. He tries to stop me, but I'm too quick.

"Give that back," he demands.

I slide the phone into my back pocket. "Oh, you'll get it back," I say. But before I do anything else, I reach down for the full can of Dr Pepper.

Bryce watches me curiously.

I pop the tab on the can, and the sound of it piercing the silence is pure satisfaction. Almost more satisfactory than me reaching up and pouring nearly half the can out on top of his head.

Bryce freezes in shock as soda dribbles down his chestnut golden-boy hair and onto his T-shirt, where his ultimate-bro Oakley sunglasses hang from his collar.

And then it's like what's happening suddenly hits him.

"What the hell is wrong with you?" he screams.

I reach for my backpack and dart out the door.

It's a second or two before I can hear him on my heels. "Give me my phone back!"

"Who is she?" I shout, not paying any mind to the fact that classes are still in session. "I know every bitch in this school! Who is she?"

Sprinting and typing in his security code isn't what I'd call easy, but I manage. "You didn't even change your code?" I say over my shoulder. And somehow it infuriates me most that he felt like there was no way he'd get caught. All I can think is that there's another girl. There has to be. Guys don't just leave girls like me unless they've got something else lined up.

I stop dead in my tracks just down the hall from the front office and scroll through his messages. He practically runs into me—all limbs as he reaches over me for the phone, but I have a sibling, which gives me the upper hand. If there's anything my little sis has taught me, it's how to be a master at keep-away.

And then I see it. A name I don't recognize. Hiding there in plain sight under a fake contact. "Who's Neil?" I ask. "New kid in school?" There are no new kids in Clover City.

"That's private property!" he says. "That phone costs more than a month of your mall-rat paychecks."

"That's okay," I tell him. "Let it all hang out. Well, whoever Neil is, I'm sure he has great boobs and a super-perky ass." I feel something boiling in my chest. Something that feels like tears. Instead of giving in, I bite them back. I scroll through the messages, but all I see are dumb memes traded back and forth and a few short texts about how the family reunion is sure to "blow."

His chest heaves and his forehead is damp with sweat. "Neil is my cousin from South Carolina, you psycho bitch."

Furiously I scroll through more text messages, and I find a little bit of flirting between him and some other girls from school—Sam included—but most of it . . . it's harmless. Nothing.

"There's not another girl," he says with finality. "But believe what you want."

I whirl around on my heels. But the fire in my belly is quieting and disintegrating into hurt. He's telling the truth. There is no other girl. He'd rather be alone than with me. I pull myself together and wear my anger like a shield, because the only thing I have left to save now is face.

"Likely story," I say. "Maybe I'll remember that before I delete all your gross dick pics from my cloud. Or I could accidentally share them. All those little buttons are so tiny and confusing." Now we've got an audience. Students and faculty are slowly creeping out of their classrooms. Great. My mom is going to kill me. But honestly, what do I have left to lose? "Oh, and here's a note for future dick pics. Everyone knows you're just trying to make it look bigger if you take it from underneath."

Someone behind me whistles, and I hear a teacher say, "Everyone, back to class."

Principal Armstrong walks up behind Bryce. "Both of you in my office."

"Not until this slut gives me my phone back."

"You want your phone back?" I ask. "Your super-expensive phone?" I'm screaming now. "The one I could never afford? I'll give you your dumb phone back."

And then I slam his phone, screen facing out, into the nearest locker. I lied when I said popping the tab on that can of Dr Pepper was satisfaction. *This* is satisfaction. The glass cracks and I slam it again. "Good thing you have so much money to buy a new one!" I throw the phone over his head and it skitters down the hallway, making a few crunching noises along the way.

I walk past Principal Armstrong and escort my own damn self straight into her office. She follows me, guiding a scowling Bryce along.

I turn around just as I enter her office. "I'm not sitting in the same room as him," I tell her.

Armstrong rolls her eyes, then nods, sending Bryce over to Vice Principal Benavidez's office.

I sit down in the chair in front of her desk, and the moment Armstrong closes the door behind her, I begin to sob. "I need . . . I need to call my mom," I say.

She pats my shoulder. "That was supposed to be my suggestion."

Principal Armstrong does most of the explaining, for which I'm grateful. I nearly tremble when she hands me the phone, but my mom is . . . calm. She tells me we'll talk about it when I get home and that she's calling Keith and my dad to see who can get to the school quickest.

I hang up, and Armstrong hands me a box of tissues. She cradles her chin in her hand and turns up the music on her computer just a little. Some kind of nineties acoustic songs with flowy lady voices dancing along to each note. "What is this? Old-lady slow jams?"

"Tori Amos," she tells me. "You're having a bad day, so I'll try not to hold that against you."

We sit there in silence for a little while.

"We can talk if you want," she finally says. "I can even send you down to the counselor. Or I can play mah-jongg and we can wait for your ride."

I sniff. "That last option is good."

About thirty minutes pass before there's a light knock on the door. A freshman student aide sticks her head in the door. She focuses on me, my tearstained face, dirty clothes, and Oreos stuck in my teeth. "Um, her dad is here."

The aide steps back and in walks my dad. Not Keith. For some reason, I'd just assumed that the aide meant Keith. But no. My dad is here.

"I was working a job just outside of town," he says.

But I barely even hear him, because all I can do is fall into his arms. He squeezes me tight. The thick black stubble peppering his chin tickles against my neck, and I let the whole weight of my body relax against him. It feels like falling into bed after a long day. He wears his everyday self-imposed uniform of a plaid button-up shirt and the same style of Levi jeans he's worn since he and my mom started dating.

"Should we talk?" he asks Principal Armstrong.

"Tomorrow. I'll talk to her and her mom first thing in the morning. And you too, if work permits. But I think it might be best to get out of here before the last bell rings."

He nods once and takes my hand. With his other arm, he hoists my backpack onto his shoulder.

He doesn't speak until we're out in the fresh air. "Made quite a scene, did ya?" He tries to swallow a chuckle as he slides on his signature Ray-Ban aviators. "Your mother liked having an audience for our fights, too."

"Dad."

"Brian had it coming." He opens the passenger door of his truck for me and tucks my backpack at my feet before slamming the door shut.

"His name was Bryce!" I say, loud enough for him to hear as he walks around to the other side.

He hops in and turns the engine on. "Guess it doesn't much matter anymore."

I sigh.

"Do I need to give you the whole he-never-deserved-you pep talk?"

"No," I tell him. "He was never in my league." But for the first time the confidence I've always put on display for the world to see feels like a complete and total sham.

"You know you'll find something better out there."

"But maybe I won't," I say, my voice tiny.

He pulls into the Harpy's drive-through without even stopping to ask if I want something.

The speaker crackles as we approach the drive-through.

"Welcome to Harpy's," the deadpan voice says. "What'll it be?"

"You never found someone better than Mom," I say.

"Two vanilla cones," he says. "One dipped in strawberry and one in chocolate." He pulls forward, but not all the way up to the window, and steadies his gaze on me. "With your mom and me, it wasn't about needing something better. Not for either of us. It was about finding something that worked. We loved each other, but we didn't work. That wasn't fair to you or Claudia. And besides, she snored too much."

"Well, you never found something that worked." I huff and cross my arms. "And she still snores, by the way." A smirk tickles at my lips.

He says nothing as he pulls up to the window and hands the grumbly woman with a name tag reading LYDIA a few bucks before passing me my strawberry-dipped cone and digging into his chocolate one.

But I let the ice cream drip onto my fingers for a moment. Partly because I shouldn't eat it, especially after all that junk I ate this afternoon. I haven't been working out like I did when I was on the team, and thinking about how many calories and how much sugar are in this thing makes me cringe.

But the real reason I'm sitting here with this uneaten cone is because—"Oh my God! Dad, you're seeing someone." I gasp. "Does Claudia know?"

He freezes midbite and then proceeds to wipe his mouth with the inside of his elbow. "I'm not seeing someone in particular," he says. "Not yet. But I am starting to see people."

I grin and smack the dashboard. "It's about damn time!"

He pulls the paper off his cone and shoves the rest in his mouth. "Well, with your abuela retired from the university, she's starting to travel more."

"So basically you're not hanging out with your mom every night?" I ask.

He winces. "Damn, you know how to make it sting."

"Well, if I'm still living with Mama when I'm your age, be sure to make fun of me too." I smile. Even though I give him a hard time, Dad actually lives with Abuela to help her take care of her land, which is her second greatest love outside of my abuelo. She's always been fiercely independent. My dad's never said so, but I know he could never bear to rob her of that and my abuelo at the same time. "We need to get you on some dating apps," I tell him.

"Yeah. No, thank you. I'll try the old-fashioned way."

"I could fill out your bio and help you take a good selfie," I offer. I deepen my voice. "My name is Marco Reyes. I like watching TV with my mom. I have two daughters. The younger one is my favorite. I'm obsessed with purchasing gadgets from infomercials and then kicking the shit out of them when they don't work."

He chuckles.

"And I'm just looking for a nice lady my age who doesn't want to make me buy clothes that might be considered in some way fashionable or current."

"Hey," he says, "my style is classic."

167

"If classic means boring, then sure. You're like a cartoon character who wears the same outfit over and over again. Like, does Bart Simpson just open his closet and have endless red shirts and blue shorts?"

He shrugs. "Never have to worry about what to wear."

"Boring," I say again as I turn up his music. My dad has different playlists for different things. Showering, cooking, mowing the yard, working. But they're all the exact same eclectic mix of Rod Stewart, Maná, Bruno Mars, Selena, the Bee Gees, the Beastie Boys, and Jay-Z. If I could only get him to throw in a little bit of Drake and Kesha, it might not be so bad.

Once we're on my street, he pulls down our alleyway behind the house. It's mere seconds before my mom is walking out the back door in her signature bright-red lipstick—which she's totally reapplied and I know it's because she knew she'd see Dad. I don't have any grand illusions of them ever getting back together, but things like her lipstick still make my gut twist over what might have been.

"Cal, wait for me inside while I talk to your dad, okay?"

I nod and give my dad a one-armed hug so as to not drip any ice cream on him. He presses a kiss against my cheek, and his stubble tickles.

"Thanks, Dad," I tell him.

"Siempre, mija."

I feel those tears prickling up again. I don't give in, though. Instead I hop out of the truck with my backpack and devour my cone as I jog up the stairs and wait for my mom inside.

"Mom?" Kyla calls from her room as Shipley trots down the stairs to greet me.

"It's just me. Mom will be back in a minute."

"Okay." Her voice pouts.

After a few minutes, the sliding glass door opens and Mom gestures for me to sit at the kitchen table.

Her whole body ripples with a sigh. "You skipped class."

I nod.

"You broke into the wrestling-mat room. You destroyed personal property. And you disrupted a whole hallway of classrooms. All at my place of work."

"It's my place of school, too," I remind her. "If anything, the lines here are a little fuzzy."

She's quiet, and that's my cue to explain myself. I squeeze my eyes shut and swallow. I can't cry again today. I can't. "He broke up with me," I say. "It's like the last year and a half didn't even happen. And there's not even another girl. He just doesn't want me anymore."

She reaches across the table for my hand. "Oh, baby. Baby, baby, baby."

"I'm sorry, Mama. I shouldn't have done any of that. I know. But I just—I have no friends and no life." My voice cracks a little on that last syllable.

"Which is your own doing," she reminds me unapologetically. But then her whole body sinks toward me as she uses her foot to tug on the leg of my chair and pull me closer to her. "But you're hurtin', and when you hurt, I hurt."

We sit there in the quiet stillness of the house where

I've spent nearly my entire life. Finally I say, "I like your lipstick. Looks nice and fresh."

She blushes lightly. "Always gotta remind 'em what they're missing."

She's right. I can't wait for that moment—because I know it's coming someday—when Bryce looks at me and he sees all that he missed out on. Or at least I hope it's coming, because I'm clinging to that. But right now I just feel like a total slob who stuffed her face with soda, Oreos, and ice cream all day and made a huge scene at school. Tomorrow all anyone will be talking about is how *crazy* Callie is and how I *overreacted*. Drama queen. "That girl has lost it," they'll say. "First the dance team. Now this."

"Can I be excused?" I ask.

She nods. "Come down and help me with dinner at five thirty."

"Yes, ma'am."

She stands and opens the cabinet above the refrigerator where she keeps her champagne flutes from her and Keith's wedding. "Hold your hand out."

She places my phone with its gold, sparkly case in my hand. "Is this a trick?" I ask.

She shakes her head. "I figure today might have gone a little smoother if you'd had a phone. And I was thinking what if there was some kind of emergency or whatnot."

I nod fervently.

"You're still on house arrest," she reminds me. "Still totally, completely one hundred percent grounded."

"Yes, ma'am. I understand." I hold the phone to my chest as I walk upstairs to my room with Shipley a few steps behind me. I feel like I've finally got some kind of lifeline back.

But then it hits me. A lifeline to who? To what? There's no one out there waiting for me to rejoin the social world. I'm grounded forever, and it doesn't even matter because I've got nothing left to be grounded from.

The thought is tragically freeing.

MILLIE

Seventeen

A bowl of mixed balled melon with a side of cottage cheese (my mom's extremely sad idea of dessert), a homemade apple-cider-vinegar facemask I found online, my fluffy notebook of achy feelings, and my completely unwritten essay for my summer program application. I am the picture of Friday-night excitement.

Callie called in sick to work today, so I was left to close the gym up by myself. I guess it's not that big of a deal. I could do that job in my sleep, but I know she wasn't sick unless you can get physically ill from your own self-induced drama.

I feel judge-y. I'm trying so hard not to be judge-y. But what kind of person trashes someone else's cell phone and causes a huge scene in the middle of school? I wasn't there to witness it, but Amanda was, and she gave me every gory detail. Breaking up with someone is bad enough . . . I imagine, at least. Seeing as I've never had a boyfriend outside of the few random summer flings at Daisy Ranch. (Translation: two awkward summers of hand-holding with Scotty Pifflin and then James Ganns the following summer and one half kiss when Greg Kassab missed my lips in the dark and instead got the corner of my mouth.) But why would you want to make it worse with a public breakup? Why would you want to draw more attention to yourself?

But maybe girls like Callie don't think about the expense of drawing more attention to themselves. It's something I consider every day. It's like a cost benefit analysis. Is this floral tunic too loud? Is me being happy wearing it worth the attention it will cost me? Is my backpack covered in patches and stitching just one more thing for people to make fun of? How much do I have to love it for that to be worth it?

I can feel my facemask hardening, letting me know it's time to rinse. After a quick trip to the bathroom, I return to my computer, where my blank document awaits me. The essay is due in a matter of weeks and I'm not the type who can just wing it the night before and I still have to figure out my audition tape. I have my suit and my script mostly written, but I still need a cameraman, and the only person I know who's familiar with AV equipment is Malik.

I scroll through my video library and land on *Legally Blonde*, starring Reese Witherspoon. A good rom-com for background noise is just as good as any playlist if you ask me, and *Legally Blonde* feels especially relevant.

I push the laptop back and reach for a fresh sheet of paper and my freshly sharpened GIRL BOSS pencil.

My mom stopped using her camcorder to record my childhood memories when I was ten years old and already shopping in the women's plus-size section of Russle's. I was the kind of fat that video couldn't hide. Pictures were still safe, though. My mom was a master of all the various flattering angles.

I stare down at the words. They're going to see my audition tape. It's not like they won't know that I'm fat. But do I have to talk about it, too? I shrug. It's just a rough draft, right?

I'm still fat. That hasn't changed. What's different now is that I'm ready to be on camera—unflattering angles and all. I've spent years dreaming of following in the footsteps of women like Barbara Walters, Lisa Ling, Diane Sawyer, Christiane Amanpour, and even my own local anchor, Samantha Wetherby. I think so many of us waste too much time dreaming of the things we believe we can't have. But I'm done dreaming. I'm ready to make my dreams my reality.

The messenger on my computer pings. I drop my pencil and push my papers aside as I pull my laptop closer.

Malik.P99: that group project in psych was the worst

I sit there for a moment, my fingers hovering above the keyboard. Why is it that he can talk to me so freely when we're both hiding behind a screen? How is that fair? Especially after everything I said last week. I know Amanda had told him I had my wisdom teeth taken out and that I was under the influence of painkillers, but still I haven't made any effort to take it back.

I know that logically he's probably just shy and everyone

thinks I should put myself out there. But I'm having a really hard time thinking about things logically right now. Maybe it's that dumb comment that Callie made in front of Mitch earlier in the week. I should have just shaken it off, but I couldn't. It stuck with me.

So now with my cursor blinking in the compose message box, part of me can't help but wonder if the real problem is me. My head pieces it all together so easily. He went to the Sadie Hawkins dance with me out of pity, and now he's reminded of it every time we see each other in class. Or maybe he really does like me. It could be that what he tells me from behind the screen is the real deal, but he's just too embarrassed to act on any of it in real life.

I know thinking like that isn't gonna get me anywhere. And it's the exact reason why I'm not going to fat camp and obsessing over diets with my mom anymore, but all those horrible thoughts still exist. I'm just trying to figure out how to live in spite of them.

Despite all my doubts, I choose to believe I'm the girl who can tell a boy that her feelings are way more swirling-heart emoji than they are handshake emoji. Also, Elle Woods resolving to go to Harvard in the background doesn't hurt. I take a deep breath and begin to type.

aMillienBucks: I feel like you're two different people. There's the Malik I see during school Monday through Friday and the Malik who talks to me at night through a screen. I can't do it anymore. Either you talk to me in person the way you talk to me through this screen or you don't talk to me at all.

I hit send before I can even check for spelling errors, which is huge, because I believe in accurate spelling just about as much as I believe in the Oxford comma and the truth that Andie and Duckie should have ended up together in *Pretty in Pink*.

It's a few excruciating minutes before he responds, and I feel like I'm about to break out into hives.

Malik.P99: Can I come see you?

My heart skips like one of Willowdean's old Dolly Parton records.

aMillienBucks: Right now?

Malik.P99: I know it's late.

I check the clock in the corner of my screen. It is super late. If my mom caught me with a boy this late at night, she would shriek until she turned into a pile of ashes before my very eyes.

aMillienBucks: be outside my house in an hour.

Malik.P99: Ok

I have never snuck out, but it's time I start doing things I've never done before. And if Malik is going to go out on a limb, I'm willing to meet him.

I'm too nervous to duck out the front door, so I make plans to climb out my window. Thank goodness we live in a one-story.

I do a quick once-over in the mirror and cover up any major blemishes with concealer before adding my favorite tinted ChapStick. Once my parents are in their room and the hallway light is turned off, I brush my teeth, not bothering to keep quiet. It's part of my nighttime routine, after all.

I sit in front of my alarm clock, which looks like an old telephone with a spin dial, a gift from my mom on my eleventh birthday. I'm always surprised by how good I am at sneaking around. It still shocks even me that I managed to keep the pageant a secret from my mom all the way up until the week before. But actually sneaking out? This is a whole new level of deception for me. I try to feel guilty, but I don't. Not even a little bit.

The clock strikes midnight, and I drop my phone into my purse. After opening my bedroom window, I carefully lift the screen.

I will be totally honest and say that fitting through a tiny bedroom window was not in the Fat Girl Manual. But as the cross-stitch hanging above the scale in my mother's bathroom reads, WHERE THERE'S A WILL, THERE'S A WAY.

Our back fence is notoriously creaky, so I'm extra careful when I open it just enough for me to squeeze past.

And there's Malik, waiting for me under the streetlight across from my house. He leans up against a dark green Toyota RAV4, which is technically his sister's, but he's been allowed to use it since she left it here when she went to college in Boston.

I can say, without an ounce of embarrassment, that I have dreamed of this exact moment. Malik waiting for me across the street from my house beneath the flickering light of a streetlamp, with his fists balled up in his pockets and his penny-loafer-clad feet crossed at the ankles.

If this were one of my movies, I'd cross the street to him

and we'd kiss and that would be the end. We'd live so happily ever after that the credits would roll and you wouldn't even need to have any more details, because the rest of our lives would be wonderful, boring bliss.

But this is real life, which means this is the hardest part of all. And one of us has to break the silence.

"Hi," I squeak.

His Adam's apple rolls forward as he swallows. "Hey." And then a second later, he adds, "I was scared you wouldn't be able to get out."

Why is the talking part so hard? Surely the kissing part is way easier to make up for all the trouble it takes to talk. I hold my arms out. "Well, I did."

"Maybe we should go somewhere."

"Okay." I hadn't even thought of where we might go or what we might actually do. "Lead the way."

Once we're both buckled in, Malik reaches for the radio, but then I guess he thinks better, because he pulls back. "Guess I came here to talk, didn't I?"

I bite down on my lips, trying to minimize my smile. He turns off my street like he knows where he's going.

"I'm shy," he finally says. "And not in some kind of endearing way. It's like crippling sometimes." He pauses. "I get so in my head and I overthink every little thing. But I don't want to be that way with you."

"I don't want that either," I say quietly.

"It's so easy to talk to you. It's like I'm not even talking to anyone." He shakes his head and lets out an exasperated sigh. "That didn't sound right. I just meant that the way I feel when we're talking online or texting is the way it feels to, like, talk to my sister or cousins. Not that I think of you as a relative or something! But like that head thing is gone. When we talk at night, I don't think about if something will look or sound stupid. I can just be me."

"I get that." I'm economical with my words. I don't want to spook him.

"But in person . . . well, first off, we're at school. And everyone there thinks I'm just . . . when you don't talk much, people make up this version of you that exists in their head. And it's especially worse when you're the only Indian kid in school. Like, I was just walking to class the other day and some kid asked me if I could look at his phone and tell him if he had a virus. Just because I look like every tech guy he's ever seen in a movie."

Something about his words comforts and frustrates me at the same time. I very much know what it means for people to create expectations of you based on appearance, but at the same time, I fit in here in a way that Malik doesn't. I'm white. So as he slows to a stop at the red light before leaving Clover City, I don't ask where we're going. I only say, "I'm so sorry you have to deal with that." Comparing my situation to his doesn't really do much, but I want him to know that he's not alone. "People have certain ideas of me too."

He turns toward me, and our gaze locks in unspoken understanding. I hold my breath, scared that the slightest sound will cause this moment to dissolve.

"Anyway," he finally says as the light turns green, "I've just never been good at showing people the real me.

Sometimes it's just easier to let them believe in the version of me they've built in their heads." He clears his throat. "You want to listen to some music for a little while?"

I nod. "Yeah, that'd be nice."

He reaches for a mix CD that's been written across in black Sharpie and says COUNTRY MUSIC THAT DOESN'T SUCK.

He holds up the CD. "No plug-ins for my phone in the car, so I gotta make my own mixes."

"You listen to country?" I ask, not doing a very good job of masking my surprise.

"Only the kind that doesn't suck," he responds with the hint of a grin.

Everyone in the world probably thinks it's some kind of requirement to love country music if you live in Texas, but to be honest, I only started giving Dolly Parton a try after getting to know Willowdean. I'm more likely to turn on a movie or a TED Talk for background noise, but sometimes the only thing that can put me to sleep is Dolly's *Blue Smoke*.

But Malik's taste in country is a little folksy and more updated. They're the kind of songs that you magically know the words to before the whole thing is even finished. And soon enough I'm singing along to an Old Crow Medicine Show song. At least that's what Malik tells me.

He looks to me and grins.

My cheeks burn as we turn into the only gas station we've seen since leaving town.

All the lights seem to flicker like the electricity is being pumped out like gasoline. The sign above the convenience store reads QUICKIESHOP, but Malik circles around to the back, where I expect to find a grimy back door and a pair of Dumpsters, but instead there is a diner called the Bee's Knees. The bricks are painted in black-and-yellow stripes and the huge window stretching from one side of the diner to the other covers the back parking lot in a warm honey glow.

"I've never even heard of this place," I tell Malik.

He turns off the music and unbuckles his seat belt. "Most people haven't. That's the best part."

I follow him inside, and the older woman behind the counter with a name tag that reads LUPE says, "Hey, hon, your usual spot is open."

Malik leads me to the booth farthest from the front door and asks, "Is this okay?"

I eye the tiny booth and hope I can suck it in enough to make it work. I nod.

Malik sits down and immediately pulls the table closer toward him to give me a little more space. "Thanks," I tell him.

I can't even bring myself to make eye contact with him. Not because I'm embarrassed, but because for once it's nice to not be the only person in the room who is aware of the space my body takes up. To me, the gesture is so sweet that I feel a lump in my throat forming.

"Of course," he says.

Love is in the details.

"How'd you find this place?" I ask.

He reaches behind the mini jukebox and hands me a menu. "Priya. My older sister. This used to be her hangout. Everything in Clover City shuts down by ten or eleven, so the only twenty-four-hour diners we have are crawling with people from school. But this place is a little out of the way."

"I'm never really out that late, but that makes sense."

"My parents aren't what you would call strict," he says. "My sister and her friends would study here all night. When I was a freshman and she was a senior, she started bringing me with her. Plus this is one of the few places still open when I get out of work on Fridays and Saturdays."

Malik works at our only movie theater, the Lone Star Four, and it's like this whole facet of him that I don't even know. "When did you start working at the theater?" I ask.

"Last spring. If Priya was going to leave me her car, I had to find a way to pay for gas. I love it there, but late-night weekend shows put me home so late I'm already jonesing for breakfast."

"Must be nice not to have strict parents. My mom is beyond strict. She would never let me have a job where I work that late."

He shrugs. "It's sort of weird. With my aunties and uncles . . . they're in their kids' business all the time. Priya says they're like ingrown hairs."

I laugh. "That's an interesting way of putting it. What makes your parents different?"

"Well . . ."

"I'll be over in a sec!" shouts Lupe from across the diner.

"Thanks," calls Malik before turning back to me. "I mean, it's not that weird for my family or for Hindu culture, really. Especially with the older generations." He pauses for a moment. "My parents had an arranged marriage."

That is definitely not what I expected to hear. I smile maybe too widely. "Wow!"

"But they love each other. They really do."

I lean in a little. "You don't have to convince me."

"I know," he says, "but it's sort of crazy, because sometimes I feel like they were meant to be. Like, they were specifically built for each other."

"Must be nice," I say. "So does that mean you'll . . . get married that way, too?"

"I don't think so," he says. "My parents told me and Priya that we can decide if we want their help or not."

"Oh. Okay." I hold up the menu, trying to cover the relief spread across my lips. I mean, it's not like I'm going to marry the guy. Or maybe I will someday! Who knows? But that's on the table still. *So that's nice*, I think.

"Anyway, my parents couldn't have kids for the longest time. It's not like all they ever wanted was kids. My mom was a literature professor up until she retired a few years ago, and my dad's an engineer. Not having kids was a bummer, but they like being the cool aunt and uncle, too. Then when my mom was forty-three and my dad was forty-eight, they had Priya. According to my dad, she was their miracle. And then two years later, I was their surprise. My mom gave me her maiden name, Malik." He pronounces it differently than me and all of our teachers do. It sounds like Mah-lick instead of Maleak. "She has four sisters and no brothers, so it was her way of passing it on."

"That's amazing." I wince a little. "But have I been mispronouncing your name this whole time?"

He laughs. "Well, I answer to both pronunciations. Even my sister pronounces it the way you do. Unless she's pissed, then she pronounces it like our parents and my aunties."

"That's such a great story about your parents, though."

His sparkling-white teeth peek out from behind his lips as he smiles. "Yeah." He nods along. "Yeah, it sort of is. So they're just a little more chill, I guess. Priya thinks it's because they're older and they've watched all our cousins grow up."

"What can I get ya?" asks Lupe as she makes her way over to our table. Her uniform is a bright mustard-colored dress with a thick black belt and black piping on every edge. I immediately like her, and I think it's because the woman is built like a snowman and that's not too far off from my apple-shaped body.

I glance down at the menu. "I'll take the funny-face pancakes and a side of hash browns and a root beer, too."

Malik takes my menu and joins it with his behind the mini jukebox. "Waffles and grits, please."

Lupe clicks her tongue. "Good choice, hon. What to drink?"

"Dr Pepper."

"Got it," says Lupe as she turns back for the kitchen.

A group of greasy-looking guys pours in from what I'm

guessing was a shift on one of the oil rigs outside of town. "Sit wherever you like," says Lupe. "Bathroom's in the back if you want to wash up first."

I watch as they all file past us for the restrooms, and most of them do that Southern gentlemen's nod I've seen my whole life.

I slide to the end of the booth and study the jukebox for a moment. "We should play a song," I say.

I reach into my purse for a quarter.

"It's free," says Malik.

"What? Really?"

He nods. "Told you this place was worth keeping hidden."

I scroll through until I land on "Under the Boardwalk."

"Oh yes!" shouts Lupe from the kitchen. "Play 'Brown Eyed Girl' next!"

"Okay!" I call back, not sure if she can actually hear me. I scroll through until I find her request.

"Thanks for coming out with me tonight," says Malik.

"I like this place," I tell him. "And I like you."

I hold my breath, waiting, waiting, waiting. I think I've been holding my breath since the Sadie Hawkins dance when he kissed me on the cheek.

He licks his lips and sucks in a breath through his teeth. "I like you, too," he finally says. Out loud. To my face. Without a single screen between us.

The table rocks as Lupe slides our plates across the surface. "Funny-face pancakes," she says, "a side of hash browns, and waffles and grits. And a DP for the gentleman and a root beer for the lady!"

We both look up and say thank you in unison.

After she leaves, neither of us says anything else. We eat our food, which is amazing, or maybe it's just this moment that makes everything taste so good. I smile the whole time. I smile harder than my funny-face pancakes.

On our way out the door, Malik takes my hand as I walk down the steps. His hand is slick with perspiration. It reminds me of when he escorted me for the pageant. At the time I couldn't tell whose hands were sweating, because I was more anxious than a hummingbird. Now, understanding how shy he really is, I see what a big challenge that was for him.

After I take the last step, I expect him to let go, but he doesn't. He holds my hand as we walk to the car, bathed in warm light from the Bee's Knees. His car is parked just outside the pool of light, and when he walks me to the driver's-side door, I eye the pitch-black flatlands that surrounds us. The sky above is stitched with endless stars, and I think that this would be the perfect moment for us to share a kiss. A real one. One on the lips.

Because he's been so brave tonight in ways that are not comfortable for him, I turn to Malik and say, "Remember . . ." I take a deep breath. "Remember my painkiller-induced text messages from last weekend?" I try not to sound as mortified as I feel.

He snickers to himself. "How could I forget?"

"Well, I still want to kiss your face." I say it too fast, before I can stop myself.

I think I hear him gulp. "You do?" he asks.

I inch closer, my mint-green-and-black polka-dot hand-painted Keds kicking up loose dirt.

"I really do." And I kiss him. I touch my lips to his, which are soft and maple-syrup flavored.

His lips press into mine and both his hands trace up my arms to my shoulders and then up my neck until he's cradling my face in his hands just like in all the movies I love so much. I fumble with my hands, unsure of what they should be doing or where they should go, until I just let them drop down by my sides. My whole body goes numb in a wonderfully tingly way, and for a moment I think Malik is actually holding me steady with his lips.

I pull back, because if I don't, we'll be here for days. He takes my hands in his, like he's unwilling to end our physical contact entirely.

"I liked that," he says. "Very much."

"Maybe we could do it again sometime?" I ask before I lean in for one more kiss. And this time I even sneak in a little tongue.

On the way home, we talk about small things like class and Uncle Vernon's gym and how Malik goes to Portland and San Diego every summer, because most of his family lives in those two places. And he tells me about how his dad moved here for an engineering job but actually took it because he's always been obsessed with westerns and has always wanted to live in this part of Texas or Arizona or New Mexico. His mom hates it, but their compromise is that they'll move to a breezy beach town when his dad retires after both Malik and his sister are out of college.

We listen to more music, and when there are a few more songs he wants me to hear, we take a couple extra laps around my neighborhood as he holds my hand.

When he pulls up in front of my house, I let out a big yawn that I've been sitting on for a while. It's already three in the morning. I don't have to be at the gym until noon, but I know that tonight I'll barely be able to sleep.

In his car, we share one more kiss. And this one feels more urgent, like we're trying to hold on to something we're not quite sure we can re-create.

When I crawl back in through the window, I lose my balance and somersault inside, nearly knocking over my nightstand in the process. It sounds like an elephant is bowling just down the hall from my parents.

I sit there in the dark for a moment, expecting one of them to rush in. But nothing. I slip back into my pj's and crawl into bed. I can't shake my disbelief. Malik and I went on a date. I think it's safe to call it a date. He said he liked me—with his mouth! Then he used that same mouth to kiss me. After I kissed him first, which—OH MY GOSH—I'm just realizing is a thing I did. (Willowdean—and maybe even Callie, too!—would be so proud, I bet.) And I snuck out for the first time ever and I didn't even get caught.

If somehow each person in the world is only allotted a certain amount of good luck in life, I'm scared I've spent all of mine tonight.

CALLIE

Eighteen

On Saturday, I get to work at noon for my shift with Millie, and I find Inga tapping her toe behind the counter. "I have to go," she says the moment she sees me.

"Okay." The door hasn't even swung shut behind me. "You don't want to fire me first?"

She squints at me like she's actually considering it. "Vernon is home with the babies and they're all sick as pigs."

"I think the phrase is sick as dogs," I tell her.

She shoves her sweater into her bag and hoists it onto her shoulder. "Well, you've obviously never seen a sick pig."

I nearly laugh. "You're right. I haven't." I glance up at the clock. Millie should be here by now. "I've never worked alone before."

She pushes open the front door. "Try not to break any windows." She points up to the camera behind the counter. "I'll be watching."

"Ha, ha," I say dryly, but she's already halfway to her car.

The only people in the gym are two older guys on the stair climbers and one dad-aged guy on the punching bags. Logically I know that nothing will go wrong, but I also hate that I'm solely responsible for this place when I've already done enough damage and shouldered plenty of the blame.

Those bitches. I know the one I should be most angry with right now is Bryce. But I can't shake that this all started with the Shamrocks, specifically Melissa. I have no way of proving they were all here with me that night. The offer from Sheriff Bell to rat out my cohorts is definitely off the table anyway. But I've got dirt on all those girls, and I think it's time to air some dirty laundry.

Out of habit, I pull out the glass cleaner and get to work. For all I know, Inga is watching me right now via some spy software on her phone. I wouldn't put it past her.

It's another twenty minutes before Millie races through the door, her hair mussed and her shoelaces untied. "Oh my gosh," she pants. "I'm so sorry. I overslept." But she doesn't look sleepy. Instead her cheeks are flushed and she's got a bounce in her step.

"No big," I tell her.

"I was out super late last night," she whispers loudly.

I can tell she wants me to ask her what kept her out so late. I can feel the energy vibrating off her. But I'm not taking the bait. Not after the week I had.

When I wasn't completely drenched in guilt from the dumb thing I said to Millie in front of Mitch, I was busy being broken up with and making a very public display of it. I suffered through school on Thursday, but my mom didn't push it when I feigned sick on Friday morning.

I cringe whenever I think about how much time I've

spent with Bryce, and what now? It was all just a giant waste? And yeah, I feel like shit. Bryce was my first boyfriend, but somehow I was always sure that if we ever broke up, it would be me who made that decision. If what I had with Bryce was so easily disposable, who's to say what's real and what's not?

But right now, the only thing I want to focus on is revenge.

Millie drops her bag behind the counter and gets busy making her rounds around the gym, wishing all three of our members a happy afternoon while she checks out all the equipment. "Callie," she calls while she's got her leg propped up on a weight machine as she ties her shoes. "Can you get started on these towels?"

I groan silently. "Sure thing." I make a circle around the gym, picking up all the towels from the various hampers and taking them all back to the utility closet where the washer and dryer are located.

"I kissed him," says Millie, like she might explode if she doesn't say it out loud.

She startles me so much I drop the detergent into the machine, cup and all. For a fat girl, she sure is light on her feet.

I reach down into the machine for the cup. "Kissed who?" I ask, not bothering to hide my bewilderment.

"The guy I said I liked, remember? The one who wouldn't make a move?"

"Oh, right, okay." I faintly recall a conversation we had before her mom picked her up for that emergency dentist appointment. Most people would probably tell Millie the best way to snag a guy would be to drop the weight. And while that might be true in certain cases, I kind of also think that there are definitely people out there who might be into what Millie's serving.

"Well, you told me I should give him another chance. So I did! And he kissed me back."

I turn around after dumping the towels into the machine. "You're not mad at me?" I ask over the running water.

"About what?" she asks. And then she remembers. I can see it on her face. "Oh, the gym equipment comment?"

I nod, trying to keep my face blank.

"Well," she says, the word coming out like a sigh, "I heard you had quite the week yourself, so I thought I'd let it slide."

I can tell from the ways her lips are pursed together that she has more to say, and I guess the nice thing would be to encourage her to talk. But I don't need another damn lecture. Especially about some stupid joke.

The bell at the front of the gym dings. "You want to get it?" asks Millie. "I've got some stuff to do back here."

I nod and shut the lid of the washing machine. "Yeah, okay." I wait a moment. "Be there in a sec!" I call. "Um, I'm glad for you that it worked out. With the kissing situation."

Millie beams and bounces on her toes. "Me too."

I head out front, where I find Mitch waiting at the counter. I'm suddenly self-conscious in a way that's hard for me to process. There's no telling what Patrick and Bryce probably told him about me. "Hey," I say.

He stands up a little straighter and flips his card out between two fingers. "Mitch Lewis, Esquire."

"Very impressive." I'm not entertained. Or maybe I am. I don't know.

"Real talk: I don't even think I know what 'esquire' means."

It means lawyer, but rather than saying so, I just take his card.

"Hey. I didn't see you in school yesterday." He coughs into his fist. "I wasn't, like, stalking you or anything. But, like, I usually pass you in the hall between third and fourth."

I nod. "That doesn't sound stalkery at all," I mumble as I sit down on the stool behind the counter and pull out the box where we keep member cards to file his away. "I was feeling kind of sick. From, like, the state of my life."

"Um, well," he says. "I hope your life is feeling better."

"Things aren't looking very good. We had to pull the plug on my social life. My reputation is basically on life support."

He grins, pushing a hand through his curls. "I'll have my people send flowers."

I tap my feet against the stool and smile with my lips closed. "Finally. Something to look forward to. I love watching dead flowers wilt."

Crickets. Nothing. I sure do know how to take a conversation a step too far.

After a long bout of silence, he knocks his fist on the

counter and surveys the equipment behind me. "Cool, cool, cool."

I watch as he heads toward the weight machines. He puts the pin in his preferred weight limit for the leg machine and studies it for a minute. Without warning, he doubles back to me and knocks his fist against the counter again.

Great. More reasons to clean the glass counter. Again.

"Hey, so are you, like, okay?" he asks.

I stare at him blankly. "Are *you* okay?" I ask, like it's some great comeback. I'm unreasonably annoyed by his concern. Something about it presumes that I'm a wounded bird after my big public breakup with Bryce.

"Yeah," he says. "I just meant after everything this week."

"It was just the one thing. So other than that super-public breakup with my longtime boyfriend, I'm totally good."

"Cool." He nods a little too aggressively. "Bryce is sort of a punk."

Surely this is a trap. I squint at him, trying to decipher how to proceed. "Aren't you friends with him?"

He pushes his fingers through his overgrown curls. "Well, I'm *friends* with lots of people."

Oh hell, do I get that. So much of living in a town the size of Clover City means hanging out with people you might not choose for yourself if you lived in a bigger city or went to a bigger school.

I stand up from my stool and grab my trusty glass cleaner to hopefully send this guy packing.

"I better let you get back to work," he says.

"Yeah," I say, my voice flat. "I'm swamped."

While he heads off to the weight machines, I get busy spraying whatever free surfaces I can find. If this job has given me one skill, it's the ability to look hella busy. I should add that to my résumé.

My phone dings, and I pull it from my backpack. I really did miss that sound.

MAMA BEAR: might be a few minutes late picking you up.

"You got your phone back?" Millie turns the corner from the office and sits down on one of the stools.

"Miraculously, yes." I wipe the last of the glass cleaner from the front door and join her behind the desk. "My mom was really feeling the guilt after this week."

"Do you want to talk about it?" Her voice sounds so concerned that it almost feels fake.

"What's there to talk about?"

"Are you, like, a robot or something?" she asks. I even sense the slightest bit of irritation. "I mean, how do you process stuff without friends to talk to?"

I whip my head around to face her. Oh, she totally just stepped in it. And she knows it. "How do you know I don't have any friends?" I ask, my voice too high, too sweet.

"Well . . . I just . . . " She stammers for a moment.

This is the problem with nice people. If you're gonna say something, you have to mean it. "Well," I say. "You just what?"

She clears her throat into her doughy fist and sits up a little straighter. "I just have noticed that since leaving the dance team, and now with all that happened this week, you seem to be, well, missing some people in your life."

Sisterhood. The word taunts me as I remember what Sam said to the whole team just hours before Melissa ratted me out and I took a bullet for all of them. "Those bitches were never my friends," I say. "Nothing in this town is real. It's not. We're all just stuck here without any better options, trying to make the best with what we have. And some of us are better at that than others."

She turns away, focusing on the (very clean, if I do say so myself) window in front of her.

She knows I'm right. The sooner she gets what the reality of living in this town really is, the better.

After a moment, she says, "Callie, I reject that."

"What?"

"You're wrong," she says simply. "And I'm going to prove it to you."

"Um, okay? With what? Scientifically gathered evidence?"

"No. Maybe. You're joining my slumber-party club."

I sputter laughter that I try to cover with a cough. "Your what?"

"My slumber-party club. Well, it's not an official club. Hannah would kill me if I actually called us that," she says. "You left all that hay in her locker last year, because your friends decided she looked like a horse. Remember?"

Oh damn. She just called me out. My stomach tenses. It was a sort of asshole thing to do. It was just a joke at the time, but something about the memory makes me uneasy. "That wasn't me."

She doesn't flinch. "Amanda saw you."

"Who's Amanda?" I ask.

She grins, but it's too polite to be genuine. "Amanda sees lots of things. But you'll know her when you see her. Anyway, tonight is Ellen's turn to host. I think y'all used to work together."

"No," I tell her. "No thank you. Definitely not." I have no interest in seeing Ellen Dryver. No one ditches Callie Reyes. Except for Ellen Dryver apparently.

"You can't say something like what you said about nothing in this town being real without giving me the chance to prove you wrong."

"I'm grounded," I tell her. "Remember?"

"For now," she says.

I roll my eyes, but she's already hard at work printing membership applications.

After work, Mom is late like she said she'd be, so I plop down on the curb and wait.

"Where's your ride?" asks Millie.

"Late."

She lowers herself down beside me. "I'll wait with you."

"That's really not necessary."

"Well, I do unnecessary things all the time."

I pull out my phone and scroll through my various social media accounts. It's moments like these that I'm happier than I can even describe to have my phone back. No awkward small talk with Millie Michalchuk. No thank you.

The first thing on my feed is a real killjoy though.

I shove the phone in my back pocket. Maybe I was better off without technology. That's fine. I can sit here silently forever. I've spent the whole afternoon with this girl. My capacity for small talk is more than depleted.

Millie leans back, bracing herself with her palms pressed into the sidewalk. If she's annoyed by my blatant decision to ignore her, she doesn't show it.

Finally, my mom pulls into the parking lot and I pounce up from the sidewalk as fast as I can, trying to avoid any interaction between my mom and Millie. Honestly, Millie's the kind of girl who you just know is parental crack. She's cheerful, polite, and fat. A parent's dream come true for their daughter's BFF. There's no way anyone is getting into trouble with Millie.

But it's too late. My mom has already rolled down the window. "Is that Millicent?" she calls.

Oh, shit.

"Yes, ma'am," calls Millie as she pushes herself up from where we were sitting on the curb. "Is that my favorite school secretary?"

"Callie," my mom says, "can you believe that last fall on Secretary's Day, Millie and her mom brought me that sweet little cactus I keep on my desk? They even knitted sweet little seasonally appropriate cozy-looking things for the pot."

I shake my head and climb in the front seat. "Yup," I say. "Totally believe it."

Millie leans through my open window and says, "You know, my mom always says succulents and sweet tea are the surest way to the heart of a true Texan woman."

"Well," says Mama, "between succulents, sweet tea, and the perfect barbecue sauce, I think your mama is right."

I turn to my mom. "I have homework. We should go."

"Baby," my mom says, "it's a Saturday night. And you're grounded. You're in absolutely no rush to be anywhere."

Millie sighs and cranes her head to the side like a perfect little golden retriever. "I sure do hope Callie's grounding is up soon. I invited her to a slumber party this evening with some of my favorite young ladies."

Ugh. She's really laying it on thick. I swear, she's a master manipulator.

"Oh," my mom croons. "That is so precious of you."

My mom glances to me, and I try to discreetly shake my head. I've got big plans tonight, and they include an entire box of microwave popcorn shaken up in a bag with chocolate syrup and a private viewing of whatever trash reality TV shows I can find, but ideally something where people have to survive in the wilderness for weeks without killing each other or eating poisonous berries.

"It has been a hard week," she says. "I bet some girl time would do you good." Mama turns to Millie with a sparkle in her eye. "I think I can make an exception."

Millie claps her hands together and twirls in a circle like a spinning-top toy. "Oh, how wonderful!" She turns back to me. "It's five thirty now. How about you pack a bag and I'll pick you up at seven thirty?"

"Great," I answer flatly. I turn my whole body to face her, so my mom can't see me mouth, *You're a monster.*

If Millie can read lips, she doesn't falter as she says bye to my adoring mother and offers me a completely vicious wink.

One thing's for sure: I have totally underestimated this girl.

When Ellen's mother opens the door to Millie and me on her doorstep, we are greeted by a petite woman in a fitted denim dress and sculpted brown hair. "I best get out of y'all's business before the real fun starts!" She squeezes past the two of us with a clutch wedged under her arm. "Bob, you stay out of the girls' way! Go to bed early or something! It's gonna be a late one for me!" She turns to us. "Off to go dancing!"

Ellen runs down the hallway, screeching to a stop in the doorway. "Bye, Mom!" And then she sees us. No, me. "Hi. Um, hey."

Millie beams. "Ellen! This is Callie."

Ellen lets out a held breath. "We are previously acquainted." She puts on a smile. "Y'all come on in. Millie, could I speak with you?"

Millie nods, and the two turn off into the formal din-ing room while I stand in the foyer. They whisper for a moment before I hear Ellen say, "If you say so."

Wow. This is like ten times worse than walking in on your parents talking about you. I'm not surprised by Ellen's hesitation, but that doesn't mean I don't feel like shit because of it.

The two rejoin me in the foyer, and Millie turns to me. "Let the fun begin!"

We follow Ellen upstairs to a second TV room besides the one opposite the dining room.

"Millie's here," says Ellen as she emerges from the stairs. "And she brought a friend."

"Is it Malik?" someone asks before letting out a wolf whistle.

Everyone laughs, and then I step forward from behind Millie.

And silence.

Willowdean grunts before looking to Ellen, her nostrils flared, like my presence is the ultimate betrayal.

I shake my head and look to Millie. I knew this would happen. Surely she did too. Or maybe this girl is just giv-ing me a taste of my own medicine after all these years, and this is her way of kicking me when I'm down— getting her whole gang of losers to shun me while I'm trapped at her stupid slumber party.

"Y'all," says Millie, seemingly unaware of the brick wall of silence and the fuming chubby Dolly Parton wannabe in the corner. "This is Callie." She touches my arm gently, like she's an adult introducing me to a classroom of hyenas. "Callie, this is Ellen, who you know."

I nod.

"And that's Amanda." She points to a gangly girl, spread out on the floor with a small plastic tub full of nail polish bottles. Then she motions to a light-skinned black girl with swoopy bangs and two long braids like Wednesday Addams. "That's Hannah." Ah, yes. Horse Teeth. "And—"

"Willowdean," I say far too sweetly. If this is how it's gonna be, then I'm ready. I put up the most valuable self-defense mechanism I've accrued over the years: sugary Southern manners so sweet they bite.

"Hello, Callie," Willowdean says from where she sits perched on the arm of the couch, overenunciating each syllable like she's spitting out each letter.

I swear, this girl brings out the best of the worst in me. "Be careful up there," I say. I turn to Ellen. "I'd hate to see Mrs. Dryver's lovely furniture get ruined from somebody cracking the arm of the couch. Furniture can be so delicate."

"The furniture," says Ellen sharply, "is just fine."

Hannah whistles low as she shakes her head and scoots closer to Amanda to claim a dark shade of purple polish.

I grin. "Good choice," I tell her. "It really reflects the whole angsty thing you've got going on."

I can feel Millie's eyes on me, but it's too late.

Amanda, who seems to be the most mellow of them all,

looks up at me from behind heavy-lidded eyes and snarls.

Willowdean throws her hands up. "What are you even doing here?"

"Callie is my guest," Millie says, her tone even.

"Well, maybe she should learn some manners," mumbles Willowdean.

Ellen claps her hands together in an effort to defuse the situation. "I'll show y'all where you can put your bags."

We follow her to her room, which I remember from our stint as friends. Her corn snake is coiled on top of a rock beneath a sunlamp in his glass case.

I shiver. The one time I had spent the night here with Ellen, the week before the pageant, I lay awake all night, thinking about that snake slithering up the blankets. No thank you.

Millie drops off her bag and then follows Ellen back out into the hallway.

"Be out in a minute," I say as I drop my bag on my bed and pretend to rifle through it.

"I'll be right back," I hear Millie say from the other room.

I look up and find her standing in the doorframe. She opens her mouth a few times, like she's about to talk, but then thinks better of it.

"I should go home," I finally say.

Millie steps into the room and closes the door behind her. She takes a deep breath and presses her fists into her hips, like she's channeling Wonder Woman—just a fatter, pastel version. "You don't have to be like this," she says.

I'm a little too shocked to even speak. I didn't know she had it in her.

"You don't have to be like this," she says again. "Every time you say some rude, biting thing, it's a choice you're making. And you don't have to make that choice. I'll be honest. I don't understand much about you or the life you used to lead, but what I do understand is what you just felt. Walking into a party full of girls from school and immediately knowing that you are the outsider."

I hoist my bag up on my shoulder. "I'm just going to go outside and call my mom."

"No, you aren't," says Millie, her hands still on her hips. "Being the fat girl—yes, I call myself fat, and I know you do, too," she tells me. "And just so you know, that word doesn't have to be mean. No offense, but it's people like you and all your old friends who make that word hurtful. Anyway, being the fat girl my whole life has never been easy, but it gave me a way thicker skin than you'll ever have. So I know that life sucks, but I just basically gave you a buffet of friends out there, and all you did was show everyone why they shouldn't even waste their time."

I could do three things right now. One, I could break down and just start sobbing. Really, I could. I've had a shit week, and being told off by Millie Michalchuk is just the turd cherry on the shit sundae. Two, I could storm out of this house and call my mom. Or hell, I could just walk home if I had to. Or three, I could suck it up. I could go out there and treat this gathering of the losers as an extension of my job at the gym—something I just have to power through. And maybe it won't be so bad. If anything, it will buy me goodwill at home. I hate to admit it, but I guess it's less than awful to be out on Saturday night, even if the company is less than desirable.

Besides, if that's the best cattiness Willowdean can muster, she wouldn't survive a day as a Shamrock. And Ellen . . . well, I might as well show her what she's missing.

I let my bag slide off my shoulder, and it makes a *thud* sound when it hits the floor. "All right. Let's do this."

Millie busts out into a grin so wide you can barely see anything but teeth. "Perfect."

I've gotta say, I have girl time down to a science. Between dance classes at Dance Locomotive, dance team in middle school (we were the Lucky Charms. Duh), and the Shamrocks in high school, I have always been on the top of every slumber-party guest list. And on a scale of one to ten—ten being pro level—this slumber party is a solid four.

In the TV room, I sit down on the floor beside Amanda. I figure she's a safer bet than Hannah, who seems to be in a constant state of brooding.

Millie stands up, holding out a movie for us to see. "Okay, as a continuation of your romantic comedy education, I give you—*Clueless*!" She turns to me. "Last time we watched *Bend It Like Beckham*."

I nod, impressed. "Good choice."

She curtsies. "Thank you."

She pops the movie in, and I reach over Amanda for the

bottle of nail polish. "You don't mind, do you?"

"Not at all," she says. She throws her body against the bottom of the sofa while the opening credits play. "I can never do my right hand. Do you think you can learn ambidexterity, or are you just born that way?"

I shrug. "Who knows? But I give a pretty bitchin' manicure. Let me."

"Oh." She tentatively holds out her hand for me, like she's deciding whether or not to trust me. "Cool. Thanks."

If I'm going to infiltrate this group for the night, I definitely chose the right girl to sit next to.

Ellen steps over me with a bag of Doritos hugged to her chest. She spreads out behind us on the couch, with Willowdean sitting on the last cushion with Ellen's head in her lap. Willowdean lets out a long sigh, and I can't tell if it's contentment at sitting with her BFF or exasperation at my presence. Probably both.

Millie takes up residence on a plush-looking armchair as I reach for a coffee-table book and a napkin to use as a flat surface to paint Amanda's right hand in the neon-yellow polish she already used on her left hand.

We watch the opening scenes of *Clueless*, and we all laugh along at all the jokes that hold up to this day and of course the nineties fashions that I secretly love. My dad is actually the one who first shared this movie with me. He says it was one of the first dates he took my mom on, and that after she went out and bought a plaid skirt just like Cher's and wore it for two weeks straight.

Outside, the sun slips down beyond the horizon and

the room grows darker, almost like a movie theater. For my nail polish, I choose a fluorescent orange. One of my favorite polish colors, despite my mother's insistence that it makes me look like I dipped my fingers and toes in a bag of Cheetos.

By the time we've made it to my favorite scene, where Cher is giving a classroom presentation, I'm blowing on my fingers, waiting for them to dry. I don't even realize I'm quoting along with Millie when Cher, with her long, perfect blond hair and her gum wrapped around her pointer finger, says, "And in conclusion, may I please remind you that it does not say RSVP on the Statue of Liberty?"

On the screen, the classroom erupts in applause as Cher puts her gum back in her mouth. In the TV room, Millie lets out a giddy squeal. "I just love that part. I want a cross-stitch with that quote on it!"

"Okay," says Hannah. "That was pretty badass. But just so we're clear, that brunette girl doesn't even need a make-over."

Maybe if the whole night is just movies and no talking, I'll survive.

Halfway through the movie, I notice Hannah struggling with her right hand as she tries to apply her purple polish. She's holding her hand up in the air the way I used to before my mom taught me how to paint my nails properly.

I lean forward and say, "The trick is to lay your hand down on a flat surface and paint a strip down the center of the nail and then thin strips on either side."

At first she just gives me this how-dare-you-speak-to-me look, and maybe after what I said to her at first, that's fair. But she doesn't reject me when I hand her the napkins and coffee-table book I used for Amanda and myself.

After the movie, we turn on a few lights, and Millie pulls out all the stops to try to get everyone to indulge in some girl talk, but no one's really interested in divulging any personal secrets, and truthfully, it's probably due to my presence.

So Millie takes her own bait and tells us all about that boy Malik, who everyone else already seems to be aware of. She blushes when she recaps the long stream of embarrassing text messages they exchanged when she was on painkillers last weekend, and she swoons when she relays the story of their first real kiss last night. She's even charitable enough to say that I'm one of the people who encouraged her to make a move—and I think she's actually serious.

"Was he your first kiss?" asks Willowdean, her voice so warm that I think she might have forgotten I'm even in the room.

Millie blushes but shakes her head. "No."

"What?" Willowdean sounds genuinely shocked, and I am, too. "Millie Michalchuk, a woman of the world!"

"I kissed a few guys at Daisy Ranch, that weight-loss camp my mom used to send me to."

Fat camp? If Millie's gone to fat camp, why is she still . . . fat?

"A few?" says Amanda. "I thought it was just that one."

"Well, he was the only memorable one," says Millie.

"But it was nothing like kissing Malik. And most of those guys at Daisy Ranch acted like I should be so lucky to kiss them. Like they were doing me a favor."

"I totally get that." Willowdean rolls her eyes. "It's like people get it in their heads that fat people can only date fat people, which is so annoying."

"Yes! Most guys treated me like they were my only shot at love. It didn't help that the guy-to-girl ratio was like one to ten."

It's so weird to hear both Millie and Willowdean use the word fat so flippantly. I don't like to admit it, but I do sort of feel like it makes sense for fat people to date each other.

"That's how it felt with Mitch sometimes," says Willowdean.

I perk up at the mention of his name but try my best to hide my interest—interest I didn't even know I had. I'm quick to brush it off. He's the one semipopular person who's not going out of his way to ignore me or ditch me. Of course his name would pique my interest.

"It's like, if I date a guy like him," she continues, "people will think, 'Oh, of course, two fatties together. At least they're not contaminating the gene pool with their fatness.' And that just pisses me off. Then people see me with Bo, and they're like, 'Well, what kind of favor does he owe her to pretend he's her boyfriend?'"

Ellen groans, throwing her hands up in the air. "Why can't you just date whoever the hell you want—or no one!—without people making assumptions?"

Willowdean sighs. "I don't know, but I appreciate your rage."

Ellen lays a fat kiss on her cheek. "Anytime."

I actually have to avert my eyes, because I can't tell if they annoy me or if I'm jealous. I just cannot fathom how this constant finishing-each-other's-sentences type of affection isn't somehow fake. No one clicks with anyone else like that. Not in a real way.

Later that night, Willowdean and Ellen sleep in her room, Hannah and Amanda take the guest room, and I take the loveseat while Millie takes the sofa.

As we're lying in the dark, slipping in and out of sleep, she says, "You survived."

And she's right. I did.

Instead of feeling proud, all that shrouds me is a deep sense of betrayal. There was a time when I thought that what I had with Sam, Melissa, and the rest of the Shamrocks was real. Dysfunctional, but real. But now the only thing I know is that they're all living my dream without me, and not a single one of them seems to care.

MILLIE

Nineteen

Callie hasn't said much about Saturday night since I dropped her off at home on Sunday morning, but I actually take that as a good sign.

In Mom's craft room, she used to have a cross-stitch hanging above her sewing machine that said IF YOU DON'T HAVE ANYTHING NICE TO SAY, IT'S BEST YOU NOT SAY ANYTHING AT ALL. And I know that's one of those quotes that people just throw around, but when I was a girl, Mom and Grandma would watch this movie called *Steel Magnolias* over and over again. There was this one line that always made Grandma chuckle. "If you don't have anything nice to say, come sit by me."

I think Callie is probably the kind of person that only knows how to tell you what's wrong and not what's right. So Callie's silence? Yeah, I can take that as a good thing. And even if she didn't have a good time, I wouldn't care. I'm still riding the high from my night with Malik. Yesterday at school, we didn't talk more necessarily, but there was just something different. Maybe in the way he smiled at me or how his fingers lingered when he passed me my worksheet.

Tuesday morning is just one of those days where I'm running two minutes behind no matter what I do, but in the world of first-period school announcements, those two minutes matter.

Amanda and I split off in the parking lot, and she waves to me dramatically. "Godspeed!"

I speed walk the whole way to the office and make it just in time for the final bell. I'm huffing a little, but I'm here!

Callie's mom, Mrs. Bradley, beams as I walk in.

"You look radiant this morning!" I tell her.

She cups her hand to her cheek and waves me off with her other hand. "Call it hot-flash glow."

I smirk and hand over the list of announcements for her to approve.

She holds a finger to her lips and gives it a quick once-over. "All looks good to me," she says. "Oh! Except for the show-choir auditions for next fall. Mr. Turner had to move those to next week." She lowers her reading glasses and her voice. "Rumor has it that Mr. Turner's husband is none too pleased about the time commitment show choir requires."

I offer a sympathetic smile, but the clock catches my attention before I can respond. "Oh shoot!" I say. "I better hop on the PA."

She reaches around and swings open the little gate that

separates the attendance office from the rest of the front office. "All yours!"

I settle down behind the desk nearest the window and pull the microphone right up to the edge of the table.

I stretch my mouth out for a minute, making ridiculous faces, before doing a few vocal warm-ups. "Unique New York. Unique New York. Unique New York. Red leather, yellow leather. Red leather, yellow leather." I overenunciate each word. "She sells seashells on the—"

Mrs. Bradley clears her throat to let me know it's time and gives me the thumbs-up.

I hit the red button. "Good morning, gold-and-green Rams! Millie Michalchuk here with your morning announcements. Show-choir auditions have been postponed until next week. Tune in here, or watch the schedule on Mr. Turner's door for updates. Today's special in the cafeteria is the ever-popular chicken-fried steak served with white gravy, mashed taters, and green beans. The Shamrocks will be selling baked goods in the courtyard, so go support their efforts to make it all the way to Nationals this year!"

I continue on with a few more items on my list before handing the show over to Bobby Espinosa from student council so he can do the Pledge of Allegiance and our daily moment of reflection.

Afterward, I'm buzzing with energy. If ever I doubted that ditching Daisy Ranch for broadcast journalism camp this summer is a bad idea, all it takes is one morning of announcements to remind me of the exhilarating buzz I get from just this little thing. Compared to this, reporting the news live on television must be pure adrenaline.

After Bobby heads back to class and Mrs. Bradley tasks me with some filing to fill the rest of my free period, she rolls on her chair over to me with her legs crossed. "That was awful sweet of you to have Callie over with your friends on Saturday night."

"Oh, we had a great time!" And it's not a lie. I don't think. . . . Mrs. Bradley and I don't talk about much else besides the weather or little bits of teacher gossip, but with Callie working at the gym, we're sort of in new territory.

"I don't want to go on making excuses for her," she tells me, "but it's been hard for her lately."

"She'll be fine," I promise her. "I don't know Callie very well. Not yet. But you raised a fighter, Mrs. Bradley."

She smiles faintly. "Maybe too much of a fighter."

"Excuse my change of subject, but I am just dying to know. What shade of lipstick is it that you wear?" I've always found something about Mrs. Bradley's lipstick a little bit intoxicating, and now that the application deadline for broadcast journalism camp is approaching, I'm having to think seriously about my audition tape, which means putting the finishing touches on my on-camera look.

"Oh, baby," she says, holding her hand over mine. "Revlon Certainly Red 740. I swear if I ever get a tattoo—which I'm too chicken to ever do—it would be this little tube of lipstick." She pulls it from the pocket of her skirt. "It's been everywhere with me. The year the Shamrocks won State when I was just a young thing. Every date I've ever been on. High-school graduation. Two weddings. Three baby births from two different daddies. Divorce court. Far too many funerals."

She holds the tube out for me to examine, and I take it in my hand. A black tube with a gold strip around the center.

"I tell you," she says, "love comes and goes, but lipstick is forever."

Something about her words makes me feel all swoony inside. "It's just the perfect shade," I tell her. "But what will you do if they ever quit making it?"

She laughs, but it comes out like a guffaw. "Die, of course." I chuckle.

She shakes her head. "I've got my babies to live for, I suppose. I would survive."

I hand the lipstick back after jotting down the number, name, and brand on a scrap of paper. We both go back to our filing and our usual talk of the weather and teacher-lounge politics.

As I'm leaving, she tugs me once more by the hand. "Don't take this as me asking you to be friends with my Callie, because trust me, she would hate nothing more than me interfering in her personal life. But just know that I wouldn't be opposed to y'all girls getting together again."

I nod confidently. "Me too, Mrs. Bradley."

As I'm walking to second period, dreaming of AP Psych with Malik after lunch, I see Callie from across the hall and wave. She stands in front of her locker with her backpack slung over one shoulder, and she's wearing a pair of leggings and an oversized tank top that says GO CLIMB A CACTUS. To say it's on brand would be an understatement.

She grins and nods back, and for a minute I'm surprised. I guess deep down I thought that when we finally did acknowledge each other at school, she would ignore me. But she's not, and it puts a lightness in my step.

And then I hear it. Oinking. Quiet at first, but then louder. Closer.

My stomach drops and my legs turn to concrete, like I'm having a nightmare and instinct says to run, but my body is frozen. I suck in a breath, hoping that somehow I will just disappear.

"Hey, fatass," says Patrick Thomas. I don't even have to turn to know it's him. "Have you thought about life as a phone sex operator? You keep doing those morning announcements all sexylike, and I might forget what you look like long enough to trick myself into thinking you're hot."

I stop. It's always been the oinking. I expect that now. And the name-calling . . . well, it's vulgar, but it's not new. But the way he just . . . he just made me feel like a piece of meat.

My gaze meets Callie's. I'm not waiting for her to rescue me or something like that, but for a brief, desperate moment, I'm hoping against hope that she'll say or do something. Just so that maybe I'll know she's not the same girl who's played along with the oinking and name-calling since grade school.

She doesn't look away, and her expression is fierce. But she says nothing. She does nothing.

So I do.

I spin on my heel. I refuse to let this guy ruin my day.

"Good morning, Patrick," I say in my most preciously polite voice. "How are you doing today?"

His vicious expression falters, and all that's left is surprise.

The guys around him roll their eyes and brush past him, but Patrick Thomas is left standing there in front of me all alone. And he's completely disarmed.

He sputters, "Uh, f-fine."

I grin. "Good to hear it."

And for one brief moment, Patrick Thomas and I are just two human beings on God's green earth sharing polite small talk. He's not a monster and I'm not his prey. I think maybe Patrick Thomas sees that, too.

He pushes past me, and I turn to head to class.

I smile back at Callie again, but she closes her locker and speeds off to her next period.

CALLIE

Twenty

During my office-aide period on Thursday, Mama asks me to run around and pick up all her attendance sheets, since her normal aide is absent.

It used to be that a chance like this to freely roam the halls for an entire class period would be the perfect excuse to rendezvous with Bryce in a utility closet. But now it's just like a torture parade around campus so that people can get a better look at the girl who trashed a local business and screamed like a banshee when her boyfriend tried to break up with her.

Yesterday I started my period three days early, so I sprinted out of class to the nearest bathroom. While I was in the stall, I watched through the cracks as two sophomores came in and hovered at the sinks, reapplying lip gloss.

"I saw Melissa posted Shamrock Camp sign-up sheets," said the first one.

Shamrock Camp was always one of my favorite times of year. Two weeks every summer, and anyone could sign up. We'd have long eight-hour days of grueling workouts and training. At the end of the two weeks, we'd host tryouts. In reality, though, the tryouts started the first day of camp, and the actual tryout was just a formality. At camp, it only takes a few days for the herd to thin.

"She totally lucked into that captain spot for next year," said the second one.

I nodded along. These girls may be sophomores, but they knew what they were talking about.

Through the cracks, I watched as the first girl scooted in closer to her friend. "Well, I heard Callie Reyes was high on pain pills when she trashed that gym. They were all just going to TP the place, but then she was on this, like, drug-induced warpath and no one could stop her."

"That girl was serious goals."

The first one shook her head. "If goals equal having a public meltdown."

The two started to laugh but stopped abruptly when I flushed my toilet and yanked my shorts up before pushing my stall door open. I took my time washing my hands, and instead of reaching for a towel, I flicked the water off my hands in their general direction. "Boo," I said.

Both girls skittered off, and the second one even shrieked, like I might turn into a pill-popping crazed cannibal.

After retrieving the last attendance sheet from the freshman hall, I turn the corner into the social studies hall to find Melissa and Sam huddled together, with Jill at the other end of the hall, hanging up posters.

"Hey," I say. The word falls flat on the ground like a

single forgotten penny. My eyes meet Melissa's, and all I can think of is that middle-of-the-night phone call when she answered Sam's cell. The two of them have treated me like the plague since I took the fall for the team, but this is the first time that there's no noisy hallway to hide behind. This time, if they want to ignore me, they'll have to do it to my face.

"Oh, hey, Callie," Sam says. "How have you been?" she asks sympathetically.

I don't take kindly to pity, but it feels nice that for the first time, someone is actually acknowledging how awful this is for me.

"Fine," I say.

Melissa stands with her arms crossed just a foot behind Sam. I sneer at her, but she doesn't budge.

Sam reaches out and takes my hand. "We just want you to take care of you," she says. "That's all that matters right now."

My brow creases. Take care of me? "I'm good," I say. "Great, even. Just sort of hoping there's some way we can get me back on the team next year. I mean, all this will blow over soon enough." I just need some other big drama to come along, and then I'll be old news.

She glances over her shoulder. Jill's looking at the freaking roll of tape like it's chemistry.

A little too loudly, Sam says, "Don't you worry about the team, sweetie. We're all rooting for you to take this chance to turn your life around." She pulls me in for a hug, but my whole body is stiff against her.

"Excuse me?" I whisper.

"We really miss you and all," she says, her voice hushed. "But we sort of just, like, need you to keep your distance. For the sake of the team."

I step back, my mouth agape.

"It was so good seeing you," says Melissa. "You're looking so much better these days."

My gaze skips back and forth between the two of them. I don't know if they started the rumor about me that I heard from those dumbass sophomores, or if that was just a fluke. But either way, Sam and Melissa are doing everything they can to make sure people think I acted alone.

I shake my head furiously. "You know what? You're both trash," I say. "And that team is nothing without me. Every time either of you fail, know that I am watching and I am absolutely delighted."

I don't even bother with the rest of the attendance slips. I take what I have back to the office and tell my mom I have some monster cramps so she'll let me hide out behind her desk for the rest of my office-aide period.

I'm done letting this shit happen to me. I'm done lying down and taking it. Not only did Melissa rat me out, but now she and Sam are trying to ruin whatever reputation I have left. But two can play that game.

The last Saturday before the start of every school year is a sacred day in Shamrock history. It is the day that the incoming team captain hosts a massive sleepover for the entire team. On the surface, it sounds like a silly party—

the type of thing wet dreams are made of. But in truth, it is the night when new members of the team commit themselves to the Shamrocks and we begin the transition from a bunch of girls in matching costumes into a sisterhood of girls who have one shared goal: to be the best.

Because no good thing comes without sacrifice, every incoming Shamrock is required to commit one secret they've never told a living soul to the Shamrock Bible—a five-inch-thick green-and-gold scrapbook. The outside of the thing is hideous. Chipped sequins, years-old chunks of hot glue, stray feathers, and an excess of glitter paint. We stopped trying to make the thing pretty years ago, and these days, we only concentrate on keeping it in one piece.

The Shamrock Bible is the deepest of all Shamrock secrets. It has existed in some form since the team was started in 1979 and contains every rule and routine and a secret from every member of the team. The current Shamrock Bible dates back to 1995.

The night I went to my first Shamrock sleepover, Isabella Perez, a senior, was hosting.

After her parents went to bed, Isabella led us all up to her attic, where she and the other girls lit a circle of candles. I remember feeling like my heart was going to beat right out of my chest.

The entire team sat in a circle. It was the first time I remember being aware of Melissa. She sat next to me. Earlier in the night, she'd been absolutely giddy about her braces coming off the day before school, but now she was quiet and reverential, even. We all were. For us, this was church.

Isabella spoke of the power of sisterhood and how the Shamrocks were the longest-standing all-female team on the Clover City High School campus. "Singular talent has no place here," she said. "As of today, you are one piece of a much larger machine, and the only way that machine works is through the power of trust and sisterhood."

In that moment, I could've been joining a synchronized golfing team. It didn't matter. Whatever she was selling, I was buying. And maybe dance was just the vehicle to get me what I was really hungry for: friends. All my life, my mother had talked about her years as a Shamrock and the friendships she made. Her bridesmaids? Shamrocks. Outside the delivery room while she was in labor? Shamrocks. Holding her hand at divorce court? Shamrocks. Crying tears of joy while I stood by her side at her second wedding? Shamrocks.

Isabella unveiled the Shamrock Bible and began to pass it around. "No feelsy bullshit secrets allowed," she said. "Hard facts. We want truth. Being a Shamrock comes with lots of benefits. Sisterhood. Eternal popularity. Legacy. But all that comes at a price."

Sam sat on the opposite side of me, and when it was my turn to write my secret down, she nodded encouragingly and smiled. "At least your secret won't be lonely. Mine's just a couple pages back."

"Can I see it?" I asked.

"Later tonight," she promised.

"Really?" Melissa asked.

"Really," Sam said. "Once you commit your secret, the book is yours to devour."

I was mystified by this one silly fact. Everyone would see my secret, yes, but I would see everyone else's.

I wrote my secret. Sam and Melissa watched as I did. And then it was Melissa's turn. When she was done, she passed the book on and said, "You saw that, huh?"

I nodded.

"I guess it's not a secret anymore," she said.

"It is," I told her. "It's a secret I'll keep forever."

It takes me almost a week to pull off my plan. The key was to only make a handful of copies every time I was in the front office. The green copy paper is the kind of thing my mom would notice if suddenly a big chunk of it went missing. But it has to be green. I thought about maybe skimming a little off the top of every color in the copy room, but the green paper is something I feel adamant about.

Millie has noticed I've been up to something, too. Yesterday at work, she got a peek at the thick stack of green paper in my backpack.

"Oooo!" she said. "Is that a craft project I smell?"

I shook my head. "Are your crafty spidey senses tingling?"

She pursed her lips and pretended to be suspicious, shaking her pointer finger at me. "You can't hide a crafting habit from me. If you're a secret crafter, mark my words, Callie Reyes, I'll find out!"

I laughed. "Trust me," I said. "None of my secrets have a damn thing to do with crafting."

MILLIE

Twenty-One

I have a deep, abiding love for routines. Or maybe routine isn't the right word? Plans! I love plans. I love opening my day planner and knowing just what to expect. Which is why I am delighted to be sitting at the front desk of the gym, doodling in the square for next Saturday.

☆ ☆ Slumber Party Numero Three @ Amanda's ☺

Callie plops down on the stool beside me after putting some towels in the dryer. "That is one intense calendar," she says.

"Slumber party at Amanda's," I tell her. "Next Saturday! You have to go."

She groans and lays her head down on the glass.

I lay my head down, too, so we're at eye level. "Is that a yes?"

"That's a I'm-a-moody-flake-and-will-let-you-know-at-the-last-minute."

I pick up my head. "I'll take that as a probably."

Callie groans again.

"Is everything okay?" I ask. Callie is a generally fussy person. But today it feels like there's just something weighing on her.

She props her chin up on her knuckles. "What does that even mean?" She doesn't say it in a rude way, though. "I shouldn't complain about this to you."

"Sure you should," I say. "Try me."

She pulls her phone from her back pocket and silently looks something up before holding it out for me to see.

"Girls in bikinis washing cars?" I ask.

"It's not just that," she says, and scrolls to another photo.

A few pretty girls sit behind a fold-out table with a bake-sale sign taped to the front. "A bake sale in the school courtyard?"

She shoves her phone back in her pocket. "The state dance competition is next week. And as of last night, they raised enough to cover the deficit from the gym's sponsorship. And . . ."

"You're not going," I finish for her. I can't help but think it's partly my doing.

She lays her head down on the glass counter again and shrugs. "I'm gonna have to clean this thing for the billionth time. Might as well get my face print on it."

I laugh. "You remind me so much of Inga."

"What? No! Don't say that."

"She is my aunt, you know."

Callie sits up. "That doesn't mean the woman isn't totally bananas."

"I'm sorry you're gonna miss the dance competition," I say.

"Normally I would say they don't stand a chance without me. Usually that'd make me feel better even if it weren't true. But . . ." She shakes her head. "I know they'll be just fine, and that somehow sucks even harder."

"That makes a lot of sense," I tell her.

"It's not just that," she says before lowering her voice a few octaves. "I didn't act alone. You know what I mean?"

I nod.

"The whole team is going way far out of their way to make sure it looks like that, though. I mean, I heard two sophomores say they heard I was high on pain pills or something and that's why I did it."

"Pills?" She doesn't respond. "Why did you do it?"

Her gaze drifts like she's looking past me. Through me. "It was stupid. I thought it was stupid to begin with. But we were so pissed. It was supposed to be a harmless prank with toilet paper and eggs, but . . . anyway, it's done."

"I'm sorry about that." I know her punishment is earned, but I still hate to see her miss out on something she worked so hard for.

She shrugs. "Not your fault," she says. "Right?"

I can feel my face getting red as I remember the exact moment I identified her to Sheriff Bell. That gosh-darn *C* necklace. "Yeah, I guess so."

Then Mitch comes out from the locker rooms and I slink back a little so that maybe he and Callie will talk. It might brighten her day. Who knows? I remember he and Will sort of had something going on for a little while, and of course I'm happy to see her with Bo. But there's just something about Mitch that makes me want to see him get a happily ever after, too. And what if Mitch's happily ever after just so happens to be Callie?

"Where are you going?" whispers Callie.

I can hear the nerves in her voice and it almost makes me squeal. Oh my goodness! They'd just be the cutest.

"I'll be right back," I call in a singsong voice.

She turns and nearly spits at me. "You literally have nowhere else to be right now."

I hold up my hand and wave with my fingers as I slip into the office. I watch through the blinds on the door as she hands Mitch back his membership card. The two of them maybe exchange all of three words before he leaves, and that's it. The perfect moment I delivered to her on a silver platter is wasted.

She storms back to the office, and I swing the door open to meet her.

"What the hell was that about?" she asks.

"I thought I'd give you two a moment," I say.

"A moment for what?"

"To, ya know, connect."

She rolls her eyes. "Just because that slumber party wasn't a total shit show doesn't give you license to meddle in every crevice of my life, okay? And Mitch? Totally not my type."

Not her type. I know exactly what that means. But I still want to hear her say it out loud. "Not your type?" I ask. "And what exactly is your type?"

Her lips spread into a thin, tight line. "Not Mitch."

"Okay," I say, choosing to let it go.

We finish up our closing duties in silence, and as I'm locking the door behind us, her phone pings. Callie checks her phone and groans. Again.

She mumbles something that I can't quite make out.

"What was that?" I ask.

"My mom is wondering if you can give me a ride home." I grin. "I'd be happy to."

Once we're in the minivan, I turn on the ignition, buckle my seat belt, and check my mirrors. I look to Callie.

"What?" she asks.

"Seat belts save lives," I say.

She sighs loudly and reaches across her shoulder to click her seat belt.

"Let's motor!" I check both ways before pulling out onto the road.

She gasps. "Wait!"

I slam on the brakes and look both ways feverishly. "Was it a cat?" I swear, I live in fear of the day I accidentally hit an animal with my van.

"No, no," she says. "Sorry. I didn't mean to scare you. I just realized I forgot some stuff at school. Could you swing me by there for a few minutes?"

I glance at the clock on the dash. "Sure thing," I say.

While I wait outside the school for Callie, I text my parents to let them know I'm running a little late. My mom responds with a frowny face and promises she'll leave a plate for me in the fridge.

I watch my clock as ten minutes pass. Then twenty. Just

as we're approaching the thirty-minute mark and I'm getting ready to turn off the car and go in search of her, Callie sprints out the main entrance and straight for the van.

I lean across the console to hold the door open for her. "Hey!" she pants. "Sorry. Couldn't find my, uh, geography workbook at first."

"I hope you found it." I don't bother hiding the annoyance in my voice.

She holds both thumbs up. "All good."

As I approach the light at the end of the street, I take the turn opposite of my house and head into the older part of Clover City, where Callie lives. I'm a little peeved with how she just took her sweet time looking for her book, but I'm determined to be her friend. "So, now that dance team is out of the picture," I say, "what are you gonna do when you're done working off your debt at the gym?"

She squirms in her seat a bit and glances in the side-view mirror at the empty road behind us. "Well, I guess I'll try to get my job back at Sweet 16. They let me take off the last few months for the competitive dance season." She sighs. "The employee discount on clothes was pretty great."

I nod. "Makes sense."

"But I don't know. I guess you could say everything was sort of riding on dance. I thought maybe it'd get me into college and—I know this is crazy—but I thought I could try dancing for a professional sports team. Like with the NBA or something." She rolls her eyes. "Those girls are barely paid anything, but I would've made it work somehow. And sometimes you even get to travel with the team."

"That would've been pretty amazing," I say.

"Well, that dream is sort of shot. It's not like I can go to another high school or something. We just have the one."

"So was dancing your passion? Like, the thing you want to do no matter what?"

She thinks about that for a long minute. "I'm really good at it. It was nice to have built-in friends . . . if I can even call them that anymore. And I liked being a co—assistant captain and telling people what to do. I like being looked at—that sounds gross, but I don't mean it like that. I just—"

"You like the spotlight?" I offer.

"Yeah." She nods.

"Well, if you're open to other options, I'm sure there are lots of things you're good at that would include bossing people around and being the center of attention."

She taps her pointer finger against her lips. "Well, that makes me sound like a bitch."

I laugh a little.

She shrugs. "But I've never really been bad at anything either."

Most people would mistake Callie's honesty for ego. And trust me. She's got plenty of ego. But there's something more to it. Something that feels like self-awareness. And I like it. Because I think maybe Callie would probably admit her flaws in the same way she recognizes her strengths.

She shimmies her shoulders, like she's shaking off whatever thoughts she's just lost herself in. "What about you? You gonna work at this gym your whole life or what?"

I tap the brake as we roll up to a stop sign. I turn to her as the car in front of me waits to go. I'm not ashamed of my dreams. But something in me has always felt like the more people you share your hopes with, the flimsier they become. Suddenly everyone else is poking holes in your future until there's not much left to hope for at all.

"I have plans," I finally say.

"Oh really?"

"Yes," I say. "I have plans."

"And what exactly do your plans entail?"

I pull up in front of Callie's house and put my parking brake on. After unbuckling my seat belt, I turn to face her. "It all starts this summer. The first domino in my plan."

And then my plans spill from my mouth like a faucet turned all the way on. I tell Callie about the broadcast journalism camp at UT Austin this summer and how I'm going there after graduation, too. I tell her my five-year goals and my ten-year goals and my lifetime goals. I tell her absolutely everything.

And then I sit back and wait for her reaction.

"Wow," she says, but her tone is hard to decipher, like she's impressed but doubtful. "You really do have plans."

"So what do you think?" I know she'll be honest with me.

"What do *I* think?" she sputters nervously. "Well, I'm not, like, some professional future-plans analyzer, but it sounds . . . good?"

"Just good?" I ask, trying to mask my disappointment.

"Well." She pauses. "I don't really know much about TV anchors or anything like that, but I bet it's a really tough industry. And you're . . ." She waves her hand around like she might just magically find the right word.

"And I'm what?" My voice carries some bite.

"Well, you're on camera all the time, right?" She looks down at her feet and swallows loudly. "People are just super shallow."

"You don't think I can be on camera?" I ask, my voice cracking. I knew that bringing this up to Callie was a gamble. But her doubt hurts. I know that in the world of TV, I will face this same hesitation at every turn, so I do my best to numb myself to it. But still, I feel it. I can't help it. Disappointment washes over me until I'm just submerged in it. I close my eyes and exhale, counting to five.

"That's not what I said." Her voice is quiet.

I open my eyes and turn to her, doing all that I can to quiet my feelings. "Sometimes it's about what you don't say," I tell her. "First you were surprised to know that I knew how to work all the equipment at the gym. Maybe it's equally shocking to learn that I want to be on the news."

She shakes her head. "You should do whatever you want, okay?" She pulls her backpack into her lap. "What does it even matter what I think? It's not like we're friends."

I hold a breath in to stop the tears prickling at the corners of my eyes. Who am I kidding? I can't numb myself. I feel it all. Every dang thing. "Yeah," I say. "I guess we're not."

She hops out of the car. "Thanks for the ride."

I wait for her to go in through her front door, but she's halfway up the sidewalk when she turns around and raps her knuckles on my window for me to roll it down.

"Did you forget something?" I ask, wiping away an angry tear.

"Listen, Millie."

Here it is. The moment where she tells me to face reality. To grow a thicker skin. Fat girls don't report the news. I shake my head. I'm done hearing from people like her about what they think I'm capable of.

She drops her backpack in the grass and says, "I actually think you're really fucking cool. And that's totally not what I expected to think about you. My whole life is a mess right now, so maybe I'm not the person you should be listening to, but I think you can do anything you want. I don't say things to make people feel good. I say them because they're true."

I'm taken aback. It's one of those rare moments in my life when I actually have no words. "Thank you? I think?"

"You're welcome," she says gruffly. She scrubs her hands over her face. "And I'm sorry about what I said at the gym awhile back in front of Mitch, and I'm sorry if I looked like I doubted you today just now. But people are assholes, Millie." She points to herself. "I am an asshole! And . . ." She takes a deep breath. "I guess my first instinct was to discourage you because . . . well, I guess I wanted to protect you from assholes like me. But that just made me an even bigger asshole, because I shouldn't be standing in your way. I should be telling you to do whatever the hell you want."

"Which means we're friends?" Doubt rings in my voice.

She nods quickly and laughs a little frantically. "Yeah. I think so."

I smile a little. I'm glad that she considers me a friend, but I've also spent my entire life living under the umbrella of my overprotective parents, and if friends are the family you choose, I choose not to be friends with people who try to hold me back. "I don't need you to protect me," I tell her.

"Good." And then she adds, "I don't think you're weak, Millie. Not at all. I just . . . I'm starting to realize that I'm the kind of person you should be protected from. I'm the jerk or the bully or whatever."

"You don't have to be"—I clear my throat—"an a-hole, as you put it."

She picks up her backpack and shakes her head. "That's what you keep telling me. Maybe someday it will stick."

When I get home, I sit in the driveway for a minute to text Malik. My mind is absolutely spinning, but somehow I still find myself focused. I have tasks that need accomplishing. I need help, and the only way to get it is by asking for it.

ME: I need your help with something.

MALIK: Is it legal?

ME: I am a strictly by-the-books kind of girl.

MALIK: Dangit. I was hoping to make my criminal debut.

ME: Do you have any access to the AV equipment at school?

MALIK: Do I have access? DO I HAVE ACCESS? I am access.

ME: You? Me? Sunday afternoon? A room full of AV equipment?

MALIK: Sounds like a date.

When I get to school on Tuesday morning, it takes me a moment to realize there's something different about the main hallway where the front office is, like my eyes are adjusting to a bright light.

It's green. The whole hallway is green.

"What is this?" asks Amanda as she plucks a green sheet of paper off the wall.

"I have no clue." But my stomach grumbles with unease.

The first bell rings, but no one in the hallway really makes any move to get to class. Amanda and I stand there as I read over her shoulder.

THE SHAMROCK SECRET SHIT LIST

1. Jill Royce has a raging crush on her stepdad.

2. Hayley Walker pooped in the community pool on Jefferson the summer after eighth grade but blamed it on Janelle Simpson.

3. Addison Caliro stole her mom's oxy and sold it to Mr. Graham, the tennis coach, who's in rehab now for a prescription drug addiction.

4. Whitney Taylor created the anonymous Twitter account that slut-shamed Chelsey Lewis until her parents sent her to private school.

5. Lara Trevino took her parents' car for a joyride and ran into a cop cruiser. When she got caught, she pretended to be sleepwalking.

6. Jess Rowley saves her toenail clippings and catalogs them by year.

7. Bethany Howard is obsessed with eating her own earwax and once even ate her brother's earwax off an old cotton swab to see if it tasted different.

8. Gretchen McKinley purposely walked into a door and broke her own nose so she could get a nose job before tenth grade.

9. Zara Espinosa flushed a cherry bomb down the toilet in the library. Not only did the toilet explode, but the priceless art on loan from the Dallas Museum of Art, which was housed on the other side of the wall, was also destroyed.

10. Emma Benjamin wanted to impress her senior friends by forking a rival team's football field, but she got too drunk and just ended up forking our own field, which resulted in a forfeit during the historic season when the football team was just one game away from qualifying for District playoffs.

11. Natalie Forrester sells her little brother's Adderall to a select few faculty members in exchange for good grades.

12. Samantha Crawford accidentally ran over the former school mascot Penelope the goat with her dad's truck, hid the body in an oil field, and then blamed the Marble

Falls High School cheerleading team. As retaliation, the CCHS cheerleading team kidnapped the MFHS's prized iguana, who was never returned.

13. Melissa Gutierrez replaced her sister's birth control with aspirin after they got into a fight. Not only did her sister get pregnant, but she got kicked out of the house too.

"Oh my gosh," I gasp. "Penelope."

Amanda nods. "That was all over the local news. She was so cute with her fake little ram horns and football jersey. This is nuts."

I take the paper from her and tear a fistful off the wall before shoving them into the nearest trash can.

My heart slams against my chest. This is all my fault.

Callie did this. It must have been her. And she did it because she thinks someone on the team sold her out.

I should have told her it was me. I should've just put it out there in the open. But now she and I are friends—real friends. And all these girls . . . their secrets. If Callie wasn't the villain before, she definitely is now.

CALLIE

Twenty-Two

When people seek revenge, they almost always make one big mistake: they go too big. They go for elaborate detail over precision. Not me. Covering the main hallway with green flyers listing the girls' secrets was simple enough to do, but also lethal enough to sting.

When Keith drops me off in the morning, I walk into the front hallway to find chaos. For the first time in weeks, I feel like normal Callie. Maybe even better than normal Callie.

Melissa is ripping flyers out of hands as fast as she can. The final bell before first period rings, and not a single person in the hallway even makes a move to budge. Right now this place is like the last day of school. For one brief moment, the students have realized they outnumber the faculty and no amount of yelling or coercion on the part of Principal Armstrong and Vice Principal Benavidez is making any bit of difference.

I see Sam a few feet behind Melissa, her arms crossed as she shakes her head furiously.

I give her my most dazzling smile and wave. Oh yeah. This feels good.

And then, because the universe is on Team Callie today, I spot Bryce a few feet away. His head is bowed, and if he had a tail, it'd be between his legs. He makes brief eye contact with me before elbowing past a few guys to get into the restroom. This whole display is a nice reminder for him. His name might not have been on this list, but I've got enough dirt on Bryce to make a list every week for the rest of the school year.

Someone yanks on my elbow and I whirl around, prepared for a fight.

"Oh," I say. "Hey, Mama."

My mother wears a long white sundress with a turquoise shawl. Her red lips are almost as intense as her gaze. "Come with me. Now."

She digs her red claws into my arm and drags me to the faculty bathroom in the front office. Once the door is closed and locked, she holds up a green flyer for me to see.

For the first time, doubt quakes in my stomach. "What?" I ask.

"Don't pretend like you didn't do this."

I cross my arms over my chest and inhale deeply. "Mama, every one of those girls hung me out to dry. They're all just as guilty as I am."

Her nostrils flare, but there's not much she can say to dispute that.

"Am I in trouble?" I ask, my voice sounding more like a squeak. I was already suspended for what happened at the gym. What's next? Expulsion?

Her lips spread into a thin line. "There's no way to

prove who did it," she says. "And it's not like you damaged any property this time. I think Armstrong and Benavidez are more concerned about damage control at this point."

"Great!" I say. "Can I go to class now?"

"No!" she snaps, and waves the list in my face. "I did not raise you to do shit like this, Callie. Not only did you violate the trust of these girls, but you broke your oath as a Shamrock." She reaches for the doorknob. "What a hurtful thing to do. I'm so ashamed."

Mama leaves me there in the faculty bathroom, and that high I was riding when I first got to school has evaporated completely. I want so badly to stick to my guns. Those girls screwed me over. They had it coming. But the regret rising up my throat like bile is too much to ignore.

I brace my hands on the porcelain sink and give myself a long look in the mirror. *They deserved it.* I say it over and over again until I almost believe it.

Since my very public breakup with Bryce and getting booted from the Shamrocks, I've spent my last few weeks of lunch periods in my mom's office. But today she's kicked me out, which should come as no surprise. She swears it's tough love. I swear it's rude.

I carry my lunch and hurt feelings out to the courtyard adjacent to the cafeteria, and for the first time in my life, I search for a place to eat. Today has been . . . interesting. While there's been some talk about who penned the list and even a few knowing glances, everyone seems more concerned with what's on the list rather than where it came from. Of course I know there's a chance of my secret getting out, too, but at this point, I don't have much left to lose.

With only six weeks left in the school year, our very short-lived Texas spring is melting away in favor of much more summery weather. It's the time of year when people are starting to get restless and rowdy. Girls (many of whom I once called friends) are spread out on the grass, soaking up the sun, while many of the guys are roughhousing with one another and playing with their food more than actually eating it. And of course a select few Shamrocks are missing in action as they assess their own personal damages.

The moment the door to the cafeteria swings shut behind me, I feel like all eyes have turned to me. No one makes a move to invite me to sit with them. Instead, they all wait to see where I dare land.

And then Millie—mother-freaking Millie!—stands up at the table where she and Amanda sit in a shaded corner that's often left alone, because with the giant tree, you run a real risk of being shit on by a bird. She waves me over with both hands.

I scan the courtyard once more quickly as I recall the conversation I had with her just last night outside my house after I wallpapered the main hallways. And then I remember painting Amanda's nails over the weekend. I like both of them. A lot. And that feeling leads to a twinge of embarrassment, which angers me more than anything else.

I roll my shoulders back and stand a little straighter, and then I walk straight over to Millie and Amanda's bird-shit table.

I block out all the whispers and all the looks. I'm Calista Alejandra Reyes and I'm untouchable, dammit.

"Y'all mind if I join you?" I ask the two of them when I reach their table.

Millie grins, and Amanda puts down the book she's reading and says, "That would be de-lightful."

Later that day, as I'm walking to seventh period, Patrick Thomas stops me in the hallway. Mitch isn't far behind him.

"I'd be careful at that lunch table you chose today."

I tilt my head to the side and decide to briefly humor him. "Oh yeah. Why's that?"

He snorts like a pig. "Millie might get confused and think you're her second course."

I cross my arms over my chest and look at him for a long moment. "Patrick, someday when we've all moved on and graduated, you'll still be here in this town, cracking the same old jokes. The only difference is no one will be laughing, because eventually everyone you know will learn what I've known all along."

"Okay," he says, taking the bait. "And what's that, Miss Hot Shit Callie?"

"You're a bully, and no one likes a bully. No one. You'll have no one left to laugh at your horribly unfunny jokes. And another thing: Millie will achieve more with her baby toe than you'll do with your entire life, so you can rinse your damn mouth out, because you're not even worthy of speaking her name."

I hear a couple of *oooooooo*s from other students, and I walk away, brushing shoulders with Mitch. "Time to find some new friends," I tell him, without stopping for a second.

By the end of the week, sitting with Millie and Amanda at lunch is no longer newsworthy. Sure, I still get a few funny looks, and every single Shamrock practically hisses when I come within six feet of her, but it's not like any of those people are rushing to invite me to sit with them, so I officially give zero shits.

And not for nothing, but the more my mom notices me settling into a groove with my new friends, the more she eases up on the whole grounded thing. She hasn't even brought up the Shamrock flyer incident since Wednesday night, when she told me one last time how disappointed she was. In fact, I've even started riding to work with Millie after school. We stop at Sonic (I get a watermelon cream slush and she gets a cherry limeade slush), and then Millie takes me home when we close at seven.

That Friday after school, as we settle into work with our Sonic drinks, Mitch walks in wearing navy-blue athletic shorts and a gold Clover City High phys ed T-shirt.

"Hey," I say. "Welcome back."

"I was wondering if you still worked here," says Mitch.

"What? I'm here every afternoon."

"Ahh, well, I know that now. I'd started coming in the morning before school, but Millie—hi, Millie!"

She peeks her head out of the office and not so discreetly winks at me. "Heya, Mitch!"

He grins widely. "Anyway, Millie let me know that you only work after school and sometimes on Saturdays."

I glance back at the office, willing my eyes into lasers. "Did she now?"

"Well, now that I know your schedule, I can plan my week accordingly."

"Oh, really?"

"Yeah," he says. "The workout burn just isn't quite as good if I can't watch you rolling your eyes at me from the front desk."

I squint but can't help the slow smile spreading across my face. "Well, my eye-rolling abilities are well worth rearranging your entire week for. I mean, no one rolls eyes like I do." Digging my fists into my hips, I make a big show of rolling my eyes just for him.

"Ah, there it is," he says. "They should list that as part of the membership benefits."

I laugh and then say, a little quieter, "I don't think I'll be sticking around here for that long."

He doesn't press me for more information, but I'm not ready to be done talking just yet. "So," I say, "you listen to my advice?"

"What advice was that?" he asks.

"About finding new friends."

He nods slowly. "Yeah, Patrick can be an asshole, but you know how it is."

I look up at him, forcing him to look me right in the eye. "Actually, no. I don't know how it is. Not anymore."

"Right," he says. "Yeah, well, Patrick is . . . I don't know."

"That's one way of describing him."

"Hey, you said you don't work every Saturday, right?"

"Yeah . . ."

"Well, what about this Saturday?" he asks.

"As in tomorrow?"

"She has the day off!" shouts Millie.

I whirl around. "I do not."

She peeks her head out again. "Yeah," she says. "You do. I just gave you the day off." She turns to Mitch. "She's spoken for Saturday evening, though." And then she disappears back into the office.

I sigh. Guess I'm in store for another slumber party this weekend, where only two out of five people can stand breathing the same air as me. With the way my mom is looking at me these days, it's better than staying home. "Well, I guess I'm off, but I'm technically grounded."

His brow wrinkles. "I can take a hint."

Guilt sinks into my chest. But I didn't genuinely want to go out with him. Did I? "I really am grounded," I say.

"Nah, it's cool," he says, and walks off to whatever piece of equipment is farthest from me.

Great. Keep pushing people away, Callie. There are plenty in your life to spare.

After he leaves, Millie rushes out of the office. "Oh my goodness!" she squeals. "He asked you out!"

"I'm grounded," I remind her.

She waves me off. "Puh-lease, your mom wants to unground you so bad. I can smell it. Yesterday when I was in the office for morning announcements, she asked me all about Saturday night and she said you came home in a . . ." She holds her hands up in air quotes. "'Not bad mood.' I really think she's very invested in your social life and is concerned for you and how well you're adjusting to post-dance-team life."

I sputter with laughter. The girl sounds like she's recapping the plot of a movie. "And you got all that from a 'not bad mood'?"

She nods with authority. "I speak Parent fluently."

MILLIE

Twenty-Three

Amanda's house is chaos, but it always is. Walking any-where outside of her room requires dodging her brothers as they wrestle each other across the house like two little tumbleweeds skittering back and forth. Which is why the six of us have locked ourselves into Amanda's room with two boxes of pizza and a chair wedged under the doorknob for extra security.

Three weeks ago, when Callie joined us for the first time, things were a little rough around the edges. Tonight Willowdean gave me a long look and a sigh when she saw her walk in behind me, but it's getting better slowly. She can't hate Callie forever. (Though if anyone can hold a grudge forever, my bet is on her.)

We each take a slice of pepperoni pizza, and Hannah goes for the box of half cheese, half mushroom. "I'm trying out the whole vegetarian thing," she says glumly. "Court-ney made me watch this awful documentary about how we slaughter animals."

"No thank you," says Ellen. "I'm happy to live in willful

ignorance with my bacon and barbecue."

"I've never taken you as one to bend your will out of guilt," says Willowdean.

Hannah shrugs. "Well, the whole no-meat thing is kinda pissing off my mom, which is sorta hilarious." She takes a huge bite of pizza, and with her mouth full, she adds, "We'll see how long it lasts. Plus Courtney says kissing a meat eater presents her with a moral dilemma."

"The only dilemma I have is between pepperoni or sausage," says Amanda.

"So are you and Courtney a thing?" I ask. "Like, officially."

Hannah keeps on eating her pizza, but she can't hide the blush in her cheeks.

I squeal and so does Ellen.

Hannah rolls her eyes. "Well, I wouldn't give up meat for just anybody. And what about you?" she asks, turning the tables.

I clear my throat. "Well, Malik and I are getting together to work on a project tomorrow."

Everyone lets out an *oooooooooo*, and I couldn't stop the smile on my face even if I wanted to.

"Well," I say, pointing to Callie, "this one was asked out just yesterday."

Callie, who is still nibbling on her first piece of pizza, sets her slice down on a paper plate. "It was totally not a big deal."

Everyone's quiet for a moment, and the whole thing just feels awkward. I need someone to break this silence, and for some reason I know it can't be me.

"Whatever," says Ellen. "Don't play it cool. Spill."

I grin gratefully in Ellen's direction.

Callie shakes her head, biting down on her lip nervously. "Just that guy Mitch from the football team."

Ellen side-eyes Willowdean, who brushes the crumbs from her pizza on her jeans and says, "He's a really nice guy. Like, way nicer than you even know." She looks directly at Callie. "Don't toy around with him, okay?"

Callie groans. "I already told him no."

"What?" asks Willowdean. "Why?"

Callie looks up to the ceiling like the answer might somehow be written there. "I'm basically grounded forever." She crosses her arms. "And I'm coming off a really bad breakup."

"By the way," says Amanda, "I saw that whole thing play out in the hallway, and you're a badass."

"Yeah," says Hannah. "I heard you destroyed him. Pretty impressive."

I nudge Callie with my elbow, and she glances at me with a shy smile. "They like you," I nearly whisper.

Willowdean leans into the circle a little more. "And, um, I saw your run-in with Patrick Thomas the other day." She nods. "That was pretty cool of you."

"What run-in with Patrick Thomas?" I ask. All I can think of is when I confronted Patrick last week and she didn't do a thing.

"Nothing," Callie and Willowdean answer in unison.

I roll my eyes. "Y'all know that I know he oinks at me,

right? Is that what you're hiding? Just because I don't usually acknowledge him doesn't mean I don't know."

Callie turns to me. "Well, just because you don't acknowledge him doesn't mean I can't."

I open my mouth to politely explain why that's not actually helpful, but Willowdean interjects. "Oh, y'all, trust me when I say that if you want anyone talking back to Patrick Thomas on your behalf, it's this girl. She takes no prisoners." Willowdean reaches across the circle to give Callie a high five.

Amanda gives me a knowing look. The two of us have spent the last few years ignoring all the looks and jokes from our peers. It's not like we don't hear it, but there came a time when we had to make the decision to pretend we didn't hear it, or just let ourselves drown in it.

Callie turns to me. "He just said something stupid to me between classes, and I set him straight."

I wait for a moment to see if she'll elaborate, but she doesn't. And truthfully, I know people like him will always exist. I don't need the details. They don't change anything for me. But still, a little bit of warmth tingles in my chest at the thought of Callie standing up for me.

That night, Amanda and Hannah sleep head to toe in Amanda's twin bed while Ellen and Willowdean share an air mattress and Callie and I take sleeping bags on the floor next to the empty pizza boxes.

I can't sleep, because it just always takes me forever to fall asleep when I'm not in my own bed, so I'm awake to see Willowdean and Ellen sit up in bed and do their best job of tiptoeing around as they gather their shoes and cell phones while still wearing their pajamas.

"Where are you bitches going?" Callie whispers next to me, scaring me a little, because I didn't even know she was still awake.

Willowdean holds her finger to her lips, telling us to be quiet. "Our boyfriends are outside," she says, so quietly it barely counts as a whisper. "We were just gonna sneak out for a little bit."

I sit up. I don't want them to go, but I'm also jealous, because what if Malik were here doing the same, and what if he was my official boyfriend? But I don't want them to miss out either. "I'll help you guys," I tell them. "I know this house better than y'all."

Willowdean looks to Ellen, who nods her approval.

"Well, I'm coming with you," says Callie.

"I'll be right back," I tell her.

"We've been cooped up in this room all night hiding from Amanda's brothers. I've forgotten what the outside world even looks like."

"Fine," I say. "Be quiet. Amanda's dad is a light sleeper."

The three of them follow me downstairs and through the kitchen to the back door, which lets out a long creak as I open it to the milky nighttime sky. I hold the door while they all shuffle through, then let it close softly behind us.

Willowdean and Ellen head to the gate on the side of the house, circling around the pool.

"Y'all, don't stay out too long," I say.

Willowdean smacks Ellen's butt as they shuffle through the gate.

"Oh my God!" says Callie.

"Shhh!" I try to quiet her.

"Amanda didn't say she had a pool!"

I smile. "It's not even warm enough out yet."

She sighs. "I know, but . . ." She sighs again. "A private pool all to yourself in the summer."

"Well, she does have to share it with her brothers."

"Can we just put our feet in?" Callie asks. "It's pretty warm tonight."

I glance behind us to make sure there are no lights on in the house. "Sure."

We sit side by side with our feet dangling in the deep end. Amanda's house is pretty old and so is the pool, but it's the reason why her dad bought the house. The tiles lining the pool are clearly older than both Amanda and I, but her dad treats this pool like a fourth child.

"Didn't your, um, ex-boyfriend have a pool?"

Her eyes light up briefly before her whole expression droops. "Yeah, but his dad was weird about having people over." She holds her hand to her chest. "*I* was allowed over, but if we wanted to hang with friends, we had to go to the community pool."

"I see."

"Which was fine," she adds. "Except for there never being enough lounge chairs, and kids everywhere. Plus they had to shut down the pool three times last summer for floaters."

I gasp. "Oh my gosh, like, dead bodies?"

She laughs. "No. More like turds."

"Ewww," I say. "Oh man, that's so gross." But it's still sort of interesting to hear about summer in Clover City. I'm usually only here long enough to go swimming with Amanda a few times before I'm off to Daisy Ranch.

"I don't think I've ever actually gone to the community pool," I say. Despite my appearance in the Miss Teen Blue Bonnet Pageant might suggest, I'm still coming to terms with wearing swimsuits in front of people. Besides, I think I was too high on adrenaline that day to process much of anything, let alone embarrassment.

"Well, it leaves quite a bit to be desired." She kicks her feet a little, letting the water splash up above her knees.

"Well, I don't think I would let it stop me from going, but I do know that the thought of wearing my swimsuit at the public pool in front of everyone from school gives me a little bit of anxiety." I sigh. "Which is silly, because it's not like I'm not used to standing out."

"I hear that."

I laugh. "Well, you stand out for things that people think are strengths. You're thin. Pretty. Smart."

"Mexican," she says.

"Well, yeah," I say, a little taken aback. "But that's not a bad thing to stand out for."

She sighs. "I know. I just . . . I know it's probably different, but I know what it's like to stand out, too. I've got my dad and my abuela and my older sister, Claudia. And there are tons of other Latinx kids at school, but at home with my mom, Keith, and Kyla . . . well, they're all super white, and I am super not. Especially with Claudia out of the house. Sometimes people think I'm not even related to them. Then when people do find out I'm Mexican, they assume my mom is a cleaning lady or that I'm here illegally. Or that I have a fiery temper or that I'm a . . ." She holds her fingers in air quotes. "'Sexy señorita.'"

"Wow. That's really crummy." In my head, Callie has had such a perfect life up until recently. Dreamboat boyfriend. Traditionally pretty. One of the most talented athletes at school. I may be fat, but no one ever questions whether or not I fit in with my family. Being white, that's not something I've ever had to deal with. "I'm sorry, Callie. I get what it means for people to make decisions about the kind of person you are based on how you look, but I'm still sorry."

Her lips spread into a faint smile. "Thanks. And hey, I guess if my BFF had this gem in her backyard, I'd keep my distance, too."

"It's not just that," I explain. "I spend most of my summer at camp."

"Oh."

"Fat camp."

I can feel her body tense up a little bit beside me.

"Eight summers," I say. "Sixteen months, if you add it all up. I even had a camp nickname."

"A camp nickname?" she asks.

"Yeah. Everyone at camp sort of chooses a nickname for themselves. Or sometimes the nickname chooses you. It kind of helps to separate everyday you from summer-camp you."

She smiles. "That actually makes sense. So what was your nickname?"

"Don't laugh," I tell her.

She nods solemnly.

"Puddin'."

"Oh my God!" she says. "Are you serious? I can't believe it!"

"You said you wouldn't laugh." I can't help feeling a little hurt.

"Oh no! It's because my grandma on my mom's side used to call me Puddin'. She moved to Arizona, but she still writes it in my birthday cards every once in a while."

I bubble with laughter. "No way!"

She shakes her head. "For real."

It's sort of wonderful that for all the differences between us, we share this one small thing.

"So, Puddin'?" she asks. "How'd you come up with that one?"

"I got caught sneaking in one of those prepackaged cups of pudding my very first year," I tell her. "The worst part is it was fat-free! It wasn't even real junk food."

She laughs then. "You really are good. Like, right down to the bone."

I nod. "Breaking the rules always requires great effort on my part. But no more fat-camp rules for me. I'm done with that place."

She's silent for a moment. "So you've, like, tried to lose weight?" Her voice is tentative.

I laugh. I can't help it. "Have I *tried* to lose weight? Up until last fall, my life was dedicated to it."

"Wow."

"What'd you think, I just went home at night and stuffed my face with marshmallows and chips?"

She pauses and shrinks back a bit. "I don't think that now, but I definitely did before."

"Before when?" I ask.

She shrugs. "Before these last few weeks? I guess?"

This shouldn't surprise me, and really, it doesn't. But it does suck. It really sucks, and I don't use that word lightly. "I probably know way more about calorie counting and how to maximize workouts and the latest fad cleanses than any other person you've ever met."

"I never thought about it that way." She shakes her head. "All that work and no results."

I let out a little snort laugh. "You know, me and my mom used to go to these ladies' aerobic classes at church on Thursday nights, and they'd choreograph the whole thing to Christian music. They'd say how our bodies were the Lord's temple, so we should maintain the temple and stay as slim and trim as possible."

"That's . . . that's kind of fucked up," says Callie.

"Well, I don't know if I'd use that exact word, but yeah. Yeah, it really was. Because not only had the world already done a perfectly good job of making me feel like I'd failed at being a human being, but then I was a bad Christian, too."

"Do you still go to church?" asks Callie. "We've never

been a very churchy family."

"I sort of stopped when I started working at the gym. I needed more time for homework, but honestly, the people at my church said lots of things I couldn't live with. Like, the way they talk about gay people and loving the sinner but not the sin. I mean, if you can't love the whole of a person, do you really love them at all? So maybe I'll go back to a different church after high school once I've moved, but I don't need a church to be a Christian. And I don't have to be thin to be a good person. Or a pretty person."

"Nope. You really don't."

"I have to ask you something," I blurt. It's something that's been weighing on me all week.

"Shoot," she says.

"Those green flyers with all those secrets. Was that you?"

She looks at me for a long moment and then nods. "I'm sorry for asking you to drive me there."

I start to shake my head.

"No, no," she tells me. "I shouldn't have dragged you into that without clueing you in first." She touches my thigh. "But no one's getting into any trouble for that. Trust me."

I gulp and nod. Guilt settles in the pit of my stomach as I'm reminded that I haven't been honest. I'm such a coward. "Okay."

"I'm serious. And if anyone does, you know I can take the fall," she adds sarcastically. "Plus those girls got exactly what they deserved."

Instead of opening my gosh-dang mouth and telling her I'm the one who spotted her on the surveillance tape, I change the subject. "So what's the deal with Mitch? You don't strike me as the type of person who needs time to emotionally recover from a breakup."

She turns to me with her arms crossed in mock insult, but I've got her pegged. "I told you. He's not my type."

I lean back with my arms spread out behind me, propping myself up. "What does that even mean? Y'all seem to really make each other laugh, and isn't that a good place to start?"

"Well, things with Bryce started in a coat closet at a party, so that was also a good place to start."

"You're avoiding the question," I tell her.

"He's just . . ."

"Fat," I say.

She grimaces. "He *is* a bigger guy. And I do like his personality a lot, and he is kind of cute. Okay, maybe really cute."

"You can use the word *fat*, by the way. It doesn't bother me."

"It seems rude."

I smile. "Because you've only ever used it in a rude way."

She looks skeptical.

"Just use it," I say. I grip my stomach and then I pinch the slightest bit of flab on her arm. "Fat. We both have it. I just have enough of it for it to be the first thing you notice about me."

She cringes, but then her face relaxes. "Fat."

"Actually use it," I say. "Like in a sentence."

Her eyes scan the sky for a moment. "I feel fat?" She says it like a question.

"Well—"

"You can't feel fat," calls Willowdean from the other side of the gate. "You either are or you aren't."

Willowdean and Ellen giggle as they fiddle with the gate before spilling into the backyard.

I turn to Callie, and in a quiet voice I say, "That's actually true. Fat is definitely not a feeling."

Callie nods. "Noted."

Willowdean and Ellen whisper back and forth, their laughter growing as they shuffle through the backyard gate.

"Shhhh!" Callie and I both reprimand them in unison.

"We had *a beer*," says Ellen.

Willowdean holds one finger in the air. "Singular!"

"Let's get them inside," Callie whispers.

I nod and the two of us guide Willowdean and Ellen back inside and up to Amanda's room.

"Does it make me a huge nerd that I'm impressed you have keys to the school?" I ask Malik.

When I asked Malik if he was sure we'd be able to get into the school building on a Sunday afternoon, he assured me that he had it all taken care of, and he did not disappoint.

"Only if it makes me a huge nerd to *have* keys to the school," he tells me as he opens the door to what was once the school newsroom.

Mr. Garvy, Malik's journalism teacher, has tried reviving the program more than once, but the district can't be convinced. Which means this room just sits here empty with an unused news desk while my announcements are the closest the student body gets to actual news, because the school paper is a joke that publishes sports schedules and quizzes ripped from the pages of magazines.

I lay my dress bag on the counter and look over my script. I sorted through old school announcements and combined some of them to make for some good news stories. "I should get changed," I say.

"There's a bathroom in the hallway," says Malik. "It shouldn't take long to get this stuff set up."

"I'll be back!" I say, and skip across the hall with my makeup and suit. The suit I've decided to wear is much more serious than anything else I own. I found it online and bought it with birthday money. Inga helped me tailor it while she was still pregnant.

The actual suit is a deep royal blue with three-quarter-length sleeves and cream trim. Thanks to Inga, the skirt hits my knees in the perfect spot and the jacket nips in at all the right places. Zipping up the skirt and buttoning the button on the jacket are as satisfying as a cherry on a sundae.

I slip into my red kitten heels, even though no one will see my feet under the desk, and I apply a coat of mascara and red lipstick, the same lipstick recommended to me by Callie's mom.

I have worn clothes that have made me feel plenty of

things. Like at the pageant, when I wore my gingham swimsuit and matching accessories. I felt unstoppable, and for the first time, everyone was looking at me—and in a good way.

I've never worn anything that's made me feel quite like this suit does. Sometimes being fat and finding clothing is like trying to ice-skate in the desert. A lot of people might think that's silly. It's just clothing, after all. But clothes are the perfect way to communicate with the world around you without having to say a word. And so much of the clothing available to fat girls assumes that we all want the same thing: floral, flowy, and possibly ready to go on a cruise at any given moment. And that's okay, if it's your style. I know there are more options now than when my mom was my age, but I still wonder what it might be like to go into a mall and shop in any store I want, instead of just the ones who want me.

This suit, though. I put it on, and I feel like no matter where I am or who else is in the room, I'm in charge. It's the kind of outfit that makes people feel like they can trust you. It's no coincidence that a simple outfit can be the first step in creating the life you want.

After fussing with my hair a bit, I head back into the news classroom, where Malik is waiting.

"Wow," he says, his voice breathy.

Anxiety spikes in my chest, and I have to remind myself to breathe. "Good wow or bad wow?"

He nods feverishly. "Good wow. Super-good wow. Like, super-foxy-good wow, but also I-feel-like-I-should-be-asking-you-to-hire-me-for-an-important-job wow."

My cheeks ache with heat, and I can't even blame it on the warm lights yet.

"You ready?" he asks.

I nod. "I've never actually sat down behind a news desk," I admit. "What if I'm horrible at this?" Because the truth is, outside of what little experience I've picked up from doing morning announcements, my career as a TV reporter has only ever existed in my head.

"Then I'll burn the evidence," he promises. "But I doubt there's anything you're horrible at."

"Just you wait and see." I take a seat behind the desk. "You didn't witness the woodcarving disaster of 2014."

He laughs. "I'm sure it was awful. I tried messing with the lights, but they're super old. Let me know if they're too bright, though, and I'll see what I can do."

I nod. My throat is dry and I feel my whole body freezing up, one joint at a time. I can't believe I thought this was a good idea. I should've figured out some way to do this on my own, without any outside help. But this is the only way I could make it look professional. Still, I can barely stand the idea of Malik watching me as I announce sort of fabricated news for a school that doesn't even have a news channel.

"I'll add in the graphics later," he tells me. "Like the little box above your shoulder. I'll start rolling now, and you can go whenever you want. I can edit out any major mess-ups, but it'll look cleanest if you can make it through without any hiccups."

I nod and clear my throat. I take a swig from the bottle of water I left under the desk. "Okay." I close my eyes and count to ten as I let out a long, deep breath. *I can do this. I can totally do this.*

I open my eyes. "Good morning, Clover City High. This is Millie Michalchuk, reporting from the Lucky Seven News—sorry," I say. "I had to come up with a name for the news channel. Is that dumb?" I ask.

"Totally not dumb," he says. "But maybe start over."

"Right," I say. Every possible doubt is racing through my mind right now. I smile, but not too hard. Just a natural, welcoming smile. I hope. All I can hear is the sound of my heart thumping, my blood pumping. Everything else is a dull buzz. I close my eyes again and count to ten. *Breathe. Just breathe.* The pumping blood. My beating heart. It all fades, and for a moment I can hear it in my head. My intro music. A cameraman doing a countdown until . . . three, two, one. I open my eyes. We're live.

"Good morning, Clover City High." My voice sounds like butter. "This is Millie Michalchuk, reporting from the Lucky Seven News studio in the heart of Clover City High." *I can do this. I can really do this.* "First up today, we have a follow-up report on the mystery-meat situation in the cafeteria. After various tests performed by both the biology and chemistry clubs, the president of the chemistry club, Jessica Banks, has confirmed that the sloppy joe meat, which also doubles as chili, among other things, is indeed ground turkey and not beef. The nonmeat substance found in the mix appears to be bean filler to save on costs, Jessica ventured when asked. When speaking with Vice Principal Benavidez, I was told that the meat is safe for consumption by everyone except vegetarians. The construction on the new indoor training facility for the football team is nearly complete and it's expected to be up and running just in time for summer training camp. Meanwhile, other teams on campus, including the incredibly successful Shamrocks, continue to fall victim to lack of sponsorship and district-wide budgetary cuts."

I continue on for another ten minutes with the boys' soccer report, the casting choices for the spring play, and rumors of an Algebra One cheating ring among the freshman class.

After I'm finished, we do it twice more, just in case, and we even do some outside footage of me reporting from the new granite reflection bench donated by the class of 1995. I can feel myself nailing it. It takes a whole lot of self-restraint not to squeal and pump my fist into the air at the end of the last take.

When we finish, Malik slides his equipment back into his bag. "You were a pro, Millie!"

"You think so?" I ask.

"They'd be crazy not to take you this summer."

I hold up my hand for a high five, but instead he gives me a light peck on the lips.

"I've been waiting to do that all day," he says.

Heat wells up in my chest. "Next time don't bother waiting," I say.

He kisses me again, and this time his lips linger. "I won't."

CALLIE

Twenty-Four

On Tuesday, there's a mandatory pep rally for the Shamrocks as a big send-off before State. I almost skip, but decide not to at the last minute. My mom was kind enough to overlook the whole breaking-up-with-Bryce-in-a-very-publicly-disruptive-way thing, but she's not yet forgiven me for the Shamrock Secret Shit List, so now isn't a good time to push my luck, especially with my birthday coming up this weekend. There are days when I am so sure that blasting that list was totally deserved, and then, at times, guilt creeps into my thoughts like an impossible-to-reach itch.

I sit as far away from the action as I can and even wave off Millie when she tries to get me to sit a little closer, with her and Amanda.

Never in a million years would I have believed you if you said that the school was holding a pep rally for the Shamrocks. This is the kind of recognition we always deserved but never dreamed we could have. In the past, pep rallies were strictly reserved for boys' football and basketball and sometimes baseball. With all the buzz building about the team being one of the top contenders for State, I guess it's hard for the school to keep pretending we're no more than a second-tier pep squad but with more costumes. This weird sense of pride over everything we worked so hard for swells up in my chest, and for a moment I think I could cry.

The moment is interrupted by the same sports-jam songs they play for the football and basketball rallies. They start up as the athletic director, Coach Culver, announces each of the girls one by one. I'd heard that after the shit list went public, a few were called in to the office for select questionable things, but the most anyone got was a slap on the wrist. With no real proof, the list is only hearsay.

Today, the girls are in what we call our Lone Star outfits. White skirt with a matching jacket and gold trim. The whole look is topped off with white dance boots. It's the uniform we use for all the various patriotic holiday parades we march in and for annual pictures. My mom and I both have portraits hanging in the upstairs hallway of us sitting in the splits on the football field, twenty years apart, in the same uniform.

"Aaaaaaand of course we can't forget our assistant and future captain for next year, Melissa Gutierrez!"

Melissa waves to the crowd, focusing in on me.

I flash her the finger, but she's unfazed.

But then I see Bryce walk in with his ever-faithful entourage of assholes, and that is a run-in I am definitely not looking forward to.

I stand up. Yup. Totally cannot do this. Mama's goodwill be damned.

Rather than squeezing my way through the crowd, I

jump the few feet off the side of the bleachers. My cowboy boots (if I have to attend this thing, I might as well wear stomping-around shoes) make a loud smacking sound just as Coach Culver announces Sam, but I barely notice because I have sufficiently startled the large, burly guy who was pacing beneath the bleachers and just so happens to be Mitch Lewis.

"Uh, did you just fall from the sky?" he asks in a bit of a daze.

"Definitely," I say, stepping under the bleachers.

Music—music I'd recognize anywhere—starts up, and I peer between random feet to catch a glimpse of the dance team performing the routine they're taking to State. The routine I worked tirelessly on all summer with Sam and Melissa.

"Of course the dance team would have to perform at their own pep rally. Don't we have cheerleaders for that?" I roll my eyes. The cheerleading team. At least that's one less thing I have to deal with now.

"Please tell me there's beef between the Shamrocks and the cheerleading team," says Mitch.

I laugh. "Oh, there is so much beef."

"Is it like the Sharks and the Jets? Do y'all have dance-offs in the school parking lot at night?"

"Mitch Lewis!" I say, poking at his chest. "Did you just make a musical theater reference?"

He smiles like a cat that's been caught. "Listen," he says, taking a step closer to me, because this time there's no front desk to separate us. "One can have an appreciation for musical theater while also playing defensive tackle for the school football team."

"Well, that's enlightening," I say.

"And to be honest," he adds, "you don't exactly strike me as a *West Side Story* kind of girl."

"Well, I'm not, but my mama is."

"I think our moms might get along," he says.

Outside the bleachers, the dance team is finishing up their routine, and now a few guys from a couple of the different boys' teams have dressed up in some very poorly assembled costumes to do their own take on the Shamrocks' routine. This is so demeaning.

"So what are you hiding from down here?" I ask.

"Who says I'm hiding?"

I give him a knowing look. "You don't just chill under the bleachers during a pep rally for no reason. Trust me," I tell him. "I would know."

"So I guess we're both hiding," he says.

"Looks like it."

"You could say my friends and I aren't seeing eye to eye."

"Oh yeah?" I ask. "How come?"

"I guess you could say I took your advice."

This pleases me. "Did you now? You found some new friends?"

"Well, sort of. I don't know. Patrick did some asshole thing—no different than all the asshole things he's done every day since the day we met. So I told him it was an asshole thing and that doing it makes him an asshole."

I whistle. "I can't imagine that went over very well."

He nods. "Hence the bleachers. Sometimes I feel bad, ya know, that it's taken me so long to just tell the guy he's a dick. I've known that guy since we were in diapers."

"You can't expect the younger version of you to know who your friends are going to be. People change. Look at Bryce. He wasn't always a dick."

"Uhhh." Mitch grimaces. "He kinda was."

I cross my arms over my chest. "Really?" I ask. "You think?"

Mitch sighs. "Callie Reyes, blinded by love."

"Well, I was sort of a dick, too. Still kind of am."

Mitch doesn't say anything. I wasn't expecting him to completely refute me, but come on, man. "Who knows?" He shrugs. "Maybe Patrick will come around."

"Or maybe he won't," I say.

"Well, if that's the case, don't forget you're the one who told me to dump my only friends in this place."

"That's a lot of pressure," I joke. "I wouldn't say I'm a shining example of a good friend. I guess I'll have to step up my friend skills."

Mitch shakes his head, his teeth tugging on his bottom lip. "Maybe." But his voice sounds doubtful.

"Hey, about hanging out . . ." The words are out of my mouth before I can stop myself. "You want to go out sometime or something?" I try to keep my voice even, but I'm not used to really putting myself out there like this, and it's got me sweating.

"Like on a date? I—I thought you were grounded."

"I was. I am. Still. Kind of. But then not really."

"Uhhh . . ."

I almost shout, "WHAT'S THERE TO THINK ABOUT?"

Then he says, "I think, um . . . I don't think that'd be a good idea right now."

I nod, but inside I'm shriveling up. No one has ever just rejected me like that. Why did he even bother asking me out awhile back if he was going to change his mind? "Okay. Well, uh, good luck hiding out?"

"You too," he says.

The pep rally isn't over yet, but I'm sure as hell not hanging out under these bleachers with him now.

I turn on my heel and take the exit right outside the bleachers into the hallway.

Maybe Bryce told him some horrible lie about me. Or even worse, maybe he told Mitch a horrible truth about me. It could be that Mitch just changed his mind all on his own, I guess. He asked me out at the gym in the moment, so maybe he's had time to come to his senses since then.

I think I might want something I can't have, and that's not a feeling I'm used to.

After school, while I'm waiting outside for my mom to wrap up a few things, I plop down in the grass with my legs crossed and scroll through my phone to delete old pictures of Bryce and me. Time for some long-overdue housekeeping. Seeing him at school is awful enough.

"Didn't see you at the pep rally today."

I look up, shielding my eyes, until Melissa comes into focus. She still wears her Shamrock uniform, but her hat is stuffed into her tote bag and she's ditched the boots for flip-flops.

"Oh, I think you saw me." I lift my hand up to give her the middle finger. "This jogging your memory?"

"Ah," she says. "That's more like it. I didn't recognize you without your shitty attitude."

I grin. "Never leave home without it."

"You know, I actually feel bad for you." She shakes her head, an incredulous look on her face.

"Wow, that's so generous of you, but I'm good without your misguided pity."

She continues, "Whatever moral fiber you have is so flimsy that you would just dump the deepest, darkest secrets of people you once called friends."

"Friends?" I ask. "You mean acquaintances who let me take the fall for something we all did?"

"Maybe keep it down?" she asks, looking around.

"Nope." I shake my head. "And besides, no one got in trouble for any of that stuff."

"You don't even get it. Maybe no one got in trouble, but you really humiliated some of those girls. Sam and Jess are both mortified. Natalie, Lara, and Addison are all in serious trouble at home. You really screwed everyone over. I mean, Bethany came to school the next day to a locker full of Q-tips."

"How horrific," I say, voice flat.

She shakes her head, her voice dropping low. "Just so

you know, my sister got wind of that list, too. She's not even talking to me right now. I'm not allowed to go to my niece's birthday party."

Up until now I was fine, but I have to admit that this one gets me in the gut. But I'm determined not to let it show. I almost blurt an apology, but instead I sit there, unmoving. I've never been that great of a sister, but the idea of Kyla or Claudia finding out I'd done something like that to them makes me feel a little bit nauseous.

"Whatever, Callie. You're off the team, you lost captain, and you're a shitty human being. I guess that's enough to live with." She walks off to where Sam and the rest of the team are waiting for her at the track.

The moment she walks off, I push my sunglasses up the bridge of my nose to let them conceal the tears burning at the corners of my eyes. Anger, guilt, shame. They all bubble to the surface at once.

MILLIE

Twenty-Five

After work one night, I drag Callie to the Crafty Corner to pick up upholstery fabric my mom special-ordered to redo our curtains this summer.

She shuffles in behind me with her nose glued to her phone. "What are you looking at?" I ask as I pull her just out of the way seconds before meeting a pincushion display head-on.

She shakes her head and huffs. "Just waiting for the stupid results from the state dance competition."

"Oh." There's that guilt again, sticking to the inside of my lungs like August humidity. "How are they doing?"

"I don't know yet. This website is so damn slow." Her voice changes as she takes in our surroundings.

One entire wall at the Crafty Corner is dedicated to yarn, while the main floor is rows and rows of every type of fabric you can imagine, and on the other side of the store is everything from raw wood dollhouse supplies to glitter paint to scrapbooking scissors.

"This place is a little intense," she says.

I can't hide my giddiness. "You know how in *Beauty and the Beast* when Belle sees the library for the first time?"

"Uh-huh."

"That's how I feel walking into this place. Like the possibilities are endless."

"Really?" she asks. "Because this place just makes me feel like the possibilities are really, really overwhelming."

I click my tongue. "I'll turn you into a crafter if it's the last thing I do."

She rolls her eyes. "Hey, speaking of you aggressively trying to manage my life for me, have you, uh, seen Mitch around? Like at the gym?"

I raise my eyebrows but keep my mouth shut, because oh my goodness, I think she actually, truly does have a crush on Mitch Lewis, and if that's the case, my instincts could not have been more right.

Callie waves her finger in my face. "If you make a thing of this, I swear I'll never talk to you about boys again. Or do whatever weird craft things you think you can get me to do!"

"Howdy!" calls Flora from the back of the store, where she cuts scraps of fabric for the clearance bin. Flora is sort of me and my mom's crafting spiritual leader. She wears her same navy-blue smock every day with her name embroidered over the chest, and she is always armed with her red scissors and the mini ballpoint pen dangling from the long, thin gold chain around her neck. She taught me how to thread my first bobbin and is actually sort of a big deal on the West Texas craft-show circuit.

"Hiya, Flora!" I call back. "Just here for my mom's special order."

She snaps her fingers. "I'll be right back!"

I turn back to Callie. "So Mitch. Okay. Mitch has been coming in early mornings before school starts." I pause for a minute to wait for her response. "I could, of course, drop a hint that maybe he should come in one afternoon."

"No," she says defiantly. "Definitely not. No meddling. Promise me."

I gasp. "What if me, you, Mitch, and Malik all went on a double date?"

Her eyes narrow. "No meddling."

Since that's a promise I can't keep, I change the subject. "Any word on the dance competition?"

She pulls her phone out and waits a moment for it to update. Her whole demeanor changes in an instant as she slumps against the bolts of fabric. "They won," she says flatly. "They're going to Nationals." She shakes her head. "Those lucky-ass bitches. How is it possible for me to be so happy and so disappointed at the same time?"

"Who's going to Nationals?" Flora asks, her voice bubbling with anticipation, but by the looks of Callie you'd think she just asked who died.

"The Shamrocks," I tell her. "The school dance team."

Flora claps her hands together. "Oh, how wonderful! I'll have to make some signs for the shop window!"

Callie sighs and slides her phone into her pocket. "Are we done here?"

"Just as soon as I pay."

"I'll wait for you outside." Her voice cracks on that last word.

I feel so bad for her that she couldn't be there with them.

After I pay, I spend the rest of the drive with a very silent, brooding Callie, as I try to dream up ways to cheer her up. Just as she's getting out of the car, it hits me—the perfect remedy. "Your birthday!" I exclaim so loudly that I scare her, and she nearly trips getting out of the car.

"Yes," she says. "I do have one of those. Once a year. Just like everyone else."

"Let me throw you a party," I beg.

She stands outside the open passenger door and shakes her head. "No can do. At my dad's this weekend."

"Oh. Well, maybe we can do something next weekend."

She studies me for a moment. "I think I'd rather just keep things simple, if that's okay, but thanks for the ride, Millie."

That night, after Malik and I proofread each other's AP Psych essays, I open up my notebook to dig into my journalism-camp personal statement again. For background noise, I turn on *The Princess Diaries*. I never get tired of the way Julie Andrews says *Genovia*.

"Genovia." I let each syllable drag, trying to pronounce it as regally as she does.

What would Julie Andrews write? Just as I pick up my pen, ready to channel the one and only Ms. Andrews, my phone buzzes.

CALLIE: I guess y'all could come over to my dad's.

CALLIE: It's far.

CALLIE: Probably not even worth the drive.

I laugh to myself. Surely by now Callie has to know that an out-of-town drive is no match for my determination. Especially in the face of an impending birthday.

MILLIE: You're talking to the girl who once road tripped hours on a school night for a Dolly Parton drag show. Your dad's house is barely an hour away. We'll be there.

CALLIE: Wow. Dolly. Parton. Drag. Show. Those are four words I never expected you to say in one sentence.

MILLIE: Don't tell my mom, but it was more life-affirming than any sermon I've ever heard.

CALLIE: Millie, Millie, Millie. Always breaking your mama's rules.

I drop my phone onto my desk and gasp. "That's it!" It's a true eureka moment.

I take my GIRL BOSS pencil and begin to write.

Sometimes we have to break the rules to get what we want. But now I think it's time we change them.

CALLIE

Twenty-Six

My abuela's house is a tiny three-bedroom bungalow on acres of land. Soon after my parents divorced, my abuelo died on a Sunday afternoon while taking a nap in front of the TV. I don't remember him as well as Claudia does. My great-grandmother, who was still alive at the time, said at the funeral that he left this world much more peacefully than he entered it. And I guess if you're going to die (because we all have to eventually), that's a good way to go.

After he died, though, Abuela couldn't let go of this house she'd spent almost her entire married life in, so rather than forcing her into something she didn't want to do, my dad moved back home to take care of the house and the property—and Abuela too, even if she swears she doesn't need it.

My dad grabs my bag from out of the truck bed, and I follow him inside through the kitchen door on the side of the house.

"She's here!" my dad calls as he walks in.

Abuela pushes past him and proceeds to squeeze my cheeks and then almost every other part of my body that's squeezable. Sometimes I think my abuela's memory is all in her hands, and if she can't touch it, she'll never truly know it. "Please tell me why the hell you haven't called to update me on your life. Everything I hear is secondhand information. Callie broke up with her boyfriend. Callie has a new job. Callie has new friends."

I look up at her. "Because I'm an awful person? And really with the guilt trip?"

Abuela waves me off and then hugs me. "Well, if you've got any awful in you, it's from your grandfather's side of the family."

I chuckle. I think she and my great-grandmother were the original frenemies.

It's easy to just melt into Abuela's embrace. She's a towering woman with broad shoulders and hands so big she can balance a pizza in each of them. Mama calls her the Mexican-American reincarnation of Katharine Hepburn, and it's true. Her deep, lightly accented voice commands attention. Her style is definitely utilitarian while still looking put together and somehow ethereal. And even though her once caramel-colored hair is grayer than it used to be, her shoulder-length natural waves still perfectly frame her long, narrow face.

My dad, though, carries my grandfather's genes, with slightly darker hair and skin and a shorter, stout physique. He's living proof that you don't have to be tall to get the girl. What he's lacking in height he makes up for in game. He's a total flirt. You should see him with the lady at the grocery-store customer service desk. It's pretty amusing until I remember he's my dad.

I look over Abuela's shoulder to see a frying pan of migas, my favorite, and her Texas-shaped waffle maker warming on the counter. Breakfast for dinner is almost as good as dessert for dinner. "Oh my God. Feed me before I waste away."

"That's the plan," she says.

After I get settled in my room, me, my dad, and Abuela all eat at the little table in the kitchen that only seats just the three of us. Abuela has a big, long table out on her screened-in porch off the back of the house, but I like when we eat in here, in her cramped little kitchen. I like the coziness of it. There's just something about being in a small space with people you actually like.

My dad circles the table, holding the skillet with a pot holder, and serves us all generous helpings. There are lots of different ways to serve migas, but Abuela's specialty is the Tex-Mex variety, with blue-corn tortilla chips, eggs, cheese, pico, jalapeños, and ground sausage alongside Texas-shaped waffles.

My abuela pats her mouth with her napkin before answering. "Last weekend, I was down at Aurelia's to help her with research for her latest article about the women of the Alamo. Looks like she's hitting a few dead ends, but . . ." She turns to my father. "She did say her daughter's divorce was finalized last month."

Dad shakes his head and waves a finger in her face.

"Stick to the politics and history, Ma. Matchmaking is definitely not in your wheelhouse." He looks at me. "She tried to set me up with Cindy."

I gag. "Isn't Cindy your second cousin?"

"I forgot!" says Abuela, her hand over her mouth. "Okay? It was an accident!" She waves a forkful of waffle at Dad. "You have to admit, if you weren't related, it would've been a good match."

Abuela hasn't always been just a mother or a grandmother. Up until two years ago, she taught political science and Texas history full-time at University of Texas of the Permian Basin, or UTPB. Now she's dedicating her days to academic publishing with her best friend Aurelia, which is really just a cover for them to try to set their kids up together.

"What are you filling your time with these days?" she asks me. "Now that you're not busy with the dance team."

My shoulders slump, and before I can even say anything, my dad comes to the rescue. "It's a celebratory weekend, Ma. Let's not—"

"Let the girl talk," she says.

"Well, I'm sort of just working for free right now," I say.

She nods. "Well, that won't last forever."

"I'm off the dance team for good." I let out a deep sigh that blows the loose fallen hairs from my ponytail off my face. "I guess I could get a job and start saving for a car."

Dad nods. "I like that idea."

Abuela tsks. "A short-term goal," she says. "What do you want to do?" Her voice overemphasizes every word, and I am easily reminded that she was used to talking to directionless young people every day from her time as a professor.

"I don't know," I finally tell her. "I'm working off my debt at this gym, and . . . and it's like the thing that everyone knew me for is gone."

"That's not entirely true," says Dad. "Your attitude is pretty notorious."

Abuela points her knife at him jokingly.

I think back to the last two months and all that's happened. I feel like a giant onion, and every day I'm peeling back a new layer of myself. Dance team and Bryce defined the old Callie. Bryce is definitely out of the picture, but what about dance? Am I done? For good?

"I don't know," I finally admit as I fill each square of my waffle with butter and syrup. "It's kind of like waking up and not remembering what foods you like. So maybe I just have to try a little bit of everything?"

She pushes a loose strand of hair behind my ear. "Find the things you love and do them every day, even if it means failing. That's all there is to it."

I shrug. "I was good at being on the dance team. What if I'm not good like that at anything else?"

"If you only love what comes easy for you, you'll find you don't have much to love. Work for it, girl."

My dad rolls his eyes. (Maybe that's who I get it from?) "You make it sound so easy, Ma. Life isn't as neat as your little nuggets of wisdom."

She crosses her arms. "Your dad is going to miss my

nuggets of wisdom when I'm not here to give them."

"All right, all right," he says. "Enough with the death guilt. Last week she told me her one dying wish was to see me married again."

"But she's not dying," I tell him.

"We're all dying," says Abuela. "It's just a slow process."

I laugh, and the three of us finish our dinner. We pile the dishes in the sink and leave them until morning, because we're too stuffed to move.

We all crowd together on the couch to FaceTime Claudia.

"My Claudia!" Abuela shouts, as if she can't hear her.

"I can't believe we caught you so late," my dad says.

Claudia's face is lit by the glow of the phone. She yawns without bothering to cover her mouth. "I was just finishing up here, resetting the stage before tomorrow's matinee. Is that Callie?"

I wave. "The one and only."

"Mom give you your phone back yet?" she asks.

"Finally."

"And you didn't call me?" she demands.

"I don't see you rushing into my missed calls either."

She nods. "Fair enough."

"Give us a tour of the opera house," Abuela says.

"I gotta make it quick. I'm one of the last people here, and this place is definitely haunted. I promised Rachel I'd call her before I went to bed."

"When do we get to meet this Rachel?" my dad asks.

"Yeah," I say. "I gotta scope out my sister's first real girlfriend."

Claudia laughs. "Uh, not with that attitude you don't."

She gives us a brief tour of the Semperoper and tells us a little bit of the architectural history, which is a snooze fest, but Dad is eating it up. I'll admit, though, with the ornate gold-gilded interior, elaborate paintings, and velvet seats, she's probably not wrong about this place being haunted.

After we hang up with Claudia, my dad falls asleep almost as soon as he pulls the lever on the recliner. I spread out on the couch with my head in Abuela's lap as we watch a rerun of one of her favorite telenovelas, *Corazón Salvaje*. I can pick up on enough of the dialogue to sort of follow along, but soon enough the three of us are all dozing, and it's a few hours before any of us even bother heading to bed.

I spend the morning and afternoon helping my dad paint the barn he and Abuela use for storage. Abuela tested every shade of turquoise before settling on mint green. When I asked why she wanted to paint her barn mint green, she said because she'd never seen a barn that color before.

While I sit on the ground with her, mixing paint, she says, "It's nice to see you have girlfriends over."

I shrug. "They're okay."

She taps the wooden stick against the side of the canister and sets it down before pouring it into a paint tray. "What's that supposed to mean? I don't speak teenager."

"I don't know. I guess the more I think about it, the more I've realized that I'm not very good at having friends who are girls."

She tsks. "Don't fall into that trap."

"They're nice. I just . . . I'm not."

"Girls don't have to be nice," she says simply. "But they should stick together." She shakes her head. "The wider world wants you to think other women are drama . . . or catty. But that's just because when we work together, we're unstoppable."

"But you have Aurelia. She's, like, your ride or die. I don't have a lifelong BFF like that."

"You will. One day you'll wake up and find that there's a woman, or maybe a few, who have outlasted every changing season in your life."

That evening, everyone arrives in Millie's minivan. I'm almost expecting to see that Willowdean is missing, and Ellen by association, but they prove me wrong when all five of them spill out of the van like it's a clown car. Well, there's no turning back now.

Amanda pours a half-eaten bag of Corn Nuts down her throat, then, with her mouth full, says, "The best road trip food. *Ever.*"

"The drive is barely an hour," I tell her.

She grins, showing off half-chewed bits of food. "Any excuse for Corn Nuts."

Millie turns to me, her cheeks flushed from unloading

bags and pillows, but still buzzing with excitement. "Lead the way!"

Hannah, Amanda, Millie, Willowdean, and Ellen all follow me inside my room, where they leave their stuff on my bed. For a minute there, Willowdean looks like she's walked into the lion's den, until she finds Ellen smiling at her. "I'm not stealing your best friend," I almost say. *Trust me, she doesn't want to be stolen.*

Out on the screened-in porch, Abuela has set up a full spread of chips, homemade salsa, guacamole, and anything else you might want, including warm corn and flour tortillas. The screen door swings shut behind my dad as he carries in a huge flank steak on a bed of peppers and onions to cut into fajitas.

"Ladies' night!" he says.

"Dad." I shake my head.

"Too much?" he asks.

Millie giggles, and so does Ellen.

"Being the cool dad is a lot of work."

I try my best to hold back my smile. "Yeah, it shows." I quickly introduce everyone, and we all take a seat at Abuela's long table.

At first everyone is quiet while we devour the spread. I sit between Millie and Ellen and across from Dad and Abuela.

Millie, with her relentless parental suck-up abilities, says, "Thank you both so much for having us all here tonight and for welcoming us into your home, Mrs. Reyes."

Abuela waves her off. "Callie hasn't brought girlfriends over in years."

Dad nods. "She used to all the time back in grade school. But it's been a while now."

For a moment, a wave of guilt hits me. I would never want them to think I'm embarrassed of them. The truth is, my time here is precious to me. Coming here is like a chance to be a new person without all the Clover City drama back at home. Even if it's just for a weekend.

"Dad would set up tents outside," I say. "For slumber parties. Claudia's friends would get one tent and mine would take another." A big smile creeps across my face. "And I remember, Abuela, you had these amazing tents that felt like mansions."

Abuela's eyes light up with memories. "The property really is wonderful." She sighs. "We're a bit of a fossil hot spot, too. During the summer, kids from town come out here with pails and shovels and go nuts. Especially down by the creek."

"Whoa," says Amanda. "What about, like, dinosaur bones?"

"We think we've found a few. Or at the very least some-one's bones."

Amanda shakes her head, eyes wide. "That's like some *Jurassic Park* stuff. Do you know Jeff Goldblum?"

Abuela chuckles. "No, but that movie got one thing right."

"What's that?" I ask.

She grins. "God created dinosaurs. God destroys

dinosaurs. God creates man. Man destroys God. Man creates dinosaurs. Dinosaurs eat man. Woman inherits the earth."

Everyone bursts into laughter.

Hannah and I both shout "Amen!" in unison.

"That's what I'm talking about!" says Willowdean.

Once the giggles have subsided, Ellen says, "I've never even been camping before."

"You're not missing out," Hannah tells her.

"We should go camping for one of our slumber parties," says Millie.

"I'm really only interested in glamping," says Willowdean. "With, like, electricity and running water."

I roll my eyes. The diva has spoken.

"Why not tonight?" Dad offers.

All of us, caught a bit off guard by his suggestion, are quiet for a minute. On the one hand, bugs and humidity and other gross outdoorsy things. But then . . . Abuela's house is so tiny, and eight people under one roof (and most of them in my room!) is no joke.

"Can we really?" asks Ellen, breaking the silence.

Dad looks to Abuela.

"All my tents are still out there in the barn. I've even got a few lanterns and sleeping mats," she says.

"I don't want to caaaaamp," moans Willowdean.

"Well," says Millie, "it's Callie's birthday, and if she wants to camp, we're camping."

"Come on," I hear Ellen whisper. "It'll be fun."

Amanda hoots and whistles.

"But first," I say, "cake!"

Abuela throws her hands up. "Yes! I'll be right back."

Dad dims the lights when she returns with a beautiful cake decorated with creamy-white whipped frosting and multicolored flowers all over, with sparkler candles that crackle and pop.

"'Happy birthday, Ashley Cheeseburger'?" Ellen asks as she reads the cake from over my shoulders.

"Oh my God." I cover my face with both hands. "Dad, what the hell?"

He laughs. "When Callie was a little girl," my dad says, "she was very upset that she didn't get to name herself, so she demanded that everyone call her Ashley, her name of choice."

"And Cheeseburger?" asks Millie.

Abuela lets out a big belly laugh. "Well, we told her she'd have to pick out a new last name too."

I turn to my dad, waving my hands in the air. "You named me Calista because Mom was an *Ally McBeal* fan. No one even knows that show anymore!"

"Calista Alejandra Reyes," says Abuela.

"So you chose Ashley Cheeseburger?" Hannah shakes her head. "That's amazing."

I shrug. "The other kids in my kindergarten class didn't exactly have an easy time pronouncing Calista, okay?"

"Middle name Puddin'," says my dad. "That was her grandmama's nickname of choice. On her mother's side."

Millie snorts knowingly. "Oh, that's good. Ashley Puddin' Cheeseburger."

"Whatever," I say. "Just sing to me before these candles melt all over the cake."

They all obey my command, but definitely not in unison. "Happy birthday to you! Happy birthday to you! Happy birthday to you, Ashley Cheeseburger!"

"Ha. Ha," I say. But I can't help the smile on my face.

"Happy birthday to you!" they all finish.

"Make a wish!" shouts Amanda.

I pull in a deep breath and blow out every one of my seventeen candles. I don't make a single wish, because I don't believe in them.

Or do I? Because all I do right now is go to school, work for free, and go home, and sometimes my mind wanders to Mitch and what the hell his deal was when he turned me down under the bleachers. So maybe a small, little wish wouldn't hurt. But as I sit here with every one of my candles blown out, I guess it's too late to bother with wishes.

My dad circles around the table and gives me a big hug before smashing something on my head. Confetti streams down over my face, tangling in my hair and sprinkling the ground.

I scream, shrieking with laughter, and touch my fingers to the top of my head to find cracked eggshell. "Dad! You jerk! You're dead, old man!"

Everyone is silent, except Willowdean, who gasps like she's watching the best kind of guilty-pleasure reality TV. (Which is obviously *The Bachelor*, just to be clear.)

Abuela places two egg crates of cascarónes on the table, which are hollowed and dried-out colorfully dyed eggshells full of confetti. "No need to wait for revenge!" she says.

Cascarónes are my favorite Mexican Easter tradition, and since my birthday always falls around Easter, they've become a birthday staple. Plus I dare you to find something more satisfying than cracking an egg over an unsuspecting person's head.

Dad backs away slowly. "Respect your elders," he reminds me, bouncing on his toes.

I grab two eggs and stand, my chair falling over behind me. "No mercy," I tell him, and race around the table. Just like when I was a little girl, he lets me catch him, and I smash a cascarón on either side of his head.

All the girls sit frozen, except for Hannah, who reaches for an egg when no one is looking and crushes it against Amanda's hair.

Amanda gasps and turns to Hannah, who is absolutely gleeful.

Amanda grabs an egg, and Willowdean and Ellen are quick to follow. I get Millie, and Abuela even cracks one down the back of my shirt.

It's like a water-balloon fight, though, and while it's furious, the cascarónes are gone in a matter of minutes.

We all collapse into our chairs, the carton of eggs sitting empty and stray confetti littering the table and the floor.

"How about some of that cake?" asks Willowdean, a little breathlessly.

"Save me a piece," says Dad. "I'm gonna take the four-wheeler out to the barn to scare up some camping supplies for y'all."

I hold up the knife. "Dibs on a corner piece."

After we eat cake, our hair full of confetti, and help clean up the mess we made, we all spray ourselves down with bug spray as Abuela pulls out her big torches to give us some "mood lighting," she says.

Setting up the tents is lots of trial and error, and by the time both tents are put together, all of our bedding is set up, and we're all changed and ready for our night in the wilderness, it's half past midnight.

The six of us lie out on a huge blanket for a bit and watch the stars while Dad and Abuela go inside and get ready for bed.

"Oh my gosh, Callie!" says Millie, shaking my shoulder. "I think that's a shooting star."

Willowdean props herself up on her elbows. "I don't know. That might just be a tiny plane."

"For the first time in my life, I actually agree with you," I say.

Millie nudges me in the ribs. "You should make a wish just in case."

I look up to the flickering light in the sky and I am 99.9 percent sure that Willowdean is right, but on the off 0.10 percent chance that she's not, I suspend my disbelief in wishes and close my eyes.

I wish to feel like this all the time. That I've found my place, and that my place isn't just a geographical coordinate, but a living, breathing thing that I carry inside of me. That is my 0.10 percent wish.

I open my eyes. "Done," I say. "Just in case."

Slowly everyone slips into their tents—Willowdean, Ellen, and Hannah in one, and the rest of us in the other—until it's just me, Amanda, and Millie lying on the blanket outside. Except Amanda is definitely asleep, and when she's not asleep, she's fighting to stay awake.

"Amanda, you should lie down inside the tent," says Millie.

"I'm awake, okay?" Amanda says, her lips barely moving. "Let me live."

Millie shrugs. "So, Ashley Cheeseburger," she says. "How does it feel to be officially seventeen years old?"

"Huh. It's after midnight, so I guess it feels pretty much the same as sixteen felt yesterday."

"But you can see R-rated movies now," Amanda chimes in sluggishly.

Millie nods. "Good point." She turns to me. "Your grandma is super stinking cool, by the way."

"She really is." I cross my arms behind my head. "I'm weirdly jealous of her. Like, I want to be that put together and know what the hell I'm doing with my life."

"Callie, you've got lots of time."

"I mean, I guess so," I say. "What if I die tomorrow? My tombstone will just read, 'She was kicked off the dance team, but at least they went to Nationals.' I just feel like there's all this pressure to suddenly know what I'm going to do now that I'm not a Shamrock. And honestly, I just don't know. Maybe I don't want to go to college. Or maybe I do, but I want to go to school in, like, Spain. Or hell, maybe I want to be a truck driver or—"

Millie laughs. "Don't you get it?"

"What?"

"It doesn't have to be pressure to find something new or be someone else all of a sudden. Maybe you do decide to go back to dance. You don't need a team to dance. Or maybe you want to be an engineer or work at a makeup counter. It doesn't matter. I know getting kicked off the Shamrocks stunk, but it doesn't have to be this dark cloud forever. It can be a chance to find out who you really want to be."

I'm quiet for a moment as all that sinks in. The only sound between us is a chorus of crickets and Amanda's light snores. "That makes sense. It does. But I just want to know who I'm going to be so I can start being that person."

"Even the wrong direction sometimes feels better than no direction at all."

"Yes!" I say. "That. Exactly that."

Millie half smiles. "But that doesn't make it right. Sometimes the best things are worth waiting for. Don't be scared to take your time."

Something about what she's said rings true, but it still puts my stomach in knots. Part of me doesn't care who I am or what I'm doing as long as I'm at the top, but maybe that's not how it has to be.

"It kind of reminds me of fat camp out here, and how quiet it was at night," says Millie, interrupting my thoughts.

"Well, I guess that means you'll have to come camping here again, since fat camp is a thing of the past." For the first time, saying the word fat doesn't make me feel anything. It's just a word. It doesn't make me feel like I'm holding it over someone as a way to make fun of them or like I'm being rude.

Millie smiles. "Yeah." It comes out like a sigh. "I'd like that."

"Hey, did you ever send in your application for journalism camp?" I ask.

"Just putting the finishing touches on my application. I made my audition video, too."

"Shut up! I want to see." As soon as the words are out of my mouth, I regret it a little bit. I've never been great at hiding my feelings and I might be a jerk, but I don't want to hurt Millie.

She checks behind us to make sure everyone is asleep, Amanda included. "Okay, but you can't laugh. The only other person who's seen it is Malik, because he's the one who helped me cut the whole thing together."

We both sit up, and she pulls her cell phone out of the pocket of her lavender hoodie and scrolls through an album until she lands on a video.

I take the phone from her and hit play. I watch Millie, in a sharp blue suit, sitting behind a news desk. Her curls are a little too tight, and at first, she's giving me deer-in-headlight vibes. But I think that's just because I know everyday Millie. She delivers stories about our school and there are even fancy graphics. And she actually has some great jokes—better than our local weatherman, who dons a yellow raincoat and cranks up a wind machine anytime storms are in his forecast. I would even go so far as to say she's charming. Her puns are cute and perfectly timed. And her lipstick! I know that lipstick.

The video cuts to a few shots where Millie is reporting "live," and then it's over, with short credits naming her and Malik.

I hand the phone back to her, and she waits in silence for my response.

"You. Were. Born. For. This," I finally say, and to my horror, I hear my voice crack. God. When did I turn into such a feelsy loser?

"Oh my gosh," says Millie, touching my leg. "Are you okay?"

I nod and laugh, tilting my head back like that might somehow keep the tears inside. "I'm great. I don't know. Or maybe I'm not." Dabbing my eyes, I look to her. "You were amazing, though. Like, if they don't accept you, they have shit for brains. I mean, how are you so good at that? I feel like I'd be a total mess on camera."

"Well," she says. "I don't know that I'm all that great, but I want to be better, which is why I *need* to get into this journalism camp. Because I want to be unstoppable. I want there to be no reason for people to say no to me. I want to be so perfect that if they're going to say no to me because of this"—she motions down to her body—"then they'll have to say so out loud to my face."

"Wow." I gasp. When did the tables turn? My life is in shambles, and Millie Michalchuk has her shit together. Like, really together. Or maybe I was always a wreck. "And your lipstick!"

"Revlon Certainly Red 740. Thanks to your mom."

"I swear that lipstick is magic."

"Something about it just made me feel . . . powerful. I didn't know something as silly as red lips could make me feel like that."

"That's what it was," I say. "You looked like you were in charge. Like you were calling the shots."

"You wanna know what being friends with all those girls has taught me?" She motions with her chin back to the tents.

"What?" I ask.

"Sometimes you have to fake it till you make it. If I want to call the shots, I have to start acting like it. And when that camera turns on, it's like someone flips a switch inside me and gives me permission to be the version of myself I only dream of."

We both lie back again.

"So," I say, "according to you, if I want people to treat me like a lobster, I have to act like a lobster?"

"No." She laughs. "But yeah, in a way. Yeah."

I think about that for a while. Acting like a queen bee definitely bumped me up the social ladder, but now it's more obvious than ever to me that I was a total sham.

So maybe after all this time faking it, I should think carefully about the person I want to be. Maybe between that and my 0.10 percent wish, there's hope for the future of Callie Reyes yet.

MILLIE

Twenty-Seven

After school on Tuesday, Callie and I make a brief stop at the post office before heading to Sonic and work.

I slide the gear into park just outside the front door and fish my large manila envelope from my backpack. I've addressed the envelope with my teal glitter marker and decided to use the limited-edition Harry Potter stamps I was saving for a special occasion.

"Nice stamps," says Callie.

"You don't have to make fun of me."

She laughs. "No, really, I mean it. I especially like the Luna Lovegood one. In fact, if Neville Longbottom and Luna Lovegood had a baby, it'd be you."

I squint. "I'm not sure you mean that as a compliment, but I'm going to take that as one, because Luna and Neville forever."

"Totally a compliment," she assures me.

"Maybe if I just pretend this letter is going to Hogwarts, I'll be able to muster up the courage to walk inside and mail the dang thing." Something about mailing this in real life feels irreversible.

Callie grips my leg. "Hey," she says, her voice no louder than a whisper. "You've already done the hard part. You wrote the essay. You did the video. Shit, Millie, you've even submitted it online. All you have to do is walk in there and mail the damn thing." She quickly adds, "And then break it to your mom."

I glance over to her. "Well, suddenly this isn't the hardest thing I have to do today."

"Didn't you need her signature for the application?" she asks.

"You could say I have a habit of forging my mother's signature. It's more of a vice, really."

"Millicent Michalchuk!" she howls. "That is the most badass thing to come out of your mouth ever."

"We've all got a rotten streak," I say as I open the door with the envelope held tight to my chest.

I march inside and hand the envelope to Lucius, who's worked behind the counter here since my mother was a little girl. "I'd like a receipt upon arrival, please."

"Yes, ma'am," he tells me.

He rings me up for the cost of certified mail and then he takes it away from me and that's pretty much it. Goodbye, Daisy Ranch. Hello, University of Texas Broadcast Journalism Boot Camp.

Callie and I rush into work, and Inga squints at the two of us, preparing to scold, but then I say, "I'm so, so sorry. It's my fault we're late."

Inga nods. "Your check is in the office."

"Getting paid?" mumbles Callie. "What does that feel like?"

I nudge her with my elbow. "Thanks, Inga. Kiss Luka and Nikolai for me."

"They're monsters," she says as she gathers her keys and things. "Little hairless monsters who just eat and poop. Eat and poop. I tell your uncle every day that if men could have babies, we'd be making people in labs instead of bellies."

Callie nods her head. "Yeah, and if they had to deal with periods, you better believe tampons would be free."

Inga nods toward Callie. "She gets it."

Callie keeps a straight face, but I can tell that Inga's slight approval has not gone unnoticed.

After I grab my check, Callie and I settle in behind the counter to see what's left of the daily checklist.

Callie gasps.

I look up just in time to see Mitch pull the front door open. He's not wearing workout clothes and he hasn't got a gym bag with him.

"Uh, hey," he says.

"Hi," Callie and I say in unison.

I shrink back a little when I feel Callie tense up beside me.

Callie holds out the sign-in clipboard. "You can go ahead and sign in."

Mitch clears his throat. "I'm, um, actually not here to work out today."

"Okay," says Callie.

Mitch nervously pops his knuckles until they won't pop anymore.

I so desperately want to jump in and mediate the situation, but I do everything in my power to restrain myself.

"Could we maybe talk?" he asks.

"Totally!" I say.

They both look to me with raised brows.

I grin sheepishly.

Mitch turns back to Callie. "Maybe in private?"

That's my cue. "I have so much to do," I say, taking the checklist. Trying my best not to sound awkward, I turn to Callie and add, "Callie, could you watch the front desk while I work on my super-long to-do list?"

Her eyes are wide with panic, and her cheeks are turning pink, but she says, "Uh, yeah. You go do that."

I skip around the gym, trying to make myself look busy. I don't purposely eavesdrop, but it's not like this place is very big.

After a while, I hear Mitch say, "What about Saturday?"

"Saturdays aren't good," says Callie.

"Saturday's good!" I say before I can stop myself.

Callie twirls around to find me cleaning the mirrors above the hand weights. Our gazes meet in the reflection of the mirror. "I thought we had our thing," she says through gritted teeth. "You know, our *thing*."

I turn around and shrug. "It's Easter Sunday weekend, so we're skipping this weekend. Plus Hannah says Courtney is demanding a Saturday date night."

"Sure, let me just plan my life around Hannah's girl-friend," she mumbles.

I smile and shrug.

She whirls around and throws her hands up a little but quickly lets them drop to her sides. "Okay then," she says to Mitch. "I'm still grounded, so I'll have to check with my mom, but maybe Saturday."

Mitch's rosy cheeks flare. "Maybe Saturday."

Callie nods. "Maybe. But probably not. You should know I am definitely a glass-half-empty kind of person."

Mitch thinks on that for a minute. "So it's a glass-half-empty maybe then?" He holds his hand out awkwardly, like he means to shake Callie's hand, but then just fist bumps her before leaving.

I wait for the door to shut entirely before I loudly say, "Is that a date?"

When Callie turns around, I expect to find her normally grumpy something-smells-bad expression, but it's clear she's brimming with excitement despite how hard she's trying to keep a lid on it. "Maybe," she says. "It's a maybe date. Glass half empty, maybe."

I rush to her and she meets me halfway, our hands clasped, as we squeal at approximately the same level of sound as a dog whistle.

After work and dropping off Callie, I sit in the driveway at home for a minute to check my text messages.

MALIK: Did you send your application in?

MILLIE: I did! Your directorial debut!

MALIK: Well, that calls for a celebration. Friday night?

MILLIE: It's a date.

A tidal wave of excitement hits my stomach. A date! Not only does Callie have a date this weekend, but now so do I. What can I say? Love is in the air.

Inside, I find both my parents getting ready for dinner. *Now*, I think. This is the perfect time to tell them. With Dad here to ease the blow.

My mom spins around the kitchen island just as my dad plants a big, wet kiss on her cheek. "Your father brought home brisket, mac and cheese, green beans, dinner rolls, and peach cobbler from Melba B's Barbecue, so I guess it's cheat night for everyone." She hums "Go Tell It on the Mountain" to herself as she runs back to the kitchen for a few serving spoons.

Melba B's is my mother's favorite—food so good she hums!—and if it's up to her, it would undoubtedly be her last meal, but she so rarely eats it and my dad is usually the only person who can convince her otherwise.

A low sigh slips from me.

I can't tell her I'm not going back to Daisy Ranch. Not right now. I won't ruin this perfect night for her.

On Friday night, Malik picks me up for our date. Well, if you ask my parents, it's a study date, and Malik is picking me up so we can go to Amanda's, but that's because I'm not sure what their opinion on dating is. If I had to guess, they'd prefer I just didn't.

After much deliberation, I settled on a mint-green

cotton dress with little daisy buttons sewn all around the collar—my own personal touch, obviously—and a pair of yellow flats.

When I get into his car, Malik hands me a fresh pair of socks. "You'll need these," he tells me.

"What are these for?" I ask. "Are we going bowling?"

His lips twitch for a second, like he's second-guessing himself. "Would it be a problem if we were?"

I shake my head. "Only if you don't mind getting beat by a girl."

"Oh, so you're a smack talker?" he asks. "Well—" His ringtone interrupts him. He glances down at his phone, resting in the cup holder. "I better get this," he says as he pulls over to the side of a residential street.

"Hello?" asks Malik into the receiver.

I listen carefully, but I can't make out the voice on the other end, so all I've got to work with is his one-sided conversation.

"Well, has he tried taking any medicine? . . . He just has to sit in a dark room and change out the reels. It can't be that hard. . . . He's sure he can't? . . . Fine. Okay. Give me twenty minutes."

Malik hangs up the phone and turns to me.

"Is everything okay?" I ask.

"Yes. No," he says. "I have to cancel tonight."

"Oh." I try to hide my disappointment, but it's no use.

"It's just there are only three of us at work who know how to change out the film reels in the projector rooms, and normally it wouldn't matter, but one guy is visiting his internet girlfriend in New Mexico and the other guy is hung over. Or maybe he's still drunk. I'm not sure."

Malik works at the only movie theater in town, the Lone Star 4, if you're not counting the drive-in. It's one of the oldest buildings in town, too, so I guess it should be no surprise that it's not equipped to play films digitally either. It's a bummer not to go bowling, but I hate even more that our night has to end before it's even begun. And then it hits me. "What if I go to work with you? Like, as your assistant."

"You don't want to do that," he tells me. "You'll be so bored."

"Not as long as we're hanging out."

He blushes. "I guess there is unlimited popcorn in it for you."

"Throw in some Milk Duds, and we have a deal," I say.

"Done." He holds his hand out for me to shake.

Malik parks around the back of the movie theater, near the employee entrance, and we trot up a dark, narrow staircase just inside the door.

I have been to this theater countless times, with its old, dusty Art Deco lobby and plush royal-blue seats, but a few years back, the drive-in on the edge of town reopened, and this place just isn't quite as busy as it used to be.

"Okay," says Malik. "It looks like Cameron got all the shows going, so I've just got to be here to change out the reels and do the late shows. Are you sure you don't mind?"

"Not even a little bit," I tell him.

"Let's get those Milk Duds I promised you."

I follow him through a tiny office and onto an even tinier elevator that drops us right into the lobby, which smells like butter and years of soda syrup soaked into the gold, red, and blue carpet.

"There's no one here," I say.

"Everyone's in their movies," he tells me. "The calm between the storms."

"Trust me," says a petite, older black woman behind the counter. "This place turns into a war zone in between shows. And you don't even want to know what the floors of those theaters look like when we bring up the house-lights." She wears black slacks, a white button-up, a blue satin vest, and a bow tie made to look like the Texas flag.

"Cynthia," says Malik, taking my hand, "this is—"

"Millie!" she finishes for him. "Darling, he has been singing your song for months now."

A sharp gasp that comes out more like a laugh tumbles from me and echoes through the lobby. "Months, huh?"

Malik bites down on his lips until they disappear and his cheeks melt into a deep shade of pink. "Cynthia is my coworker."

"And friend," she adds.

He turns to me. "And general sentence finisher."

Malik fills a large tub full of popcorn, pours us each a soda, and retrieves my Milk Duds from the glass case. I know this isn't how our date was supposed to go and that this is just concession food, but something about this feels decadent. My mom never buys movie theater snacks. Instead, she sneaks in bags of sliced apples or, if she's splurging, a SlimFast cookie-dough bar.

We take the elevator back upstairs and settle onto a small couch in one of the projector rooms.

"So should I be worried about you and Cynthia?" I ask as the ninth movie in an action-adventure car-chase franchise plays in the background behind us.

He cracks a smile. "I guess we're not two people who you would expect to be friends, but you try spending half your summer here and not bonding with the closest set of lungs you can find." He shoves a handful of popcorn in his mouth and washes it down with a swig of Dr Pepper. "But I'd like to think that me and Cynthia would've found a way to be friends even if I didn't work here."

"Is she married?" I ask. "Any kids?"

"Two kids. A daughter in Houston and a son in Fort Worth. She took a job here after her husband passed away."

I don't know if this makes me feel better or worse. Knowing that she has people and is alone anyway. "Why does she stay here then? She could go be with one of her kids. And I'm pretty sure they have way better movie theaters in Houston and Fort Worth. No offense."

"Oh, I'm offended," he says. "Experiencing a film on thirty-five millimeter is the purest movie-watching experience there is. Even if it means sitting in our broken seats and your feet getting stuck to the floor. But actually, Cynthia and her husband went on their first date here, so she's kind of serious about keeping this place up and running."

That's so sweet," I say. "But I had no idea you were such a hipster snob about your movie-watching preferences."

"If we lived in a big city, I'd be a total hipster snob, but out here, I'm just the weird kid who works at the movie theater and is boring enough to be trusted with keys to the school."

I take a few pieces of popcorn and toss them in my mouth with a Milk Dud, because I'm an enlightened genius. "I don't think you're boring. Heck, I didn't even know you were this into film stuff."

"I wasn't always, but working here and watching old Westerns with my dad has kind of had an effect on me."

"I for sure thought you wanted to be a politician."

He sets his drink down on the floor by his feet and rotates his whole body toward me. "I did. I do." He shakes his head. "Maybe I still will be." He holds his lips in a firm line for a moment. "I always wanted to change the world. I know that's so corny. Of course everyone wants to change the world."

I place my hand on top of his. "No," I say, my voice dead serious. "Not everyone wants to change the world."

"I just always thought the only way I could do that was by being a senator or a mayor or something like that, but there's something about movies and stories. I want to help change the rules, you know? To help make everything more fair. But no one cares about evening the playing field or changing the rules unless they have some kind of connection. I guess . . . well, that's what stories do. They connect people. Stories change hearts and then hearts change the world."

I didn't think I could fall harder. But I am. I know that

lots of folks look at people like me and Malik and think we're just silly idealists who want more than we have any right to have. But let them think that. "I bet you can have it both," I tell him. "I bet you can change the rules and the hearts."

He leans toward me and our lips brush—just as the credits in the theater begin to roll. "All I'm changing tonight," he says, "are these film reels."

My heart hiccups. And then I begin to hiccup.

"Are you okay?" he asks, holding back a laugh.

I nod, only a little mortified. "Too much fizzy soda."

He takes my hand and pulls me up. I follow him to each of the projector rooms and watch as he carefully changes the film for the 9:00, 9:10, 9:20, and 9:30 showings, which is right about when my hiccups die down.

We hang out for a bit in each room and catch a glimpse of each movie: action adventure with street racing, a cartoon about cats, a World War II romance, and a slasher movie about a cheerleading summer camp.

At the end of the night, Cynthia closes up the concessions and the ticket counter while Malik and I sweep up the four theaters.

"I'm sorry this didn't turn out exactly as planned," he tells me.

"Hey, at least I got a free pair of socks out of the whole thing."

"And Milk Duds," he reminds me.

Cynthia pops her head into theater four. "I'm all done up here," she says.

"You head on out," Malik tells her. "Just lock up the front and we'll leave out the back door."

"You got it," she says before turning to me. "Millie, it was a pleasure."

Once she's gone, Malik asks, "Do you have to be home soon?"

I glance down at my phone to find a text from my mom asking how much longer I'll be. I shoot off a quick response to tell her we're studying late at Amanda's. That should buy me a few hours. "Nope, I'm good!"

"What's your favorite kind of movie?"

"Promise not to laugh?" I ask.

"That depends."

I clap my hands over my face. "Romantic comedies."

Between my fingers, I watch as he leans the broom against a chair and takes a step toward me. One finger at a time, he pulls my hands from my face. "Romantic comedies," he says, "are entirely underrated. "

"Right?" I feel my whole face lighting up. "It's like, just because they're marketed toward women and end with a happily ever after, they're somehow silly or frivolous."

"I'm always game for a good HEA."

I sigh. He even knows the lingo.

"Stay right here," he says. "Pick any seat you want."

As he races up the aisle, I settle on a row in the middle of the theater and even choose the exact middle. I squeeze my hips past the armrests of the tiny old seat. I'm not squished exactly, but I just barely fit. A gold star-shaped plaque on the wooden armrest reads 13P, and the one next to me reads 13Q. It's such a small detail, but I want to remember these two seat numbers forever. I think about Cynthia and her husband, and I wonder which seats they sat in on their first date.

The houselights dim, and it's actually a little spooky in here by myself. And then the screen comes to life with intro studio music playing. Malik runs back down the aisle and flops down into 13Q.

"Which movie did you pick?" I whisper. I feel immediately silly, because it's just us and I can talk as loud as I want.

"Well, I almost chose my favorite," he says, "which is *The Princess Bride*, which we keep on hand for annual anniversary showings, but then I figured maybe we should watch one I hadn't seen. So we could expand my education."

"Next time we have to watch your favorite," I tell him.

"In which category? Sci-fi? Horror? Suspense? Bollywood? Comedy?"

"You're into Bollywood?" I ask. I've only seen a few on TV, but to say I like what I've seen would be an understatement.

"Strictly the classics," he says. "I don't do remakes."

And then the opening scene starts before I can ask for more details. We see the back of Drew Barrymore's head as the camera pans down to reveal she's standing on a baseball mound as she narrates. "You know how in some movies they have a dream sequence, only they don't tell you it's a dream? This is so not a dream."

"Oh my gosh!" I squeal. "*Never Been Kissed*! Drew Barrymore plays a journalist—well, technically a copy editor—who goes undercover at her former high school. You're going to love it."

"We'll see," he says. "I'm kind of annoying to watch movies with. At least according to my sister. She says I find a flaw in everything. But we had this one on hand for a Drew Barrymore marathon."

"Just watch," I tell him.

We've held hands. We've kissed. And still my stomach is spinning in circles when I hold my hand palm up on the armrest—the universal sign to oh-my-gosh-please-hold-my-hand-already!

It takes as long as it takes Drew Barrymore to show up to school with her fresh makeover in her outlandish white fur outfit before Malik's hand inches closer to mine and our fingers finally intertwine.

We sit there and watch the movie—the whole thing. I quote along to a few lines before I can catch myself, and I don't even get up to pee because I'm scared I'll somehow ruin this moment and it won't be the same when I return.

After the credits roll, I let out a big, unstoppable yawn.

"Just one last thing," Malik says. "I just have to show you one more thing before you turn into a pumpkin."

I yawn again, but I nod. "Okay."

He takes me back through the employee staircase we initially went up, and then he leads me to an even narrower staircase. Before he opens the heavy metal door, he reaches for a brick sitting on top of the doorframe.

He grunts as he opens the heavy door and holds it for me as I step out onto the rooftop. Carefully he wedges the brick in place to stop the door from swinging shut.

"The best view in Clover City," he says.

I take a few steps closer to the edge of the roof where the LONE STAR THEATER letters stick up over the roofline. A few of the letters have little birds' nests inside and a couple of the lights need replacing.

But he's right. The view is amazing. At this hour, only a few buildings are still lit up, but you can still see all the way to the edge of town, and then it's like the rest of the world is just swallowed up in darkness. Like this little town exists on a planet all by itself.

Malik pulls over two old office chairs. "Cameron and the other guys take their smoke breaks up here," he explains.

The two of us sit down, and for a few minutes we just live here in this moment without a word between us.

Finally I break the silence. "How is it I've lived here all my life and I'm just now seeing this view of Clover City?"

A soft smile plays at Malik's lips. "You think you know a place," he says. "You think you've got it all figured out, but it's like with camerawork. You just adjust your position, even slightly, and suddenly you're telling a different story. Seeing a new world."

And funny as it may be, this reminds me of Callie. I thought I knew just the kind of person someone like her was. I thought I had her pegged. Pretty girl, dance-team assistant captain, dream boyfriend, and just sharp enough to intimidate you. But that was only the story of herself she wanted me to see and not the Callie I've come to know.

"Perspective," I say. "Perspective is everything." I want to stay here forever, but I can't stop myself from yawning again. I glance down at my phone to see that it's well past two in the morning.

"I better get you home." Malik stands up and offers me his hand.

"Only if you promise not to be greedy with this view." I take his hand and stand.

"We can't tell too many people," he says. "Can't have everybody trying to steal our spot."

My mouth goes a little dry. I've been waiting for another chance to kiss, ever since we were interrupted by the movie coming to an end earlier. We haven't kissed, like really kissed, since we filmed my audition tape. I thought kissing him again would get easier, but try telling my nerves that.

If Malik's nervous, it doesn't show. His head tilts to the side as he pulls me closer to him, holding me tight. It's way too warm out to have this many goose bumps, but my body defies science as Malik's lips meet mine. I almost forget to breathe through my nose as he deepens the kiss and combs his fingers through my hair.

I can have it all. I decide in that moment. Everything I want can be had.

CALLIE

Twenty-Eight

When Mitch came by the gym to talk to me, I was completely caught off guard. After Millie left me totally stranded with him—I gotta teach that girl how to be a proper wing woman—Mitch blurted, "I'm sorry about acting so weird at the pep rally."

I nodded. "It is what it is." Instinct told me to play it cool, but somehow I didn't think Mitch was the kind of guy to respond to playing it cool.

"Listen," he said, "I'd really appreciate it if you gave me another chance."

And that was about the time Millie piped in, stealing away whatever shot I had left at playing it cool.

So I'm giving him a chance. Partly because what the hell else do I have to lose? And also not many people outside of Millie and her friends are clamoring to hang out with me. And there's something about the boy that makes me want to get to know him better.

The real obstacle now is getting my mom to agree to lifting my grounding enough to let me hang out with a member of the opposite sex.

I decide the best time to strike is Saturday morning. I wake to a flurry of text messages from Millie. She included me in a group text with Amanda in the middle of the night.

MILLIE: If everything is horrible every day for the rest of my life, just remind me that this night in April was perfect.

MILLIE: Is it silly to think that you can find true love in high school?

MILLIE: Have y'all ever thought about how weird it is that birds are just little feathery dinosaurs?

MILLIE: Okay, that last text wasn't relevant. But I think I'm in love. Real love.

MILLIE: happily ever after romantic comedy love #HEA

ME: What's HEA?

MILLIE: HELLO?? Happily ever after!

I laugh to myself. So I guess it's safe to say her date with Malik was a success. I don't get how she just *feels* everything so hard. That must require some serious energy.

I can smell my mom's omelets from where I sit upstairs in bed. My door creaks open, and Kyla pokes her head in and then shouts down the stairs, "She's awake! Can we eat already?"

I push myself out of bed. "You didn't have to wait for me," I tell her, yanking on her ponytail as I jog past her and down the stairs.

"Mom said so. She said to let you sleep in."

That makes me perk up. Maybe it will be the perfect morning to ask for a reprieve. Maybe I do deserve to sleep in and even go on a date.

Downstairs, I find my mom setting the table while my

sister examines each omelet to be sure she gets the best one.

"Keith had to run into work for a bit," says Mom. "So it's just us girls."

The three of us sit down, and my mom pours two glasses of orange juice, for herself and me, while Kyla demands to pour her own. I think this is the first time we've all sat together for a meal in weeks. Mom's always busy with work and running Kyla to dance class and soccer, and Keith has been picking up extra shifts to save for the vacation he and my mom have talked about taking us all on for years now.

"I don't want to take dance classes anymore," announces Kyla with her mouth full of egg and cheese.

"Excuse me?" asks Mama. "Swallow your food and try again."

Kyla takes a sip of orange juice and then sits up on her knees, so that she's at eye level with both of us. "I want to quit dance."

I slink back a little. This is definitely my fault. "You'll regret it, Kyla bear," I tell her.

"And just what brought this on?" Mama asks. I can hear it in her voice, the way she's trying not to overreact. But truthfully, Mama is a dance mom. She even has the bumper stickers to prove it.

Kyla shrugs, oblivious to the tension mounting around her. "Callie doesn't dance anymore."

Great. One more thing for Mama to blame me for.

"Well, I wouldn't exactly say she quit of her own volition," Mama reminds her.

"Well, it's not like that was my choice," I remind her.

Kyla looks to me. "Well, you don't seem to miss it very much."

I shake my head. The kid misses nothing.

"Well," says Mama, "after the spring recital we'll look at taking some time off of dance. But you've already made a commitment, and we always follow through on a commitment. Don't we?"

"Only 'cause you make us," says Kyla.

Mama stares her down into submission.

Kyla huffs. "Okay." After a few more bites, she hops down from her chair and announces that she has television to catch up on.

"Don't watch *Tiny House Hunters* without me!" I call.

"Put your plate in the sink," Mama tells her.

With Kyla in the living room and the TV turned up a little too loud, I watch as my mom scrapes her fork around her plate, not really eating anything.

"I'll talk to Kyla," I tell her.

She doesn't look up. "I think you've done enough damage."

That stings. I pull in a deep breath. "You can't be mad at me forever."

"No," she says, "but I can be disappointed in you for an awfully long time."

I slump back in my chair. Why can't we just have a conversation without her slinging guilt on me from every direction?

She's in a shit mood, but this is the only chance I've got.

"A friend of mine wanted to hang out."

"Is it that sweet little thing Millie? She's welcome here anytime."

I clear my throat. "It's a boy."

"Oh Lord."

I put the orange juice away and try to sound as casual as I can. "It's not even a real date, Mama. We just wanted to hang out."

"What's his name?" she asks.

"Mitch Lewis."

She pauses for a moment with her arms elbow-deep in the suds-filled sink. I can see her flipping through the mental files of every student she's had an interaction with. "That big ol' boy with the cheeks?" She looks at me. "He is very sweet . . . and not someone I ever thought I'd see you spending time with."

I decide not to take that as an insult. "I'm full of surprises these days."

"That you are." Mama takes her time as she weighs her options. "Okay," she finally says. "Y'all can hang out here tonight. At the house."

"But—" I stop myself. "Yes, ma'am."

Mitch arrives at seven thirty on the dot. The doorbell rings, and Kyla races from the kitchen, where she's dyeing eggs with my mom and Keith. She peeks through the window beside the door and shouts, "He's here! He's here! He's here!"

"I heard you the first time!" I yell down from my room.

"I'm sure he did too!" I give myself one last glance in the mirror hanging on the back of my door. I haven't honestly tried to look this decent in weeks, but with Mitch coming over to my house I didn't want to look like I tried too hard, so I kept it simple with a pair of denim shorts and a fitted gray T-shirt with the outline of Texas across the front. I curled my hair and painted my fingers and toes the shade of red my mother swears was made to match her lipstick perfectly.

I run down the stairs, but Keith beats me to the door. He turns to me. "You girls and your mother only let me answer the door when it's a steak salesperson or a Jehovah's Witness. My turn." He swings the door open. "Well, aren't you a big fella," says Keith.

"Keith!" I smack his arm and push him out of the way.

Mitch takes off his sweat-stained baseball cap and shoves it in the back pocket of his khaki shorts. "Mitch Lewis, sir."

"You're a Lewis boy," says Keith. "Theresa," he calls over his shoulder, "didn't we go to high school with a Lewis?"

Mom steps out from the kitchen in a food-coloring-stained apron. "You know, I think your father was a few years ahead of us," she says.

"Class of eighty-nine, ma'am."

"Hey," I say, interrupting their trip down memory lane.

Mitch grins. "Thank y'all for having me over tonight. My mama sent over some of her cranberry-orange muffins for Easter morning or just whenever a craving hits ya, I guess."

Mama clicks her tongue. "Well, that is the sweetest dang thing ever. You come on in. We just ordered some pizza and are dyeing eggs, but I'm sure y'all would rather—"

Kyla takes Mitch's hand. "You should dye eggs with us. Will you, please?"

Mitch's broad shoulders cave in a little and he says, "Sure."

I groan. Wrong answer.

"Actually," Mama says, "why don't y'all go for a walk or something? Pizza won't be here for a little while."

I squint at her, trying to figure out if this is some kind of trick question.

"Go on," she says. "Y'all get outta here before I change my mind."

Keith raises his brows, and his whole expression tells me he's just as surprised as I am.

I shove my feet into my boots and throw on the sweatshirt I left hanging on the railing.

Outside the dusky sky is nearly dark enough to be nighttime, but daylight still burns at the edge of the horizon, which is only visible because everything around here is so damn flat.

"It was cool of your mom to let me come over," says Mitch, once we're a safe distance away from my house.

"It would have been even cooler if she would have let me go out."

"Haven't you already been everywhere in this town?" he asks.

"Well, sure," I say, "but isn't the whole point of a date so you can show me some magical hidden gem of Clover City that I've never seen?"

"Would it be horrible of me to say that maybe you're the hidden gem of Clover City?"

"Very cheesy," I tell him, but I look away and do that thing where you stretch your jaw out to stop from smiling.

"Well, then I won't say that." He bites down on his lips until they disappear.

"Okay, good," I say. "I mean, at the very least, we could have made out in the back of your car."

He clears his throat, and his cheeks turn so red they're practically purple. "I . . . uh . . . that's not why I asked you out. Of course it's not like I don't want to do that. It's just that . . . it's not . . . I don't think you're some kind of—"

I laugh a little too hard and touch his arm. I can almost feel his heart beating right there in his bicep. "Hey, I was just messing with you. Chill."

He lets out what appears to be a long-held breath.

We reach the end of my street and I lead us toward the aging man-made water feature at the center of my subdivision that's supposed to be a lake with tons of fountains, but the fountains haven't been turned on in years.

A few ducks splash around in the water and then chase each other onto land and then back into the water.

"You wanna sit here for a bit?" asks Mitch.

"Sure. My ankle monitor electrocutes me if I go any farther."

"A joke," he says. "I got that one."

I cock my head to the side and nearly tell him he's kind of cute, but I fear it might send him into a frenzy all over again.

He takes off his letter jacket and lays it on the grass for us both to sit on. "You don't have to do that," I tell him.

"I don't have much use for the thing anymore," he says. "I finally quit the football team."

"Wow. Really? But you only have one year left. I mean, you could probably not even go to college and just be like a spokesperson for one of Bryce's dad's car dealerships for the rest of your life. Is that why I haven't seen you at the gym much?"

"Partly." He pauses for a moment. "But that wasn't the only reason."

"I don't do well with coy," I tell him.

"Well, I quit the team. And then things were weird with us."

"Which was your doing," I tell him. "And what was that about anyway?"

"I don't want to make you mad," he says.

"Oh, don't worry about that." I laugh. "I'm always a little mad about something."

He clears his throat. "I had a sort of falling-out with Patrick and all those guys. They were planning some awful hazing prank for the incoming freshmen at spring training. It wasn't right. I've known for a long time that I didn't like the kind of people they'd become and the way they treated others, ya know? It's embarrassing how long it took me to act on that, though. Like, I've been over their bullshit for a long time, but I just played along, because I was scared of not having friends. Not having a place to sit or whatever. And then you told me to start looking for new friends, and it just made me really think."

"Well, good for you," I say. "Those guys are pretty big assholes. Especially Bryce. Not like I'm biased or anything. But what does that have to do with you shutting me down?"

"So . . . okay. Well, you shut me down the first time I asked you to hang out, which is cool and totally fine. But then I started thinking about that joke . . . you probably don't even remember, but it was this joke you made about Millie."

"On your first day at the gym," I say. I let out a heavy sigh. "Oh, I remember." I feel at once both guilty and defensive.

"And then—"

"Oh, great, there's more?"

His lips form this soft little half smile. "Then there was that day at school when the hallway was covered in those green flyers with all those secrets, and I assumed it was you. But maybe not?"

I twist my boot into the grass until it hurts dirt. "Nope, that was definitely me."

He sighs. "I just . . . I started thinking that if I was gonna go to the trouble of cutting all these guys out of my life, maybe hanging out with you wasn't exactly the best thing I could do. Like, it was cool how you stood up to

Patrick that one day. But . . . man, I don't want you to take this the wrong way."

"You're already halfway there," I say. "Might as well finish me off."

"We've known each other for a long time, Callie. Maybe we've never been close. But we went to grade school and then middle school with each other, and you were never . . ."

"A very nice person," I say.

He clears his throat. "You've just always kind of said and done whatever you want. To anyone you want. And part of me really admires that, but it doesn't always sit right with me either."

I'm quiet.

"You're mad, aren't you?"

I pause for a long moment. "No," I say. "Yes. But at myself. But also you. Just a little bit. Even if that's unreasonable."

"I decided to go back to the gym and see if you wanted to hang out again because I got to thinking what would happen if people just judged me on the little they saw of me and the company I kept. You're funny and smart. And pretty, too. But mostly I liked how funny and smart you were."

"Flattery is good," I say, and this time I can't keep from smiling. "Keep that up."

"I knew you were experiencing a little of what I was, so I thought that maybe getting to know you would be a good idea after all." He stops for a moment, and the only sound is the ducks squabbling back and forth. "Say something. Please."

"Well, all of that kind of sucks," I say. "But I can't blame you, really."

"Yeah?"

"And at least you're not hanging out with those assholes anymore."

"We can agree there."

"But why football?" I ask. "Why did that have to go?"

"Isn't there anything in your life you just do because you've always done it?"

"Um, are you kidding?" I ask. "I was born wearing a Clover City Shamrocks uniform."

"Yes!" he says. "You get it. Football has always been that thing for me. I finished out the last season, and I was going to go back and just do my senior year to make my dad happy and maybe even get some scholarships out of it. But then I'd be stuck playing for another four years at the very least."

"But free school," I tell him. "And don't you enjoy it? Even just a little bit."

"If I don't get injured," he says. "I guess it felt good to win. But I kind of wonder what it feels like to love something so much that you're even happy to fail at it."

I shake my head. "That sounds all nice and good. But I don't know how that's possible."

He shrugs. "Guess I'll have to let you know. And I've always wondered what I would do with a whole year of high school if I got to call the shots. Like, have you even taken the time to imagine what you'll do with your time when your grounding is up? No dance-team commitments to worry about?"

"I have thought about it," I say. "A little." But not fully. Maybe I'll take dance classes on my own. Or write for the school newspaper. Or join the volleyball team. I don't know.

"Video game designer." He nods to himself. "It's this thing that I've always wanted to try, but I don't even know how someone does that. And, I mean, my dad would give me so much shit. I can practically hear him. 'What kind of bullshit job is video game design?'"

I think for a minute about what I could do if I could do anything. I wonder if Claudia has ever felt like this and if she could choose who she was going to be today, if she would still choose opera.

Once the sun sets completely, Mitch and I stand up to walk back home. He offers me his arm like a true Southern boy, and I loop my arm through his. For a moment, I even rest my head against his shoulder.

"I better get home," he says once we've made it back to my house.

Suddenly I feel like I've wasted my whole night. Like, what if he decides he doesn't want to see me again after this? Breathlessly, I stand up on my tiptoes and kiss him on the cheek.

When I step back, he touches his hand to the spot I just kissed. His cheeks burn with blush.

Heat spreads down my neck, and it takes all kinds of

willpower to not do things that would really make him turn red.

We could do more. We could get in the backseat of his Bronco or we could get back to the lake and roll around on his letter jacket. And all that would be fine. It would be fun even. Because there's nothing like tumbling around in the dark with someone you like.

But I feel like I'm stepping out of my house for the first time after a colossal storm. I just want to take my time. Survey my new reality. Most of all, though, I want to savor it. I want to go to bed tonight and dream about the way a simple kiss on the cheek made everything tingle all the way down to my toes.

MILLIE

Twenty-Nine

Two weeks have passed since my epic date with Malik, and I take another turn hosting a slumber party. I can tell my parents are a little perplexed by my friendship with Callie. I hear my mother referring to her as a criminal in hushed tones to my dad the next morning, but no one says a word to me. Willowdean promises to host once she cleans her room (though she says she can't make any promises when that will be), and Hannah swears to have us over in a few weeks, once her mom gives away the litter of kittens their cat just gave birth to. I argue that this is actually the best time for us all to come over, when there are kittens to cuddle, but Hannah's mom thinks otherwise.

So that means this week is Callie's turn to host, and not to be a nerd or anything, but I'm weirdly excited for Callie's mom to see that she's made friends.

I take my time getting ready for work on Saturday morning. I slept in a bit and I wish I could've slept longer, but I'm still buzzing from last night, which was the third Friday in a row I spent hanging out with Malik while he worked at the Lone Star 4.

Last night when he pulled up in front of my house to drop me off, he said, "I know you're going to be gone for most of the summer and that I'm going to be off visiting family, too, but I just want you to know that I don't want us to take a break."

"Well," I said, "what exactly would we be taking a break from?"

He coughed into his fist and squirmed in his seat a bit. "From us."

"And what are we?" I asked.

He looked to me, his eyes questioning. "In a relationship?"

"Good," I said, letting out a squeal.

As I relive the interaction over and over in my head while I finish off my cereal, I barely even notice my mom coming in from the grocery store.

I pop up from my seat. "Let me help you."

"Oh, I've got it all," she says, "and you can sit your behind right back down, young lady."

"Um, okay. Is everything all right?"

Mom puts her low-fat fruit Popsicles in the freezer and her almond milk in the fridge before saying, "No, ma'am, everything is not okay."

"Did I do something wrong?" I'm starting to work myself into a panic. She found out about broadcast journalism camp. I don't know how, but she did.

She crosses her arms over her chest and leans against the kitchen counter. "You tell me, missy. Where have you been the last three Friday nights?"

Oh crap. "At Amanda's house," I lie. *Stupid, stupid, stupid.* I should've just told her the truth. If she's asking, she definitely knows something is up. "Studying with Malik. You know that."

"Really?" she asks. "You want to think real hard about that for a minute?"

I don't say anything. My mom doesn't care that I have a social life, but she would definitely care that I'm going out on dates by myself with a boy. Literally no one else's parents care about this, but I'm pretty sure my parents expect me to abstain from dating until I'm thirty.

"Well," she says, her voice as sharp as a razor, "I ran into Amanda's father, and I thanked him for hosting you for the last *three* Friday nights. And do you want to know what he said?"

I shake my head, because no, I actually don't want to know.

"He said you haven't been over a single Friday night in the last month, Millicent. So not only is my daughter—my own flesh and blood who I provide for and care for—lying to my face, but I had to humiliate myself and find out from another parent."

"I'm sorry," I whisper.

"Well, honey, sorry just doesn't cut it. You're gonna have to tell me where in Hades you've been for the last three weeks."

I push my cereal out of the way and stand up. "I have been with Malik. That part is true. But Amanda wasn't there and we weren't studying."

"So what in the H have you been doing?"

I smile. I can't think of the last Friday nights without smiling. "I like him, Mom. A lot. We like each other."

She gasps. "Are you telling me that you're dating a boy right under my nose? Without even going to the trouble of asking your father and me or even introducing us to him? And what type of gentlemen courts a girl without meeting her parents first?"

"Mom." My voice drops an octave. "You met Dad in a parking lot and went on plenty of dates before introducing him to your family."

"I was an adult," she says.

"Barely!" I take a deep breath. "I want you to get to know him," I say. "He's smart and passionate and a good listener, but I was scared you'd say no. And I like him too much."

Her whole face hardens. "Well, I say no. You lied to me. You went behind my back. Lord knows what else you're fibbing about."

Something occurs to me, and it makes me cringe. "Mom, is this because Malik isn't white?"

She gasps. "Of course not."

I study her for a long while. Even if the color of Malik's skin does have something to do with this, she would never say so. And I know for a fact that me dating anyone at all would send my mother into a tailspin, but I refuse to leave a prejudice like that unspoken, even if it's unintentional.

I inhale deeply. Well, I might as well get this over with. "It's not exactly a fib, but I guess it's time you know that

I'm not going back to Daisy Ranch," I say.

"What?" Now that shocks her. A boy wasn't so surprising, but this nearly bowls her over. She braces herself on the counter. "Where is this coming from? Is this you trying to rebel? I knew this would happen. I told your father. We had it too easy with you. Is this your uncle's doing? Is this his influence on you? No. It's this boy, isn't it?"

I shake my head. "Mom, no. Listen. Hear me out."

"This is that Willowdean, isn't it? Baby, you love Daisy Ranch. What about all your friends there?"

Now I'm mad. I just want two stinking seconds to tell my side of the story, to be heard for once. "I'm not going back. I am thankful to both y'all, you and Dad, for always trying to do what you thought was best for me. But this summer I've applied for broadcast journalism camp at the University of Texas in Austin. It's a six-week program. I wrote an essay. I paid for the application fee myself and I even filmed an audition tape."

She slumps into a chair at the kitchen table, shaking her head. "Lose the weight first. That's what we always said."

I sit down across from her. "Mom, I've been waiting to lose the weight for as long as I can remember."

"Baby, I want you to go to journalism camp or wherever your heart desires, but I just know you'll enjoy it so much more if you can just shed the pounds first. There's a thin girl in you just waiting to get out."

I shake my head. "No. No." My voice is soft but firm. "There's no skinny girl trapped inside of me, Mom. Just

336

like there's not one in you. This . . ." I grip my thighs and my thick arms. "This is me. And I'm done waiting to be someone else. I know what I want to do with my life. Isn't that incredible? Some people wait their whole lives, figuring out who or what they want to be. But I know."

"You lost six pounds last year," she says. "Maybe this summer it'll be twenty. And you know that keeping it up at home is the hardest part, but it's worth it."

My eyes burn, but I swallow back the tears. Now isn't the time for crying. "I'm okay with this body no matter what package it comes in. I just wish you would be, too."

"Sweetie, you know I love you just the way you are, but I always want the best for you. That's why you're going to Daisy Ranch this summer. I already put the application in the mail."

"Mom! That was for me to fill out."

"Oh, don't pretend like you're the only one who can sneak around in this family."

I stand up and yank my keys off the counter. "I'm not going back to Daisy Ranch. I'm going to broadcast journalism camp. And you wanna know what else? I have a boyfriend. His name is Malik. And we kiss. With. Our. Tongues." I feel my cheeks growing flushed with embarrassment, but that doesn't stop me from storming off.

When I get to the gym, I push through the front door and plop down on my stool behind the counter without even stopping to say hi to Callie.

"Whoa, whoa, whoa," she says. "What's your deal?"

"I told my mom," I say. "About this summer. And Malik. And making out with Malik."

"And I'm guessing it did not go well?"

I close my eyes and breathe in and out through my nose, trying to calm myself. I shake my head after a moment. "It was just about as disastrous as you can imagine."

She throws an arm over my shoulders. "God, I'm sorry, Millie."

"It's okay," I say. "Because last night Malik and I DTRed."

"DTR?" she asks. "Is that like something between first and second base?"

I laugh. "No, we defined the relationship."

"Ohhhhh. So I guess that means you're someone's girlfriend?"

"Not just any someone." But instead of excitement, a cloud of disappointment hangs over me as I remember my mom's reaction this morning. "What about you and Mitch?" I ask. "I didn't want to make a big deal when I saw you guys at the movie theater last night, but OH MY GOSH! Your mom let you out of the house."

"Ugh. Finally!" she says, spinning toward me so that our knees brush against each other. "It was my first night returning to civilization in like two months now."

"And you looked amazing in that yellow romper," I tell her. Malik and I ran into them in between shows, and Callie wore this dreamy yellow lace romper with her long hair down and curled at the ends. She was a vision. She and Mitch walked with her arm looped through his, and it was maybe the cutest thing ever. "Did you guys kiss finally? Like, on the lips?"

She grins devilishly. "Not yet. I'm thinking next week."

"No shame in making him wait," I say.

The bell above the door dings, and I open my mouth to recite my greeting, but it's only Uncle Vernon. And then Sheriff Bell a few feet behind him.

"Hey?" I don't bother to hide my surprise. "What are you doing here on a Saturday?"

Vernon winks at me. "Just some business to attend to."

"Callie," says Sheriff Bell. "You mind following us back to the office?"

"Surely I'm not in trouble," she says. "I've been way too grounded to do anything interesting."

Sheriff Bell chuckles. "I don't think there's much more trouble left for you to get in."

I grab Callie's wrist as she stands up.

"It's okay," she whispers.

Nodding, I let go. It's probably just about her paying off the damage. Maybe she's all done working? I could talk to Inga and Vernon about actually hiring her part-time. I wouldn't even mind taking a pay cut.

I smile to myself as Vernon shuts the office door behind them. Callie and I are friends now. Almost best friends, I'd say. We don't have to work together for us to keep seeing each other. My mom might be unhappy with me, but

I have an amazing boyfriend—I! Have! A! Boyfriend!—
and a group of friends who could hang out with the best
of the best girl squads around.

I just have to stay positive. It's like one of my mom's cro-
cheted pillows says: GLASS HALF FULL, GLASS HALF
EMPTY. BE THANKFUL YOU'VE GOT A GLASS AT
ALL.

CALLIE

Thirty

Sheriff Bell takes the seat behind the desk while Vernon shuts the door, then leans against a particularly precariously stacked pile of boxes.

I've got that achy-pit-of-my-stomach kind of feeling I had the moment I saw Sheriff Bell standing in my kitchen a few months back, the day this whole mess started.

"Have a seat," says Vernon.

"Am I somehow in more trouble?" I ask as I move the stack of binders from the chair opposite the desk and sit down. "I swear to God I've been living like a freaking nun since I started working here." A few memories pop into my head. Specifically of Melissa. And the main hall of the school covered in green paper. "Well, mostly."

Sheriff Bell laughs, but it comes out like more of a grunt. "Not this time."

Vernon coughs into his fist. "Inga did the, uh, math, and it looks like if we were paying you the same wage we pay Millie, you'd have paid off the insurance deductible by now and whatever damage they didn't cover."

"Okay?" Cautious optimism tingles in my toes. "So what does that mean for me?"

"Well," says Sheriff Bell, "you're a free woman."

"We're not pressing charges," confirms Vernon.

"So my life is back to normal?" I ask, totally unable to conceal my excitement.

Sheriff Bell purses his lips together, which I think is his version of a smile. "The school board decision to ban you from the Shamrocks still stands, so you won't be able to rejoin for your senior year, but other than that, your time is your own."

I jump up and squeal. "As of, like, right now?"

Vernon nods. "Well, in about ten minutes, so yeah." He whips out a paper. "I just need you to sign this, saying you understand that you were not compensated for your work and that your labor was in exchange for the insurance deductible and miscellaneous damages."

I'm signing on the dotted line before he can barely finish his sentence. "Can I ask you something?"

"Shoot," says Vernon.

"You didn't really need my help around here, did you?"

He's quiet for a moment. "You could say business is slow."

"So why'd you agree to this? It's not like you were saving money on labor you didn't even need."

Vernon shrugs. "There were a lot of you. Didn't seem right for just one of you to carry it on your record. Guess I wish someone would've given me a second chance at that age."

"Hell," says Sheriff Bell, "if it weren't for your Millie's sharp eye, we wouldn't have caught any of you."

I snap my head toward him just like our dog Shipley does when she hears the crackling sound of my mama cooking bacon. "Excuse me?"

"Slip of the tongue," he says. "Don't you worry about it, girly."

Girly. The word is like a hot coal on a fading fire. It stokes the anger that's always rumbling inside me, even when it's only a low murmur.

I follow Vernon and Sheriff Bell out of the office, and the two of them head straight for the front door.

"Callie," says Vernon, "just leave your name tag with Millie."

Before the door can even shut all the way, Millie turns to me with that deer-in-headlights panicked look. "You're leaving?"

Suddenly I don't buy it. I don't buy any of this after-school-special friendship bullshit she's been selling.

"You." I say. I don't even have all the details or the facts, but I know Millie well enough to know that she'll spill the moment she knows her secret's out. "You're the reason I'm off the dance team. And why I'm stuck working in this body-odor hellhole. And why Bryce broke up with me! I humiliated Melissa! And Sam! And most of the team! Do you remember that? And you let me do that. You didn't even tell me that you were the one who knew it was me after I spilled all their secrets. I . . . I . . . ." Suddenly the weight of exactly what I did to the Shamrocks hits me.

"My mama is never going to forgive me for that, Millie. I violated her trust. All their trust!"

Her eyes fill with tears immediately. "I didn't know how to tell you," she blurts.

I have no pity for her. In fact, seeing her cry only makes me angrier. I'm the one who should be upset! I don't know the what or the how. But Millie is the one who turned me in.

"Your necklace," she says. Her whole face is flushed red and splotchy. "I saw it on the security footage. I wanted to tell you, but then we became friends and I was too scared to lose you."

I rip the name tag off my shirt and slam it down on the counter, making the whole glass top shake. "Well, you should've been scared," I say. "Because I'm done, Millie. With this gym. With slumber parties. With you. It's over." I stomp toward the front door. I was fine before Millie, and I'll be just fine without her now.

"How will you get home?" she asks. "Let me give you a ride."

"I have two legs," I snap. "I can walk."

I grab my bag and shove my cell phone in the back pocket of my jean shorts as I march out the door and out of the parking lot. Millie watches me the whole time. She even walks out onto the sidewalk and tries calling my name.

A few heads in the parking lot turn, but I don't stop. I just keep walking.

Honestly, though, it is hot as hell outside and my home is at least a six-mile walk. I keep moving until I know I'm far out of sight. Millicent Conniving Manipulator Michalchuk will never see an ounce of vulnerability from me ever again.

I finally stop walking when I find myself in front of Harpy's Burgers & Dogs. I think, for a minute, about going in, but quickly remember that Willowdean works here. Yeah, no thanks.

I look both ways before jaywalking across the street to the Chili Bowl—quite possibly the one Clover City establishment I've never given a try.

Inside, a bored-looking guy behind the counter says, "What can I get you? Our summer special is two for one bowls of white chili."

Chili in May when the temperature is nearly scraping the triple digits already? I'm good. "Just a large fountain drink," I say.

I hand him $1.27 in exchange for an empty cup, which I fill to the brim with Diet Dr Pepper—possibly the only good thing left in the world.

I settle into the booth nearest the window to just enjoy the air-conditioning for a little while before I decide on my next move. I could call my mom, but then I'd have to explain all this drama to her, and she is very clearly Team Millie.

Across the street, I watch as Willowdean's boyfriend, Bo, squats down on the curb with a soft drink. A few minutes later Willowdean follows him in her red-and-white uniform dress, her blond curls spilling out of her baseball cap.

The two share a soda and make a sort of contest of kissing each other on the cheek until their noses collide and Bo breaks out in a big gut-busting laugh.

Watching the both of them is like watching the cheesiest montage in one of Millie's romantic comedies.

And it only makes me angrier.

The one person I thought was different from all the other waste-of-space assholes in this town, and she turns out to be just as bad as everyone else. I reach for the napkin dispenser on the table and try pushing away the tears brimming up. But once they start, they don't stop. I turn my body away from the guy at the counter—not like he's paying attention to anything besides his phone anyway—and I let the tears spill down my cheeks.

My life wasn't perfect before. And, yeah, Bryce was a jerk. But who knows what I missed out on besides State and Nationals when I was banned from the dance team? Travel, scholarships, awards to beef up my college applications. And I guess Melissa and Sam weren't all that bad. They weren't great friends, but they were friends. And Millie took all that away in a moment, without a single thought as to what kind of consequences might lie ahead. Logically, I know that I trashed the gym and that's my fault. But did she have to be the one who pinned it on me? Something about that just stings.

But what hurts most of all is that she never said a damn

thing. All those hours at the gym and talking in Amanda's backyard or out at my abuela's house, and she said nothing. I've never even taken Sam or Melissa or even Bryce to meet my abuela. Not even after Millie knew what I did to the Shamrocks for the whole school to see! That really kills me. I like some good revenge as much as the next person, but only when it's well deserved.

I watch as Willowdean and Bo share their soda before heading back into work. I try to muster up the old Callie and think of some truly awful thing to say, about how a girl who looks like Willowdean has no business with a guy who looks like Bo, but the truth is I think they're nauseatingly cute together. The thought alone feels like some kind of betrayal of self. Like I've shed the person I once was, and maybe that's supposed to be a good thing. But instead I feel like I've lost the layer of skin that protects me and keeps me safe from the rest of the world. My whole body feels like a skinned knee with too-fresh skin exposed to the elements—so much so that even an innocent breeze stings.

The sun is slowly beginning to dip below the horizon, and I still have a long walk ahead of me. I don't need my mom out patrolling the streets, looking for me. I refill my fountain drink once more, and the guy behind the counter doesn't even look up when the bell above the door rings as I walk out into the parking lot.

I tighten the straps on my backpack and head off toward home. I make it four blocks before a Ford Bronco rumbles to a crawl beside me.

The passenger window buzzes down as another car

honks as it speeds past. "Hey!" shouts Mitch, unfazed. "You out here training for a survival show or something?" He points to my Chili Bowl cup. "I see you've come prepared with rations."

"Yeah," I say as I walk alongside the car on the sidewalk. "Diet Dr Pepper is my survivalist elixir. My life blood, if you will."

"Ah," he says. "Well, I don't want to interfere with your oneness with nature." Another impatient car speeds past him while the driver practically sits on the horn.

I can't help but laugh. "You might be the cause of Clover City's first official traffic jam."

"Finally, something for my father to be proud of," he says. "Let me give you a ride."

I stop. And so does he. Walk six miles, or take a ride from the one person in this town who hasn't thrown me under the bus at some point in time? (Yet.) I'll take the ride.

"I think you and Dr Pepper might be the only trustworthy things left in my life. Sure you don't mind?"

"I mean, not to objectify you, but I also like watching you walk, if that's what you prefer. But your company is great, too!"

I feel an almost smile forming on my lips.

He reaches over his center console to open the door for me, and I hop in.

I throw my backpack in the backseat, and it crashes against piles of empty cups and clothes. "Whoa. That's a lot of shit."

"Listen," he says, "my mom does not mess around when it comes to how clean she keeps our house. My room included. The backseat of this baby is like my own slovenly dirty secret."

I shrug. "So you're like a hoarder, but just your backseat."

"Well, I like to think of it as more of a junk drawer."

"A really big junk drawer."

He smirks. "To your house?"

I nod. "Yep."

"Are you going to tell me why you were walking, or are you going to play it cool and mysterious?"

"Cool and mysterious," I tell him. "For sure."

He nods silently to himself and turns the radio up. We've been spending more time together, but I don't trust myself enough right now not to turn into a sobbing mess. And maybe a little part of me is scared he'll tell me I'm being ridiculous.

When he slows to a stop in front of my house, he turns the radio down to a murmur. "Hey, um, I don't know what exactly happened today, and you don't have to tell me. Unless you want to at some point," he adds. "But, um, I know you don't have a lot of people right now, and I just want you to know that I can be your person." He coughs into his fist.

I stare at him for a long moment. I can feel my whole body turning to mush. Like I could just nod and let this life with Mitch happen to me in the same way it did with Bryce. I like Mitch a lot. But I liked Millie, too, and look where that got me. "I need some time to think," I tell him. "But thank you. Because I really don't have any people at all. Not anymore. Can we just keep taking it slow?"

He tilts his chin down toward me. "As slow as a turtle race if you want."

MILLIE

Thirty-One

I'm not saying my life is perfect or drama free, but I'm used to knowing where I stand, and for the first time I don't know if I should be demanding an apology or giving one. For the first few days, I tried texting. I even tried approaching her at school. I swear, for as good as she is at pretending I didn't exist, I think she could be an actress. I probably tried every form of contact outside of flat-out asking her mom to lock her in her closet with me.

Three days after the incident, I decided to forego texting and just give her a call, but I was promptly greeted with a message saying the person I was trying to reach had blocked my number. One thing I can say about Callie is when she's in, she's all in. She's cut me out of her life with as much swift efficiency as my mother can repurpose a pile of old camp T-shirts into a summer quilt. (I've got the Daisy Ranch T-shirt quilt to prove it.)

I haven't had a ton of friends in my lifetime, but I've never failed so miserably at being a friend. I know that what Callie did by vandalizing the gym was wrong and that I wasn't doing anything bad by pointing out her necklace in the video footage.

Heck, we wouldn't have ever become friends otherwise. But after I saw what she did to the dance team and how deep that cut, I should've said something. I was so scared to lose what we had, because it's not a friendship that's been tested or even lived in a little. The balance with Callie has always felt fragile, like something might just randomly click one day and she would turn back into the person who humiliated me in eighth-grade gym, or the girl who went out of her way to make Willowdean miserable last fall.

I don't think that version of Callie is a different person, like some kind of evil twin. I believe the bad parts of us always live inside of us. It's just up to us to take those flaws and repurpose them for good. I was scared of losing Callie, so I wasn't honest with her. And I lost her as a friend regardless.

Oh, and because everything is a mess, Mom is giving me the silent treatment, too. She goes so far as to even talk to me through my dad. *Will you ask Millie to pass the margarine? Please remind Millie to empty the dishwasher. Has Millie finished her homework?* And somehow she's still spying on me enough to make sure I don't have any solo time with Malik.

When I get home after work, waiting for me on my desk is one single envelope from the University of Texas. When I slipped in through the garage door, my mom didn't even bother saying anything to me or offering me any hint that the fate of my summer was waiting for me in my room.

The envelope is large. I try not to read too far into it, but I know the law of college acceptance letters is big envelope = good and small envelope = bad. I sit down in my big wicker chair and take a few deep breaths. Maybe I should take up meditation?

And then I tear into the envelope. I've pictured this moment for months now, the same way lots of girls imagine their engagement or wedding. In my head, I'm surrounded by friends, and they're the kind of friends who are so sure that I'll get into this program that after I read my acceptance letter and we all cry tears of joy, there's a luau-themed surprise party waiting for us in my backyard. Malik would be there. My parents would be overjoyed.

Instead I'm here alone in my room. I slide a single paper out of the envelope.

Dear Ms. Millicent Michalchuk,

Thank you for applying to our summer broadcast journalism program for high school students. Each year our applicants are more and more impressive, making for a rather competitive program.

We regret to inform you that you were not selected for our program this summer; however, we encourage you to apply again in the future and

My eyes are a tearful blur as the page drifts from my fingers to the carpet below.

We regret to inform you. We regret to inform you. We regret to inform you. The words of rejection are seared onto my heart. I know that I should turn to some sort of tried-and-true motivational book or post or video that has gotten me through tough times in the past. I know I should refocus this pain into motivation.

But for right now—for this exact moment—I just need to hurt. I just need to feel bad for myself and roll around in my own self-pity. I feel so foolish for ever believing they would even accept me. This is what I get for trying so hard and demanding so much.

I don't know when I started crying, but I am and I can't stop.

After a while, my mother knocks on the door and says something to me for the first time in weeks. "Dinner's ready, sweet pea."

"I'm fine." My voice wobbles. "Thank you."

It's a few moments before I hear the floor creak as she makes her way back toward the kitchen. I hear a few hushed whispers exchanged between her and my father before my dad says a little louder, "Leave her be for a bit."

I sit there unmoving, letting the tears fall down the front of my dress. The sun floats below the rooflines of my neighborhood, and I should probably turn a light on, but I think my whole body is frozen.

My phone dings a few times and I hear a few alerts on my computer, too. Probably Amanda and Malik messaging me about silly things. Neither of them has any idea that the goal I've been racing toward for the last few months has just been snatched out of my reach. It almost reminds me of the treadmills at Daisy Ranch. There was this huge screen at the front of the room, made to look like we were walking down some picturesque New England trail. You'd walk over one hill and then another and then another, hoping to reach your goal. But the scenery never changed. You conquered one hill only to do the exact same thing over and over again.

When it's almost pitch-black in my room, my mom quietly lets herself in and turns on the lamp on my bedside table. Even that little bit of light burns my eyes.

She sits on the bed and gives me space to talk. But I'm not ready. I don't even know what to say.

"Did you open your mail?" she asks.

I nod.

"I'm guessing it wasn't the news you were hoping for."

"No," I mumble. "It wasn't."

She presses the palm of her hand to my back and rubs in circular motions, just like she always has when I'm sick. After a long pause, she says, "I spoke with Ms. Georgia from Daisy Ranch. She said it's well past the deadline, but that they were holding a spot in your cabin, hoping you'd change your mind."

I can picture my bottom bunk at Daisy Ranch like it's an extension of my own home. My wooden sign above my bed painted baby pink with teal letters that spell out PUDDIN'. I'll always be that girl. I've run from her for the last nine months, trying to be someone else. A beauty queen. An aspiring news anchor. A girlfriend, even. But I'll always be that girl who shows up every summer, hoping that this is the year everything changes.

It feels like defeat. And what's harder is that I resent myself, but more than that, I resent my mom. I resent her for not believing I could be more. I resent her because I'm scared she's right.

"That's kind of Ms. Georgia," I finally say.

"So I can let her know you'll be back this summer?"

I nod. "Okay."

"I'll send in your deposit this week." My mom pats my leg and then stands to leave my room, but then she stops and turns around. "I don't want this to be some sort of 'I told you so' moment, but you know your father and I are strict for good reason. This is the exact type of pain we've been trying to keep you from. I'm glad that the pageant was a . . . positive experience for you. But, baby, the world just doesn't work like that in real life. People are rude and hateful, and I don't want that for you. I don't want the world to miss out on you because of their own silly judgments getting in the way. You know that, right? That's why your dad and I pay to send you to Daisy Ranch. We just want the world to see the girl we know has been inside you all along."

My eyes well up with tears. But this time it's anger. It's all anger. Because my mother thinks some thin girl is living inside me when the truth is, I am right here. I am the same Millie inside and out. I want to believe that. I want so badly for it to be true. But I have to confront the possibility that maybe my mother is right. Maybe it's too much effort to change the world. Maybe the only way to survive is to change myself.

I have an awful taste in my mouth at the thought.

Mom interprets my angry tears as self-resignation, and when she hugs me, it takes everything in me not to roar at her to get away from me.

In the end, she was right and I was wrong.

CALLIE

Thirty-Two

I'm in San Francisco. The whole team is buzzing with energy. Of course we all want to win the big prize, but at this point the fact that we've even made it all the way to Nationals is a dream so surreal none of us can quite believe it.

I groan into the carpet.

Except I'm not in San Francisco. I'm lying facedown on my bedroom floor, counting carpet fibers with my eyelashes. I have literally nothing scheduled for the foreseeable future. No dance practice. No loser sleepover party or whatever the hell it was. No job.

I've even studied. FOR FINALS THAT DON'T START FOR TWO MORE WEEKS. I have a research paper on natural selection due next week, and I turned it in nine days early. My teacher asked if it was a prank. I assured him it was not.

"Callie!" my mom calls from downstairs. "You've got company!"

"I don't have any friends," I call back, but my voice is muffled by the carpet.

After a moment, there's a faint knock on the door. "Come in."

The door creaks open.

"Whoa," says Mitch. "Quite the situation we have here."

I flip over onto my back.

I'm wearing a holey T-shirt, my most stretched-out sports bra, and paint-splattered jean shorts from when my mom decided she wanted to redo the bathroom but took nine shades of blue to find the perfect shade. Basically, I've sort of ghosted Mitch since he gave me a ride home, because I just have zero will to be around anyone right now.

"Well, I saw the national dance-team competition was on ESPN 2. You weren't answering my texts, and I thought you could use some company." He pulls a bag out from behind the door. "And as many obnoxiously flavored chips as I could find."

I sit up. I still don't really feel up for hanging out, but I'm not going to send him home and ruin the only decent friendship/unlabeled sort of romantic thing I have going. "You got any Flamin' Hot Cheetos in there?"

"If they sell it at the Grab N' Go, I've got it."

I squint at him for a long moment. "How do you feel about hate-watching this dance competition?"

"You're looking at a Guy Fieri hate-watching pro here."

"Well, let's hope we get ESPN 2." I hop up and swipe the bag from his hand and race down the stairs as he follows me.

I stop abruptly halfway down the stairs and spin around.

He stops short just a step above me, and my nose is practically pressed into his chest.

"Sorry," I say. "I just wanted to say thanks for coming over."

"Why be miserable alone when we could be miserable together? With chips?"

I smile.

"Baby," Mama calls from the kitchen, "Kyla and I are running some errands. Y'all okay by yourselves?"

I look up to Mitch, our bodies pressing together with every exhale. "Yeah," I say. "We're good."

Yeah, if we don't kiss pretty soon I'm going to explode.

Which is why it makes no sense when the two of us settle on opposite sides of the couch, just about as far away from each other as we can manage. My first physical interactions with Bryce were usually lubricated with alcohol, so these skittish butterfly feelings I'm having right now are not something I know how to combat.

I flip through the channels until landing on ESPN 2, which is definitely not part of our basic cable package, but something Keith must have snuck in when my mom wasn't paying attention.

I dig through the bag of chips and pull out some pineapple-and-ham-pizza flavored ones. "I want this to be my job," I say. "Coming up with ridiculous chip flavors."

Mitch laughs. "I can't believe someone gets paid to do that. I would want, like, holiday-themed chips. Like Thanksgiving dinner or hot dog with all the fixings for the Fourth of July."

"Oooh! Or like pumpkin-spice chips for Halloween."

"Oh, gross. You lost me there!"

I toss the Grab N' Go bag to him. "You mean you can fathom Thanksgiving dinner chips, but pumpkin is just too much of a stretch of the imagination?"

He shrugs. "It doesn't suit my palate."

I shake my head. "Well, just you wait. When I'm lead chip scientist or whatever, pumpkin-spice chips will reign supreme."

I turn up the volume a little as the announcers talk about their top contenders for first place. A team from Harlem, another from Southern California, one from Miami, and the current title holder, a team out of Savannah, Georgia. I take way too much satisfaction in the fact that Clover City doesn't even get a brief mention when they discuss possible upsets.

"So they just dance?" asks Mitch. "How do you judge something like that? Like, objectively?"

"Well, there are two major categories: technical ability and artistic presentation. And then in each of those categories, they judge things like technique, difficulty, precision, creativity, use of space, and the elusive energy. Which is actually frustrating as hell."

We watch a few routines in silence. I glance over to see Mitch's gaze wandering as he studies a not-at-all-interesting painting of a desert landscape above the television. Yeah, even for someone who's into dance, this is pretty boring.

I scoot across the cushion that divides us so that I'm

sitting right next to him. "Okay," I say, snapping his attention back to me. "See that kick line they're doing? It's actually super hard, because I bet they're all going to land in the splits like a domino effect, but there's always one girl who's gotta go and screw the whole thing up."

We watch as the team on television in their multicolored neon glittering costumes do one last fan kick as each dancer falls into the splits one by one.

"Ow, that does not look comfortable."

"Anyone can do the splits," I say. "It's just about stretching the right muscles." I point to one girl in the middle as she lands into the splits. "Look. She's the one who threw them all off. Bye-bye, perfect score."

"They're barely off, though!" says Mitch.

"Doesn't matter. When other teams are perfect, the smallest mistake comes with a big price tag."

"So anyone can do the splits, huh?"

I chuckle and bounce up from my seat, sliding right down into the splits and then rotating on my hips effortlessly. "Voilà!"

"Whoa. If the whole team is half as limber, I think the Shamrocks might be more athletic than the basketball and football teams combined."

I throw my hands up. "This is what I've been saying for years!"

He nods. "Teach me something."

"Seriously?"

"Hell yeah!" He stands up and holds a hand out for me, pulling me up from the splits with one quick yank.

"Okay. I'll teach you how to do those kicks," I say.

He shakes his head. "No way. I can't kick that high."

I shake my head. "Kicking high is impressive, but it's about kicking in unison." I start pushing on the coffee table. "Let's get this out of the way."

He comes along beside me and helps push the table to the wall.

"Okay!" I take his arm and loop it around the back of my waist. His hand curls around the front of my stomach. My breath hitches.

"Is this okay?" he asks.

"Perfect." I cross my arm behind his.

He gasps. "I'm ticklish. Embarrassingly ticklish, actually."

"Note to self." I smirk. "Okay, so just kick straight out from your hips. We'll save the fancy fan kicks for later."

He kicks out clumsily.

"Keep your leg straight," I say. "But your support leg should be bent a little."

He tries again.

"Better!"

I kick with him a few times as we alternate. He smells like boy deodorant and sour-cream chips. And somehow, I'm really into it. Boys are straight-up sorcery.

"So you've got straight kicks," I say. "Let's try changing directions. It's just a matter of rotating your hips."

Mitch fumbles a bit as he tries to change kick directions without steadying himself or taking an extra step.

After a while, he collapses onto the couch, a little out of

breath, and I plop down beside him.

"That wasn't so bad!" I say.

"Well, if you count not bad as completely forgetting what the purpose of feet are, I guess I did okay."

"Let's take a break from all things dance." I use the remote to flip through the channels until settling on a marathon of *Shark Tank* reruns.

"This show is awful." Mitch shakes his head. "These people come on this show with these awful ideas that they've like invested every penny they've ever made in, and then that awful bald dude just shuts them down."

"I love this show. And to be fair," I say, "that's not always what happens. Some of these people become millionaires!"

"But most of them leave rejected and knowing they've wasted tons of money and energy on a dumb idea like swimsuits for cats."

"You know," I tell him, "the idea that cats hate water is a very harmful stereotype about cats, and I reject that."

He laughs. "I just hate watching people be embarrassed or lose out on something they'd really thrown themselves all in on."

"I kind of like it. There's just something about watching other people fail."

He turns to me but says nothing.

"You're looking at me like I'm a monster. I'm not a monster, I swear! But we're all scared of failure, right? Isn't it comforting to know it happens to everyone?"

"And for some people, on national television."

I smile. "Well, that's their gamble. Not mine."

"Gamble, huh?" he asks, his voice lower now with his gaze fixed on me.

I swallow, but it comes out like a loud gulp.

He leans toward me, not breaking eye contact. "What kind of odds would a guy have if he asked to kiss you?"

I take a deep breath. "I can't make any promises. But I think the odds would be good."

His body inches closer to mine as he stretches his arm along the back of the couch. "Still good?" he asks.

I should probably let the moment play out a bit more. But I've wanted to kiss him since that day under the bleachers, and I've been patient long enough. I don't wait for him to lean in any farther. I kiss him.

The kiss goes from zero to sixty in a matter of seconds. I pop up onto my knees on the couch and pull his face to meet mine. At first, he lets me take the lead and waits for me to initiate each new touch or deepening of our kiss, but soon he drops the gentleman act and pulls me closer to him.

My whole body is full of heat, and I am lost in this moment. Which is why I gasp and jump back almost a whole foot when my mom and sister come in through the back door.

"We're home!" my mom calls.

Mitch and I look at each other and share a moment of exhilarated panic. Flushed cheeks. Swollen lips.

Kyla plops down between us. "Why are y'all out of breath?" she asks. "Were you running?"

"Yup," I tell her. My eyes are locked with Mitch's over

her head. "Just went for a quick run."

She grabs the remote from the floor. "Mama said the Shamrocks are on soon."

"Any minute," Mama says as she settles into Keith's recliner. She turns to me. "Keith's cousin and his wife are in town tonight."

"The rodeo-clown cousin or the accountant cousin?" I ask.

She sighs, rubbing her eyes. "The rodeo-clown cousin. Keith wanted to have them over, but I thought maybe he and I could just go out with them if you could hang back and watch Kyla."

Kyla crosses her arms. "I don't need watchin'."

I shake my head and ruffle my hand through Kyla's hair. "I don't mind watching Kyla."

"Date night!" says Mitch.

Mama laughs. "With a rodeo clown and his fourth wife! Lucky me." She turns to me. "Thank you, baby."

I nod. "No prob."

Kyla flips over to the right channel, and the four of us sit back to watch. I rest my arm on the back of the sofa behind my sister, and Mitch coyly stretches his arm behind mine, tracing circles up the sleeve of my T-shirt. He leaves a trail of goose bumps everywhere his skin touches mine.

My phone buzzes and I find a picture of Claudia and her girlfriend, Rachel, attempting to paddleboard, except that Claudia is mid-fall and she is definitely taking Rachel with her. My super-serious older sister, who never took time out to do anything that didn't move her one step closer to her dream of becoming an opera singer, is paddleboarding somewhere in Germany with the girl she loves.

> **Wow**, I respond, **what possessed your body and forced you to do an outdoor activity?**
>
> **CLAUDIA: I guess you could say I'm diversifying my interests. You could probably stand to do the same.**

I smile to myself and tuck my phone into my pocket.

We watch as the Shamrocks do their routine—the one I spent so many hours perfecting. They're not perfect. They won't place. But they're still good. They don't look out of place, like they made it there on some kind of fluke. I'm angry all over again about how underappreciated the whole team was and is. And then part of me is sad over the missed opportunity. I look over to Mama and I see it in her eyes, too. She would have done whatever it took to fly out to San Francisco and watch me and the rest of the girls. But instead both of us are here in this living room, watching other people live the life we'd both bet on.

I'm kind of surprised, though. Sitting here, watching my whole team at Nationals without me, isn't quite as miserable as I thought it would be. I'm glad to be sharing this couch with Mitch, our kiss still fresh on my lips.

On the television, the cameraman focuses in on an immaculately crafted sign made to cheer one of the teams on. The fluorescent letters are piped with glitter and read WHY NOT US? GEAUX SOUTH BATON ROUGE! It's craftsmanship Millie would've appreciated.

If I'm missing anything at all right now, it's not dance or

having a boyfriend or being one of the most popular girls in school. It's a fat girl who surprised me in ways I could never expect and who I think might just have somehow become my best friend.

MILLIE

Thirty-Three

Mom is no longer giving me the silent treatment, which is convenient, because she has imposed a new rule stating I'm not allowed to go anywhere with anyone unless she confirms my plans with the other person's parents. Basically, if you're trying to read in between the lines, all that means is no more date nights with Malik.

I haven't had the heart to tell him that I don't think this will work anymore, so I've done about the worst thing I can imagine and lied, telling him I've been busy with family stuff and schoolwork. There are nights when he messages me online and I just let the open messenger box sit there for hours, blinking at me. During the day at school sometimes he'll ask me if everything is okay, but I just put on my usual positive, cheerful face, except this time it's nothing more than a costume. "Yes! Of course!" I tell him. "I'm so fine. I've just been so busy."

Since my blowout with Callie and receiving my rejection letter, I haven't exactly felt like wrangling the whole gang for a sleepover. I've spent a lot of time over the last few days wondering why I bother. Sure, I love Willowdean,

Amanda, Hannah, and Ellen, but the more I think about it, the more I realize that I'm the only one trying to make that friendship circle happen. Maybe it's for the best that I just let them all go back to their normal lives and let the slumber party tradition die, just like my short-lived friendship with Callie.

The good news, though, is that school is nearly over, and while Daisy Ranch isn't what I had in mind for this summer, maybe it will give me a chance to reset and somehow remember the things that are most important to me.

After doing my opening duties at the gym, I pull up outside Amanda's house to pick her up for school. It's the end of May, which means the end of the school year is so close, I can practically taste sunscreen.

I turn up the radio to some bouncy pop I know she's sure to love. I can fake smile the whole way to school so long as I don't have to talk.

Amanda hops into the passenger seat, and over the music, she shouts, "My parents finally said yes to two weeks at soccer camp! Me, the Kansas plains, and tons of balls!" She pauses. "Soccer balls! Not, like, actual balls."

I give her two thumbs up and a huge grin before taking off down her street. I'm happy for her, I swear. Amanda's wanted to go to this camp for years, and it's not a cheap thing either. But I have to blink aggressively until the sting of oncoming tears is gone. I've told Amanda about the Callie situation, but I just can't bring myself to tell her about the rejection letter. Something about saying it out loud makes it too real.

When we finally make it to school, and I put the van in park, Amanda hits the power button on the radio, enveloping us in silence.

"I better get in for the announcements," I say.

She hits the lock button on the door. "Not before we talk."

"I really can't miss this. It's an obligation."

"Millie, I don't know what the heck is up with you. It's like some kind of alien has taken over your body and he got the cheat sheet on how to impersonate you, but he's failing miserably BECAUSE HE'S A DAMN ALIEN."

I clasp my hands together, my palms slick with sweat, but I say nothing.

"What's the deal?" she asks.

I shrug. "I really have to go."

"All right, listen, you're my best friend. You are literally the only person who I would give my last piece of pineapple-and-ham pizza to even though I really don't want whatever other kind we ordered. I've tried really hard not to be weird about the Callie thing."

"The Callie thing?" I ask. Is she mad at me too? I guess in a way Amanda also lost a friend when Callie stopped hanging out with us.

"Ya know," she says, "you basically replacing me with a super-hot ex-Shamrock bad girl. I thought maybe it was like some weird phase, or that once you guys had been friends for a while longer . . . it wouldn't feel so intense, but . . . and I'm sorry that y'all had a fight, but, like, hello? I'm still here." She points to herself repeatedly like a flashing sign. "Your longtime BFF is still totally here for you, even if you treated her like hand-me-downs for a few months."

First, I'm shocked. Replace Amanda? I could never replace Amanda. She is one of a kind. I couldn't find a match if I searched every corner of the earth. But then slowly I begin to see it from her perspective . . . and oh my word. I've been an awful friend. "Amanda," I finally say. "No, no, no. I could never replace you. I never meant for you to feel that way."

She shrugs and gives me this sad half smile. "I get that you didn't mean to, but I still felt that way. Hannah thinks so, too."

"Hannah too?" That stings.

She nods. "It was like watching you trade up for the newer model who didn't have an LLD." She motions to her shorter leg. Then she pauses. "Or wasn't asexual."

I gasp. "I would never."

"I just figured with you going to your hotshot broadcast journalism camp and with your new BFF that you didn't really need me, and I don't want that. So I need you to start being mindful of the friends you do have. The ones who aren't mad at you over a thing that was their own damn fault in the first place."

The way she says it, that the whole thing at the gym was Callie's doing, eases the guilt I've been carrying. I should've told Callie that it was me who identified her, but that doesn't mean she wasn't guilty. But none of that matters now. Amanda's here and Callie isn't. Amanda's always been here. "You're right," I say. "I just really loved being friends with Callie. She was funny and way different than what I expected, but if I've learned anything, it's that you can't force someone into being your friend."

Amanda sighs. "I really did like Callie. Even if she sort of stole my best friend."

"I'm not going anywhere," I tell her. "And about broadcast journalism camp . . ." I take a deep breath. "I didn't get in."

Amanda gasps. "What? How is that even possible? You are literally the most qualified person to do everything ever."

I shake my head. "I don't know, but they were not interested in Millicent Michalchuk." Even though, deep down, I know they took one look at that audition tape and that was it. They didn't see my talent or charisma. They saw the size and shape of my body.

Amanda's nostrils flare and she growls a little bit. "Well, I don't know if I can fix journalism camp, but I can try to fix at least one thing that's gone wrong." She pulls her phone from the front pocket of her backpack.

"What are you doing?" I ask.

"Calling in the troops."

As I sit in AP Psych, waiting for the final bell to ring, I read over the note I wrote Malik one last time. I've carried it in my backpack for over a week now, but I have to give it to him, and I have to do it today. Waiting any longer feels selfish, especially after talking to Amanda and learning about how she felt like I ditched her. I know this will hurt, but it will only hurt more if I wait.

Malik,

First, I want you to know that I think of you as one of the most important people in my life. The time we've spent together has felt like a dream I never thought could come true.

Unfortunately, though, my mom doesn't think I'm ready for the type of relationship we have. I've tried sneaking around and it's just not something I can do anymore.

Also, I didn't get into the University of Texas Broadcast Journalism Boot Camp. I can't say for sure why, but I think I have a hunch, and it definitely wasn't because of your amazing directorial skills. You made me look better than I could have ever imagined. I guess this means I'll be headed back to fat camp this summer.

I hope we can stay friends, though, and that you'll keep in touch while you're visiting family. You are one of my most favorite people.

Always,
Millie

As he rushes in just before the last bell, I set the note down on his half of our desk. He grins at the folded piece of paper and my bubbly handwriting. Once Mr. Prater dims the lights and turns on the projector, Malik opens the note. I guess it makes me a coward, but I just can't bring myself to watch him read it.

Maybe working hard and wanting the dream career and that sickeningly sweet rom-com love story isn't enough.

I keep picturing the wooden toys my mom bought for Luka and Nikolai. It's the kind of shape toy where you push a block through a matching hole. The triangle goes through the triangle hole and so on and so on. Last Sunday, I sat there with the boys all afternoon, mesmerized by the small shaped blocks and how, truthfully, they could fit through almost any size hole. Bigger shapes, like the circle, could only fit through the matching shape. No matter how hard Luka or Nikolai tried, the circle couldn't fit through the star or the triangle or the octagon. It reminded me that no matter what I want to be, to the rest of the world, I will always be a circle.

All throughout class, Malik is completely silent and makes no effort to acknowledge the note. I guess he read it loud and clear. Guilt burrows deep in my chest at the thought of hurting him.

After class is over, I wait for him to leave first. I should give him space for a little while, before I try to pursue the whole friends thing. But once I've said good-bye to Mr. Prater, I walk into the hallway and Malik is waiting there. His hair is a little more disheveled than normal, like he's been running his fingers through it. Other than that, he is completely put together, from his forest-green sweater vest, gingham button-up shirt, and creased jeans down to his penny loafers. Without a word, he takes my hand.

This is the first time we've held hands at school. I try not to be giddy, because this is definitely not how I expected this first time to go, but still a little spark of delight lives inside my chest.

"I need you to come with me," he says.

"Okay?"

Malik leads me by the hand to the AV studio, where we filmed my audition tape.

Inside, he leaves me at the center of the room while he turns on a few lights, and then he paces. I've never seen him like this, so intense and deep in thought.

I watch as he paces for a few moments more, and then he stops in his tracks and pulls the note I just gave him out of his pocket. I don't know what I expect. Maybe that he'll read it to me? Or try to give it back to me? But instead gentle, soft-spoken Malik rips my note into a million furious pieces.

My eyes widen. "What—what are you—"

"No," he says. "This is not a note-appropriate situation. This is a conversation. God, Millie, you know I'm not built for confrontation. Did you see just then how much I had to psych myself up? I need, like, a shot of steroids."

"Malik," I say, suddenly finding myself a little annoyed that he's upset that I gave him a note instead of talking to him. "All I did was present you with facts. My mom doesn't want me to date. I can't keep sneaking around. I didn't get into journalism camp and she didn't even want me to go in the first place, so I'm going back to Daisy Ranch."

"Weight-loss camp," he says.

"Well, yeah."

"The camp you've sworn up and down that you're done with?"

I pause for a moment and then nod as I study my sneakers far too closely.

"Millie, you love rules. It's one of my favorite things about you. The way you find comfort in order. But whose rules are you even following?"

I throw my hands up. "You're telling me to lie to my mom? To keep sneaking out?"

He shakes his head. "That's not what this is about. I mean, yeah, you're my girlfriend, I want to see you, but you shouldn't waste another summer at Daisy Ranch if you don't want to."

"Well, then what the H am I supposed to do, Malik?"

He begins to pace again. "Protest your rejection to journalism camp. Or just don't go to Daisy Ranch! Stay home this summer. Help at the gym!"

He doesn't know how impossible his suggestions are. "And what am I supposed to do about us?" I ask.

His voice is tiny, but his words aren't. "Fight for us? Let me meet your mom. I'll do whatever it takes. But we're almost seniors, Millie. She can't expect to run your life forever."

He's right. This last year has been this precarious balance of trying to be her little girl forever while still becoming a functioning adult. But I don't know. My whole life feels impossible right now. Like one giant uphill battle. "I can't make any promises," I tell him.

"I can," he says. "I promise to not give up on you and to never let you give up on yourself, Millie. And that means all your larger-than-life dreams, too. But you gotta stand up to your mom. That's where it all starts."

He steps forward and kisses me on the lips. It's a silent plead. He wraps an arm around my waist, but then he pulls away too soon, leaving both of us breathless. He walks out, leaving me alone in the AV studio.

CALLIE

Thirty-Four

If my mother were to describe herself this afternoon, she'd say she was *all in a tizzy*! After school, I meet her in the front office. She grabs me by the elbow, and I have to practically run to keep up.

"Okay," she says as she's pulling out of the parking lot. "I've gotta pick up Kyla and then grab her recital costumes from Rosie Dickson. She put a rush on the alterations for us. And then I've gotta get dinner going somehow and get Kyla to her dress rehearsal." She clicks her tongue. "I just hate to leave her there, but Keith won't feed himself. Well, he will, but if he does it will be delivery pizza. And he doesn't even order the good kind."

Mama and I haven't spoken much lately except for the sake of logistics. Who's giving me rides where. Whether or not Mitch can come over. If I've done my chores or if I can stay home with Kyla. It's not that I think she's mad at me anymore. Just a little disappointed still, and that's turned out to be harder to live with than I thought.

She glares up at the traffic light, willing it to change as she taps the steering wheel impatiently.

"I can make dinner," I say, surprising even myself. Claudia always helped out with things like dinner and packing lunches, but I've never been quite so domestic.

"Pfft. It'll be fine. I'll just have to time it so that I'm taking Kyla while the casserole is in the oven." She looks over to me. "Maybe with all this extra time on your hands this summer, we can finally get your driving test over with."

"Really, Mama, just leave me the instructions. You've got plenty going on tonight."

The light turns green and she takes off. After a moment of thought, she says, "I'll write out each and every step in detail. It's just King Ranch casserole. You oughta be fine." She glances over to me. "You're sure you don't mind?"

"I wouldn't have offered if I did."

Mama runs me home and writes out detailed instructions down to every minute and measurement for her casserole. As she's walking back out to the car to pick up Kyla, she turns back for a moment and says, "Keith won't be home for another couple hours." She pauses. "Callie, I appreciate this a whole lot."

I nod firmly. "No problem."

I keep waiting for this one big moment when she won't be disappointed in me anymore, but maybe that's not how you gain back someone's trust in real life. Maybe it's a slow, frustrating thing that takes lots of King Ranch casseroles, so I guess this is a start.

Things with Mama have gotten slowly better. Since I'm not sitting with Millie and Amanda at lunch anymore, I'm back to spending lunch period in Mama's office. She said she wouldn't kick me out as long as I helped her file and answer phones, which is a fair trade for me. I think she knows something's up with me and Millie, but she hasn't pried. (Yet.)

Today during lunch, I was sitting behind the desk while Mama ran off to the cafeteria to get a refill on her sweet tea.

The office door swung open and someone said, "I, uh, have that doctor's note from yesterday, Mrs. Bradley."

I stood up to see Bryce approaching the attendance desk. "Oh," I said. "Hey." We'd seen each other in the hallways a few times, and I even dumped a box of his sweatshirts, some pictures, and presents he gave me on his doorstep. But this was the first time we'd actually spoken.

His face turned sheet white. "Um. I was just giving your mom this note."

I took the note from him. I wanted to say something sharp or biting, but any hate I had for Bryce is in the past, and it's just not worth resurrecting. "I'll pass it on."

He nodded. "Cool. Thanks." He was quiet for a moment. "You look good."

"I know," I said, without skipping a beat. Having those last words satisfied my ego in a very delicious way, but I still had one last thing to add. "I'm sorry about your phone, by the way."

He grunted. "Time for an upgrade, anyway."

After cooking and shredding the chicken for my mom's casserole—can we just agree that raw chicken is just about the grossest damn thing ever?—the front doorbell rings.

I sort of feel like doorbells are as useless as landline telephones. I mean, if you're going to come over, wouldn't you just text me? And if you don't have my number to text me, do I even want you coming over?

All of this flawless logic is the exact reason why I let the doorbell ring eight times before I finally shout, "What? No one's home."

Then come three swift, pounding knocks on the door.

"For fuck's sake," I mutter as I check to make sure I'm not leaving the kitchen in a the-house-might-burn-down situation.

I jog over to the door in my mother's ruffled red-and-white polka-dot apron and swing the door open.

"Oh, hell no," I say the moment I see what's waiting for me, and I swing the door shut again, locking the deadbolt and the chain.

"Callie," says Ellen through the door. "We come in peace."

"I don't know about peace," says Willowdean. "But could you at least pretend to have an ounce of manners and let us in?"

"What do you want?" I shout back.

"Tell her," I hear Willowdean whisper.

Ellen says something too quietly for me to hear.

"We're here on a mission," Amanda shouts.

"Not for you," Willowdean clarifies.

"We're here for Millie," says Hannah.

"Millie who?"

"That's it," Willowdean says. "Callie Reyes, I swear to

Dolly Parton that if you don't open this door, I'll sit my ass here until your mama gets home, and if your mama is anything like mine, I'm sure she'd love to meddle all up in your personal business."

I huff through my nose and unlock my door one lock at a time before finally opening it a few inches. "Well," I say, not making any motions to welcome them inside. "Let's get this over with."

I open the door and find the four of them standing there with stern looks and crossed arms.

Hannah rolls her eyes. "This is such a waste of time," she says under her breath.

"I agree," I mutter as they all file in.

In the kitchen, we all sit down at the table, but there aren't enough chairs. "I'd prefer to stand," says Amanda.

I shrug and plop down into the chair I'd held out for her. "Is this some kind of intervention?"

Willowdean looks at Ellen with big wide eyes, telling her to go first, but Ellen nudges her forward with her chin just like my mom does when she's trying to communicate with me in a room full of people.

"Never quite took you for the domestic type," Willowdean finally says.

"Are you here to offer cooking tips or for some other God-ordained reason?" I spit back.

Hannah drums her nails, which have been colored in with black permanent marker. "No, but if you could go ahead and complete my Life Skills final and make me a casserole while you're at it, I wouldn't be mad."

Amanda sniffs the air. "It does smell pretty good in here."

Willowdean crosses her arms and looks to Ellen once more. "We don't think you're awful. And that turned out to be a really big surprise."

Ellen rolls her eyes. "What my girl is trying to say is that we sort of got to know you over the last few months, thanks to Millie. And, well . . . Amanda filled us in on everything."

Amanda leans against the counter, crossing her legs at the ankles. She digs into the fruit basket and takes an apple. "Like, right down to your necklace on the security footage at the gym." She points at me, her eyes squinted as she bites into the apple, and with her mouth full, she adds, "By the way, I totally knew it was you who wallpapered the main hallway with that Shamrock shit list or whatever."

"Okay," says Hannah, "but that was, like, super obvious."

"What do you want?" I ask, my tone exasperated. "I got shit to do."

Ellen fidgets in her seat, crossing her legs back and forth. "What we're getting at is that somehow we started to consider you a friend."

"A friendly acquaintance," says Willowdean.

Ellen swats at her thigh before continuing. "And friends tell friends when they're being ridiculous."

My eyes ping-pong back and forth between the two of them. "Friends?" I ask. "Ha! Are y'all delusional?" I know I'm playing it tough, but I can feel myself softening just a little bit. Maybe it's the weeks I've spent without Millie, but this sudden, very tiny dash of . . . not kindness . . . but not awfulness . . . well, it's tugging at my soft bits.

"I wouldn't push your luck," Willowdean tells me. She pauses before adding, "At first, we—"

Ellen nudges her.

"I," Willowdean continues. "At first *I* didn't get what Millie saw in you."

"Nope," says Hannah. "That's definitely a *we* statement. Cosigned."

A deeply satisfied grin spreads across Willowdean's face. "You're kind of selfish and rude and, like, really not that funny. But then you started coming around more and . . . well, you ended up being sort of funny."

Amanda holds her apple up like a gavel. "For the record, I think you're pretty damn funny."

"And smart," adds Ellen. "And loyal," she says.

"Well, there's something you don't have much experience with," I say.

Ellen swallows hard. "You're right. After Willowdean and I mended our fence, I was certainly not loyal."

"You ditched me," I tell her, my voice flat, because I can't risk letting her know how awful that really made me feel.

She nods. "Yeah. Yeah, I did. But gosh, Callie, you also gotta know that you haven't always been the easiest person to be friends with. Hell, if anyone was gonna crack you, it would be Millie. So I'm sorry that I just ghosted on you after the pageant, but I'm also glad that I got a chance to get to know this new and improved version of you, too."

"I get why you're mad," Willowdean says. "About Millie not telling you she was the one who recognized you on the security footage. You could say that I have a little bit of a temper, too. But would it have changed anything?"

"I might not have made that list," I tell them. "With all the secrets. Or wasted so much time being pissed off at the Shamrocks—girls who were my friends."

"Girls who let you carry that blame all alone," says Ellen in a soft voice. "Listen, I don't think there's any use in pointing your anger in one direction or the other. The whole situation sucked, but it happened."

My arms fall limp at my sides. I hadn't realized that this whole time I was crossing them so tight over my chest.

Willowdean clears her throat. "And you gotta get over it. No use wasting a perfectly good friendship on yesterday's history."

"And Millie needs you." Amanda tosses the core of her apple into the trash can from across the kitchen. "She didn't get into camp at UT, and now she's going back to Daisy Ranch. You get what a big deal that is, right?"

And that hits me right in the gut. I shake my head. "Oh my God. How could they not accept her? And she swore she wouldn't go back to Daisy Ranch!"

Amanda nods. "Exactly. I tried talking some sense into her, but if you really care about Millie, maybe you should try, too."

Ellen and Hannah stand up and join Amanda.

"Listen," says Ellen, "if you ever want to—"

"I'm, like, super territorial," Willowdean interjects,

still sitting firmly in her seat. "Like the day we learned to share in elementary school? I was probably absent. But what Ellen is trying to say is that if you ever want to hang out . . ."

"We don't mind having a third wheel," Ellen finishes. "Or a fourth or a fifth or a sixth or whatever."

I watch the four of them suspiciously. "Thanks for ringing my doorbell relentlessly."

After they leave, I slide down the door and onto the floor, still wearing my mother's apron. Shipley sniffs me, searching for scraps, before plopping down beside me, and I stroke her soft ears.

I can't make my brain shut up. The dance team and whoever's fault that it was that I was caught. Millie getting rejected by the broadcast journalism camp. Ellen. Willowdean. Hell, even Amanda and Hannah. All of it swirls around in my head and I can barely process any of it, so I do what I would do in any time of Shamrock crisis. I prioritize.

What is the one thing I can actually fix? I don't know if there's anything left to salvage with Sam and Melissa. And Millie . . . well, I know I need to go to her. I gotta make it right somehow. Not just because of me lashing out at her, but I can't let her go back to Daisy Ranch. Not after the way she talked about all those summers there and how this would be the year everything changed. She was so damn positive and determined. There are a lot of people who could probably stand to be knocked down a few pegs, but Millie is not one of those people.

I push myself up off the floor and head to the kitchen to finish up dinner. After Keith and I eat, I set aside leftovers for Mama and Kyla.

As I'm sitting at the desk in my room with a pen in my hand and a pad of paper in front of me, Mama knocks on my already cracked-open door. "Not bad for your first try at my King Ranch casserole."

I smile. "Keith said he couldn't even tell the difference."

She rolls her eyes. "His taste buds are about as refined as a hog's." She leans against the door and crosses her arms. "I really appreciate you picking up the slack tonight."

I nod. "I didn't mind."

"You working on some homework?"

I slide my arm over the paper and lie. "Yes, ma'am."

"Good girl," she says. "Night, baby."

"Night, Mama," I whisper as she shuts the door behind her.

As the house quiets for the evening, I text Mitch and ask for a favor before reading over what I've written one last time.

Mama,

First, I haven't run away. Don't panic. I like your cooking way too much. But I've gone to do something important, and I'll be gone for the next day or two. I know I've been all sorts of trouble lately, but I want you to know that this thing I have to do isn't for my own sake. It's for Millie. She was there for me when I didn't even have the sense to know I needed her, so now it's my turn to be there for her.

You can be mad at me. You can punish me when I get back. I'll spend the whole summer cooking dinners to your liking if I have to, but I gotta do this one thing. I promise to text and let you know that I'm safe.

xo,

Callie

MILLIE

Thirty-Five

I lie perfectly still in my bed, holding my breath. The light scratching on the window doesn't stop. It's been happening for about five minutes now. Someone is outside my bedroom window.

I'm going to die. I'm going to die at the hands of a window-scratching killer.

"Millie," a voice whisper-shouts.

Then comes a light knock on the window.

"Millie!" the voice says again.

This time I sit up and tiptoe to my window before yanking the curtains to the side and jumping back into a boxing stance in one swift motion. What am I going to do? Box the window-scratching killer from inside my room? Well, at least Uncle Vernon might be proud.

My eyes adjust to the moonlight as the figure in my backyard melts into focus. "Callie?"

She motions to the window, and I step forward and slide it up.

"What are you doing? How did you get here?"

"Mitch dropped me off," she says.

I gasp. "Are you two, like, a thing? Oh my gosh. I've missed so much."

She smiles just a little. "Are you going to let me in or what?"

I step back and she crawls through the window gracefully.

"You're good at that."

She shrugs. "If the Shamrocks left me with anything, it was balance and leotards." She sits down on my bed. "We need to talk."

I pull on my fuzzy pink robe and plop down beside her. "I'm so glad to see you," I say. "And I'm so sorry I never—"

She shakes her head. "First, you really don't have anything to apologize for. Second, we're gonna have to save the heartwarming reconciliation for later, because we're on a time crunch."

"What?"

"It's a seven-hour drive to Austin." She glances at her phone. "It's just past midnight. Once you pack a bag and we get on the road, it'll be quarter to one. With stops, that puts us getting in around nine."

My eyes go wide. Did she hit her head? "Austin? What are you talking about?"

She takes both my hands in hers. "We're getting you into that damn broadcast journalism camp, Millicent Michalchuk."

"They already rejected me," I tell her.

"No," she says. "I reject them rejecting you!"

"What would I even say?"

"How about 'My name is Millicent Fucking Michalchuk, and you made a mistake. Lucky for you I'm here to help you make that right.'"

I smile. "Well, maybe without the F-word."

"We'll figure out the details on the way. The point is, I checked online, and applicants who have been accepted have until tomorrow to respond, so I figure if we can make it there by then, we still have a chance."

"I don't know." I shake my head. "My mom already paid the deposit at Daisy Ranch, and she would kill me if she knew I ran off to Austin in the middle of the night."

Callie takes my hands again. "Millie, you are the most badass person I know. Your mama would be disappointed in you for doing pretty much anything she herself hadn't specifically planned out for your future. But you've got to live the life you want. Not the one she thinks you should." She closes her eyes for a moment and bites down on her lip before continuing. "I've never had much faith in religion or school or heck, people. But, Millie, I have faith in you. People aren't always gonna get it right on the first try. They're not always gonna say yes when they should. And sometimes you just gotta swallow rejection and move on, but sometimes you have to refuse to take no for an answer. For the next twenty-four hours, 'no' is not in our vocabulary."

I let out a shaky breath. "Give me a minute to pack a bag and grab my keys. Guess we're driving to Austin?"

"I promise to keep you awake the whole time and sing

whatever music you choose as loud and obnoxiously as I can."

"Deal," I say. "Austin or bust?"

"Austin or bust."

After packing my lavender overnight duffel bag, I sneak out through the garage, which I open manually to cut down on noise, and meet Callie in the driveway. She's got a small backpack and two bags of chips.

"I should grab some bottled water for us," I whisper as I open the van for her.

I make a quick trip inside and grab an armful of water bottles and a few bananas, because if I'm really doing this, maybe a little extra potassium wouldn't hurt.

We settle into the car and I check every single mirror twice and then I turn the ignition. My parking lights come on, illuminating the figure standing just in front of the hood. I don't know if it's adrenaline or what, but my nerves have taken a hike.

"Millie?" my dad calls.

I gasp. *Crap.*

"Let's just go," Callie says. "We can explain later."

Dad stands in his sleep pants and DAD OF THE YEAR shirt I made him in middle school using iron-on letters. I can't imagine just leaving him here without even a brief explanation. "Give me a minute," I tell her.

She grips my shoulder. "You're doing this for all the right reasons, Millie. Don't forget that."

I turn off the car and get out.

Dad rubs his eyes. "Where are you going at this hour?"

"I'm going to contest my rejection from the UT broadcast journalism camp."

"You're . . . you're going to Austin? In the middle of the night? Millie, that's a six-hour drive!"

"Closer to seven hours," I correct him.

"What's seven hours?" My mom appears behind my dad, framed by the door leading into the house. She pulls her robe—a perfect match for mine—tight over her chest. I can see the fuzzy sleep still there in her eyes as she looks from my dad to me to the van to Callie sitting in the passenger's seat. "What's going on here? And why is that girl in our van? Millie, what are you doing?" With each word, the panic in her voice builds.

"The drive to Austin," I say. "It's seven hours. I'm driving to Austin with Callie to protest the decision from the broadcast journalism camp."

Mom takes a step closer to me. "Oh, honey, we've already talked about this. You're going back to Daisy Ranch." She looks to my dad for backup. "This is the summer. I can feel it. Isn't that right, Todd?"

But my dad says nothing. He won't even make eye contact with her.

I brace myself. "I'm going," I tell her. "I can't live with myself if I don't at least try."

She takes another step closer, and this time she puts an arm around me, but my shoulders are stiff and unforgiving. "My Millie, my sweet Millie. They passed on your audition tape. They said no for a reason."

I take a step back, out of her reach. "Then I at least deserve to know why."

Her expression hardens. "I forbid this," she says. "I forbid you from driving to Austin with that girl—the same girl who destroyed your uncle's place of business—in the middle of the night."

I close my eyes. I don't want to hurt my mom, but I don't know how else to make her understand. "This isn't about me," I tell her. "That's not why you're trying to stop me. This is about you and trying to shape me into the person you always wanted to be. But I'm not you. I love you. But I'm not you. I can't spend the rest of my life obsessing over diets and searching for the miracle fix."

My mother is shocked. She looks like I just slapped her in the face with a frying pan.

"Mom," I say. "Think of all the energy you've spent trying to lose weight. It's who you are. It's your whole identity. But it doesn't have to be. Dad loves you. And I do too. And it's certainly not because of your low-carb lasagna."

Her whole face looks like she's about to either erupt in anger or crumble entirely. "This discussion is over," she says, overenunciating every syllable through gritted teeth. "Back inside. Your father will drive Callie home. And we will certainly have a word with her parents."

"No." My voice is firm. "I can't live with the person you want me to be. Especially not when I know exactly who I want to be."

"Millicent. Amethyst. Michalchuk," she says through furious tears now.

"Millie," my dad says.

I almost forgot he was there.

"You have money for gas?" he asks. "Meals?"

I nod, trying my best to conceal my absolute glee. Mom might be wrong, but there's no use rubbing it in her face. "Yes, sir."

"You go there. Stop if you get tired. I don't care if you have to charge a hotel room to your emergency credit card. I want a phone call every hour. I don't care what time it is."

I nod, forever thankful to him for this one moment. Dad has never been the type to speak over Mom or undermine her parenting decisions, but if he's going to step on her toes, I'm so glad he chose this moment to do so.

My mother guffaws. "Todd, you can't be serious."

He turns to Mom. "As serious as I was the day I married you."

Oh, he's definitely sleeping on the couch tonight.

I hug my dad. "Thank you," I whisper.

My mom stands there, her lips stiffly pursed and her arms crossed.

I hug her. It's like hugging a dang stone pillar, but I hug her. "I love you, Mom."

She doesn't say anything back.

I get in the van and back out of the driveway, always careful to watch my mirrors.

"Buckle up," I tell Callie.

"Are you okay?" she asks.

I wave to my parents as my dad closes the garage door. The moment they're out of sight, I hit the gas. "Yes." I wipe away the last of my tears. "I'm okay."

She rolls down the window. "Austin or bust!" she howls.

I roll down my window, too, and take one hand off the wheel, which I rarely do. My arm hangs out the window as it slices through the warm air, and I leave town with Callie Reyes under the cover of night. I'm okay.

CALLIE

Thirty-Six

For the first two hours of the drive, the energy pulsing between the two of us is absolutely tangible. I navigate and play DJ while Millie belts along to old Britney Spears, Destiny's Child, and even a little Dolly Parton, which Millie swears helps her channel her bravest self.

Around hour three, we stop for gas and a few snacks, including one of those bouquets of Tootsie Pops. I've made this drive a few times with my family, so I know that there's not much but flatness and a little bit of hill country just outside of Austin, but making this drive at night feels like we're speeding through a velvety black hole. Out here there's nothing but the random town every once in a while, and sporadic truckers making the long drive across Texas.

As we're pulling back out onto the road, Millie reaches for the volume to turn the music back up, but I hit the power button. I don't want to distract her from the task ahead, but I also have something to say.

"I shouldn't have blown up at you the way I did," I tell her.

"But I should've just told you. Early on. I could've gotten it out of the way."

"I can see how you would be nervous to do that, though. I'm not what you would call easygoing."

She laughs. "Well, yes. But that's exactly what I like about you. You're intense, and you don't care if other people know it."

I laugh. "I don't know that most people would call those desirable qualities."

Millie shakes her head resolutely. "Do you know how many people spend their whole lives pretending they don't care? You're not like that."

I sigh. "Well, I do care a little bit, I guess. I just wish I hadn't released that list of secrets."

Millie's lips turn downward. "Me too. I feel awful about that, I do."

"It's not like those girls didn't screw me over. They let me take the blame for the whole team. But . . . I don't know. What I did . . . was wrong."

"Maybe you could make it up to them," says Millie.

I laugh. "Like how? Become their water girl?"

"I do think you'd make a really cute water girl, but no, I mean something different. Like, it sucks that the gym had to drop its sponsorship and it sucks that y'all reacted the way you did, but neither of those things are the real problem."

"Try telling Inga that," I mutter.

"The real problem is that the school board budgets so

much for the football team and all that's left for everyone else is peanuts! The Shamrocks have the best competitive record of any team on campus. Y'all should have been way better funded. Frankly, it's bull—"

"Shit!" I shout. "It's bullshit!" She's right. That is the real problem. I've been saying it for years. The whole team has. But no one would listen.

"Well, I was going to say bologna, but it is also bull doo-doo."

"But what can I even do about that?"

"If there's anything I've learned from watching local politics, it's that decisions are made by those who show up."

"Okay?"

"And no one shows up to school board meetings," says Millie.

We spend the next few hours hashing out talking points if I do decide to speak in front of the school board. I'm doubtful, though. To them, I'm just the girl who trashed a local business. Why would they listen to me? When I change the subject and ask Millie about her mom, she goes quiet, which is entirely out of character, but I don't push.

Soon we're lowering our visors and reaching for sunglasses as we drive into the sunrise and closer to our destination.

The traffic in Austin is awful, and I'm not just saying that because I live in a town where the biggest traffic jams are caused by school zones and the rare busy drive-through lane overflowing into the street.

Mama says Austin was made to be a tiny-big city, but now it's trying to be a big-big city in tiny-big-city pants, which actually makes some weird kind of sense.

Millie is the model driver, of course, and turns down the music. Both hands are wrapped so tightly around the wheel her knuckles are turning white.

When we finally do exit for the university, Millie and I both marvel at the size of the campus.

"I think this place is as big as all of Clover City," I say.

"I think you might be right."

We take a few wrong turns before finally finding the School of Journalism, but parking is another story. The nearest parking is almost a mile away from the actual building.

"Wow," says Millie. "If having a car in college requires this much effort, I think I'll ditch the van for a scooter."

And for just a brief moment, I picture a future version of Millie zipping all over Austin on a baby-blue Vespa. "You'd be a vision," I tell her.

She maneuvers the car into a parking spot and pulls the parking brake. "Well, before that happens, I have to make myself presentable." She looks around the lot. "Keep an eye out while I change in the back?"

"What else are friends for?"

While she wrestles around in the back, I check my phone. There's only one message.

MAMA: I read your note. We will talk when you get home. I spoke with Millie's parents. Please be careful. This doesn't mean you're not in trouble.

I breathe a sigh of relief. That wasn't so horrible. I'm definitely grounded again, but I can live with that.

"Okay!" Millie says. "Let's do this."

When she hops out of the van, Millie's wearing Mama's red lipstick and a black dress with daisies all over. "Wow," I say. "I don't think I've ever seen you in black."

She nods seriously. "I wanted to go for something that said serious but fun."

"Serious fun."

"Precisely. And the daisies felt like the perfect amount of irony." She takes a deep breath. "We gotta move before I lose my nerve."

We walk through the campus and find our way back to the journalism building, and as we stand at the steps, unsuspecting students stream past us. They're all so close in age to us, but somehow so much more grown-up.

I squeeze Millie's hand.

She nods, and we walk in shoulder-to-shoulder, straight to the faculty offices.

We stop in front of the office of Dr. Michelle Coffinder.

Millie squares her shoulders and lands three solid knocks on the door.

After a moment, a younger, round Asian woman opens the door. She wears a black-and-white checkered pencil skirt and a pineapple-patterned neon-yellow blouse. Her curly, short turquoise-streaked hair frames her face, while managing to be unruly yet cool.

I watch as Millie's face basically turns into the heart-eyes emoji. If this is Dr. Coffinder, she's also Millie's long-lost edgier twin.

"Dr. Coffinder?" Millie asks in confused wonder.

The woman lets out a full belly laugh. "Oh, hell no. I'm her TA."

"Oh, right," says Millie. "Of course. Well, I'm here to speak to Dr. Coffinder."

The door swings open to reveal a tall, thin but muscular guy with sandy-blond hair. If this guy isn't already on the news, he will be one day. "Do you have an appointment?" he asks.

"N-n-no," says Millie, suddenly cowering.

"But it's an emergency," I interject.

The guy looks dryly from me to Millie. "What?" he asks. "Daddy's gonna ground you all summer for failing mass comm?"

"Actually, we're not students," says Millie. "I'm here to speak to Dr. Coffinder about the summer broadcast journalism camp for high school students. She's the head of the program."

Something clicks for both of them, like they suddenly recognize her.

"Grant, Iris, I'm taking an early lunch," a lofty voice void of any accent calls, before a petite woman with quintessentially Texas hair appears from an adjoining office. "Well, this is quite the traffic jam," she says, motioning to the four of us in the doorway.

"Dr. Coffinder," says the girl who I'm assuming is Iris.

"These girls are here to see you, but they don't have an appointment."

Dr. Coffinder turns to us. The curls of her blond hair are so perfect I swear she must sleep with Coke cans in her hair. She wears a cream pencil skirt with a tulip hem, and a silk sleeveless burgundy blouse shows off her well-defined arms. Even I'm a little intimidated by how perfect she is.

"Girls," she says, "I can't do anything once grades are posted. I gave plenty of chances for makeup work. If you failed, you'll just have to spend another semester with me."

"No," says Millie. "This is about the summer program you run for high school students. Please." Her voice is even, yet urgent. "I just need a moment of your time."

Dr. Coffinder. "And you?"

All eyes turn to me. "Emotional support."

Dr. Coffinder thinks for a moment. "You'll have to make it quick. There's a taco truck calling my name, and when they run out of their barbacoa, that's it. They close up shop for the day."

Millie nods. "Yes, ma'am."

MILLIE

Thirty-Seven

I leave Callie in the front office where the TAs work and follow Dr. Coffinder into her office. I wish I didn't have to do this part on my own, but I do.

I take a moment to absorb the room, with its dark wood panels and expansive windows. Every surface is covered with folders and stacks of paper. Almost every inch of wall space is covered with some type of certificate, degree, award, or picture with one of my all-time sheroes.

I gasp. "You're friends with Christiane Amanpour?" A picture of them on the deck of a beach house is wedged between a framed article and an award from the Associated Press.

"Chris is an old friend," she says with a warm smile.

Dr. Michelle Coffinder is somehow even more beautiful in real life than her picture on the school's website led me to believe. But more than that, she runs one of the most competitive journalism programs in the country.

"What can I help you with . . ."

"Millie," I say. "Millie Michalchuk."

She smiles. "Millie. What can I help you with, Millie?"

"I was rejected for the summer program, and I came to see why."

She nods. "Well, that's not normally a request we cater to." She huffs out a breath, blowing her bangs up. "Our admission decisions are final, but you can always apply again next summer."

I shake my head. "No, ma'am. It has to be this summer."

"Are you dying?" asks Dr. Coffinder.

I think for a moment. "Aren't we all?"

"Right answer." She chuckles. "Good girl."

"Ma'am, with all due respect, I am the hardest worker you will ever meet. I'm clever and thorough and . . . and . . . I drove all this way."

"All the way from where?"

"Clover City, ma'am."

"Well, damn, that's all the way out by Marfa."

"It is," I say.

She shakes her head. "But I'm sorry, Tillie—"

"Millie," I correct her.

She smiles apologetically. "Yes, I'm so sorry, Millie, but our decisions are final."

"Did you even see my audition tape?" I ask, and my voice comes out a little too accusatory.

Dr. Coffinder pushes back from her desk, like she's about to stand up and dismiss me. "Well, no. Not in full."

"What? Seriously?"

"Well, it's not our process," she explains. "Iris and Grant, my teaching assistants, do the application intake, and I'm their tie-breaking vote."

"You mean you rejected me without even reviewing my application in full?" I think back to how awful my nerves were the day I sent in my application. What a big deal it was for me. How much effort I put in. And then how quickly it was probably just discarded.

She smiles again, but this time it's a bit more sour. "Welcome to academia."

"Can you at least just watch my tape? After I drove all this way, can you at least do that?" I wish I could channel Callie in this moment. She would know just what to say and just what to do. Callie's the kind of person who doesn't think of the perfect comeback five minutes too late. She's got her response ready to go before the last syllable is even out of the other person's mouth.

I take a centering breath. *One thing at a time, Millie.* "Please." I persist once more. "It would mean so much to at least have your opinion."

She checks the thin silver watch on her wrist. "Well, they'll definitely be out of barbacoa by the time I get there and wait in line. All right. Let's see it."

Frantically, I dig through my backpack and hand her my phone with my audition tape pulled up.

She sighs and hits play, slumping back in her seat.

I hold my breath, studying every twitch of her face, but she's unmoved entirely.

After I've done my sign-off, she tosses the phone back to me and I fumble to catch it.

"Well, I've definitely seen worse. Your puns were awful, but somehow . . . cute?" She studies me for a moment. "I was the tie-breaking vote on your application, Millie."

"Oh." Somehow I hadn't expected that. She'd just been so warm and accommodating even though I had stopped her from going to lunch. But it was her. She was the one who rejected me.

She lifts herself onto her desk and crosses her arms. "Grant," she says, "the Ken doll–looking TA out there, voted against you, and Iris voted for you." She smiles at Iris's name, and I can see she has a soft spot for her. "They both made their case for you, and I agreed."

"Their case for me?" I ask.

"Grant said you'd be better suited behind the camera or on radio. Iris disagreed." Her brow furrows, and I can see that for the first time she's feeling a bit uncomfortable. "You see, Millie—and you should know I don't agree with this— there's just a certain look that reporters have. It's archaic, but it's what sells. And being on television is all about ratings and ratings are all about ads and ads are all about money."

I don't respond. I don't quite know how to. I feel like I've walked into a brick wall.

Dr. Coffinder must see how stunned I am. "When I was a girl, the only thing I was serious about was ballet. I loved it. I breathed it. My parents spent so much money and time carting me to classes and sending me to prestigious camps and workshops, but at the end of the day, when the time came to turn pro, no one wanted me. Bad feet. Too short." She says it so simply, like it's been said to her so many times that she hears it in her sleep.

My heart aches for her. "That's awful."

She nods aggressively. "Yes, exactly. It was awful. Someone could have saved me years of pain and suffering. I could've spent all those years concentrating on something I was actually capable of achieving. Do you see now?"

"No," I say quietly. "Not at all. What's awful is that you have to be a certain height or have certain kinds of feet to be a dancer. Your height and your feet, though. Neither of those things is awful."

"Try telling my podiatrist that," she mutters. "Millie, maybe you'll thank me one day. You're a smart girl. There are so many things you could do. You know, half the people on the news are just talking heads. Some of 'em are real journalists, but it's a dying breed. I'm really doing you a favor. Saving you some valuable time."

"I know what you're trying to do," I tell her. "But my mind is made up about broadcast journalism." I stand up and shoulder my backpack. "I don't know if anyone has one true calling. I can't say you were destined to be a ballerina or a journalist or a rocket scientist or whatever, but what I *can* say is that you should be able to be any of those things regardless of your height or your feet." I motion down the length of my body. "Or your weight."

"I didn't say it was right," she says, her voice more timid than I expect.

"Think of all those times you tried to become a professional ballerina and someone said no to you. What would your life have looked like with just one yes? There's no telling." I point to her desk, like my application might magically appear there. "You know I've got the chops.

Heck! I know I've got the chops. All I need is for you to say yes. Someone closed the door for you, but you have the chance to open it for me."

Her phone rings, breaking the loaded silence between us. She leans back and hits a button. "Yes?"

"Dean Gomez is on line three," says Iris through the speaker.

"Thanks," says Dr. Coffinder. "I'll be right with him." She looks back to me. "Millie, I must ask you to leave. I'm sorry to say my decision stands. Even if I wanted to change my mind, we've reached capacity. Maybe try applying for a different track in the program next year."

I nod. *I will not cry. I will not cry. I will not cry. I will not cry.* I will stand here in my serious fun dress with my lipstick that is the perfect shade of red and I will square my shoulders and say, "Thank you for your time, Dr. Coffinder. This won't be the last time you hear the name Millie Michalchuk."

Dr. Coffinder gives me a stiff smile and motions for the door.

I walk to the front office, where Callie waits for me. I hold my hand out for her to take, because I think the only way I can carry this disappointment is if I am somehow physically connected to her and she is carrying this ache right alongside me. I don't look at Iris or Grant. I just head for the exit and squeeze Callie's hand so, so tight.

"Well?" she whispers.

I shake my head, and as the door shuts behind us the first tear falls. "No. It was a no."

She squeezes my hand back, and we walk in silence out of the building and through a canopy of trees to my van.

I count my tears as they fall. Twenty-eight before my eyes are finally dry. I count them because I want to remember what the cost of this heartbreak was. I hope and pray that someday, when I count up all my tears, that whatever life I'm living will have been worth it.

"Wait!" a voice behind us shouts. Neither of us turns around. There are so many people on this campus. No way is that one single voice directed at us.

"Wait!" it says again. "Millie."

Callie stops before I do. We turn around to find Iris running up the hill toward us. Her glittery cat's-eye sunglasses shimmer quietly from the sunlight shining through the trees. If I was in a better mood, I might ask her where she bought them.

Once she makes it to us, she pushes her sunglasses into her curls and clutches a long white envelope to her chest. She holds a hand up for a moment to tell us to hold on while she catches her breath. "Here," she says, handing me the envelope. "Lesson for you, kids: pencil skirts were not made for running."

"What?" I open the envelope, sliding out the papers. "What is this?"

She rests her hands on her hips. "It's your welcome packet," she says in a matter-of-fact way.

"But I just—Dr. Coffinder just—"

Iris swallows, still catching her breath. "I was eavesdropping the whole time, and, like, side note, you are just as rad as your audition tape led me to believe. So after you left, I went in there and told Dr. C we had one student decline their spot. And, like, she's my PhD mentor, so I didn't want to really step in it or anything, but I very politely told her that I thought she was wrong about you."

"Oh my gosh, you didn't have to do that."

"I did, though. Millie, I voted for you because you were good. Not just because you're a fellow fat girl." She holds up a fist. "Don't get me wrong, though. Fat girl pride. Riots not diets and all that."

"Riots not diets? I like that." Note to self: add to my to-stitch list.

Iris continues, "Dr. C's always been cool with me, and that's probably because my concentration is more behind the scenes with production, but she was wrong about you. And she knew it, too. She sent me out of her office and called me back in a few minutes later before agreeing to give you the spot." She rolls her eyes. "Listen, Dr. C won't admit she's wrong anytime soon. She'll probably treat you like you've got something to prove all summer, but I think you're up for the challenge, no?"

I hold the envelope to my chest like it's made of gold. I don't even bother wiping away the tears now. "Thank you. Thank you so much!"

"You don't have to thank me," she says. "Just prove me right this summer."

I nod feverishly. "I so will."

She motions to the envelope. "And get a jump on that paperwork. Parental signatures and everything."

I gulp.

"She'll get it all back ASAP," promises Callie.

I'd almost forgotten she was there.

I thank Iris once more and ask if it's okay to hug her, before squeezing her to death.

As we're walking back to the car, our arms linked, I turn to Callie. "I have to get them to say yes."

"You will," she assures me. But even Callie doesn't sound so sure.

I know my dad would have probably preferred if I'd stayed the night in Austin instead of driving right back, but I've got too much adrenaline to even think about sleeping. And with my parents' signature on this form looming, I'm feeling antsy about just getting back home.

Callie and I stop to eat on South Congress at a place called Home Slice Pizza. It's the first time I've ever parallel parked the minivan on a busy street, and that definitely inflates my ego a bit. Before heading out of town, we stop at Amy's Ice Cream, where we each get a scoop of sweet cream, mine mixed with Oreos and Callie's mixed with strawberries.

When we get back to town, I drop Callie off first.

"Your mom is going to be so upset," I tell her.

"It was worth it," she says. "Besides, you're, like, her favorite person, so she might just support the cause."

I don't know how to say thank you. I keep trying to think of the perfect way. Putting the car in park, I turn to her. "I love you, Callie, and I'm so glad you're my friend."

I shake my head in disbelief, remembering her scratching on my window just last night. "I would've never done this without you. I spend a lot of time telling myself to be brave, but you make me brave."

She laughs, and it almost comes out like a sob. "You jerk. You're making me cry. I love you, too, Millie. How ridiculous is it that we've lived in this town together for so long and it took us all this time to become friends?" She uses her knuckle to wipe away a tear. "You make me brave, too. You make me brave enough to be the person I am and not the one I think I'm supposed to be."

I pull her to me for a hug before she heads inside.

Since I've been in contact with my dad every hour, like I'd promised, my parents knew I would be arriving soon. They're waiting for me at the kitchen table when I get home.

"Hi," I say before dropping the welcome packet on the table in the hopes that it will speak for me.

My dad motions for me to sit down, and my mother looks like she hasn't showered, slept, or even done her hair since I left. She sits with her arms crossed, but she doesn't look angry like she did when the garage door closed early this morning. More confused than anything else.

"They let me in." The words burst out of me like an impossible-to-keep secret.

"Well . . . wow," my dad says, and it comes out like a gasp. "They're better off for it."

"Thanks, Dad." I look to my mom. "But I can't do it without y'all. I need your permission, of course. And then we'd have to see if we could get our deposit back from Daisy Ranch. And this counts for college credit, too. Just so you know."

My dad takes the envelope and looks over the papers briefly, including the tuition payment plan. "This looks manageable," he says. "Certainly not as pricey as Daisy Ranch." He chuckles and nudges my mom to try to get her in on the joke, but she's nonresponsive.

I appreciate my dad's willingness. So much. But he's not the only one I want to hear from. "Mom?" I ask. "What do you think?"

She looks me in the face for the first time since I walked in. "I think you're a different person than the girl I raised." Her voice is flat.

That knocks the wind out of me. I feel it right down to the bone.

She drags her hands down her un-made-up face. "But maybe that's not such a horrible thing." My dad squeezes her shoulder before she continues, "I don't know what to make of everything that you said today and, honestly, things you said even weeks ago, but if this is what you truly want . . ." She pauses. "I support you, Millie."

I stand up and rush to the other side of the table to hug her. I squeeze her tight, and after a moment she reciprocates. Because I'm always getting ahead of myself, it's hard for me not to think of a future when me and Mom are out doing things like shopping and she's having a great time, not huffing over the size of her jeans or the way her stomach pooches. Maybe it's a long way off, or maybe she'll

415

never quite get there, but the fact that she's agreed to support me is all that I've ever wanted.

I take a few steps back. There's one last thing I have to say. "And y'all should know: I have a boyfriend. His name is Malik, and he's nonnegotiable."

Mom eyes me suspiciously. I might be pushing my luck. "Well, I don't know about that. There are some serious ground rules to consider."

"How about we start with inviting him over for dinner and go from there?" my dad says, and then turns to my mom. "What do you think?"

"Well, I guess we better officially meet this mystery man."

I shriek with excitement before heading back to my room to message Malik. We have so much to squeeze into our last few weeks together before I leave. And of course I have a going-away party to plan!

I crash-land on my bed, watching as the ceiling fan spins on low. For the longest time, I thought the power of positive thinking would get me by. And it helps, that's for dang sure. But it takes more than thinking and hoping and wishing and praying. You need a whole lot of doing.

CALLIE

Thirty-Eight

A week into June and two days into summer vacation, Mama pulls up in front of city hall and parks in a two-hour parking spot.

I reach for the door handle. "I thought you were just dropping me off."

She chuckles. "If my baby's gonna address the school board, I'm gonna be there to watch."

She checks her lipstick in the rearview mirror and holds it out for me. "You want some?"

"Sure." I don't know if lipstick will do much to make these old farts listen to me, but I'll try anything at this point. I pull my mirror down and carefully apply.

Mama tussles her hair to add volume and shuts the car off. "Showtime."

When Millie dropped me off after our truly epic road trip, Mama was doing the dishes before bed. She pulled a plate of food from the fridge labeled CALLIE and sat with me as I ate. Finally, as I was finishing up, she asked me where I'd gone and why. When I explained, she sat there for a long moment and finally said, "Two weeks grounded."

And that was it. That was the cost of doing business.

I decided to take a page out of Millie's book and let my clothes do some of the talking, which is why I'm wearing my white Shamrock uniform with matching white boots. I ditched the hat, though, because some heads were made for hats, but mine was not, so I opted to just wear the bun I'd normally don beneath the hat.

But I needed more than clothes. I needed facts. For those, I went to someone who I still can't believe texted me back.

ME: I know you probably never expected to see me pop up in your phone again, but I need your help. First, I need to say that I'm sorry. I should never have shared everyone's secrets like I did. I was mad and I felt betrayed, but that wasn't right.

She left me hanging for a good long time before texting me back.

MELISSA: Why should I even consider helping you?

ME: It's for the Shamrocks. I swear.

MELISSA: Keep talking.

For the rest of our interactions, Melissa was all business. She didn't even acknowledge my apology, but she did help me gather the facts and research I needed.

Inside the town hall meeting room, sitting in the middle row, I find Millie, Amanda, Hannah, Ellen, and Willowdean. "What are you guys doing here?" I ask.

"Couldn't let you embarrass yourself alone," says Willowdean.

Ellen elbows her in the ribs.

Hannah laughs. "Millie made us come."

"We wanted to," says Amanda. "So here we are!"

"You're going to do great," Millie says, giving me two thumbs up.

I look at the five of them. These girls were never the friends I asked for, but they're definitely the friends I needed.

"Nice outfit!" calls Hannah as I'm walking down the aisle.

Without my mama even noticing, I give her the middle finger behind my back. And then I turn around and smirk at her.

Mama and I sit in the front row, in the seats marked for members of the public who would like to speak during the open forum.

The budget meeting is long and boring. Who knew it cost that much to fund a cafeteria? And why is everyone always trying to take money away from libraries? Aren't books sort of the reason we're even in school at all?

Finally, Laurel Crocker, an old white man who always matches his cowboy hats to his boots, wears expensive blazers with starched jeans, has never taught a day in his life, and who also happens to be the president of the school board, bangs his gavel. "And now we'll take the required twenty minutes to hear input from the citizens of Clover City."

The only other person here to speak stands up, a short, graying woman who has the horrible sense to wear a tur-tleneck during June in West Texas. "I would like to speak on behalf of abstinence-only education in the classroom."

Someone behind me groans. My bet is on Willowdean or Hannah.

I catch Mama discreetly rolling her eyes. As someone who's had to sit through sex ed in Clover City, I can attest that we don't need to make it any worse than it is. As it stands, the teacher treats the diagrams like a game of Pictionary because he can't bring himself to say the word vagina out loud.

The woman drones on for another five minutes, detailing obviously made-up statistics and a few Bible verses before she takes her seat again next to Mama.

"Do we have anyone else before this meeting is adjourned? Perhaps someone who would like to speak about something relevant to the topic of the meeting?" asks Mr. Crocker.

I stand, and my boots click against the linoleum as I walk to the center of the room. I steady myself at the podium and reposition the microphone.

"My name is Callie Rey—"

Feedback from the microphone shrieks and echoes, interrupting me. Everyone groans from the intrusive noise.

"Try taking a step back, hon," Laurel suggests.

"I'm not your hon," I almost find myself saying out loud. But I take a step back and start again. "My name is Callie Reyes, and I am a former member of the Shamrocks. A legacy member, in fact. My mother was on the team that won Nationals in 1992. You may have heard of me. For good and bad reasons. Um . . ."

I lose track of my thoughts for a moment and glance down at myself. I look ridiculous in this uniform. There's probably lipstick on my teeth, too. For a second, I glance back and catch sight of Mama, who winks at me. A couple rows back, Millie is smiling and giving me thumbs-up.

I turn back to the microphone.

"You've got about six minutes left," says Mr. Crocker.

Great. Not only do I have to be profound, but I'm being timed as well. Millie would know just what to say. She'd say something meaningful and important. Something that would almost sound emotionally manipulative coming from anyone else, but from Millie it would be nothing but sincere.

I sigh into the microphone. For as much as I love Millie, I'm not her. I'm Callie. Prickly and uncomfortably honest.

I try again. "I'm here today because for as long as I can remember, the Shamrocks have had to seek outside fund-ing for everything from costumes to travel. I understand that the school district isn't a money tree, but when we lost our sponsor a few months ago, we were pissed."

"Language," warns Mr. Crocker.

"Sorry, sir." I clear my throat. "We were very upset. I was the co–assistant captain at the time, and I had sunk my whole life into that team. So yeah, I was upset. And because I was so angry, I did some things I regret, like vandalizing a local gym, which I'm sure you're aware of. Y'all and Vice Principal Benavidez made the decision to remove me from the team, and I can't blame you. What I did was wrong. But what I can do now is to help fix the real problem."

Mr. Crocker chuckles. "The real problem?"

No, sir. You will take me seriously. "Yes," I say defiantly. "The real problem. The real problem is that the Shamrocks are the most winning team from Clover City of all time. We hold the most District and State titles. And we hold the only National title in the whole city. In fact, we're the only team that has ever been to Nationals. And! We've been four times." My boots clack as I double back to my empty chair and grab the folder I brought in with me, which Millie helped me compile in a rush. "I brought all of the statistics here with me for you to see."

"Well," he says, "I'll admit that's rather impressive."

"But, sir," I say, "what's not impressive is our budget. I'm all for rolling your sleeves up and doing some good ol'-fashioned fund-raising, but the Rams, our football team, is allotted a budget twelve times the size of ours, and you're even building them an indoor training facility."

Behind me a few people clap, and I think I know just who they are.

"So, Mr. Crocker, today I stand before you wearing my Shamrock uniform for the very last time, and I ask you to consider where you spend taxpayer dollars. I daresay the Shamrocks have more than proven themselves worthy." I nod to him and the rest of the board. "Thank you for your time." I step forward and place the folder in front of him, which not only includes Shamrock stats, but also the team's budgetary needs, thanks to Melissa.

"We thank you for speaking up, Ms. Reyes, and we'll be sure to consider this as we finalize next year's budget." He bangs his gavel. "Meeting adjourned."

I twirl on my toes, and Mama is right there to meet me. She holds my face like she would when I was a little kid and she'd squish my cheeks together, except this time without the squishing. "Callie Alejandra Reyes, I am so damn proud of you."

There's so much between us that's unsaid, but this feels like a good first step.

Just two weeks after the last day of school, and it's already time for us all to see Millie off. Amanda hosts a pool party in her backyard the night before.

Millie wears a bright-yellow high-waisted bikini swimsuit with a ruffle top. She's lying out on a lawn chair beside Malik with huge red heart-shaped sunglasses pushed up the bridge of her nose. Willowdean, in her bright-red polka-dot swimsuit, is canoodling with Bo on the tiny bench built into the deep end of the pool, while Hannah sits on her girlfriend Courtney's shoulders as they battle Ellen with Tim on her shoulders in a game of chicken.

I sit on the steps in the shallow end with Mitch (whose amazing swim trunks look like the Texas state flag, by the way) on the steps above me so that I'm resting between his legs.

I'm actually 100 percent twinning with Millie today and wearing the exact same style and color of bikini that she is. Her idea, of course. She had tried to get all the girls to join in, but I was the only one who agreed. But I agreed to go all in on the whole obnoxious twinsie thing. I guess you could say I'm pretty accustomed to wearing identical outfits with at least twenty other girls, so the idea of matching bikinis seemed sort of normal to me. Millie mostly marveled about the fact that she found the same thing in both our sizes.

Amanda steps down into the pool beside us, presenting us each with multicolored plastic beads and neon shutter sunglasses. "Much better," she says.

"You didn't look festive enough!" Millie yells from across the yard.

Mitch swaps his neon-green sunglasses for my neon-yellow pair. "Feeling very festive right about now!"

"Amanda," I say, "it's not that I like you only for your pool, but I also hope you invite me over all the time this summer to go swimming."

"Your wish is my command! As long as you can deal with my brothers."

"Where are they, anyway?" I ask.

"My mom bought them a new video game so they'd leave us alone."

"Good woman," I say.

"She'll need all the pool breaks she can get with her new work schedule!" calls Millie.

I cup my hands around my mouth. "Either come over here and be part of this conversation, or stay over there and flirt with your boyfriend."

Her cheeks are nearly bright enough to match her lei.

"She's really good at multitasking!" yells Malik. "Flirting with me and butting into your conversation at the same time."

She swats at him playfully.

"I approve!" I say.

Tim crashes into the water, falling from Ellen's shoulders as Hannah and Courtney whoop victoriously.

"I can't believe the elusive Courtney has finally made an appearance," says Willowdean as Tim surfaces and dunks Ellen.

Hannah hangs on Courtney's arm like a koala, both their chins skimming the water as they move toward the deep end. It's the most affection any of us has ever seen her express. Ever.

"Oh," says Courtney. "Don't be fooled." Her bleached hair is nearly white and spreads in the water like tentacles. "Hannah tries to keep her social circles like her food. Separate and never touching."

"No fun!" says Amanda.

Courtney turns to her. "Thank you!"

Hannah rolls her eyes but can't stop herself from smiling.

Tomorrow is my first day back at the gym. Vernon agreed to let me take on Millie's shifts, and, most surprising of all—it was Inga's idea. I've already started to pitch them some ideas about student discounts and a few other things we can do to grow membership over the summer so that maybe I can stay on in the fall.

Millie calls it a night early, since she and her parents are leaving town way before sunrise, and even though I'm not grounded anymore, I've got an early curfew until my mom says otherwise. As we're all saying our good-byes, I run back inside for my bag to get the small going-away gift I made her. Yes, *made* her.

Just as I'm about to walk outside, my phone chirps.

I expect it to be a text from my mom, asking when I'll be home, but instead I find an email.

To: CallieHeyyyes@zmail.com
From: ShamrockCapt@zmail.com

Word is the district is upping our budget for next year. It won't be much, but it's more than we had. Thanks for what you said at the budget meeting.
Melissa
Clover City High School Shamrock Dance Team Captain

I laugh to myself a little. I can appreciate the fact that she went out of her way to use the official team captain email address. Serious alpha-dog move. Maybe she'll make a good captain after all.

I don't know if Melissa and I will ever be friends again. It's hard to say if what we had was strong enough to salvage, but after the last few months, nothing surprises me.

I run out the door barefooted into Amanda's front yard, where Mitch waits for me. I stand in front of him with his arms wrapped around me.

"You got it?" he asks, eyeing my bag.

I lean against his shoulder. "Yup."

Millie makes the rounds, saying good-bye to everyone, including Amanda—they share some kind of secret handshake and a tight hug—until it's just me.

Hesitantly, I reach into my bag. This particular gift is not what I would call my best work. "You better not laugh. Hold out your hands. Close your eyes."

She does as I say with a wide grin.

It took me six hours, three trips to the Crafty Corner, and a binge of the first few episodes of *Parks and Rec* on Millie's advising. (She swears I'm the Ann to her Leslie.) But in the end I created the world's shittiest cross-stitch. It's no bigger than the size of my palm, and in simple black thread, it reads AUSTIN OR BUST.

Millie opens her eyes and gasps, swinging an arm around my neck. "Oh my goodness! It's perfect! Did you make this yourself?"

I nod.

"I witnessed the whole painful thing," says Mitch.

Millie giggles and claps her hands together. "I love it!"

I beam, blinking away a few fresh tears. It wasn't so long ago that I was chanting "SAN FRAN OR BUST!" with all the Shamrocks. I'll make it to San Francisco one day, I know I will. But for now it feels just as sweet to see Millie off to Austin.

I hold both her hands. "Message me every day. Promise me."

"At least twice a day," she swears. "And I want pictures of my nephews when you see them."

"If I can get close enough without them biting."

She laughs before pulling me close for a hug. We stand there in our matching bikinis, two girls whose friendship was never meant to be, but it is. It really is.

I watch as she and Malik get into the van and drive off toward Malik's house, where they'll have their own private good-bye. I certainly hope it involves lots of kissing.

I lean back against Mitch's chest. Something tells me my night will end in some kissing, too. I don't know if I'll end up with a happily ever after, like in one of Millie's rom-coms, but I am definitely happy for right now. And that feels pretty damn good, if you ask me.

ACKNOWLEDGMENTS

I have many people to whom I'd like to express thanks, and in true Millie fashion, I will do so in the form of a list.

JULIE'S LIST OF THANKS

✓ Alessandra Balzer, my editor and ultimate cat-lady goals, you know when to challenge me and when to let me roll around on the floor, fussing, until I'm ready to move on. Thank you for everything, but mostly thank you for never leading me astray, especially when it comes to good food, pet products, and facemasks.

✓ John Cusick, my agent, who works tirelessly and cheerfully on my behalf, and I am equally thankful for both. Thank you for breathing new life into my career and for color-coding my life.

✓ Molly Cusick, my former agent and my friend, thank you for all the years you spent nurturing my writing career and for leaving me in very capable hands.

✓ Dana Spector, my film agent, who is absolutely ferocious.

✓ Caroline Sun, my publicist, who is always busy working magic behind the scenes. Rumor has it she can exist in two places at once.

✓ Aurora Parlagreco, Alison Donalty, and Daniel Stolle, who create my truly divine covers. Your work inspires me. Thank you.

✓ My whole huge Harper family, whose passion absolutely invigorates me, but especially: Donna Bray, Bess Braswell, Audrey Diestelkamp, Patty Rosati, Molly Motch, Stephanie Macy, Kelsey Murphy, Gina Rizzo, Maggie Searcy, Bethany Reis, Laaren Brown, Veronica Ambrose, Andrea Pappenheimer, Kathleen Faber, Kerry Moynagh, Heather Doss, Caitlin Garing, the Harper360 team, Kate Jackson, and Suzanne Murphy.

✓ The HarperCollins Canada team, whose enthusiasm and hospitality are unrivaled.

✓ My sensitivity readers for their thoughtfulness and care.

✓ Natalie C. Parker, thank you for always answering when I FaceTime and for reading a very early draft and for all the endless troubleshooting.

✓ Bethany Hagen, thank you for always staying up too late with me and never making me feel guilty about sleeping in. Also, thank you for all the reading and insights and for all those good secrets.

✓ Preeti Chhibber, Sona Charaipotra, and Amy Spalding, whose feedback proved invaluable. (And who are also just really funny, badass ladies.)

✓ In no specific order, I would like to thank the following people, who have made my life and my books better just by merely existing: Kristin Treviño, Veronica Treviño, Tessa Gratton, Jessica Taylor, Dhonielle Clayton, Jeramey Kraatz, Jenny Martin, Angie Thomas, Corey Whaley, Adam Silvera, Brendan Kiely, Justina Ireland, Becky Albertalli, Katie Cotugno, Zoraida Córdova, Jason Reynolds, Tara Hudson, Robin Murphy, Nic Stone, Jennifer Mathieu, Ashley Lindemann, Laura Rahimi Barnes, and Heidi Heilig.

✓ The following fat women, whose writing and work in the fat community has changed the way I look at and talk about my body and live my life in general. I cannot recommend their work enough: Lesley Kinzel, Marianne Kirby, Roxane Gay, Jes Baker, @yrfatfriend, Bethany Rutter, Sarai Walker, Stacy Bias, Gabi Gregg, and Nicolette Mason.

✓ Thank you to my family, Mom, Dad, Jill, Bob, Liz, Emma, Roger, Vivienne, and Aurelia, for all your support and love.

✓ Dexter, Opie, and Rufus. Yes, I would like to thank my two cats and my dog for all the cuddles, even when they weren't willing participants. And to my sweet Stevenson, the cat I'd had since my senior year of high school. I will miss you always, my favorite grumpy kitty.

✓ Ian, my partner and love, thank you for hopping all over the country with me and for all the late-night drives with seat heaters and for letting me be the version of myself that not many people get to see because she's messy and boring. I love you.

✓ If *Dumplin'* was about coming to terms with your own body, *Puddin'* is about demanding that the world do the same. I wrote this book for all the fat kids who have waited too damn long for the world to accept them. Stop waiting. The revolution starts with and belongs to you.

TURN THE PAGE
FOR A PEEK AT

Ramona Blue

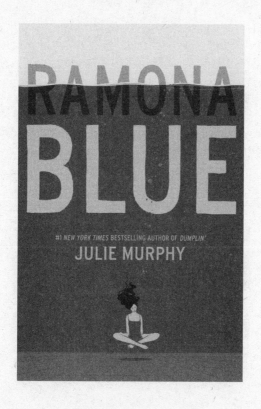

AUGUST

ONE

This is a memory I want to keep forever: Grace standing at the stove of her parents' rental cottage in one of her dad's oversize T-shirts as she makes us a can of SpaghettiOs. Her mom already cleaned out the fridge and cabinets, throwing away anything with an expiration date.

"Almost ready," says Grace as she stirs the pasta around with a wooden spoon.

"I should probably leave soon," I tell her. I hate prolonged good-byes. They're as bad as tearing a Band-Aid off one arm hair at a time.

"Don't pretend like you have somewhere to be right now. Besides, you should eat before you go." Grace is like her mom in that way. Every time we've left the house over the last month, her mom has tried to unload some kind of food on us, like we were taking a long journey and would need rations. "Don't make me eat these SpaghettiOs by myself."

"Okay," I say. "The thought of that is actually pretty pitiful."

She takes the pot from the stove and drops an oven mitt on the kitchen table before setting it down in front of me. Scooting in close, she winds her legs between mine and hands me a wooden spoon. We're both white, but my legs are permanently tanned from life on the coast (though a little hairy, because shaving is the actual worst), while Grace's normally ivory skin is splotchy and irritated from all the overexposure to the sun. And then there are her feet.

I grin.

"What?" she asks, tilting her head. Her raven waves brush against her shoulders. She's obsessed with straightening her hair, but even the mention of humidity makes her ends curl. "Don't look at my feet." She kicks me in the shin. "You're looking at my feet."

I swallow a spoonful of pasta. "I like your feet." They're flat and wide and much too big for her body. And for some reason I find this totally adorable. "They're like hobbit feet."

"My feet are not hairy," she insists.

I almost come back at her with some dumb quip, but the clock behind her melts into focus, and I remember.

Grace is leaving me. I knew she would leave me from the first moment we met on the beach as I handed out happy-hour flyers for Boucher's. She lay spread out on a beach chair in a black swimsuit with the sides cut out and a towel over her feet. I remember wishing I knew her well enough to know why she was hiding her feet.

This is our last meal together. In less than an hour, her mom, dad, and brother will all wake up and pack whatever else remains from their summer in Eulogy into the back of their station wagon, and they'll head home to their normal lives, leaving a hole in mine.

"I'm gonna be miserable without you," says Grace between bites. We're both too realistic to make promises we can't keep. Or maybe I'm too scared to ask her to promise me anything. She tugs at my ponytail. "And your stupid blue hair."

"Not as much as I'm going to miss your hobbit feet."

She smiles and slurps the pasta off her spoon.

Grace loves this shit. It's the junk food she craves after growing up in a house where her mother fed her home-made meals like stuffed salmon and sautéed asparagus. SpaghettiOs or any other kind of prepackaged food marketed toward kids—that was the kind of stuff Hattie and I grew up on. With Dad working and Mom gone, we ate anything that could be microwaved.

I think I'm in love with Grace. But sometimes it's hard to tell if I'm in love with her or her life. Her adorable little brother, Max, who is still sweet, because he has no idea how good-looking he will be someday, and her mom and dad, always checking in and leaving out leftovers for us. And this house. It's only a vacation rental, but it still feels so permanent.

Grace tucks her black bob behind her ears. "Did you ever look up any of those schools I put on that list for you?"

I shrug. This is our sticking point—the one thing we can't get past. Grace says the only thing keeping me here after high school is me. And I can concede that, in a way, she is right, but Grace is the kind of girl who never has to look at a price tag or tell the clerk at the grocery store to put a few items back.

We sit here curled into each other as the clock on the microwave melts into morning.

"I should go," I finally say.

She nudges her forehead against mine.

If we lived in a world where only my rules applied, I would kiss her. Hard. And leave.

Instead we walk hand in hand to the porch, where my bike sits, and then we make our way down the gravel driveway to the mailbox still shrouded in darkness.

I rest my bike against the post.

"Text me when you get a chance," I tell her.

"Olive juice," she says. *I love you*, her lips read. Her mother used to mouth it to her when she was dropping Grace off at school so she didn't embarrass her in front of all her friends.

"I love you, too," I whisper back with my lips already pressed into hers. She tastes like SpaghettiOs and the cigar we stole from her dad's portable humidor. Her lips are chapped and her hair dirty with salt water from our midnight swim just a few short hours ago. I feel her dissolving into a memory already.

TWO

I leave Grace's house and ride past the trailer park, where my dad and Hattie are asleep. My days always start like this—before everyone else's, in the moments when the only thing lighting Eulogy is the casino on the waterfront. Today, I'm a little earlier than usual, so I take the time to ride straight down to the water. Carefully, I lay my bike down on the sidewalk and kick my flip-flops off before walking down the rickety wooden steps to the beach.

My Mississippi beach is very rarely love at first sight, but an endearing, prodding kind of affection. Despite her lack of natural beauty, there are many like me who love this place more than she deserves. It's the kind of place people on a budget choose for vacation. Thanks to the line of sandbars trimming the shore and our proximity to the Mississippi River, our water is brown and murky. Nothing like Florida's blue-green waves. But a family like Grace's can get a lot of vacation for their buck if they're willing to overlook the imperfections.

Sand kicks up around my ankles until I reach the water's edge. I press my toes deep into the sand as the cool water rinses over them briefly before pulling back. The moon hangs in the sky, chasing the horizon, as the sun whispers along the waterfront.

Water has always been my siren song. Any kind of water—oceans, lakes, pools. There's something about being weightless that makes me think anything is possible. My whole body exhales in a way that it can't when I'm standing on land.

The brightening horizon reminds me that I have somewhere to be. Shaking sand from my feet, I run back up to the sidewalk and slide my flip-flops back on.

A continuous stream of tears rushes down my cheeks as I direct my handlebars around the corner and down the hill to where Charlie waits in his truck. I hate crying. I mean, most everyone does. But some people, like Hattie, feel better after a good cry. When Hattie cries, it's like watching a snake shed its skin. Tears somehow let her regenerate, whereas crying only makes me angry I cared so much to begin with.

"You're late," Charlie calls. He wears his usual uniform of coffee-stained undershirt and twenty-year-old jeans. With his shaggy thinning hair, he looks like an old white guy who either traps little kids in his van or grows weed in his backyard. Thankfully it's the latter.

I squeeze the brake on my handlebars and push the tears back into my eyes with my other fist. "Overslept."

I don't have a history of being late, so Charlie shrugs it off. Maybe a five a.m. start time is earlier than most teenagers could commit to, but I treasure all my little jobs. My paper route, busing tables at Boucher's, and working whatever under-the-table cash gigs I can find. I guess, growing up, most kids wonder what they will do for a living. But for me, there was never any worry over what the job would be, just how soon I could start.

Charlie loads the basket on the front of my bike with papers for the second half of my route, while I fill my messenger bag. Charlie is the kind of man who will always look like a boy, and the uneven whiskers lining his upper lip don't do anything to help the matter.

"Going for the mustache look?" I ask.

He strokes what little facial hair he has. "Wanted a change. You like?"

"Change is good," I tell him as I swing my leg over my bike and wave good-bye.

I weave up and down the streets on my route, letting my memory guide me until almost every house has a paper waiting in its yard. The routine of it keeps the thought of Grace at bay, at least for a little while.

At the corner of John Street and Mayfield, I pass Eulogy Baptist, a bright-white building with perfectly manicured lawns and flower boxes under each windowsill. Dim light from the back office bleeds into the street, and I wonder if Reverend Don is getting in or leaving.

I turn the corner down Clayton Avenue, pedaling as I lean back in my seat and gently tap the brake while I careen to the bottom of the hill. It's in this moment when I always feel like I'm flying. But then the bottom of the hill brings me back to reality.

Standing in front of my last house, which was recently added to my route, is a black woman in an unzipped terry-cloth cover-up with a bright-yellow bathing suit underneath, watering her flower bed. I always love morning people. They feel solid and reliable. Not like my mom, who sleeps past noon if no one wakes her up. Grace wasn't a morning person either. It was a small detail that always bothered me for some reason.

Grace. Grace, who I might not ever see again. I feel the tears begin to threaten.

"Mornin'," says the woman as the paper hits her lawn.

"Mornin'," I call back, pedaling past.

"Hey!" she shouts. Something hits me square in the shoulders, knocking the wind out of me.

"What the hell?" I mutter to myself as I loop back around to find I've been hit with one of my own papers.

As I reach down to pick it up, the woman's voice says, "Ramona Blue! Get back here!"

Her voice. I know it. And that nickname. Ramona Blue is what my dad called me when I was a little girl, because he could never get me out of the water. It's a name not many people know.

The woman walks to the edge of her yard and as she does, I see past the ten years of wrinkles. Dropping one foot to the ground, I stop my bike from rolling any farther as memories trickle back. "Agnes?"

"You get your heinie over here and gimme a hug!"

I drop my bike right there on the curb and fall into an embrace.

Agnes used to come down every summer from Baton Rouge with her husband and their grandson, Freddie, who they were raising. She was as much a part of my childhood memories as my own grandmother until the summer I turned nine and they just stopped coming. That was the first time I'd really understood that even if it feels like summer lasts forever here in Eulogy, Mississippi, it doesn't.

I can't think of many moments when I've looked in the mirror and taken an inventory of all the ways my body has changed. But here and now with Agnes squeezing me tight, her forehead barely brushing my chest, I feel like I'm some giant cradling a baby doll.

Agnes pulls away but holds my shoulders tight, examining me. She tugs on my long, wavy ponytail, and says, "Of course I'm not surprised. Your daddy always did let you get away with everything short of murder."

My cheeks burn, and even though the ache in my chest is as heavy as an anchor, I smile. She's referring to my hair. Ramona Blue with the blue hair.

Depending on when you catch me, my hair could be any shade ranging from royal blue to turquoise. I was thirteen the first time I dyed it with Kool-Aid mix and a little bit of water. To no one's surprise, I was sent home from school, but my dad came to the rescue despite how much he hated what I'd done to the blond locks I'd inherited from my mother. He fought with my principal until the whole ordeal had eaten up more time than it was worth. And my hair's been blue ever since, thanks to Hattie and her amateur understanding of cosmetology.

Today, though, I am in need of a dye job. The sun, salt water, and plain old time have left my hair a powdery shade of turquoise.

"You sprung up like a weed." She shakes her head, and I wonder what it is she's seeing in her memory of me. She points to my empty messenger bag. "Last house on your route then?"

I nod. "Yes, ma'am."

"You come hungry tomorrow morning." She pats my belly. "We're gonna have us a big ol' breakfast."

"I can do that," I say. "Okay."

Agnes's lips spread into a wide, knowing grin. "Freddie is going to die."

Freddie. All my memories of him are sun bleached and loud, but I try not to let myself be fooled by the past. Growing up can change you.

FROM *NEW YORK TIMES* BESTSELLING AUTHOR JULIE MURPHY!

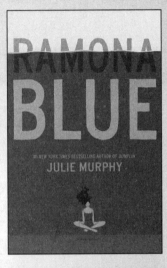

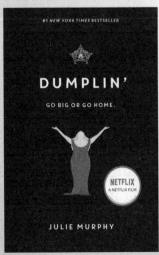

JOIN THE

Epic Reads

COMMUNITY

THE ULTIMATE YA DESTINATION

◀ **DISCOVER** ▶
your next favorite read

◀ **MEET** ▶
new authors to love

◀ **WIN** ▶
free books

◀ **SHARE** ▶
infographics, playlists, quizzes, and more

◀ **WATCH** ▶
the latest videos

www.epicreads.com